Samuel Sullivan Cox

The Isles of the Princes

The Pleasures of Prinkipo

Samuel Sullivan Cox

The Isles of the Princes
The Pleasures of Prinkipo

ISBN/EAN: 9783337407902

Printed in Europe, USA, Canada, Australia, Japan

Cover: Foto ©Andreas Hilbeck / pixelio.de

More available books at **www.hansebooks.com**

THE

ISLES OF THE PRINCES;

OR,

THE PLEASURES OF PRINKIPO

BY

SAMUEL S. COX

LATE UNITED STATES MINISTER TO TURKEY, AND AUTHOR OF "BUCKEYE ABROAD;" "WINTER SUNBEAMS;" "WHY WE LAUGH;" "FREE LAND AND FREE TRADE;" "ARCTIC SUNBEAMS;" "ORIENT SUNBEAMS;" "THREE DECADES OF FEDERAL LEGISLATION;" "DIVERSIONS OF A DIPLOMAT IN TURKEY;" ETC.

"Summer isles of Eden, lying in deep, purple spheres of sea."
Tennyson.

With Map and Illustrations.

NEW YORK & LONDON
G. P. PUTNAM'S SONS
The Knickerbocker Press
1887

TO MRS. JULIA A. COX.

THIS volume faintly describes the delights of our Grecian home at Prinkipo, among the Isles of the Princes. It is intended as a souvenir and record for each of us. It recalls our pleasant sojourn in those classic isles, and the many courtesies bestowed upon us,—"strangers in a strange land." We both desire to give our appreciation and thanks a form more substantial than that of a memory merely. Here we can attempt this, and make our response in grateful recognition of the kindness with which we were received and the happiness of our sojourn.

It is fit, therefore, that to you, my dear wife, I should dedicate this volume ; for if we have achieved any measure of success, socially or otherwise, in our island home, may I not say that it is due to those qualities of kindness and complaisance which you possess, and which have made our lives one in an ever increasing circle of felicity ?

S. S. COX.

iii

PREFACE.

THIS little volume is the episode of a summer's enjoyment and observation among the Princes Isles, in the old Propontis. It is intended to be a recital of the many diversive excursions in and around these islands and the adjacent places in Asia and Europe. It is supplementary to a more complete account of the author's experience while minister of the United States to Turkey. That account, in its fulness, is to be found in a volume entitled "Diversions of a Diplomat in Turkey," published by C. L. Webster & Co., of New York City.

These Isles of the Princes lie in sight of Stamboul and its splendors, and of the mountains of Asia, dominated by the Mysean Olympus. They are glorious in physical loveliness. They are still the "Isles of Greece," although under Ottoman rule. Out of their blue waters, at morn and eve, the beauty of the Grecian myth arises, to grace the isles with her smiles. Upon them burn "the larger constellations." They are fitly named "Isles of Princes." Upon them the palaces of the princes of old Byzantium were erected. Here, too, were their monasteries and prisons. The relics of these lines of civil and ecclesiastical empire are nearly all faded; but the monasteries of the Orthodox Greek Church still hold here their eminences, as well by virtue of their antique titles as by their superb situations.

Under the light of these associations, and with the fantastic glimmer of human caprice and passion which the pages of Gibbon best picture, and under the constantly recurring phases of the "Eastern Question," the summer of 1886 was passed by the writer.

The impressions herein recorded cannot, perhaps, be of more than fleeting interest to the reader. Their very diversity indicates the separate and distinct hues of a prism, and these give their colors to the author's pages.

S. S. Cox.

NEW YORK, *May* 1, 1887.

CONTENTS.

vii

LIST OF ILLUSTRATIONS.

ix

THE PRINCES ISLES;

OR,

THE PLEASURES OF PRINKIPO.

CHAPTER I.

THE ISLES OF THE PRINCES IN THE PROPONTIS— THEIR GOVERNMENT AND PEOPLE.

THERE are nine of these isles, of which five— Prinkipo, Halki, Antigone, Proti and Terevinthos (Androvichi)—are inhabited; the other four— Oxia, Plati, Nyandros and Pita—are uninhabited. The five first-mentioned have been inhabited for ages past. The great Doge, Henry Dandolo, who was the soul of the Fourth Crusade, advised the Crusaders, who were then encamped at San Stefano, just beyond the walls of Constantinople, " not to forage in the Thracian plains, but rather to try these islands *qui sont habitées de genz, et laborées de blez et de viandes et d'autres biens.*"

They were called in ancient times " Demonisi," and under this appellation they are mentioned by Aristotle, who says of one of them : " Demonisos, an island of the Chalcedonians, deriving its name

from its founder, Demonisos, famous for the gold
dust it produces, which is most valuable as a cure
for those suffering from the eyes."

The Turks call them collectively "Khizil Ada-
lar"—Red Islands—from the peculiar color of
their soil.

The early Roman had a taste for beauty.
When he became master of the East the mythical
and mystical beauty of the Greek islands allured
him.   He liked the climate, which the sea softened
alike during summer and winter.   The islands of
the Bay of Naples became favorite abodes for the
opulent of Imperial Rome, and Lesbos, described
as a noble and pleasant island by Tacitus, was a
royal retreat for a Roman governor in exile.

Some liken these isles and waters to those of
the Malayan archipelago.   There the scenes are
tropical and the waters luminous with phospho-
rescent beauty.   Those who have seen the inland
sea of Japan, compare its charm of water and sky
to the deep blue sea and overarching glory of
the Grecian isles.   I have often been reminded,
while sailing amidst these isles, of the sunny
sheen and the verdant hills and mountains of our
Antilles.   In praising the Princes group I give
the palm to no other scenery, for to the beauty
of nature in the islands of Greece, like those of
Prinkipo and the other Isles of the Princes, there
is an added charm : it is that of historical and

poetical associations. Their historical associations are the annals of ancient empire, Asian and European ; and their poetical associations have as their aureole a golden radiance, under which

> " Mildly dimpling, ocean's cheek
> Reflects the tints of many a peak,
> Caught by the laughing tides that lave
> These Edens of the Eastern wave."

There were nine muses. The Princes Isles are the same in number as those sisters. The muses had various functions in the hierarchy of song. These isles have a similar condition in the economy of nature, not to speak of their artistic utilities. Their beauty and allurements are as varied as the hues of the waters around them. Yet they are similar; and, notwithstanding differences in history, size and cultivation, they cannot be accounted aliens to each other. The same geology, the same sun, the same production, the same insects even, give them a unity in variety which would be as pleasing as one of Sophocles's plays to a scholar—or as the *E pluribus unum* to a patriotic lover of our starry ensign. Like the Iris— which is seen with every dash of the clear water of the Propontis (or Marmora)—*varios insula colores*, this group, unless we except the bay of Naples, is without a peer in the archipelagoes or waters of our globe.

The isles are on the latitude of New York
but they have not its winter sleet, snow, chill, and
inclemency. They are a little south-east of Constantinople. They are sheltered from the harsh
winds of the Black Sea, as the Bosphorus is not, by
the northern range of Asiatic mountains. They
take on the climate and characteristics and have
the same people that inhabited the Isles of Greece
of which Homer and Byron delighted to sing.

It is difficult to affirm after the lapse of many
hundred years that the people who reside upon
the shores of the Greek islands are other than
a mixed race. They are of the Greek, Roman,
and Turkish races. Their only sign of patriotism
is a fervid attachment to their own islands and
the emotion by which they are bound to their orthodox religion. One must go inland upon these
isles of Greece to find the Greek of our classic enthusiasm and patriotic frenzy. In this respect the
Isles of the Princes are exceptional. The body of
their population is of unmixed Greek origin. It
needs no ethnographical chart to show this; the
features of the people demonstrate it. The population is nearly all Greek. It numbers over ten
thousand. Their government by the Porte is
hardly felt.

Mohammed II., the conqueror of Constantinople, was wiser than his contemporaries. The
Greeks were allowed by him, through their own
officers, to supervise their own ceremonious relig-

ion in the very city of Constantinople. That Sultan pensioned many of the Greek clergy to keep up the establishment of their faith. He did not antagonize the millions in the provinces of Greece who were under the crescent. He was content to exact from them only the recognition of his secular power. These isles were given in fee to the Greek population. Thereupon they flocked hither, with such wealth as was spared to them from the sacking of the city. Here they found already built their religious houses and churches, sacred for a thousand years to their faith. Here they built their villas, and thence daily sailed in their pinnaces to the city, when on business or pleasure intent.

What kind of a government have these isles? Upon some of them, the smaller ones, like Pita, Androvichi, Nyandros and Oxia, there are no residents. Upon Plati—Sir Henry Bulwer's Isle, so called—there are a few folk cultivating the soil under an Armenian peasant. This peasant is the gentle castellan. He watches the tumble-down castles which the English minister erected in one of his eccentric moods. Consequently upon only four of the isles is there need of a government or police. What do the police here?

One of their functions is the protection of the few trees from the goats. The islands are traversed daily by herds of these voracious animals.

They are generally associated with the gentlest of big-tailed sheep. Both are under one shepherd. But as the goat will eat anything, even an American petroleum can, and especially as he will climb the rocks and almost trees for anything verdant, he is the pest, not only of these isles, where some verdure is left, but of the Orient. When the young boys and girls who are shepherds are aloof from the forester, owner, or police, in remote places, they help the goats to make havoc of the woods and foliage. In these countries, almost denuded of trees by fire and war and reckless peasants who know and care nothing for the sanitary, climatic and agricultural value of trees, this devastation was simply inevitable. Cyprus was, until the English control, almost ruined by the greedy goat. Last summer, when venturing up the pretty creek out of the Bosphorus, whereon are situated the "Sweet Waters of Asia," a mile or more with the meandering stream, I saw a couple of gentle shepherd youths, with a flock of goats, on the beautiful hillside. The boys were in the trees. They had "little hatchets" and saws. They were cutting off the limbs for the sustenance of their flock. Thus passeth away the glory of these little Lebanons of Asia!

These isles, however, are now pretty well guarded. They bid fair to preserve what bosky beauty and sylvan shade they have.

The Sultan is wise beyond most of his subjects. He preserves the grand Belgrade forests, in whose cool haunts, from the borders of the Bosphorus to the Black Sea shore, there are miles of splendid roads through deep, verdurous alleys and paths, for equestrians and carriages. Deer still frequent these woods. These Belgrade woods are made famous by the vivid descriptions of Lady Mary Montagu, who sojourned there when her husband was minister. Besides this forest, the Sultan has made his grounds about Yildiz palace umbrageous in trees and shrubs, and tasteful in pretty lakes and fountains. Photographs of these he has had taken. He requested me to send to the President these pictures. This I have done. He desires some of our American indigenous trees, being partial to *conifera*, as he contemplates enlarging his forest domain, to remove the reproach of barrenness from the hills which overlook the Bosphorus above the palaces of Beckitash and Dolma Batché. To make this plan a success, the omnivorous goat must go! But as long as the peasant relies on the goat for milk, he is loath to let him go.

Although the Bosphorus is fifteen miles away to the north from our Prinkipo home and isle, still it is within my bailiwick, though not within that of the police system which obtains here. Formerly these nine Princes Isles were attached to the

"Sixth Circle," or Prefecture of Pera—the city on
the hill opposite Constantinople proper, or Stamboul.   It was owing to the skill of Blacque Bey—
the Prefect, or Mayor, of the "Circle"—that these
isles improved.   But recently the isles have been
added to the Prefecture of Ismid, whose capital,
at the end of the gulf of that name, is famous
in the annals of Bithynia, in her earlier Roman
and more recent Byzantine ecclesiastical history.
However, the rule is nearly the same as when
Blacque Bey was the Prefect.   The government
is still based on the ideas of municipal rule, with
considerable freedom about taxation ; for the people are allowed *voluntarily* to pay for their own
improvements.

The government of the isles is so much mixed
that it is more difficult to understand its philosophy than autocratically to administer it.   To
understand its combined central and local character you must study its Turkish features.   In the
old Arabic legislation municipal rule was not the
exception.   The Ottoman did not greatly change
the general polity and administration of affairs
when Turkey was conquered from the Greeks.
Both systems were decentralizing.   In the old
Greek system there was much reserved to the
provinces and the people of the localities "respec-
tively."   This was the mainspring of Grecian sur-
vival and of Turkish continuance.   One of the

changeless things in this country is the fixed fact
that, while the Greek emperors ruled there were
the same capitulations or privileges extended by
the Greeks to the Turks as the Turks now extend
to the Greeks and Franks. The concessions went
almost as far in religious matters as those of Lord
Baltimore and Roger Williams ; so that the Moslem had the privilege of erecting mosques within
the very heart and walls of the Stamboul triangle ;
just as now the American Bible House and Female Home School, not to speak of the American
(Robert) College, are tolerated within its jurisdiction.

The Sultan is, when he chooses, practically
absolute. He controls purse and sword. Although the " Gotha Almanach " puts the government down as a constitutional monarchy, it is so
in form only. There was a constitution adopted
on the 23d of December, 1876, under some up-
heaval, but it remains a dead letter. The Sheik-
Ul-Islam represents the spiritual power of the
Caliphate. He is neither priest nor magistrate,
but an interpreter of the sacred Koran, which is a
law for the realm, except when the Sultan dis-
penses with the interpretation. There are titles,
but no nobility, no hereditary lords. " Effendi,"
the name by which the princes and even the "honorable women " are called, is no more than
" Esquire." Other titles, such as Aga and Pasha,

are only convenient handles to names like Tewfik, Ali, Mustafa and Mehmet. There is a title representing the controlling power, by which the administration is known—viz., the Sublime Porte. It is a locality, on or near the Seraglio Point, where the Bosphorus flows into the Sea of Marmora on one side, and the Golden Horn flows into the same sea on the other But as all names of places in Turkey have an inner meaning, so Sublime Porte means the exalted seat of justice. As the Bible tells us, justice was administered "at the gate," or "porte." It was the Oriental custom. So that this gate is known as the gate of justice *par excellence !*

The empire in its grand divisions is made up of *vilayets.* These are governed each by a Viceroy. There are subordinates, like governors of counties, called Mudirs, or of divisions of counties called Kaïmakam. The Governor of this isle of Prinkipo is a Kaïmakam. Sometimes these officers, especially in Christian neighborhoods, are Christians. Many of the Turks are descendants of Christians, and one-half of the population of Turkey, which is estimated at thirty-six millions, are not Turkish. The idea of the government is patriarchal, whether it is practiced or not. What would seem anomalous in other countries is here a rule, viz., that there are governments within the government. These are patriarchal, and both civil and ecclesiastical in their functions. The Greek subjects in their internal affairs are ruled by their own laws and magistrates. There are heads to the Armenian, Hebrew, Greek and Latin communities. There is a Greek nation, *Ooroom Milletti.* It is ruled by a Council. In this the laity have much control. The Patriarch is called "His Holiness." With his bishops he forms a Synod in religious matters. Throughout the country, in every district, city and village, civil relations are regulated by these councils and synods, along with the ecclesiastical. The civil representative may be a Turk. The Kaïmakam, or chief of this isle of Prinkipo, is now a Turk. He used to be a Greek. You scarcely see him or hear of him. He called on Admiral Franklin, when he anchored here with the "Kearsarge," but informed him that he had no residence, only an office, on the isle. He did not expect, therefore, the Admiral to return his call. I have not received a call from His Excellency; but I have heard from him, in an unpleasant way, when he interfered with my comfort and courtesy, without suspecting from my modest demeanor that I represented some sixty millions of free-born Americans. I was cautioned against as the man with a high silk hat, who was guilty of some misadventure, not entirely in accord with his sense of decorum. When he learned his mistake, the correction was

prompt and adequate.   More of that hereafter.
It is one of the mysteries of Asia; and as these
isles are in Asia, let us not pluck out its heart too
suddenly.

Prinkipo, like the other eight "Isles of the
Princes," has a good deal of Home Rule.   It is in
the form of a Council, which is elected by the
householders.   It has power, in some way, to levy
some of the taxes, but it takes care not to do it
to any great extent; for the revenue is taken to
the city and becomes a common fund.   This fund
does not always inure to the good of the island,
for there the, taxes—wherewithal to light, police
and improve the isles, or at least this isle of Prinkipo—are voluntary contributions by the rich folks.
There are taxes—the old *octroi*—levied here upon
donkeys and carriages.   They pay for the removal
of the garbage and to improve the streets and
roads.   Altogether the system is not the perfection of municipal home rule.   There are some
thirty police, called *zaptiehs*, in the town which
is near the shore.   These keep the peace, watch
the *scala* (or quay) and shipping, and light the
lamps.   They seldom penetrate into the interior
of the island, which is a dozen miles in girth.

Once in a while, when sauntering over the
heights of the island, or among the pines, there
comes on you, unexpectedly, a strange-looking man,
as if he were lost out of one of Ulysses's pinnaces

in an erratic way, or just from Albania, or had
been tossed out of the Cyclades by an earthquake,
or swam ashore by some help of the Homeric
gods or goddesses. He is in the old Greek costume, with embroidered vest, large red sash, and
baggy pants. As a sign of his Turkish subjection,
he wears the red fez. In his sash he has some
Damascus pistols, silver-mounted. They are as
handsome and as harmless as those of our Cavass. There protrudes from the sash the jewelled
handle of the Damascene dirk, or *yataghan.*
There is a sword, or scimitar, by his side, and
altogether he appears quite voluminous at his
middle. He wears low shoes, adorned with silver
buckles. He has them turned up at the toes, and
high black silk stockings. His brow is corrugated
with care. His hair and mustache are blonde.
His frame is stalwart. Two dogs follow him
about. What is his business? To protect the
forest from goat, fire and spoilers. The trees must
not be disturbed. Fig and olive, pine and pomegranate, on the road or by-paths, or over the stone
fences, each and all are precious. The world does
move!

This elaborate forester is from the Albanian
mountains. He is too proud to make his avoca-
tion known. He is yet to arrest any one. He
trudges along as independently as if he were in
his native Croatia. He is one of the hardy race

of mountaineers which has seen much fighting. He is on good terms with my Dalmatian *serviteur*, Pedro Sckoppegalia. I hope the forester's name is not so unpronounceable as Pedro's.

Besides guarding the forest, vines and fruits of the isles, these men act as private guards to houses and grounds. They are good, orthodox Greek Christians ; and whether as Slavs or Greeks, I suppose they love Russia more than Turkey. There are not many of them, but they give picturesqueness to the scene.

No robbers are on the isle. As some one said to me : " If a robber should make a raid here, how could he get off the island without being caught?" The beggars are few and are easily satisfied. They are a law and a police to themselves. There does not seem much necessity for these guardians of the vine and pine, fig and pomegranate, for few people here lock their doors at night, much less their garden gates.

Altogether the population seems to be happy and contented. Whether it be the fisherman sitting on the sand, mending his nets after the apostolic method, or the little girls plucking the grapes in the vineyard and figs in the orchards, or the women attending their children and their washing, the song ever goes up from cheerful throats and well-fed stomachs. The prevalent song is Greek. It has a weird, quaint melody of which I have

ALBANIAN POLICE.

heard snatches in some comediettas at the Casino in New York.

There can be little use in having much police on the islands, as at nearly every point you meet groups of honest people. The carriers with their kegs of fresh water on their donkeys, the fruit venders and foot peddlers, and the donkey-drivers or parties are everywhere. Bevies of girls and children are in the woods, sitting on or playing among the rocks, or ensconced amidst the aromatic shrubbery. There are no Naiads here. All are Dryads; for there are no fountains, only wells; and trees in plenty, where the wood nymphs cluster and chatter and laugh their golden moments away. Sometimes, when the bands play at the restaurants, or a Bohemian comes along with his hand-organ, the young folks have a dance. There is much provision on the isle for picnics and parties. The steamer from the city, especially on Sunday, brings its thousands to the isle for pastime, and they make the hours fly on winged feet.

Although there are many and various people sojourning on the isle—some of whom are occasionally addicted to *bier de Vienne*, and the horrid mastic or whiskey of the country—I have not seen one case of drunkenness, fighting, or quarrelling. The policeman, therefore, when not a gay and happy forester is almost supererogatory.

The roads are in admirable repair, and fit for

the finest vehicles.   Occasionally an invalid lady
ascends the mountain in the old sedan chair.   The
paths up and down are for donkeys and promenaders, who flock over the island from morning till
evening, in search of cool spots and *al fresco* dining.   Now and then these social amenities indicate
a church *fête* or love making ; for the women of
the isle have rare Hellenic beauty and coquettish
ways.   Besides these promenaders, you meet frequently the peddlers of all kinds of wares, cakes,
confections, fruit—and water.   Everything you
want here, from a needle to a pair of shoes, from
a peach to a glass of ice-cream, is brought to your
very hand.   The water that you drink is drawn
from wells in the valleys on the north and south
sides of the isle.   The proprietors own a donkey
drove.   They fill four casks of pure cool water
from the deep wells, rope the casks with equipoise
dexterously on the donkey's back, and dispense it
around to the private houses and restaurants.
Water costs about half a *piaster* a keg, or two
cents.   Some of these venders of water and things
are *hamals.*   They bear great loads from the *scala*
and ferries to any part of the island.   They are
duplicates of the stalwarts of Stamboul, who can
carry 600 or 700 pounds of furniture, trunks, or
what not up the hills and never turn a hair.

In my summer life here, I have yet to meet
from the people, old or young, one act or look of

discourtesy, or observe one Bad Boy made after the similitude of Peck's. The Greek origin of the people has given them graces beyond the reach of art, and my summer at Prinkipo has been a revel in the very heart of nature.

CHAPTER II.

ISLES OF THE PRINCES—THEIR GEOGRAPHY AND HIS-
TORICAL ASSOCIATIONS.

THE map will show the relative position of the
isles to Prinkipo and to each other and to the
main land and city of Constantinople. Oxia and
Plati seem from the other isles like barren rocks
in the sea. This is one of the illusions. Proti,
Antigone and Halki are about of equal size.
They are nearest the city. Androvichi lies east
of Prinkipo. It has but one resident on it. You
may guess his occupation by the great gash he
has made on its western side, from whence comes
the marble and out of which he makes the lime for
transportation to the city. This isle has no cultivation, unless the smoke that ascends from his
lime kilns indicates an ancient cult and a pious
sacrifice which Homer so frequently records.

Nyandros, another island, is off the southern end
of Prinkipo. From the top of this latter island
Nyandros seems to be a part of Prinkipo, but it is
really two miles away. Pita is a very small islet,
between Halki and Antigone. It is not peopled.
The other islands are visited by strangers as sum-

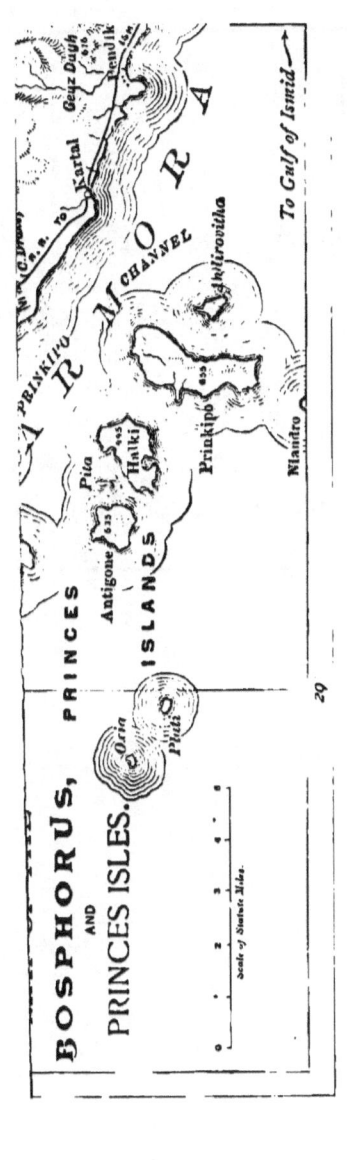

MAP OF THE

BOSPHORUS,

PRINCES

AND

PRINCES ISLES.

Scale of Statute Miles.

0 1 2 3 4 5

20

To Gulf of Ismid →

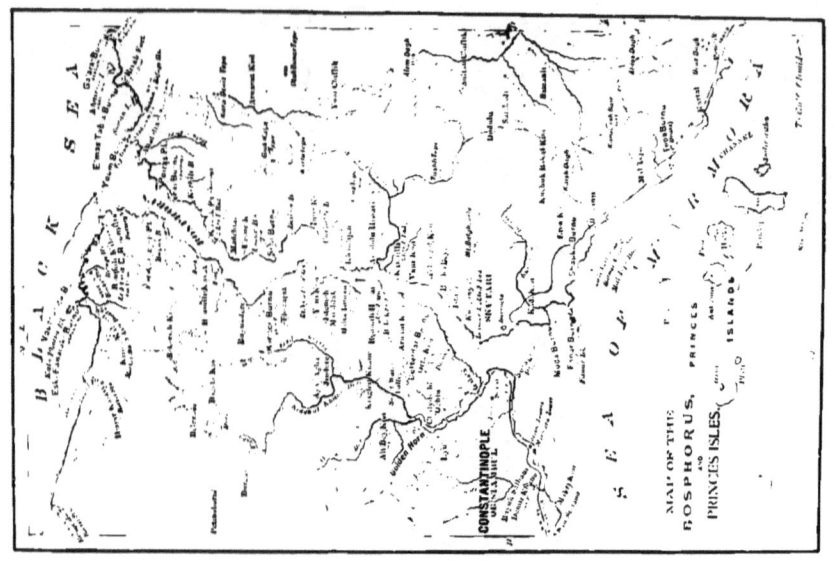

mer resorts, besides having a goodly number of inhabitants who live there the year round. Prinkipo, however, is the chief. It is *facile princeps.* The island is some ten miles around, with a rare variety of mountain and intervale.

The Turkish name for Prinkipo is Buyuk-Ada, or "Large Isle." This is the appellation given to it by the ancient Byzantines. The history and reminiscences connected with the ancient nunnery established in this place, and to which the Empress Irene was provisionally confined, are more or less accurately given in Schlumberger's "Iles des Princes." Where the monastery of St. Michael's now stands, on the northern side of the isle, there existed in former times a large village. It was called by the Byzantines "Karya." The church attached to that monastery used to serve as the parish church of the village. The monastery now belongs to the patriarchate of the Greek Church and is rented by an abbot.

The monastery of Christos is also of very ancient date. Beginning from just beyond our villa, on the mountain side, its premises run down to the *Diaskalon* or picnic grounds. The surrounding lands belong to this monastery. Up to 1870 the building was a perfect mass of wooden ruins, including the church. In that year the present Patriarch of Alexandria, then Patriarch of Constantinople, having been deposed from his bea-

tific title and place, retired to Prinkipo. He set to
work to restore the tumbledown wooden hut which
served as a chapel. With the help of contributions from wealthy friends, the church, under the
personal superintendence of the ex-Patriarch, was
rebuilt of stone as it now stands. The monastery
itself was only restored last year, 1885, by the
present abbot, mostly at his own expense. This
abbot is an active and hard-working man. He
devotes his whole time to the cultivation of the
lands belonging to the monastery. He is also a
large wine and spirit brewer, and the products of
his brewery are renowned all over Constantinople
for their purity and excellence.

I am sure from observation and taste that the
wine of the isle is more plentiful and delicious
than the water. The latter is nearly as costly as
the wine.

I have been told by those who have dug on the
island for water that Prinkipo is somewhat different
from the other islands geologically and mineralog-
ically, and that parts of it differ from other portions. This is accounted for, of course, by some
remote cataclysm. Like the other isles it has its
depressions and elevations. These give a curva-
ture to the horizon which adds many a grace.
Upon the tops of the mountainous portions are
situated Greek colleges and monasteries. These
give the name of "Scholastic" to Halki, and would

give that of "Pious" to Prinkipo were not Prinkipo so superb in her worldly adornments.

Halki has three seminaries of learning: two
Greek and one Turkish. The last is a naval
school. Prinkipo has three monasteries. These
isles, especially Halki and Prinkipo, are accessible
from the city of Constantinople by the Shirket
ferry. It leaves the bridge over the Golden Horn
several times a day, and makes the trip in an hour
and a-half. The Turk sets his clock and watch by
the sun. He begins his day at sunset. The time,
therefore, varies. This produces, until you are
accustomed to it, many misadventures. The population who come to these islands consult the daily
journals for the exact minute when the boats leave
the bridge at Constantinople and the *quai* at the
isles. There are two good hotels in the town of
Prinkipo, and these are well patronized in summer. Of the other isles, besides Prinkipo, I will
hereafter dilate at pleasure, for from Prinkipo
with our steam launch, which Congress was good
enough to vote the minister, we can take our time
to visit and revisit these gems of the sea.

What historic events have these isles witnessed
during the thousand years of Greek empire in the
East? What palaces and prisons were here erected
for living and fallen greatness when in power or
banished? What did the Empress Irene in the
ninth century for Prinkipo, when it was at the sum-

mit of its splendor?   What has become of the very
dust of these Grecian worthies and rulers, since
the conquest of Constantinople in A. D. 1453, by
the Moslem?   How happens it that only a few
old monastic relics remain upon this consecrated
ground?   These are questions under a veil of tradition, if not history, which even the regeneration
of these lands has failed to bring fully to the light.

The tourist who travels with Murray's red-book
in hand will be disappointed at its meagre mention of the Princes Isles.   It gives hardly a stick-
ful to Halki; and as for Prinkipo there is scarcely
a finger's length of matter, and that has reference to
the Empress Irene.   That reference is all too brief,
for the empress was a grand figure in history at a
grand epoch.   It hints at some spectacle of fallen
greatness and vanished splendor witnessed in the
first year of the ninth century, when Irene, the
contemporary of Charlemagne and Haroun-Al-
Raschid was banished from the throne of Byzantium to the convent which she had built at Prinkipo.   The convent remains on the north-eastern
side of the island, and from its lofty site sweeps a
splendid horizon of continent, isle and sea.

This description was provocative.   I sent to
London and Paris, and scanned the libraries here,
to find a full account of the antiquities and *per-
sonnel* of this once regal isle.   I heard of but
one volume in French, by a German, Gustave

Schlumberger, which would serve to elucidate the spectacle. But even this volume is faulty. I doubt if the writer ever visited the isles. Gibbon is always near, and so I turn to his grandiose picture of the Eastern Empire ; but even he fails to give much of interest about the empress and other great personages, in their relation to our isle. In his forty-eighth Chapter, he makes a *résumé* of five centuries of the decline and fall, and he has eight more centuries before Constantinople succumbs to the Turk. He pursues its "tedious and uniform state of weakness and misery." He has "cornered" the great Roman name in the lonely suburbs of Constantinople. "As in his daily prayers, the Mussulman of Fez or Delhi turns his face toward Mecca," so the historic eye, as he phrases it, " is always fixed on Constantinople." Making this prelude the historian proceeds with stately step to open the prologue of swelling drama in which, then as now, Latins, Greeks, Bulgarians, Russians and Turks play their parts. Upon this stage moves Leo IV., son of the fifth Constantine. This Emperor Leo took an Athenian orphan girl to wife. She had great personal accomplishments. He was feeble ; she was not. It is the old story ; she was the ruler of the Emperor, and at his death, by his will became Empress-Guardian of all the Eastern Empire. The Prince, their son, Constantine VI., became her anxiety and care, next after the restoration of the worship of images, of which she was the champion. This image-worship was the burning question of her time. Upon this question thrones were upturned and synods thundered. The iconoclasts had been in arms and had been successful. After many trials the Prince succeeded in obtaining the throne and humiliating his mother, but he was soon dethroned by a counterplot of the wily Irene. She had his eyes put out. She had him assassinated. Ambition stifled all the good in her nature. Her crimes were horrible, but not more so than the crime of many other rulers at Byzantium during the Greek dynasties. Putting out the eyes and banishment to monasteries seem to have been the favorite penalty and pastime of princes in those days of unparalleled cruelty. Irene held her ill-gotten power only five years. She was wont to pass through Constantinople in her golden chariot, drawn by four milk-white steeds. Their reins were held by patricians who had been made eunuchs by her edict. These eunuchs, with the cunning of that class, conspired against her. The great treasurer, Nicephorus, led the conspiracy. He was secretly invested with the purple and crowned in St. Sophia. Irene sought a retreat from her perfidious treasurer. This, her prayer, was granted; but when she requested her treasures, they were refused her; for was he not a good

treasurer? But he graciously allowed her to retire honorably to the monastery of Prinkipo.
It seems that this was too near Byzantium for his
comfort, for he banished her to the Island of Lesbos. There, like good Penelope, she endeavored
to atone for her unnatural crimes by a life of labor
at the distaff. With this simple implement the
empress, who had revelled in all the splendors of
the Blachernal palace, was enabled to earn a
scanty subsistence.

What remains of the old Byzantine civilization?
Nothing but the walls, and even their eternity of
strength has been broken. When the spring
comes with its foliage, the moat around the towers
that once protected the great city is a vegetable
garden, and the blossoms of the peach, plum and
the pomegranate give to its grassy mound their
beauty and fragrance. What changes have taken
place! Who can tell whether man or nature, the
sword or the earthquake, hath produced them?
When I was in Constantinople in 1851 I saw a
large porphyry sarcophagus. It was once the
tomb of the Empress Irene, when she was buried
in Prinkipo. It had been converted into a water
tank. It was in the old hippodrome. It is no
longer even there. It matters not to us in America or elsewhere now, what became of her tomb or
of her treasurer. There may have been a Lord
Elgin for the removal of the one and a convenient

Canada in the archipelago for the other. One
reign was similar with that of others. Another
ruler soon follows. Eye after eye is put out with
red hot irons ; and so on, until the Turk comes,
though with a scimitar—yet with some clemency—
about the year that Columbus went to seek Ca-
thay.

The purple robe of the Orient which enveloped
Constantinople, and whose resplendent fringes
hung over these isles, was associated with the
orthodox Greek religion. There was a closer
relation of Church and State here than the union
of civil and religious power at Rome. At no age,
or country, was there ever so permanent a system
with so much of intrigue, cruelty, bloodshed and
war, as at this historic point. It is the verdict of
history that the incoming of the Turk was a blessing to mankind.

In all these phases of power the monastery
has played a great part. Nearly all that remains
in these Islands of the Princes of the evidences
and emblems of ancient empire are these old
religious houses. They are not numerous, but
they are monuments of Greek rule, long in continuance, and at times resplendent in scholarship
and jurisprudence. The Turks were iconoclasts.
They spared little. Few of the images of the
orthodox church escaped their spoliation. They
were religionists. They came with fire and fury.

Manuscripts, pictures, statues, altars and structures fell before the Sultanic bâton.   Blindings
and mutilations, however,—crimes so horrible as
to make Gibbon's page blush,—no longer incarna-
dined the azure Bosphorus or Propontis.   In
looking here for relics of those regal and monastic
eras we find few.   Even the pictures which the
muse of history paints are but meagre, grimed
and almost colorless.   Open a page of Gibbon.
Read the story of these emperors.   Select one
whom you may call a sample.   Take Manuel.
He was a Comnenus.   In war he could not fight
for peace; and in peace he was incapable of war.
He was an anchorite in the camp; a Sardanapa-
lus in the palace.   No sooner did he return from
the field to Constantinople than he resigned himself to the arts and pleasures of a life of luxury.
The expense of his dress, table and palace surpassed the measure of his predecessors.   Whole
summer days were idly wasted on these delightful
isles of the Propontis, in the incestuous love of his
niece, Theodora—gift of God, in the euphony of
this rich tongue.   Here and there we have such
horrible hints as to these lovely isles, in the front
of history; but in vain have I looked for the
grand palaces, or even their ruins, in this isle.
Outside of the monasteries I have found but one
old tower of doubtful tradition, and the foundations of what is known as Irene's palace.   The last

are on the north side and in the vale that divides
the two high points of the island, a half-mile from
our humble villa. You will know the spot by a
dark-looking cave out of which much iron has
been extracted. It is on the left hand of the road
as you drive eastward from the village. As you
cross the stone bridge you see the tower and the
wide foundations nearly hidden beneath the red
soil and abundant foliage. If you desire some
mosaics—or something else archæological—take a
pick, and do as my neighbor, Mr. Edwin Pears,
author of the "Latin Conquest," has done : dig
away the dirt and you will be rewarded for the
delving.

When this palace was in the meridian of its
existence, and before the Turks razed all these evidences of Greek luxury, this isle was as picturesque as art and opulence could make it. Being in
sight of Constantinople, and with a climate where
even winter smiles, it was the resort of princes
and, of course, of the troop of hypocrites, parasites
and favorites which Walter Scott has well pictured
in his "Robert of Paris."

What a race the Greeks were and are ! For a
thousand years, and within my sight upon yonder
Seraglio Point, and here upon these isles of their
princes, they struggled and survived, after many
an exhaustive contest with the Barbarians of
the North and the Moslems of the East. Their

colonies were their glory. Here the Ionian children of old Greece still held supreme honor. Pre-
cocious often, but always intellectual, they ad-
vanced in nearly all that modern philosophy can
teach ; while Athens, the eye and soul of their polity and art, "arose to an empire that can never
perish until heroism shall cease to warm, poetry to
delight and wisdom to instruct the future."

CHAPTER III.

THERE are 250,000 Greeks in Constantinople, of whom there are 120,000 *rayahs*, or Turkish subjects. When Mohammed II. captured Constantinople, as I have said, he reserved the Isles of the Princes for the use of the Greeks who chose to remove there. Some thousands sought these isles as a residence; their descendants yet seek them as such. These residents are the cream of the Greek population of the city. Their features, especially the rich complexion, the straight nose in a line with the symmetric brow, seem copied from one model, or rather that model is copied from nature. I find that model upon the wall of the Greek villa of which the writer is at present the occupant. It is a Minerva. It is grace, dignity and wisdom in one.

Thirty years ago, just at the conclusion of the Crimean war, a lady—Mrs. Hornby, wife of an English loan commissioner who was afterwards a judge in Constantinople—wrote a brief chapter in her book about the delights of a farm on this isle of Prinkipo. She said: "We could buy half the island, with a garden and vineyard, for £500, and build a good comfortable house with a fire-place and every comfort." Now, five million pounds sterling would not buy the property of the town proper, much less the splendid mansions which rise and front street on street. The streets are terraced from the sea up the mountain side to the pine forests which crown the summits.

Upon the north-western side of Prinkipo there is a little city whose villas are rare in elegance and architecture, whose gardens have a hesperidean fruitage and bloom, and whose red-tiled roofs over the white or yellow buildings add a refinement to the town and isle which the bath houses at the water's edge, upon the jutting crags, themselves ornamental, in vain try to dispel. The rich Greek merchants and bankers, together with the English, German, French, American, Armenian and Swiss families, who summer here, have not only spent their money freely to decorate their own homes and grounds, but they have made winding roads, up hill and down, which cross and encircle the island. These roads are embowered most of the way by fig, olive and stone-pine trees. The culti-vated country is green at the opening of the season with the fig bearing its fresh fruit. The vines are putting forth their tender grapes. The pomegranates blaze with scarlet flowers. Hun-dreds, nay thousands, of people come to the isle

from the city for health and recreation, attracted
by these *parterres*, mansions and pineries.   They
often bring their provender along.

There are several extensive restaurants on
the island, where, upon the smoothed terraces,
in the open air under coniferous canopies, with
convenient tables and seats, there is plentiful and
breezy room for picnic parties.   Many invalids
from all parts of the East are ordered here, to
drink in the resinous ozone, while they lie on rugs
under the groves which cover most of the isl-
and elevations.   While the carriage roads are as
good as those of Central Park, the principal feature of the isle is the donkey ride.   This style of
locomotion is quite as common here as in Egypt or
the Riviera.   The donkeys require much prodding
and are not comparable with those of Egypt.
The company for a donkey promenade may be
made up of a dozen or more.   It is guarded by
the Greek donkey man, who, whether the animals
go fast or slow, keeps up with the pace, and steers
the beast cunningly by the tail, up hill and down,
from the quay on the north-west to the rocky top
of St. George on the south-east.   Upon this
height is a monastery of old associations, and an
out-door restaurant with its conveniences for rest.
What a prospect is here upon this point, overlooking land and sea, reaching from San Stefano in
Europe to Mount Olympus in Asia ; and from the

north, where the Alem Dagh lifts its mountainous
observatory of 1460 feet for the tourist from Constantinople to the mysterious islets of Oxia and
Plati, which leap out of the western sea, rock-
ribbed but lovely !

The French have a proverb that a man who
drinks once will drink again. It applies to travelling adventures. I began my travels to the Orient
in 1851. Since then, from Hammerfest, the north-
ernmost town in Europe, to the Atlas Mountains
in Africa and the Nubian Cataract of the Nile, and
from San Francisco west to Damascus east, I
have viewed many rare scenes. These travels
have been inspired by an unrest that belongs to
my nature, by a curiosity begotten of reading, and
by a romantic sentiment that defies the practical.
Bayard Taylor's " Views Afoot " started me to this
land of the Orient thirty-five years ago. But the
most interesting journey of my life carried me to
the Riviera on and along the Corniche road, and
from thence to Corsica, Spain and Algiers. That
trip was a search for " Winter Sunbeams." It was a
sanitary tour, under Dr. Henry Bennet's direction. The same prompting from an eminent
physician of Constantinople impelled me to this
isle of Prinkipo, here to summer. I had not seen
these isles in 1851, nor when I again visited Turkey in 1881. Last summer, 1885, we made a
hurried visit here in the launch of an Armenian

3

banker. He is an American citizen and flies our flag, when the Kaïmacam of the isle permits, over a grand tower at his villa overlooking the sea. I had then a glimpse, in the gloaming of the evening, and in a ride behind his high-stepping bays, of the rare mountains and valleys over which these roads run. But I did not dream then of the affluence of loveliness and sanitation which the isle possesses.

The question may, perhaps, be asked: "How could you, as an officer of your country, accredited near His Majesty at Yildiz, live so far from your post as the island of Prinkipo, which is fifteen miles away?"

To this inquiry of the anxious tax-payer I respond:

First: It is not so very far. I could reach the Legation Office within two hours from my home in Prinkipo.

Second: In the summer season, and by the instructions, I was not required to be at the Legation more than twice a week; only to be in call. I could go every day, as I generally did in the summer, if not for business certainly for recreation. The bulk of my business is done at the island, which I tried to make an agreeable resort for all Americans who came that way.

Third: It was a health resort; and health is indispensable beyond all things. In the summer Constantinople itself, or Pera, where the ambassadors winter, is uninhabitable by reason of its stenches, dogs and heat.

Had I arranged to spend another summer at Therapia, on the upper Bosphorus, with its endless round of visits, I might have made many more acquaintances and been more useful, perhaps, in gathering information about the endless Eastern imbroglio. But as health was predominant in my mind, I concluded to forego all this, in order to enjoy the refreshing and isolated delights of Prinkipo. This the steam launch, voted by Congress, happily seconded.

Among the requisites for health, and especially in pulmonary and rheumatic disorders, is the resinous quality of the pine. Bishop Berkley saw the poetic Star of Empire on its western way; but he made also some practical observations about the use of tar-water in consumption. It is an old remedy. It is one of the virtues of Prinkipo. Every breeze is laden with its essence; every pine needle distils it. Some years ago an attempt was made in Germany to utilize the pine-needle for making paper. It becomes apparent that the workmen in the factory, who had been sufferers, are by handling the fibres made well. A learned doctor makes investigation. He discovers that the tissue of the leaves of the pine is composed largely of resinous and oily particles with curative properties. He separates the fibres.

He finds that they resemble cotton or wool. He
gives them a new utility. He weaves the wool
into underclothing.   He establishes a health-cure
at Lairitz.   He is hailed as a benefactor and is the
recipient of many medals.   Out of this seeming
quackery cometh the pulse-warming underwear
which is now working its marvellous results.   But,
as I found out for my own comfort, it is much better to inhale this subtle property than to wear it
in flannels.   And hence my sojourn at Prinkipo.

Yet for all that, it cannot be disguised that the
beauty of the isle and its social allurements had
much to do with separating our home from those
of the other Legations which summer on the upper
Bosphorus at Therapia and Buyukdere.   In glanc-
ing over the diary of my wife, I find some para-
graphs which describe these attractions.   At that
time we made the journey under the crescent flag,
in the hospitable launch or *mouche* of our host.
The voyage thus depictured allured us hither for
our second year in the Orient.   Along with some
housewifely suggestions it will not be uninterest-
ing to the female reader to scan a page or two of
this diary :

At ten A.M. we are afloat.   There is some question as to the proper flag to sail under.   We naturally prefer the stars and stripes, but our *Capitano* has already hoisted the crescent and the star,
and as our host is of the Sultan's realm, though an

American citizen, we acquiesce. Beside, it might be difficult to explain our wishes to the captain or sailors, since all on board are Greeks or Armenians except ourselves.

We leave the dock at Buyukdere and secure the middle of the stream for the strongest current. It is a little misty toward the opening at the Black Sea, but the waters are indigo. The hills on the Asian shore are seamed and scarred by quarrymen. Out of their rocky sides many ribs have been taken to give life to the city below and the villas and palaces around. Upon the European side the hills are green, in varied shades, from the orange trees in the gardens at the water's edge to the dark umbrella pines above upon the hills and mountains. Here and there are some tints of a pale green. It is a double sign, first of the Mahometan color, and next of a Turkish barracks and fort. This is Sunday and all the flags of the Legations are flying. Jason's Mountain, tipped with a minaret, has a magic look and a far-away expression. Are these birds, which we see flecking the blue water as if a part of it? Yes, flocks of the "condemned souls," so called, which never seem to alight. They fly close to the wavelets. A few crows cross the stream without any noise. Some gulls of various species ride like Halcyon on the wave or dart down swiftly after schools of fish which fret the water in dark spots. Porpoises

come up and tumble back, enjoying their Sunday
out.   These are but transient objects, and the eye
returns to the curving lines of beauty which the
hills   make   on   either   shore.   We   meet   many
strange, fantastic sails—the vessels full of lumber
from the Black Sea or fruit for the city market.
The palaces of white marble seem to rise out of
the blue water.   We come to the narrowest place
—Roumeli Hissar, with its grand old towers and
walls.   It is a most picturesque spot.   It combines
with sky, water and land, a well-kept cemetery of
the Moslems ever so unique, and antique houses
ever so strange, dominated by these towers of Mohammed II., above, which are fit associates with
the running, clear, potential stream below.   Then,
above all, we see the Robert College.   It is
American, as we know.   I ask a friend :

"What is that long row of twenty white houses,
all alike, over in Asia?"

"Warehouses for American petroleum."

Ah! if they should take fire at night Edwin
Arnold would have to rewrite his "Light of Asia."
Now and then the landscape is smirched by
the black smoke of passing ferry steamers, which
ply up and down and across the Bosphorus.   We
pass the big boats which under French, British,
Russian and Austrian ensigns are going out to
breast the waves of the Euxine on their voyages
to Trebizonde, the Crimea, Odessa or Varna, for

cargoes of grain and cattle to supply the millions
of mouths in and about the capital. Far off, under their guise of misty beauty, lie the mountains
of Asia—Olympus towering with a double crown!

The day is a choice one as to wind and water.
Our chat goes merrily round. The soldiers are
drilling at the barracks on the Straits by the sound
of the trumpet, the fishermen and venders of vegetables ply their trade, and the city grows dim
and dimmer in the distance. Now a quietude settles over our company. Some draw out their
books, and others recline on the divans and lazily
watch the plashing waves in the wake of this little
dapper darling midshipmite of the sea.

But we are nearing our island. Lovely terraces
and vine-clad hills greet the eye in every direction.
We are closing up packages and gathering shawls
and coats, when a sudden cessation in the machinery creates as sudden a surprise. " We are
stranded," says our *Capitano.* Our friend on board
immediately lowers the flag to half-mast, and in ten
minutes we see a little sail-boat bearing speedily
towards us. Our host had seen the mishap. We
are soon transferred and landed at the *scala,* or
quay, where in carriages we are rapidly driven to
our destination. The gravelled drive to the steps,
the warm greetings on the balcony and the chaffing
as to cold luncheons, are soon over. We settle
down to a most thorough enjoyment of this lovely

island home. We are a party of ten, and yet
abundant room is found for night entertainment as
well as day. The grounds without are terraced to
the water's edge. Arbors, fountains, rustic bridges
and cool grottoes tempt the straying feet. A lawn-
tennis court is ready for its devotees. The *caïques*
lie rocking idly on the water within reach of
those romantically inclined. Even a small *barca*
is unloading its generous supply of oats for the
stables hard by at this private wharf.

The house is large and airy—filled with bric-a-
brac of every description. I notice one peculiarity, similar to our Southern homes! The "cuisine" is apart from the house ; but connected there-
to by a bridge.

I ask the hostess, "What is it?"

She replies: "Oh! we call that the Bridge of
Sighs."

I think it is well named, if the mistress has often
to entertain as generously as she is doing to-day.
To my relief I found out afterward that there was
a capable housekeeper on the premises to aid our
lady hostess.

One thing here strikes an American as peculiar,
and yet it is a custom that might well be introduced
with us. I refer to the breakfast hour. Each
guest descends to the dining-room when he or
she may choose, or may ring for coffee in their
rooms. As coffee or tea, with eggs and bread, or

some kind of confiture, jelly or jam only are given, it is not so difficult to serve one's guests. The custom gives ease and comfort to the lazy ones, and does not interfere with early risers.

A drive around the island develops more beauty and shows us the most luxuriant vegetation. As we are lavish in our admiration, our host seems to enjoy our pleasure with us.

"And to think," says he, "it is only four years since, that I took these bare rocks in their savage estate and have thus transformed them. All the growth of tree and shrub is in that four years."

It is indeed marvellous. But it belongs to the islands. It is entirely characteristic—this luxurious growth of plants and trees of every clime.

"But," I ask our host, "where did you get this beautiful finish of room and hall? It is not of the Turk—Turkish? It looks more like a home in America."

"Ah! you are right there," he answers, "for every door, window and floor was imported from the United States."

Our host and hostess are citizens of the United States. The orders given in the Turkish language seem quite musical to the ear, for as yet I have not heard much beyond street cries, which do not seem melodious.

All visits must end. The pretty little three-year-old son of the host prattles away; the young

maiden daughter receives our parting adieus, the
host and hostess are hospitable with renewed in-
vitations, while we can only express our thanks
and pleasure for all we have enjoyed.   It has been
a day of enjoyments unique indeed.   The launch
brings us safely to the city.   Another day has
gone by, idling in the Orient, but one rich in
delight of sun and wave, sky and atmosphere, and
charming entertainment.   As I turn my eye to
the East, to leave these bluest of waters and skies,
" I drag at each remove a lengthening chain."

     *   *   *   *   *   *   *   *

Would you know how a cosmopolitan thus introduced to the Orient settles down into snug
quarters at this end of the world?   It is not difficult, after such an experience as the foregoing.
At the risk of being tedious I will tell in the next
chapter, in my own words, something more of our
domesticities.

CHAPTER IV.

HOME LIFE IN PRINKIPO—OUR NEIGHBORS—LITTLE
GREEKS—FISHERMEN AND SONGS.

IF our jaded American citizens can race across
the continent to the Rockies and Sierras to find
the domes of the Yosemite and the geysers of the
Yellowstone, or wander amidst the Alps of Switzerland and the Highlands of Scotland, or sail over
the Bay of Naples and through the fiords of Norway in search of health and change of scene—
why may they not venture here, to these " Isles
of the Princes?" They are only a fortnight
from New York, or four days from Paris by the
Oriental express railroad *via* Varna to Constantinople. A day at Havre or Liverpool, a day at
Paris or London, another at Vienna, another at
glorious Buda-Pesth, a dash at Varna on the
Black Sea, and the next morning, at daylight, you
are at Cavak in the Bosphorus. A rest at Stamboul, and in another day here you are! in a villa
of your own choosing, or at a hotel where there is
every comfort, and where the scenery is unparalleled and the air balmy.

Appreciating this suggestion, the American citi-

zen, who pays for his minister abroad, will allow me
to make a picture of our new home at Prinkipo.
Already many of his compatriots of both sexes
have been within its sanctuary.

"Ah!" exclaims the travel-tired tourist from
Oregon or North Carolina—"ah! what a solace
and a joy to see the blessed old banner. No such
beautiful ensign have I seen since I left Sandy
Hook. God bless the stars and stripes! It is
all the dearer because no longer streaming upon
sea or land outside of America."

Thus is the loneliness of absence from home
relieved by a little color, and a symbol which ever
recalls to us our nation's pride and honor.

Our house does not rival, nor, indeed, equal by
many degrees, the superb chateaux of these fair
demesnes, or other mansions wherewithal the isle is
decorated ; but for seclusion, scenic prospect and
proximity to the pine forests,—as well as nearness
to Legation work,—it is all that the student, the
doctor, or the æsthetic could desire. Half way up
the mountain,—it faces to the sea and the north.
From its windows, if one could pierce the mountain
range of Asia Minor, there would be seen the olden
towers of Roumeli and Anatolia—the ancient
warders of the Bosphorus. But who would dispense
with these beautiful ranges of mountains even for
such romantic and historical additions to the view.
The highest peak is about fifteen hundred feet.

The range is crescent-shaped, as if emphasizing the national emblem. The foot hills and open vales reach to our Marmoran shore. They are covered with cultivated fields from the Pendik village and Phanar banks near Kadi Keüi to the side opposite, far across the Prinkipo channel, which is here over two miles in width. What a view from Stamboul and its minarets to the white houses of San Stefano on the European shore! The Prinkipo channel, along with the isles of our small archipelago, is a lake in seeming. That illusion is kept up as the sea runs south-easterly into the Gulf of Ismid, making the waters appear enclosed on every side. Along these shores are the remains of empire and commercial greatness.

The mountains on this coast close our view. But is not the sea blue here, and the bays and harbors charming enough, without seeking to unroll the endless panorama of land and sea, city and country, towers and mosques, mountains and clouds, which this terrestrial paradise furnishes to the enchanted eye? Within a mile from our eyrie of observation we can view the waves shimmering in the morning sun and snowy sea birds riding on the deep blue waves. Then the Asian mountains are meshed at dawn in an airy web of many hues; at noon, behold them radiant in celestial light; and at eve,—see the glow upon them from the west is one unclouded blaze of roseate and im-purpled living light!

I forget our household! One cannot live upon the whip-syllabub of descriptive scenery, however entrancing the view may be.

We found a villa ready to be rented to one who could "house-keep" it neatly. We were approved as apparently the proper tenants by the owner, an elderly Greek lady of refinement and courtesy. She lets her villa to us as she is about to depart for the summer, to visit relatives in Athens. She leaves it as tidy as any New England dame could wish. In fact, as we alight at her gates about five o'clock in the afternoon they seem to fly open magically, and as we cross the threshold what a charming picture is presented by the little dining-table already prepared for its hungry guests, with its hot, steaming soups, and *étagères* and vases all redolent of flowers, spice and fragrance.

But how can the masculine pen describe the inner sanctuary of a home? I call to aid the new house-keeper and from her house-book quote under protest:

I said to a friend: "Is this a Greek house?"

"Oh, I do not know that you would call it that exactly; it is a house of the country."

Let me then describe this "house of the coun-try": The tall stone walls and iron grating com-pose the barrier and gateway. They are decorated with huge pots of hydrangea, in full bloom. The bell-knob hangs at this outer gate. You enter a tessellated plaza before the house. This admits you to the lower rooms, which are the servants' quarters. As the house stands on the side-hill, to find the front entrance you turn to the right and ascend the white marble steps. These steps are kept immaculate by Miche333alis, our bright *factotum.* Here the high portico offers the main entrance. A summer arbor covered with that house-decorating plant, the wistaria, reminds us of home, and graces the terrace. Above it waves our own red, white and blue bunting, for which Admiral Woods Pasha, a neighbor, has already kindly provided a lofty staff. Some symmetrical fir-trees, a fountain with gold-fishes playing in the basin, and the garden in miniature, complete the terrace of the entrance. The black and white pebble-stones set on edge after the Pompeian manner, form fanciful designs of flower and foliage in the pavement which extends around the house. The tessellated walks remind us of the harem gardens of Cairo and the deserted earthquaken streets of Chios. A huge catalpa and a drooping willow adorn the kitchen court. The steps to the upper terraces are lined with fuchsia, geranium, snow-white jasmine, verbena and other gay flowering plants, while the terraces are fringed with lemon and orange trees, whose golden fruit would have tempted Adam as well as Eve. It is quite beautiful to see the fruit and flowers at the same time upon these trees. They give present odor and promise for the future, even though we may not be the happy recipients of their favors.

Enter the house and you are at once in a large square hall. This serves in summer-time as the general social room of the family. On the left and right are four large rooms. In some of the more palatial houses of the isle the entrance-hall includes two such end rooms, thus making one large airy apartment. Upon the ground floor we find a library and dining-room, both green and beautiful with foliage and flower. Folding glass doors at the end of the hall may be closed for winter or left open for summer. In either case, they reveal the stairway which leads to an equally open and airy hall above, supplied with wide divans in addition to other furnishings. The bow-window here extends over the portico. It makes an exceedingly attractive lounging or smoking room. In the cities of the East it is the practice to build this bow-window projecting over the street below, and at four or five o'clock in the afternoon, it is always occupied by a merry group taking tea, sweets, fruit, or Turkish coffee. Here they receive visitors. or survey the outside world of gay promenaders, and make laughing comments on all that meets the eye.

We are happy in finding our island home far up in the pure, dry air of the mountain amidst the forests of pine. Every room has the indispensable divan ; and from the windows we have the ever lovely views of the Sea of Marmora and the Asian land, with their never tiring and ever changing phases. Even now, at the outset of our experience, we have oranges, figs, and many vegetables from the gardens above, which are included in our leasehold.

It is amusing to hear the juvenile street venders call out in their long drawling falsetto some of these vegetables. The simple word *bamia*, becomes ba-ha-mi-a-a-ah ! This vegetable is a novelty to us. It is not among our American products ; but it proves to be relishable. All vegetables and goods are "cried" before sold. They come to your door on the numerous donkeys that throng the island, or on the backs of the peddlers who carry great show-cases of their wares. The cries of the venders are monotonous, but they are often varied by the recitation of some blind strolling beggar. The latter goes his customary rounds and enlivens the intense quietude of our surroundings by his plaintive appeal, in some verse of the Koran inculcating charity. I must say that he merits some reward, if it is only for his forbearance to ring the area-bell, with which our street mendicants of New York are all too familiar.

4

Our gardener comes to us daily with his floral
offering for the table.   There is always efflores-
cence enough for change and variety.   This morning, for instance, Xenophon's bouquet consists of
the snow-white, sweet-scented jasmine.   He looks
quite pleased when I compliment its beauty and
his taste.   I ask to see his manner of arranging
the flowers.   He has cut a pine branch with its
needles, and each tiny blossom is strung on each
needle point, thus saving the ravages of the scissors on the plant, and making a neat cluster
bouquet in quicker time than our laborious gardeners with their broom-stick stems could rival.

      *   *   *   *   *   *   *   *

Thus far you have been favored with a glance
into the diary of the newly inaugurated mistress
of the house.

It may be interesting to know upon what we
Greco-Americans subsist for food.   Our milk and
butter come cheaply enough.   They come across
the channel from Asia, from the fine farms upon
the slopes of the distant mountains.   These farms
are in sight.   They are rich in fruit as well as in
kine.   We were told that we should find one treasure in our Greek home—a goat.   For awhile we
tried our domestic sheep's and goats' milk.   Bah!
There is nothing like the original cow.   There
lies before me, in the shape of a foot-long pine
stick, our milk account!   It is marked with many

notches. On it my wife has written " 56 oks."
An *ok* is about two and a-half pounds, or in liquid
about a quart. The month's account is on the
stick. This is not an original plan of keeping accounts. It is aboriginal in many lands. It struck
us as convenient and honest ; and when rendered,
there was no need of calling in arbitration. The
amount due at the end of the month was summed
up in notches and *piasters*.

The *caïques*, which whiten with their sails our
lake-like sea, bring to our docks the finest melons
of every variety. Among them is our nutmeg ;
but the best is the *cassova*. Its color within is
golden and its meat honey, with a dash of musk
and spice. Grapes soon begin to adorn our table.
They are of various kinds ; but there is one peer-
less kind. No fruit has ever been grown upon
other parts of the earth equal to the fruit which
September welcomes here, chief of which is the
grape known as *tchaouch uzum*. While Europe
and America may excel in pears, apples and plums,
Asia has the most delicious fruit of royal clusters.
The *tchaouch* is of pure gold and of plum-like size
and rotundity. Its very pronunciation makes the
mouth moisten. The hills around Tcham Lidja,
where these grapes grow, are the Mecca of
crowds of the lovers of this Bacchanalian fruit.
Here the harem makes its visit, breakfasting on
these grapes and bread. Sometimes this exquisite

fruit is dried for winter use, but generally it is too rich to be spoiled in that way. Amber is not more beautiful in color. The cluster is very large and weighty. It seems bursting with a fruity bloom and gives such aroma and flavor that the bees follow it into the very *penetralia* of our *salle à manger.* This luscious vintage inspires poetic fancies, even before it is trodden in the wine-press—

" Less fragrant scents the unfolding rose exhales."

Peaches, plums, apricots and nectarines make up a picture for the table as well as a feast for the epicure. For meats, we have lamb and mutton, beef and chickens; for vegetables, there are varieties not known to the cuisine of the West, among which is the *bamia,* only not our bean, but more unctuous and toothsome than the marrow-fat pea. What could we wish for beside? Fish? Yes, the Propontis is the resting-place of the " fishy Bosphorus," as it was called in ancient days. It is the home of the fish called the mullet, as well also of the turbot and the mackerel, and a dainty, shining, nameless little beauty, quite delicate even without sauce. These disportively abound. The fishing with hook and line is spoiled by the nets which one sees actively employed at all hours, and wherever the shelving, pebbly shores and eddies invite. Indeed, the isles are surrounded with fishers' nets. You may see their high poles standing in the bays, and

PEDDLER OF MEATS.

a platform or lookout attached, where a fisherman watches for the schools late into the night. These nets are placed so as to catch the current, and as the water is clear it is easy for the experienced eye of the watchman to see when the fish enter the net. He then pulls the string and the finny fellows are entrapped. These platforms, or watchtowers, are seen on the upper Bosphorus as well as here. They are called "Talliens." This is a corruption of the word "Italians," as that race were the first fishermen here to use this peculiar tower of observation.

We often fish in another mode, in company with these Zebedees. When the *caïque* is sufficiently far out from shore, they throw out one end of the net, this end being buoyed up by a cork or gourd; and then, after the boat has described a circle, they throw quantities of stones into the water within it,—stones which they always carry in the boat for this purpose. These startle the fish from their quiet depths, and drive them swimming hither and thither, and thus they are more than likely to be ensnared. Fish, like our milk, meats and vegetables, are brought to our door, and are less costly than in America.

From the fishermen of Judea the world has learned much. The Greek fishers who convey us about these isles are not picturesque, nor statuesque, but they are Hellenic in many ways, and

chiefly in their worship of the waters.   As they sit
on the sandy beaches carolling their weird songs
and mending their nets, they bring to memory the
apostolic employment.   They are both   classic
and biblical.

What boatmen, what fishermen, what male
nereides these Greeks are !   How deftly they ply
the oar ! how neatly they untie a string or fix a
hook ! with what taste they arrange the fish when
caught ! For example : "I go afishing " with old
Nicholi on the east side of the island ; we catch
about fifty of all kinds, including some *rouget*.
These *rougets* are dainties fit for Lucullus.   They
are worth, in the parlance here, twenty-five *piasters*
per *ok*.   A *piaster* is nearly five cents and an *ok*
between two and three pounds.   In arranging them
in the basket, Nicholi turns up their heads and lays
out their tails, so as to make gold and silver radii.
The big shiny fish are the centre, they form the
hub.   Then with a stick he strips the scales from
the *rouget*.   The *rouget* immediately blushes a
rich crimson, at the indignity of this disrobing.
Then he arranges the colors so as to make every
other spoke in the radiant " mess " fiery with the
red hue.   Is this the result of that inborn love for
the beautiful which is Grecian ?

When the army of Xenophon on its famous retreat reached these very waters, their inborn love
of Neptune's element burst forth in shouts of joy

—"Thalassa ! Thalassa !"—The sea ! The sea ! I get this not from Xenophon my gardener, but from old Anabasis himself, who reposes on the shelf of the library.

The Greeks still love the sea. Not to speak of pirates who used to infest the archipelago, one need only look at the inimitable big sailing ships which plough toward the Euxine, after their own peculiar golden fleece,—which is horned cattle and grain from Russia,—to appreciate their spirit of marine adventure. With their isles and coast lines how could they do otherwise than love the water ?

They had fountains which were sacred to their genii. Was not Arethusa the nymph who, when chased by her lover, turned into a fountain ? Diana changed her, chaste goddess that she was ! Water was ever sacred to her. It is the emblem of purity in the East. The rivers of the earth are the children of Oceanus and his sister, besides having three thousand oceanides—little ones of the sea. Maury must have descended from the Greeks of Maronia, to have discerned the thousand streams and currents in the bosom of the deep. When Peleus would dedicate a lock of Achilles' hair, he bore it to the river Sporcheios. Peleus was a relative of Neptune and the father of the irascible hero of Homer. The Pulians sacrificed a bull to Alpheios, which was a river of Peloponnesus. It had a knack of running under ground, very

near the scenes of classic Olympus. It excited
mystery and devotion. Spenser, in his "Faerie
Queen," makes some rare stanzas about a congregation of the rivers of Britain. He copies the picture from Themis, the goddess of law and justice—
the first personification of a virtue—who summoned
the streams of Greece to a great Olympian Legis-
lature—I suppose, for improvement and appropri-
ations. Oceanus and the fountains were regarded
as divinities. How much the people of a dry
land like Greece must have appreciated streams!
Mr. Gladstone in his "Juventus Mundi," regarded
this water worship of the Greek as coming from a
different race; but Sir John Lubbock, who is better authority on this point than Gladstone, says
that this water worship was only an earlier stage
of the development of Grecian mythology.

The question is likely to occur to the reader :
" How do you get along with your household
and neighbors as to language? Do you speak
ancient Greek, and will that answer for modern
uses?"

Let me rise to a personal explanation. Mr.
Speaker!—Ah! Oh! I beg pardon,—Ladies and
gentlemen :—

There are two kinds of language spoken by the
modern Greek. One is called the Nooheknia.
It is the regeneration of the ancient language, and
is said to be the more classical and elegant of the

two. It is called "regenerated" because it differs
from the other—Romaic. The regeneration of
this language is supposed, in part, to be the elim-
ination of all Turkish words and phrases. As a
vehicle of thought it is growing rapidly; but it is
very unlike the ancient Greek, except in its printed
form. It is more or less tinctured with the French
in its modes of expression. Hearing it spoken in
the theatre at Constantinople, I have been struck
with its vivacious turns of expression. That it
is capable of great eloquence, tenderness and
music I do not doubt. In the provinces where
Greek is spoken it is said to be very difficult for
the peasants to understand a Greek newspaper;
while in Athens among the *élite*, the most
ordinary word familiar to the provinces is unintelligible. It is said by one who is conversant with
these dialects that the younger Athenians of to-
day would have greater difficulty in communi-
cating with the Greek peasants or fishermen in
Turkey, or even in Greece, than with foreigners
possessing a superficial knowledge acquired in the
mountain districts.

Judging by certain plays which I have seen performed in the modern Greek language, I think
the sense of pathos is more predominant in that
language than humor, although there is a close
alliance between the two. As one not unobservant of humor, I may be allowed to say that the

Greek has it, but not in the refinement, which is one of the last or highest reaches of civilization. The Greeks are not wanting in broad fun. There is much amusement in their ballads. They have a quickness or vivacity somewhat like the French or Irish, which is the spirit of witty retort; but of that kind of humor or wit which sees the incongruity of things there is not much trace in their nature. This may be accounted for by the condition of the people, living as they do in a state of insecurity, and their experiences tending toward the lugubrious. And yet, like the Irish, the Greeks, with all their disappointments and oppressions, are not wanting in a sense of that liveliness which is the source as well of poetry as of humor. Their every-day language bears the same relation to the written modern Greek language as the Saxon did to the Norman, or the Turkish to the Arabic. As for understanding the special Greek *patois* of these isles, we do not dare to begin its study. A few words of daily use at the table or about the house are all that we need, as our own servants, Pedro, the Dalmatian Slav, and Marie, the Armenian maid, both speak the modern Greek in its simplicity, as well as the Turkish language.

Who and what are our neighbors? They live along the road and up the mountain side. They too are Greeks. All make courtesy to us. From the day we enter our green-grilled gate to the present writing, there is the uniform bow and salutation, "*Kale mare !*" Good day ! or "*Kale spero !*" Good evening ! It is pleasant to receive salutation from the children. It puts one's politeness to its best vigilance, as the children are plentiful. Our three nearest households have between them—eighteen !

Had I come to Prinkipo when younger, say three decades ago, nothing but my sex could have stopped my maternal instincts. The isle is celebrated in that respect. These little Greeks bear grand classic names. Let them be perpetuated. Some few have ecclesiastical names, but the classics are in the majority. If I had to canvass Prinkipo for Congress, I would first cultivate the classics, then orthodoxy. For every Michael there are two Herodotuses ; for every Antonio, two Lycurguses ; for every Nicholas, two Pisistratuses. The Marys are plentiful, but the Helens are more so. The equivocal reputation of Aspasia has not prevented many namesakes. Our *femme de chambre* is called Theano! One of the fishermen is called Phaon, from that jolly mariner or ferryman of Lesbos, with whom Sappho fell in love before she fell into the sea. How sad ! Her love was unrequited. Our gardener rejoices in the name Xenophon. He is neither historian nor philosopher, and he never heard of Socrates. In fact, he had never heard of his own great namesake. My wife said to him one day : " Did you ever hear of your ancestor Xenophon, who was not only a handsome soldier but a great writer many hundred years before Christ?"

He smiles, ponders a little and with a slight play of fancy, as if he thought the madame were humorous, says: "I know no such man; but I know Xennie, who carries water to our garden." And this was the nickname for the pupil of Socrates, the historian, and soul of the Anabasis! This is the pet name of the hero who twenty-three hundred years before, had visited Byzantium, after his famous retreat over rough lands for fifteen months, making 1155 parasangs. In one thing our gardener resembles his namesake. He has that simplicity of style which was the relief of my callow college days, and an integrity of character worthy of Socratic teaching.

One does not enjoy his beef less because his butcher is called Pausanius, or his beans more because his gardener is called Xenophon. Nor do we enjoy our ice-cream, fruits, music, or the little courtesies of the isle the less, because they come to us upon the hills of Prinkipo tendered by Anastasia and Euphrosyne; or depreciate our purchases because Demetrius and Theodosius stand sponsor for the wares which they peddle along the highways of the isle. Our cook is named Katarina. Is it a German name? No: it is Greek. She has been cook in the family from whom we

ICE-CREAM PEDDLER.

rent for thirty years. They call her Amty,—which
is modern Greek, I suppose, for "Aunty." Thus
our South is reproduced with its nomenclature.
Of the children who play around our house in the
alley above and in the valley below, you may read
their names in the Odyssey or in Mitford; or, call
the roll of the Amphictyonic Congress, and they
will not be absent, like so many of our American
Solons, when their names are called.

While musing upon the various names which
are rich in classic and historic lore, I pick up a
volume which is a part of my diversion occasionally. It is that of a literary tourist, travelling in
the neighborhood of Athens. He is repeating, of
course, some of Childe Harold's exclamations
about "Fair Greece!"—sad relic of departed
worth, immortal, though no more! when he is
tapped familiarly on the back by a so-called son
of modern Athens, very likely a composite of Dalmatian, Saracen, German, French and Italian.
This Athenian speaks to him in the vilest French.
He points out, at the entrance of the harbor of
the Piræus, the tomb of Themistocles, saying:
"*Voilà!* the tomb of our greatest man!" The
tourist thanks him, and asks him for his card.

"I am," said he, "Miltiades."

The tourist starts back.

"What!"

The stranger smiles a savage grin and says :

" At your service."

" Who are you ?" I inquire.

" *A laquais de place*," he replies.

" Is it possible ! the hero of Marathon **so re-**
duced !"

" Oh !" says he, " I knew them all."

" Who—all ?" I ask.

" Those poor gentlemen of Marathon."

He confesses—this tourist—that his dream of
Grecian beauty and greatness is over ; but that
is the hard English way of looking at the world.

The sports of children are typical of their lives.
Even bankers' sons fly many-colored kites, and
fly them skilfully, as their fathers do on the
bourses of Europe. The little urchins in our
vicinity are histrionically inclined—inchoate Sopho-
cleses and Æschyluses. They play house-keeping
and horse, and occasionally have a Greek funeral,
with priest, corpse and pall-bearers. They show
their classic heredity, for they are running over
with dramatic mimicry.

The other day the children were much excited.
They gathered on the hill side in front of our
house, and began to clear away the pine needles
and cones to make a smooth floor for a restaurant,
or *Diaskalon*. Ropes were extended, upon which
hung from the trees in colored papers the flags of
the different nations.

"What are they doing?"—we inquire of our domestics.

" Oh, Excellency, it is a fête day among the Orthodox."

The children had caught the contagion. They are copying the *caffanées* on the mountains, whither to-day streams of pious Greeks are wending.

" Why this fête?" we ask.

" Excellency, it is the beginning of the grape season."

The people of the isle gather at the monastery and church of Christos, above, where the good Papa has baskets of the succulent vintage, in rich golden and purple clusters. These are blessed, and each person comes up to the altar and receives one of the blessed bunches.

Is this one of the Pagan rites which the orthodox Greek covers with a thin veneering of Christianity? If so, is it so very bad to be a little Paganistic? Indeed, it savors of the " first good and first fair," and deserves to be celebrated ; as much so as our Thanksgiving, with its turkey roast and pumpkin rites.

Between our point of view at the villa and the sea, there is nothing to interrupt the vision. We overlook the eastern end of the elder village by the shore. Immediately on the east is a Swiss valley. It is Swiss in its depth and picturesqueness. In its hollow are a few cottages, and on its sides some villas. This vale is a mile long, and runs up to the middle depression of the island. It is covered by a vineyard, interspersed with fig-trees now bearing fruit; and rich in their large fresh green leaves. Olive trees here and there silver the scene, and mingle with the few stately cypresses, once marking tombs which are now lost in the cultivation and changes of the soil.

Out of this valley there comes tripping a little fairy of the vineyard and fig-tree. She is singing a song whose evanescent music, with its quavers and turns, none but a Greek girl can master. Her mother is a donkey proprietress, and she allows her pet to salute our flag and its interterritoriality with her favorite roundelay.

This little one is my nearest neighbor. When I walk up through the groves and take my place, with a book, upon the circular stone seat under the umbrage of the pine trees, " midway up the mount," I hear her voice from the valley gradually nearing, until that voice becomes embodied, as she stands half panting with her race up the acclivity, yet trilling her " Pipini " roundelay! I insert a translation and notation of this popular song and its melody; * but the donkey queen will not allow me to transport to a New Atlantis her little Prinkipo princess.

* See pages 66 and 67.

It is very touching to see how, from lip to lip, simple verses like these will awaken a whole population to the influences of music in its quick and vivacious expression. With the simplicity of a primeval ballad, the " Mother Goose " melody conquers all tongues and hearts.

Another of these peculiar melodies or poems reminds me of the ballads which are sung in the nursery. I cannot translate it, for I do not understand the original.

The burden of the song is about an old man who keeps a cock, which wakes the lonely old man. A fox comes by and wakes the cock which waked the lonely old man. Then a dog comes along; it killed the fox that ate the cock that crowed and waked the lonely old man. And so on, until the log falls down and kills the dog, and the furnace burns the log, and a river quenches the furnace, and an ox drinks up the river, and a wolf eats the ox, and a shepherd kills the wolf, and at last the plague carries off the shepherd who killed the wolf, that ate the ox, that drank up the river, that quenched the furnace, that burned the log, that killed the dog, that ate the fox, that ate the cock, that crowed and waked the lonely old man ! Something after this manner is not unfamiliar to the little ones of all lands.

There is a folk lore among the Greek peasantry, which has its moralities, and this is assimilated in

5

THE BIRD SONG.

" Tò Πttìvt."

The little bird that I loved, that I still adore—
    Little birdie, my darling;
    For thee, birdie, I'm sighing.
The little dear bird has fled and will return no more:
    Come back, birdie, my darling,
    Oh! where are you flying?

Oh! cruel birdie! Oh! come back, before it is too late,
    Little birdie, my dear;
    My prayer won't you hear?
Return, my pretty bird, to me, seek not a better fate;
    Come back, birdie, my dear,
    For thy fate I fear!

You have, birdie, my heart; it has for long been thine,
    Birdie, my heart you carry:
    To come back, oh! do not tarry.
Return me, birdie, thine heart and come to nestle in
        mine.
    Come back, birdie, come back, darling,
    For thee, birdie, I'm sighing.

THE BIRD SONG.

" *Τὸ Πεπίνι.*"

67

many ways with that of the Orient. Of course it
is more or less influenced by magic, and hence it is
Persian, or Arabic. It has in it a whole circus of
interjected horses, and bevies of maidens in wilder-
nesses or in shipwrecks. It is full of wicked subject matters, but everywhere it is replete with
the marvellous. The myths of ancient Greece
or the Sagas of Norseland are not more pene-
trated with the supernatural than are the ballads and fables in the modern Greek language.
Many of these fables and stories are the same
which we hear repeated in our own tongue. They
are, in other forms, the substance of Uncle Remus'
stories of the fauna of our own woods ; and these
stories have an Oriental flavor, which came to the
original Guinea or Congo slave when the religion
of Mahomet spread through the Dark Continent
to these unhappy exiles of our ante-revolutionary
years.

CHAPTER V.

How is the island watered? For so fruitful a spot, it must have water. There is some dew, and that refreshes the vines, which are in great abundance. The vine does not seem to need showers, for in summer there are none worth noting. Wells of water are dug, and the Egyptian mode of pumping by ox, horse or man power is resorted to in the best places. On the east and west sides, where the isle is lowest and the gardens of melons and vegetables are many, the water is drawn by hand. We start with full cisterns, but these do not hold out long, and we are soon obliged to join the numberless households around us who live by this locomotive irrigation. Twice a day the picturesque scene presents itself at our garden gate—Antonius and his four pet donkey companions, with their surroundings and not unmusical voices. The gold-fishes must live in the fountain and the flowers must flourish on the terraces. Ergo, the cistern and fountain must be supplied. And Xenophon, like his great namesake, must work on a great scale, and so, with

69

lavish hand he distributes to his cherished wards
that which costs him nothing and which gives them
beauty and fragrance.

But where are the beautiful lawns of other
lands? Where the fresh green grass to cool the
hot air and relieve the eye? These are not. The
grass will not grow at all on this island. Under
the pine trees the needles are so thickly strewn
that they pave the ground and make the walks
quite slippery. The shrubbery is of a larger variety than elsewhere. It reminds me of the fragrant
machie of Corsica, of which Napoleon said, that he
"could shut his eyes and smell it," when he was a
prisoner in far off St. Helena. Nearly all of the
islands are covered by this shrubbery, where the
trees and rocks permit. It is a sort of heather.
I see the women and men folk gathering it for
"yarbes," as its roots are medicinal.

There is a *quasi* grass grown here, perhaps quite
as pretty as our grass. It is called *Lepia.*
Whether this is the right spelling or not, I do not
know. Whether it be derived from *lepus,* a hare,
which feeds on it ; or *lepas,* a shell-fish ; or *lepidus,*
pleasant—it makes no difference, so long as
it makes a pleasant lawn, whether for rabbit or
barnacle. It is very *petite* and delicate, and of a
pinkish white in color. Upon its tiny petals
the bees and other honey-suckers buzz all day
long. Butterflies of gorgeous hues and large size

WATER-CARRIERS.

vie with the tiny humming-birds of purple tint which invade our garden. This *quasi* grass can be shaven, and then it makes a pleasant lawn, but in so doing the little fragrant flower must fall with the gardener's knife for awhile, until the new blossoms come again. It forms a very attractive addition to the *parterres* of these island homes.

Our villa is a miniature compared with the superb villas which line the lofty terraces by the seashore, and within whose enclosures the tamarind, magnolia and oleander flourish. The best houses are roofed with red tiles. They are gay with verandas and covered with creepers. They are either pink, white or yellow with fresh paint. Everywhere embowered, they make pictures worthy of the Greek gardens of Antinous.

It is neither pedantry nor exaggeration to compare these island villas to the classic garden of Homer's Alcinous in the Phæacian Isle (Corfu), where that "much experienced," wise old man, Ulysses, was harbored for a season. To be prosy, let me make an inventory of that famous epical garden : It has four acres edged with green, and tall trees, cypresses, we suppose. There are reddening apples, ripening to gold ; blue, luscious figs ; red pomegranates ; heavy pears, and perennially verdant olives. Whenever one fruit drops, another takes its place. The seasons are so mild that blooms, buds and fruit appear together. The

vines are ranked in order, some fit to pluck, some
to make raisins, and some for wine. While some
are in flower, others are in grape. Some are just
coloring and some are purple with autumn. Beds
of herbs are ever green. Fountains shake their
silver in the sun. Streams abound as visitors to
the roots of the plants, and pipes with water connect with palace and city.

All this, and more, is here, with proper hydro-
statics and irrigation, in the palatial gardens of
Prinkipo. There are windmills, colored like Iris,
perpetually pumping, with a grateful sea breeze as
the motor. The breeze is a good worker and seldom "strikes," except for a few summer days.
Attached to house, stable and office are mystic
lines for telegraph and telephone, which deep-
browed Homer never vouchsafed to his heroes or
gods, with all their lording over lightning and
thundering oratory from Olympus.

There is one house here upon the island which
has on the outside, what most mansions have
within, viz. : exquisite colored tiles. This is very
unique. Its doors, porticoes and windows are
richly gilded and gracefully carved. It is but a
cottage, but it ever excites comment and admiration, followed by the exclamation : "Why does an
old bachelor keep so much of beauty to himself,
instead of sharing it with a wife ? "

Many years ago this isle was thickly peopled.

The people disappeared and the isle became a waste, remaining thus until only a few short years ago. It was a mountain of pine trees in a land denuded of other vegetation. Like all such places, it had to have a pioneer. Out of his enterprise, within a half century, Prinkipo has become a second garden of Eden. His name will be perpetuated, for the first hotel of the island is named after him, though it is located back and above that of Signora Calypso, of the Homeric epic. Signor Giacomo started early here. He kept goats and loved America. He was a Maltese. That means that he was more or less of a mixed race. Doubtless he was mostly Italian. He was a devout Catholic. He came to these waters of the East a little ragged, sailor imp. He was employed at a store in Galata. There is a Maltese street there yet, and through its fragrant purlieu I often ride, but seldom walk. I hurriedly go through this rueful *rue*, where Limburger cheese exchanges its odor with herring, and onions help assafœtida to dilate the nostril, *ad unco naso.*

After Giacomo's successes at Galata, he came here and constructed houses around his own larger house, and upon terraced plateaux that rose in loveliness to the mountain top. He decorated his terraces with a profusion of his favorite white roses, whose fragrance was wafted far out at sea ; thus in some manner, as it were, compensating in

his opulent days for the infragrance of his work in
the time of youthful poverty. What forty years
ago was " Giacomo's Delight " is now no more.
It is gone ; but the Giacomo Hotel with its pretty
terraces survives. It overlooks its rival, " The Calypso :" so, when Greek meets Maltese there is
a tug. Giacomo had a wife. She loved him and
music passing well ; but the island or her talent
did not furnish as much music as her husband did
diamonds for her adornment. So she bought a
barrel organ, and turned the handle. Handel
would have turned in his tomb if he had heard it.
The husband cultivated plants and statues. She
looked after the barrel organ and ironing. When
he came home and hung up his broad-brimmed
hat over a plaster cast of Diana, she quit her laun-
dry and took to Handel. He, Giacomo, had a
gun. Quails filled his larder, and the gun seldom
hung at rest near the statue of the divine hunt-
ress. With due regard for the religious cultivation of his own household and his neighbors' he
caused a church to be built. He made a very
happy speech in its honor on the opening of its
doors to the Catholic community. It was the first
Catholic church on this isle.

As I pass the hotel bearing his name, I take off
my hat. Why not? Giacomo loved America. I
wander over the terraces, among the umbrageous,
gravelled walks so cleanly kept. I receive the

greetings of mine host of " The Giacomo," who proves to be a brother of mine host of the " Hotel Royal," our winter home at Constantinople. He bears the Greek patronym of Logothetti—or " word bearer."

Everywhere upon these isles we are reminded of our classics, and of Homer especially. "Calypso" carries us back not merely to our college days, but four thousand years.

There has been much discussion between geographers and other learned men, as to which one of the Grecian islands was inhabited by Calypso. Some have supposed the Island of Fano was the fateful isle. This has been denied strenuously, for it is admitted that there is nothing very attractive about that rocky island. An American in passing by it, called it a " darned spot, only good for sharpening a slate pencil." Still the classic books generally regard Fano as the old Ogygia. The argument to prove that this unpronounceable and unmusical Greek island was that of the alluring Calypso, is its position. It lies between the south of Italy and Corfu, in the middle of the channel which leads into the Adriatic. Another argument, quite weak, however, is the fact that Ulysses took twenty-one days to get from Ogygia to Corfu. To know whether this was or was not good sailing, one should make inquiry as to the kind of vessel he sailed in, and the kind of weather he had. According to Homer, Ogygia, where resided the beautiful-haired goddess, was supposed to be the *nombril* of the sea, ὀμφαλός θαλάσσης, just as Delphi was called by the Greeks the navel of the earth. Calypso, as we know, was the daughter of Oceanus; and Oceanus was a river-god, and according to a correct knowledge of our rotund star, whose roundness Herodotus laughed at, the river was supposed to flow swiftly around the earth. One thing, however, is proven by a learned pundit, and that is that this island of Calypso occupied a prominent position between Cadiz and Troy. This is as much as to say that the town of Kalamazoo is situated somewhere between San Francisco and Boston. Pliny has something to say about this remarkable island. He asserts that it was not far from Cape Colonna, at the entrance of the Gulf of Tarento. There is nothing against this learned supposition, except that no such island can now be found on the charts. However, it is not unusual in the Mediterranean for an island to pop up in the day, and pop under over night. In fact, the island may be nothing but a myth; but the myths of Homer, to one who lives upon a Grecian island, become so real that we forget they are mythological. Here, we regard his heroes, divinities and localities as real personages and solid facts. Especially are they so regarded when

such a substantial and festive modern Greek tavern is called "The Calypso."

The gardens around many of the more splendid
edifices of Prinkipo extend down to the grotesque
rocks on the shore, upon which hang, in quaint style,
summer *kiosks*, or bath houses. Nearly all the elegant houses have in the corners of their grounds
summer houses, where in the evening or after
dinner the family gathers and visitors are welcomed, and where tea and coffee are served.

At the *scala*, or on the verandas, or in these
kiosks, you may observe the consummate charms
of this isle. Murray, in his hand-book, says of
Prinkipo : "The air is mild and healthy, and the
heat in summer by no means so oppressive as at
Constantinople ; and the women are said to be the
most beautiful in the world."

This last sentence shall be the text of a chapter
by itself, dedicated to the beauties of the isle.

CHAPTER VI.

THE traveller to the Arctics notes the glory of
the aurora borealis, the stupendous glaciers, the
superb fiords, and sublime mountains ; but he
notes also the absence of running water. Without this element of beauty, no landscape, however
grand, is perfect.   Even in the upper Alps, where
the tintinnabulation of the sheep-bells is faint, and
the torrents give only a murmur from below, the
eye tires of the frozen rigidity of all within its
range.   Here, on these isles, there is this drawback ; yet running water is not missed so much,
as nature supplies so many other beauties.   No
brooklet here sings between osiers and alders ; no
mountain stream bounds between crags and over
boulders, making motion and music.

Along the mountain sides we perceive long
lines and piles of broken stones.   What are they ?
The *débris*, or *moraines*, left by torrents of a past
age ?   Are these the relics of a once watery way,
or are they the ground-rubble of a glacial age ?

It was some time before my unscientific mind responded to these queries. Pedro, whose very name signifies a rock, inclined me to the opinion that they were the once gathered yet now scattered remains of boundary walls, when Prinkipo was in the height of her refinement and culture. What have we to do with such puzzles here? Have we not the magic climate, the narrow girth which confines the essential beauty, the atmospheric tints which color the mountain features, beautiful flowers in cultivated gardens, refreshing nooks under the umbrage of pine, olive, oak and fig, groves of endless variety, gray stones and moss-covered rocks, shrubbery whose fragrance sweetens the sense, and a shore whose indentations remind one of Prospero's isle, where the lover may load the air with sighs in the " odd angle of the isle ? " All these we have; but alas! no running streams, no tinkling fountains with thin sheafs of prismatic silver, and no lakes and cascades to give the isle more melody. But we have sea water of the loveliest tint—the celestial hue of blue. Should not that of itself suffice?

The ancient Greeks made much out of their restricted water privileges.

What classic, historic and poetic splendors surround the rivulets of Cephissus and Ilissus! They were monstered into wonders. They had nymphs and naïads innumerable. The Missouris and Danubes, Amazons and Rio Grandes are as

nothing comparable to the Scamander of Troy.
What will not genius expand and fancy glorify!
If the aqueous sterility of Greece conduced to its
greatness, what will be said of the aggrandizement
of America, with its Ohio, Hudson and Mississippi,
its lakes and its gulfs, its Atlantic and Pacific?

The voices of the isle are numerous. In such a
secluded spot, even the hum of a bee is noticed.
When the north-west wind comes to make its
streaks of shadow and its dimples of beauty on the
sea, the sighing thereof is soft-noted; and when
evening comes, and the sun with a ruddy, violet
haze makes charming silhouettes out of the nine
isles of the archipelago, the wind begins to play
on its piney keys, with an autumnal solemn sound,
like that of a rich-toned organ. In its pauses you
sometimes hear the sonorous tremolo of the train
across the channel in Asia, as it rumbles along the
railroad between Hadji-Ali and Ismid, and sweeps
the chords of another age and civilization. In the
evening, as we pass the venerable church of Christos, we hear the chants of the parish *Emphemerios.*
They sound as if half hushed within a sepulchre,
like the service for the dead, with its piteous *Kyrie
Eleison ; Christé Boétheson.* Breaking in on the
solemnity comes the pertinacious, shrill, rasping
monotone of the cicada. This insect is as old as
Homer. He likens it to a piping old man whose
voice is thinned by age. He describes it as be-

longing to a bloodless race, which in summer days
"rejoice with feeble voice."

This insect, from the midst of the isle, and by
the sounding shore, sends up its scrannel piping
through the pines of the *Diaskalon* to arouse the
monks of Christos for their matins. The very
roosters of old Asia, across the channel, respond
in greetings to the god of day and the isles of the
sea. These cocks act as if they were the chartered
libertines of the East, because nearest the auroral
gate. Thus nature salutes the sacred sun, as
through Heaven's portals he blazes to give the
cheering ray and golden day. This sentiment is
Homeric ; but the chanticleer has become a sign
and clarion of patriotism ; for his voice arouses
our Dalmatian *serviteur*, who prepares to raise our
flag upon its staff to continue the salute. Along
with the domestic flap of our neighbors' fowls, I
can hear from my open window the patriotic flap
of our bunting, as I sink off again in dreams of
home.

This grasshopper, alias locust, alias katydid,
or alias cicada, is a sign of dry weather. In these
Greek isles, as in Cyprus, Necessity has taxed her
maternal solicitude to find some mode for its destruction. It spoils the crops. I do not know
that it is so destructive on these as on other islands, but it is very numerous, and it must live
on something green. Hence, there is much con-

6

cern about the cicada. Judging by the sound, it is as dry as a militia regiment on a muster day. Some one — is it Tennyson ? — generalizes by saying :—

"At eve, a dry *cicala* sung."

Cicala is Italian for katydid, grasshopper or cicada. The latter is the scientific term. *Cicala* philologically indicates that the bird wants a drink. You can never see the insect ; it is as green as the tree on which it chirps. Chirp ? Yes ; for it does not sing. Its hemipterous membranous transparency is in a *scrape* on the under side of itself, and grates out by friction a shrill monotone, which on this island is only equalled in its annoyance by the unmelodious bray of the festive jackass. Its falsetto is relieved by snatches of sprightly Greek songs, trilled in girlish glee by shoeless little Calliopes, which rise in treblous hilarity from the cottages of the valley below.

At dawn we are awakened by three peculiar sounds. One is the "strain of strutting chanticleer." This is Shakespeare's expression in the "Tempest"; so that the herald of the dawn belonged to other enchanted isles. It is literally a strain—which means an effort ; for the firstlings of the chicken tribe try their tiny throats with a feeble agony which soon arouses the ire and ambition of the elder cocks. These make the isle ring from side to side with their clarion voices; and St. George's Mount takes up the shrill crow, which St. Nicholas echoes. Dreams here? Dreams in the early morning? Mayhap;—but not rosy.

Another noise begins. At first it is an equivocal sort of bruit. Is it the distant thunder from Olympus? Is it the rolling of the Ismid train again? It starts afar. It approaches! It is—no! —yes! it is the jackass Diapason! "It frights the isle from its propriety."

Be it known that nearly all the locomotion of these isles is done by these meek children of misery. I am prepared to defend them for their patience, industry and docility. I am ready to die believing in their good sense, despite the libels upon their long ears, as significant of obtuseness. I have been familiar with them at home and abroad —in and out of Congress. They are not insensible to kindnesses. They are not donkeys in the sense of dulness. I am in sympathy with Coleridge's elegy to the ass's colt. In monumental Egypt; around thy walls, O Jerusalem; and over the mountains of these princely isles, I have become their confidant and familiar. When Athanasius, our donkey driver,—long may he be immortal!—brings from below his white jackass arrayed in gold cloth, with blue beads on its noble forehead and around its milky neck—to keep off the evil eye—I know that I have a safe companion for the pleasant paths of the pine woods. But there is something too much of this animal on the isle, if one would seek quiet rest in the morning. When donkey parties meet on the roads, there is much recognition and confusion. I demand of Athanasius the reason of this sonorous braying. He responds :

"You ought, Excellency, to hear them in the month of May, when Jack salutes his Jenny, a mile or more distant, and when the general jubilee of affection begins its vociferate attentions;" or words to that effect.

After all, it is their affectionate nature that must speak out in these inharmonious numbers. It is said that in the isle of Crete, whence Homer imported Stentor for his epic, the shepherds, owing to the pure air, can be heard calling to their flocks three miles and more distant. The undulations of the air here furnish the same facility for sound. The isle, by conformation, is a vast microphone. Nothing is lost in the limbo of silence.

When Monsieur Chanticleer has quit his strutting and crowing; when Madame Poulet has finished clucking her morning "lay;" when the wind is quiescent and the star-spangled flag hangs limp by its staff, and the cries of the bread and vegetable mongers are stilled—then, as if by some infernal pre-concert this ear-benumbing noise of the amorous and jocund jackass begins again. It starts with an exaggerated case of asthma. This rasps the soul. It is as if the beast would lose and then catch his bated breath, with a harsh, squeaky sibilation—until a roar, as of forty hungry lions of the desert, comes to its infinite relief. It would seem as if all the powers of wheezy, whistling, gasping suction were exhausted. And so it is; but then follow the terrific expirations of the bellowing monster! This process of suction and emission is repeated with "damnable iteration," until it dies out in an agony unutterable— long drawn out. I can recall in adolescent association with the paternal saw-mill, agonizing creakings of ungreased timber-wheels, and the filing of saws on a frosty morning. I have had recent experience of the screaming *shadoof*, turned by blind buffaloes, pumping the Nile upon the fruitful land. In time I became accustomed to these chromatic eccentricities; but no one, not even the inhabitants of these isles, can ever become tolerant of this braying. When the *Equus Prinkipo* begins, as he does by lifting the upper lip and showing his white teeth, the driver takes precautions against too prolonged an agony. He makes a wild and desperate rush for Asinus. He beats and kicks him. He jerks his head up, down and awry. But still undaunted, the animal roars again and again; and his congeners from the town below on the shore, yea, even afar off to the *Dias-*

kalon on the summit, take up the horrid refrain, until one would think Enceladus had walked out of the sunless chambers of the earth to bellow upon the affrighted air. Oh! that these donkeys were like the lion indeed,—not of natural history, but of the species Bottom would have played in such an " aggravating voice" that he would roar you as gently as any sucking dove, or any nightingale. Certainly, Shakespeare, who was fond of locating his midsummer fancies upon enchanted isles, must have heard of these donkeys of Prinkipo, when he said : " The isle is full of noises."

I am not prepared to join in the general objurgation against this animal. He has excellent qualities. It is the duty of just criticism to discriminate and not judge too harshly. It is said of the mule that he is the meanest of brutes. I would not be unjust to him even. I admit that he has plenty of total depravity in his hind legs. I further admit that he is more obstinate than his step-brother ; but has he not the same evangelical expression of countenance? As the mule is only half an ass, dispraise of him must be discounted at the beginning fifty per cent. I assert boldly that there are good mules as well as good donkeys. It is a great mistake to suppose that the obstinacy which belongs to both animals is a vice. On the contrary, it is a virtue. Does not this quality of nature give strength of character and courage ?

Much has been said and written of the pride of birth. Much wit has been expended in relation to that pride. But it has never been applied except in derision of the donkey. This is unjust. Humble though his present station may be, he is of an ancient family. Royalty is shown in the thistle of his escutcheon. He has much more reason to be proud than the mule. He has no bar sinister on his shield. It may not be generally known that the mule has an arrogant and offensive pride, which amounts to vanity. The pride of the mule is in some respects justifiable. It is inherited. It comes from his maternal connections. Perhaps it is because of this that the mule joins in the general objurgation against his father, the donkey. If an ass is thrown with a pack of mules, he is sure to be badly treated, kicked and cuffed like a poor relation; while the horse is treated with the most distinguished consideration. The mule is always anxious to be near his equine relative. Those who are accustomed to these animals will verify this remarkable statement. Yet with all his faults the mule is a true patriot; he served gallantly in the late war, and has not applied for a pension! He took rank in the quartermaster's department and became a "brevet horse."

The ass is by no means a stupid beast; he is contemplative. He belongs to the tropical climate. The horse belongs to the colder latitude

and supplies almost its every emergency. The
ass is Oriental. His progenitor is from Central
Asia. He has long served as a domestic in its
regions. From there he went down into Egypt.
He is the offspring of a splendid civilization. The
Bible, which is a Semitic book, has many references
to him, both in the satire in relation to Baalam, and
in the beautiful entry into Jerusalem. The ass has
been exalted by the Arab. He came in with the
Caliphs. He shared their honors. My recollection
is precise that when I was asked to ride to the Pyramids, or to make a tour around ancient Thebes,
the admiring and eloquent donkey contractor never
failed to dignify the animal with such names as
" Washington," " Grant," and " Yankee Doodle."

The donkey of Egypt is quite an improvement
on all other donkeys that I have observed in the
Eastern world. His breeding is of high antiquity.
Great attention is paid to his pedigree : as much
as to that of the horse. In that warm climate
there are donkey barbers, who clip his hair in
order to prevent him from suffering from the
heat. When kept for private use this quadru-
ped is sometimes dressed in splendid housings,
rich and gaudy,—having on a high pad or saddle upon which one may even lie down in comfort. This aristocrat is by no means a sample,
however, of the ordinary animal, even in Egypt,
much less of those we find in Prinkipo.

DONKEY RESTING HIS HEAD IN AN EGYPTIAN TEMPLE.

I am inclined to tell a story at the risk of in-credulity. When in Egypt, in the winter of 1886, the donkey I rode,—which was named Sardanap-alus, because he fared so sumptuously,—became overweary in our long ride to the temple of Abydos, on the border of the desert. He was taken into the cool chambers and hitched amidst its cyclopian pillars. Under the very eye of a painted Rameses, he hung up his head by his upper teeth to a ledge of the structure, and thus rested. I thought at first he was fascinated by the double-crowned king of Egypt, who peered down at him with almond eyes; but no! it was a little contrivance of his own to hold up his heavy head.

I once served on a Committee on Foreign Affairs in the House of Representatives with a member from Nevada. He has since been Minis-ter to the Sandwich Islands. In the absence of better business before the Committee, he on one occasion entertained that body with a description of a contest between a grizzly bear and a jackass. The idea that the grizzly had failed in the contest gave great satisfaction to the Foreign Affairs Committee. It has been my constant delight since that time to review the terrific contest as depicted by the then member from the Sierras. If he did not exaggerate, as doubtless he did not, there never was in the history of animated nature a beast with such belligerent propensities. They

reached even to his extremities. How he defeated the grizzly bear; how he won the hearts
of the Nevada people; how he pursued his enemy
until the last element and microbe of its being
was annihilated, can only be told by the ex-editor
of the Nevada *Enterprise*, whose "lecture" on
that subject deserves to be filed with his diplomatic correspondence with King Kalakaua!

My memory of his description of this fighting
animal, recalled in the land of the Homeric Greek,
makes me tolerant of its vociferation in the early
morning. I have been told that after this victory,
Nevada seriously contemplated giving a place to
the donkey in her armorial bearings; and that it
was only prevented by a chivalrous spirit of inter-
State comity which would avoid offence to California's grizzly shield.

Every defence of this patient animal, by persons in or out of authority, has been welcome.
When questions are asked by his representative
in Congress, when the heads of departments send
in their reports, when a constituent writes for
the agricultural report—which frequently contains
his portrait,—when a newspaper makes inordinate
or irrational humor, well,—I feel like defending
the donkey against the attacks which the inconsiderate may make. Æsop, in his fables, and the
world, with its satire, have made light of his ra-
tional attributes. He is yet to be thoroughly vin-

JACK AND GRIZZLY FIGHT.

dicated.   A French poet once said : "*A force de malheurs l'âne est intéressant.*"   Some of our comic papers in New York have shown that the ass is conspicuously an ass when he does not know it.   Oftentimes an irrational person may call a man an ass.   He does not intend to, but generally he wrongs the animal.

I like the theology of India.   It reverences all animals.   The souls of men even inspired and often ventured within the precincts and anatomy of the animal after death.

I am proud to confirm the statement of the member of Congress from Nevada, that the ass is a warrior.   On the authority of Voltaire, I may allege that Mirvan, the twenty-first Caliph, was called "The Ass" for his valor.   Homer compared the coward Paris to a horse ; but when he sought for a heroic synonym to glorify Ajax, he likened him to an ass.

Greece and Rome were careful to produce the best breed of these animals.   They were more precious than slaves in the market.   Our own Bible has many allusions to this animal.   It makes him sacred.   The wild ass of Job may not have the equine thunder in his neck ; he may not snuff the battle from afar ; but he is, nevertheless, good at a fight when it is near.   He is a magnificent figure in Biblical history.   We know his relation with the life of the Holy Family.

Any one who has seen the Arab, or the donkey, whether in Egypt, in Syria, or in these isles, will understand that the family is not less holy by the presence of this animal.

Why is it that the ass's head never figured among the gargoyles and other strange carvings in the architecture of the Middle Ages? There must have been a prejudice at that time against all sedate and reverent objects. Coming down to a later time, it is not unusual to see the ass led in grand procession in the solemn ceremonies of the Church. Chants were sung in his honor. Even imitations of his braying, certainly more musical than those of Prinkipo, were heard in the responses of the assistants who took up the melodious noises and gave harmony to the mediæval mind.

What though this animal have the power by its voice to arouse us in the early morning; why should we be sluggard, when the virtues of patience and humility, which are typified in his life and manners, are given for our instruction? Let us not be iconoclasts. Let us believe in the dignity of the ass. Let him be rewarded, not as a degenerate horse and the subject of universal ridicule, but as an illustrious object of all the ages, having the qualities of antiquity and goodness, faithful among the faithless, and by no means to be disregarded because of his capacity of hearing.

It cannot be denied that the ass does sometimes allow us inhabitants of Prinkipo a respite from his music. It is at eventide. When the day begins, the donkeys are at their useful work, as carriers of water, provender, materials, furniture and persons. When the evening comes with its soothing light on the hill sides and amidst the pine shades, when families begin to pack up their rugs and dishes, preparing for a descent from the picnic grounds; when lovers begin softly to steal away and coo amidst the rocks; when the flecked and shaggy trunks and limbs of the old pines begin to cast their long shadows over the sinuosities of the paths— oh! then comes the quietude beyond all other spots of earth. Then each person may wander at will over the cliffs and under the silent groves, utterly isolate with the summer sea that makes no murmur against the placid shore.

I have the same fondness for birds in which George Sand delighted. They are almost as indispensable in a landscape as trees or running waters. When we first came to Prinkipo, in the late spring, there was at daybreak, in the olive trees of our neighbor, a bird which I persisted in recognizing as a nightingale. Such "liquid sweetness long drawn out," must have belonged to the *bulbul*. He made love to our roses like a true Oriental. He made love to a whole garden or harem of roses—the profligate! However, he departed as mysteriously as he came. The little brown *rossignol*, which our "Amty," the cook, kept caged under the catalpa tree in the back court, refused to sing any more responses. Her heart was off in the further East, where the seven rivers of Damascus are accordant and these birds sing the summer-time away.

Then we have swallows, who make their dudish toilets early in the summer. They cleave the clear air of the mountain sides, dart out of the vine-yards, and flit amidst the pine trees, never seeming to alight. They are quite tame and fearless. One morning while sauntering up the mountain I notice that two of these birds are following me. When I stop they hover about my head; sometimes within arm's length. I marvel. What does it mean? Am I near a nest? Are these the mother and father of a brood, as to whose safety the parents are apprehensive? I move on. Still they follow, darting far down into the valley, then sweeping on their electric wing to the very crown of the mountain and about the crown of my hat. I reason that they have been domesticated at the hearthstone or in the chimney, and so I solve the problem. A month or so ago, one morning, a cloud of blackbirds, our own cornfield larcener, took possession of the woods of the isle. They are known here as petty crows, and do much damage. They soon left for better foraging.

This isle is distinguished for quail. They come about the first of September in great flocks. Already some of the pioneers have heralded their approach. From the hills opposite our villa shots are heard in the morning. When the season is full it is dangerous to be about the woods, the shots are so numerous. These birds are migrating from the grain plateaus of Russia to the balmier fields of Egypt. Their resort here reminds me of the wild pigeons in the West—in Ohio, in my old district in Licking County, where for years they were wont to come and roost as regularly as the seasons came. They made the air black. They covered trees and fences with their multitudes. The quail here are not so numerous; but they fill the shrubbery. Some of the rich folk of the isle are buying up preserves to limit their destruction. After a few weeks' rest, during which they are massacred by the thousands, —even by boys with sticks,—the survivors take flight over the sea to San Stefano, or the shores of the Hellespont, *en route* for "winter sunbeams." Their flight and multitude raise a question about the quails of the wilderness, when Israel was hungry.

CHAPTER VII.

ALTHOUGH, as I have said, the mass of the population and visitors upon these isles are Greeks, yet there are many sojourners belonging to other nationalities. These are French, Italian, English, German, Russian, Greek and Armenian. It is not infrequently that we hear a veritable Pentecost. In these polyglotical accomplishments the Levantines are pre-eminent. They are the descendants—somewhat mixed—of all the commercial and adventurous people who have sought the Orient and its capital for occupation and emolument. Many wear the fez ; these are the subjects of the Porte. As we take our excursions by carriage and donkey, horse and foot, over these mountains and through these valleys, we often meet, ascending the hill in a palanquin, some aristocratic lady. She is loath to quit the old custom, —one by no means inconvenient or abandoned in Constantinople. We meet families and groups of these Levantine people. Most of them—of both sexes—dress like Europeans. Until they speak,

it is difficult to tell one race from the other.
Even then, as most of them speak Italian, French
and Greek, it is difficult. The Greek predominates even above the Levantine. The Italian is
next. The French tongue is used mostly among
the wealthy and official classes. The Levantine
inherits from his ancestor facile organs of speech.
So easy are these organs that it is no trouble to
form, in a mechanical way, by the *chordæ vocales*,
with tongue, mouth and lips, the various sounds
and the words of the various dialects of the " seven-
ty-two nations," of which Constantinople boasts.
Whether this be one of the evidences of heredity,
certainly it is remarkable how open-mouthed and
comfortable these people are, who for generations
have talked a dozen languages, and can roll the
words, spread the syllables and intone the sentences
of these different tongues. I know of children
who, while accomplished in French, English, Greek
and Turkish, revel in Russian and grapple with
German, as with their playthings.

My first tonsorial experience is in a barber
shop of the old town of Prinkipo. Most of the
barbers are polyglotically inclined. My particular
barber is either a Greek, a Maltese, a Sclav, a
Bulgarian, or a Montenegrin. It is impossible at
first to tell his native tongue. He has French
glibly. He speaks a "leetle Inglis" and understands less. He is well up in Italian, as many of

7

the families in this vicinage are. He has some
knowledge of Spanish as kindred to the Italian.
This extraordinary learning always gives me a
shudder, and especially when under his razor or
shears.   Being a stranger on the island, and having no very pronounced national features, it was
equally difficult for him to ascertain my nationality, except by inquisition long and pitiless.   All
I could do was to arm myself with the affirmatives
and negatives of various languages.   With these,
I made myself complaisant, to save my face from
bloodshed.   My first conversation with this artist
confirmed the general reputation as to the gossipy
quality of the Barber of Seville.   He had all the
gossip of the isles, including its languages.   The
conversation ran somewhat after this style :

BARBER :   "You have been here long ? "

I reply in Bohemian, "*Ne !* "

He easily understood that.

"You are here for your health ?"

I reply in Danish, affirmatively and negatively,
"*Ja !* " "*Nei, minherre !* "   "Yes, sir," and "No,
sir."   This puzzled him.

"An army gentleman, perhaps ? "

I reply in German, "*Nein, mein herr.*"

"O, then you are a navy officer?"

Having in view my position as Admiral of the
launch, I reply in Hungarian ; because, *lucus a non*

lucendo, Hungary is an inland country and like our own, without a navy,

" *Igen !* "—" Yes."

" Your vessel is at Constantinople ? "

Remembering that there was an Italian emigrant named Christopher Columbus of naval renown, I reply : " *Si, signore.*"

" You will bring your vessel to Prinkipo ? "

Ah ! here was my opportunity. It is the modern Greek in which I reply : " *Nae vevayos.*"

He is thunderstruck. It is evidently his mother tongue. Likely he has a Polish father; who knows ? When he asks me in French :

" Will your vessel touch at Athens ? "

I respond in Polish, " *Tak !* " No.

And then, with some hesitation, I add the French word " *Peut-être,*"—Perhaps.

" You will visit Egypt ? "

" *Sim, senhor.*" This is Portuguese for " Yes, sir."

The gesture or the manner with which these responses are made encourages him ; for he immediately asks whether I have ever been in Albania. I have no negative or affirmative in any of the languages of the Adriatic. My Dalmatian servitor, Pedro, is absent and my next best affirmative is in Russian.

" *Do prawda.*" Perhaps, being affiliated with the Sclav, he understands this language.

" You have never been in Egypt ? "

As the pine and the palm are associated in my mind, and having connected the Polar Midnight Sun with the Pyramids of the Pharaohs, I respond in Swedish, making it intense,—

"*Ja !*" Adding a little affirmative in Roumanian to give intensity to the remark, "*Gic.*"

After a pause in the conversation he resumes. He believes that he has my nationality fixed. He surmises that I am from some Balkan province, and he asks :

"Have you been in Roumelia, Bulgaria, Servia, Montenegro and Herzegovina?"

Knowing that I could not answer this truthfully, and not being able to answer it partially, I give him back in Roumanian an emphatic negative :

"*Na canna, bucca.*"

"You have been quite a traveller!"

This suggests the Chinese as the fitting language for the affirmative, and I say :

"*She !*"

Having no reference to Haggard's novel ; for it was not then out. To make the "*she*" expressive, I add another affirmative which I had carefully studied while boarding with the Chinese Legation in Washington.

"*Ta Jin !*"

"You like the Chinese, monsieur?"

Having succeeded so well with the Chinese, I answer promptly in the negative :

" *Puh!* "

This monosyllable disgusts him. His subordinates gather around the chair where I was being shaved, interested in this composite conversation. The artist then asks if I had visited Jerusalem. Here was my great break-down. Notwithstanding I had represented a Hebrew community in New York, with more synagogues than Jerusalem had in the time of Solomon, I was at a loss for a Hebrew affirmative. Happy thought! I respond promptly in the Arabic tongue, with its guttural peculiarity :

" *Na'am.*"

It sounded to me after I uttered it like profanity, and I fell back as gracefully as I could, waiting for the next attack, and equipped with a Japanese expletive.

" You like Constantinople ?"

I respond in a sweet Japanese accent :

" *Sama, san!* "

" How long have you been in Constantinople ?"

I give it to him in English.

" I arrived there in the year 1851—thirty-six years ago."

" *Mon Dieu!—mon Dieu!—mon Dieu!* " he exclaims.

" Have you lived there ever since that time ?"

" *Beaucoup, monsieur!* "

He has not yet learned my nationality. I am

afraid every moment that he will strike America. It comes :

" Perhaps you have been in America ? "

" Wa'al, yaas, I guess ! "

He could not understand this, for he had not been educated at Robert College, nor had he abided in Vermont.

I ask him in French which America he means. He says :

" South America. I have a cousin of my wife's there, and I would like to know how the country looks."

" *Le nom du cousin de votre femme ?* " I ask.

" Pierre Moulka Pari Michipopouli. He is like you, monsieur, quite a traveller."

Then began a fusillade of questions and rattling replies.

" You have lived in Paris, monsieur ? "

" *Jamais !* "—Never. " Been to Genoa ? " " *Si, signore.*" " Ah, you are English, are you not?" With the intense Turkish negative I respond : " *Yok !* " " French ? " " *Non.*" " German ? " " *Nein.*" " Sclav ? " " *Nee !* " " Italian ? " " *No, signore.*" " Ah ! Espagnol ? You look like one." " Pardon, monsieur, I am not." " Well," said he, taking breath, " will you tell me, monsieur, where you do come from ? "

" Don't you remember the only nation in the

world where the barber is as good as a king?" I said proudly.

"Oh, Switzerland. *Sapristi! Corpo de Bacco!*"

Understanding that last remark perfectly, I offer him a cigarette and say: "No, I am not Swiss."

"Brazeel?" "*Jamais.*"

The way that barber rubs the unguent into my hairless scalp and hirsute beard shows that he is a disappointed man.

The next time I visit the shop I receive marked attention. The hands all rise up. They pick up the earth, in a Turkish *salaam*. They distribute it in courtesy to the American Minister, whom they had meanwhile discovered. As I had been frequently turned away from the doors of our American Congress after twenty-five years' service, because I did not act or look like a member, so I was unrecognized here, by the "*Oi Barberoi,*" as having no national characterization. America was the last race or people to which this Greek barber assigned me.

Let me illustrate further. My wife and myself start out in a carriage for a turn about the isle. We drive over the Christos road toward what is called "The Saddle." There the vale spreads into gardens, and leads, on either side, by gentle depressions, to the sea. Here are two *caffanées* or *diaskalons*. Upon terraces, and under the shade of the pines, are sev-

eral hundred tables, with seats all temptingly arranged.   At various angles the blue sea is visible.
Here you may call for coffee, lemonade, wine or
milk.   From the peddler, dressed in his spotless
robes, you may buy an ice, for he has a small
confectionery shop on his back, with dainty spoons
and dishes.   Or you may do more : buy the toy
dishes, as Madame does, to carry home as souvenirs.
Our carriage has stopped on a terrace where there
is a picturesque family group of a dozen or more.
They are sitting or reclining on their mats or car
pets.   The outer wrappings of the females are
hanging from the trees near by.   They are having
a day's outing.   A faithful white hound, at the foot
of the tree, keeps watch over the clothing.   The
grown daughters are off climbing the neighboring
peak of St. George.   We hear their laughter and
fun far up the mountain.   The men are smoking
about in utter ease, while grandmother, mother,
servant and children roam about the woods.   That
which attracts us most is the odd costume of the
children.   It is made up of very gay-colored stuffs,
red, white and blue stripes alternating.   It recalls
our own national emblem.   Madame is enchanted, and calls one of the children to her for
examination.   As the child cannot talk French
or English, only Turkish, Russian and Greek, her
petite teacher, dressed in the same ruddy trainless
garb, comes up courteously.   She adds French to

her accomplishments. Her name is Minerva Kypriadés. She is a Greek, twenty years of age, and looks sixteen ! Her eyes are as black as her raven hair. She is now on a vacation. She teaches school in Odessa. She will not, however, be called Russian, much less Turkish, although born in Constantinople. She is Minerva —helmet, spear and all, without the Gorgon shield. She explains her costume as Russian, —a dress not for the city, but for the *campagna* — and of the country of Mordovski. It consists of a dark blue cotton skirt, with a wide red border, heavily embroidered in gay colors, red predominating, inserted above a very deep hem. The waist is of blue cotton, with the same style of gay collar as the trimming or border of the skirt. Her flowing sleeves are of alternate bands of red, white and blue, edged with the lace of the country. A very large square *tablier*, or apron. falls to the edge of the skirt. This completes the attractive picture. I must not forget the red silk scarf. It partly confines her heavy black tresses. The same fabric is worn by all the children. The young teacher has a heavy cincture, *à la Grec*. The buckles are big and of silver. Around her neck are several heavy gold chains of peculiar workmanship. This temporary governess of the children, whose grandmother sends them all to us in turn to make their

pretty obeisance, seems nothing loath to chat
fluently.

"Will not the children," I ask her, "give us a
specimen of their acquisitions?"

"Yes, with pleasure."

She makes them form a circle, and they commence their recitation. They make the pine
woods echo to their tender Demosthenic philippics
against the Turk. She has taught her little
charges patriotic and other verses, in which the
hated Ottoman comes in for vehement denunciation.
A small ten-year-old pupil recites an appeal to Grecian patriotism. She casts furtive glances around
lest some furious Ottoman with big turban and
terrific scimitar should leap from the bushes.
Luckily, all are Greeks upon the grounds. The
youthful declaimer is allowed free range. Only
upon sympathetic ears falls the stirring and furious waves of Grecian *anathema*. Then a dialogue
is recited. Then the small child, in costume, recites
a Greek song,—in the modern Greek, of course—
which is in strange contrast with her infantile
voice and mien. "How does it sound, compared
with the ancient Greek?" you perhaps ask. That I
can hardly answer. It is not unmusical. Its cadences, at times, are quite like the Italian, and in
places it had some tough and harsh Teutonic
tones; but on the whole it is quite musical.

The conversation of those we meet, especially

GREEK GIRLS.

that of the Greek women of this isle, is soft and sweet in tone. Perhaps these young Græco-Russians have given to the modern Greek pronunciation some jagged and ragged consonants which are foreign to the broad vowelled, *ore-rotundo* speech of the sweet South.

The performance of the children being over, we call for ices and lemonade. A hurdy-gurdy approaches. We improvise a Russian dance of the little ones *en costume*. Then, after much courtesy from the group, we bid them "good-bye."

The young teacher promises to call at our villa, where she has seen the flag. This she accomplishes at a propitious time with her pupils. We receive them in the arbor overlooking the road, and while listening to other recitations, we are fortunate enough to see the Turkish "Punch and Judy" approaching. The show is stopped and a few *piasters* serve to reciprocate their entertainment of us in the forest. And a funny one it was.

The Turkish "Punch" is very grotesque. He carries on his show through all the details from the cradle to the wedding, and from the wedding to the grave, with all the alternations of funny episode.

We saw our little Greek teacher no more ; but she kindly remembered our admiration of the pretty Mordovski peasant costume, and sent

Madame an apron of many colors, embroidered by her own cunning skill.

It is said that this isle is much changed since the Crimean war. Then it was Turkish embarrassment and Greek opportunity. The soldiers of that war helped to give piquancy and adventure to the pleasurable gatherings upon the isle. Then the Greeks of both sexes met at these places of recreation and diversion, with all their bravery of talk and toilet. This was especially the case in the old town of Prinkipo, which of late years has lost much of its prestige and attraction. Still its immense plane tree in the old *plaza* spreads its shadow, and the restaurants around it do a good business, amid many amusing escapades.

The old town reminds one of a town in Italy. It has narrow streets ; the markets are crowded with fruit, fish and meat stalls, and the street is full of donkeys and carriages, awaiting the arrival of the boats from the city. There are many saloons and coffee-houses, for the body of the folks are Greeks, and Greeks dearly love a tavern. There is in the homes of these traders and denizens much to remind one of the Dutch *housen.* They have a balcony or bay-window overhanging the street, with lights and beauties looking out at each end. The balcony is generally full of black-eyed, black-haired girls, who gaze curiously at the

passers-by. The old town once had its own pier
of debarkation and embarkation. That pier is
now in ruins, having given way to the more pretentious stone *scala*, in the new town.

What merry times those were when the Maygar
coffee-house supplied with its music, viands and
intrigues the company which met around the big
plane tree for coquetry and deviltry.

Then husbands and brothers here met wives
and sisters, to say nothing of lovers, to smoke
cigarettes, drink lemonade and sherbet, and eat
the walnuts already peeled and cracked. Then it
was crowded of an evening, not as the *scala* restaurant is now, to hear the music of the brass
band, discoursing operatic airs, but to listen to an
Arab band of tomtoms and flageolets. This barbaric music seems to encourage the drinking of
raki by the men. This white whiskey of the
Orient is worse than Jersey lightning. Whether
it was the music or the liquor that made them " rak-
ish," is not told by gossipy tradition. But at the
time of which I speak, it was the mode for the
fashionable beauties—Greek and Armenian—to sit
amidst the smoke and the *raki* fumes, on the little
stools yet in vogue along the Bosphorus, for the admiration of the ruder sex. The Maygar hotel yet remains, not far from the present *scala ;* but it lacks
the great overshadowing plane tree, whose roots and
boughs were protected as all old trees are here, by

a stone wall, and whose wooden seats and stools about the trunk were dimly lighted by lamps from its spreading branches. *Caffanées* surrounded the tree ; and while the Arab band played, torches burned and threw their shimmering light on the Greek and Armenian beauties seated around. Then there was a scene unknown to the witcheries of the present wooing world. These torches were called *madahs*. We still see them on the hills upon all festal nights. Then the Greeks burned them in honor of their " flames." The color is light blue, and much favored by those who represent Hamlet's father, in a proper ghostly style. When, therefore, in the good old time, a lover wished especially to honor his inamorata, he confidentially informed the master of the *caffanée* that he must burn so many *madahs* at his expense, and throw the light so as to designate and honor the " She "— whose " fair divided excellence lies in him." Then the elected beauty shone out as a star. Envy glittered in other eyes. The swain arose and made his Oriental *salaam* toward the dark-eyed beauty, while the tom-tom of the tambourine and the scraping of the viols celebrated this novel mode of election. On some occasions, when too much *madah* or *raki* was on board, little fortunes were spent by rich young Greeks, in honor of their favorite Helens. This was the mode of courting by the light of the moon ; for *madah* means " moonlight."

When enacted by droning music and crazy mastic its spectral light must have been effective. All that is changed now.

When the United States man-of-war "Kearsarge" was here about the Fourth of July, at the request of the citizens I asked Admiral Franklin if he could send his brass band to the *scala*, to play for the assembled islanders. He acquiesced. Its music made our flag known and popular. When I went down on the Sunday evening promenade, after the performance, I found our flag gracefully entwined with the Turkish ensign over the archway of one of the *cafés*. The stars add their glow to the crescent. This conjoint patriotism is as inspiring as the heaven above is glorious with the crescent moon and the brilliant constellations of the deep Oriental sky. There is an Arab band of six robustious Maltese performing. Our patriotism succumbs to curiosity. The crowd seems entranced by the weird music of the strange instruments. There are two fiddles, a tambourine of fish skin, and a sort of zither. These make tinkling noises to the rapid movements of the vocalization which are appetizers to the thirsty Greeks. The Arab music brings Egypt to my memory. All that is wanting to make the illusion perfect is a bevy of brown-browed dancing girls. The dim lamp in a sepulchral hall displays strange cross-legged folk, smoking on divers divans. This

Arabic style of droning scarcely changes a note for an hour. The words sung are loose love-words. It is fortunate that the Arab tongue is not well known. Mendelssohn's "Songs Without Words" would have been more decorous.

At every turn and angle in these isles and waters there is something to remind one of Italy; and especially of Naples, Genoa, Pisa and Venice. There is, *vice versa*, much in superb Genoa, and palatial Venice in her primal bridal beauty, to remind us of these Grecian isles and Orient lands. Ischia and Procida are the hand-maidens of Naples, veiled with a violet haze, which gives them their witchery of loveliness. The Genoese tower at Galata dominates the Golden Horn with a proud and ancient glory. Upon the Moslem Sunday this tower flies the ruddy crescent,—a symbol of dynastic change. You cannot tread the narrow declivities of Galata without coming upon evidences of Italian supremacy there in the elder time, for Galata was once an Italian city, and the seat of an immense commerce. The Venetian palace is almost concealed by its plebeian surroundings. It has remained as the property of Austria, whose Legation is therein established; for on the secession of Venetia from Austria, Italy did not reclaim this Oriental possession. The most significant reminder of pristine Italian glory in these lands it was my fortune to find in the upper gallery of St. Sophia.

The other day, in walking over the worn stone pavement of the women's gallery of the old Greek edifice of St. Sophia—lo! Dandolo, the blind nonogenarian of the Latin conquest of Constantinople at the beginning of the thirteenth century. Not in the body do we discover him. The place of his burial is unknown; although it is known that the heroic old doge and ambassador to Constantinople had St. Chrysostom's church for his sepulchre. There at my very feet, almost dust-hidden, I spell out his name! His name is quite legible. It gave a spell to the "Stones of Venice," which Ruskin has not catalogued. Like the stones of Memnon, even in the dim light from the dusty windows of that immense corridor,—it gives its music from another sphere. Captor of Zara, soul of the Fourth Crusade, and Nemesis of the Comnenus, it was his fire and vigor, when blind and aged, which compassed the fall of Stamboul, despite its 478 towers, its eighteen miles of triple walls, its fosses and fortifications, and its thousand years of immunity. Here he lies—somewhere under the spacious dome; but his fame has not died. The dragoman of our Legation, Gargiulo, who was with me when we discovered his monumental stone, is himself of Italian descent. He

8

has promised me to rescue his bones and indite his
history.

This incident is mentioned that the reader may
not marvel at the quantity and quality of the
musical dialects spoken in and around Constantinople.   The variety of speech is the consequence
of the enterprise and eminence of Italy in the Middle
Ages.   Why, St. Mark's at Venice is but a copy of
St. Sophia, almost its original!   The latter was
spoiled to decorate the former.   What spoils!
what opulence and imagery! what pillars and altars!   "Ouida," who lives and writes at Venice, and
receives much of her weird and luxurious fancies
out of its very stones, has stormed against the
abolition of the fairy gondolas and the introduc-
tion of steam tugs with their Cardiff smirch upon
the poetic and, I may add, the unfragrant canals.
She protests in vain.   It is like my lady of the
twelfth century in her boudoir, embroidering a
shepherd and his love, hurling furious obloquy
against the loom of Jacquard.   Let her Venetians
restore St. Sophia!   But no!   It is Venice that
is being "restored."   Since 1840 St. Mark's, which
had been sinking into the mud, has been under-
going repair to establish its stability.   Many a
strange inscription appears in the transformation.
Art not architecture, it is said, gave St. Mark's to
the world.   It was rather artifice than art.   Its
foundations and dome stand amid the changeful

dynasties and religions. No shoving or bracing
is needed at St. Sophia ; what is needed is that
which once glorified it. When the Moslem white-
wash is scraped off and the stolen property returned, what a wealth of art will reappear in the
church of the Divine Wisdom! When that is
done we will all join in the *Te Deum Laudamus*,
even though it be chanted in the sweet tongue
of the Italian spoiler. "Ill got, ill gone," says the
proverb. In spite of all efforts to save the splendid pile of St. Mark's it is cracked irremediably
The lagoons, like time, are slowly hiding its
beauties. No Mosaic wand can drive back the
Adriatic. No Dandolo, like the Danish king,
lives to say to the Adriatic : "Thus far! and no
farther!" Under the great dome of St. Mark's
the tide ebbs and flows, or such tide as the Mediterranean has to ebb and flow. No sealed
crypt keeps out impermeably its ooze. The floors
are breaking up. The invaluable decorations will
soon follow. The mosaics are being effaced by
the tourists' feet. Soon St. Mark's must be a new
structure, on new foundations, or she will perish.

It is not the Genoese tower, that stands on a
treeless promontory of Halki, looking toward
Stamboul, that alone marks the footsteps of Italy
over these isles and lands. The hotels and the
tinge of the Levantine *patois* show the recent

prevalence of Italian trade and growth on these shores.   Wordsworth sung of Venice:

" Once she did hold the gorgeous East in fee."

But now Italy is impotent to stay the great white Czar, or to do more than make the protest which she helped others to enforce in the Crimean war. Still Italy, next to France, is the relict radiance of European domination in these waters of the commercial Orient !

CHAPTER VIII.

THE mist rolls away from my enchanted isle by five in the morning, if there be a mist; or if not, the morning star sings "its spirit ditty of no tone," and departs. Then there is a reproduction of the evening before. It glows and glories over the Asian mountains. Their outlines are revealed in roseate tints; and when the sun-god is fully adrive in his car, there appears a series of pictures on water and on land from minaretted Stamboul to the scattered villas at the base of the Bithynian mountains. Windows glance with their diamond splendors, morn and evening, like Prince Arthur's shield, whose brilliancy was so dazzling that it was covered with a veil, and "which to wight he never wont disclosed." The sails of the *caïques* show whiter as they sail. The sea-mews glisten, blanched in the light, as they sport on wave and in air. The early shepherd carols, as he goes his rounds for the pasturage of his mixed flock of goats and sheep. There is a fresher scent to the wild shrubbery and to the pine odor. The arbu-

tus and cistus take away the stony glare of the
ground. They garland the very vertebræ of the
isle. The vineyards come forth in the morning
lustre, with new dew, all prismatic ; and the olive-
trees give to their peculiar dull verdancy a fresher
than their normal legal-tender tint of silver. The
lidless eye of God looks upon the prospect and it
rejoices. It is new born of a night of starry splendor !

As the sun rises in the heavens, it is canopied
with fleecy clouds. The ferry comes laden with
Greeks and Armenians intent on picnics. Donkeys are in demand. Gardeners sprinkle and
dress their favorite beds *en toilette* for the day.
Around goes on the "chirp! chirp!" of the cicada. We have dedicated this superb day to an
excursion to the remote end of the isle on the
east. There St. George's monastery holds high
court.

The early Byzantine monks, and the emperors
who sometimes became monks, always sought the
highest mountains for their monasteries. There
was one built on the summit of Mount Olympus,
I mean the Mysian Olympus—just as there had
been one built on the peak of Athos.

The monasteries in all parts of ancient Greece,
as well as modern Greece, including those of the
Princes Islands, were always built on elevations.
In this the modern Greeks copy their pagan

ancestors, who consecrated with temples the highest peaks. The Acropolis was always especially honored. In fact, there are upon Mount Olympus to-day, as well as upon Mount Ida, monasteries whose cells are beautiful in their ruins. When the snow melts upon Olympus there are traces of the convents yet to be seen.

The inaccessibility of some of these monasteries is beyond description. There is one known as the Convent of the Pulley. It is on the banks of the Nile. You approach it through the rocks, or rather you are received by the worthy brethren who jump, one after another, into the Nile to assist you to secure the boat with ropes and anchors, so that you may scramble up the heights with the aid of the blue-robed monks.

Sometimes these monasteries are reached not without risk from the brigands of the neighborhood. Sometimes they are reached by ascent through hundreds of airy feet with the aid of ropes. The idea of being hoisted into or near heaven with the aid of fragile hemp is not altogether unknown in our country to sentimental sympathizers with martyrs who have been convicted of murder in the first degree. There is a monastery on the Gulf of Corinth, under the shadow of an overhanging precipice. There are the monasteries of Meteora, and Mount Athos, both remarkable for their wild inaccessibility.

Many of the convents in Syria and the islands
of the archipelago are associated with those of
the Princes Islands, as unrivalled for the beauty
of their position and the splendor of their surroundings. Besides, there are many others in
Bulgaria, Asia Minor, Sinope and other places
on the Euxine, which remain as curious monuments of a wonderful era, when men sought exile
in strange places from the eventful social life.
Curzon, whose " Monasteries of the Levant " is
still read, found one in Persia, ensconced in the
fissures of a rock, with odd gardens adjoining the
buildings, displaying the horticultural intelligence
of the monks, the whole having the appearance of
a *bas relief* against a wall. He calls it a large
swallow's nest. There are other hermitages of the
same description among the precipices of the Jordan. These houses he studies, because they are
the most ancient specimens of domestic architecture, next after the houses at Pompeii. Their antiquity is illustrated by the monasteries on Mount
Sinai, at Cairo, at the head of the Euphrates,
and wherever the Greek faith prevailed. They
date back to the fifth and sixth centuries, with
contemporaneous relics, and crosses of rare workmanship, illustrative of the peculiar art of those
early periods.

It is to be noted in this connection, that the
monasteries, especially those which are our neigh-

MONASTERY OF METEORA.

bors on the Princes Islands, have undergone much
trial and trouble from the subjugation of the
Greek to the Mahometan. This has kept down
the splendor of the Church and oftentimes destroyed the establishment itself. Many of these
monasteries were regarded as castles. Curzon
himself says, that once while dining inside one of
them he heard, even at his meals, and while the
brotherhood were reading homilies from St.
Chrysostom, shouts and shots fired against the
stout bulwarks of the walls by enemies from without. Was not this in strange contrast with the
cadences of the good fathers within ?

But we have started to investigate St. George's
monastery,—the most celebrated of those located
on the Princes Isles.

We are hospitably received by Father Arsenius, who alone is in charge. He invites us to his
cool chambers in the second story of his monastic domicile. The views through the large window
are far-reaching and splendid. He shows us the
images of his shrines in the old church. They
are black with the holy-candle smoke of centuries.
An old parchment Testament, illuminated, of the
year 600, is produced. It is his chief joy. It
is a volume quite worn. It was brought by Father
Arsenius from his old home in the Peloponnesus.
Its text is in the Greek. The illuminations in red
and blue indicate its antiquity and consequent

sanctity.   In the little chapel there are a half-
dozen pictures ; but the gold is tarnished, and the
flesh colors also dimmed with the sacred grime of
smoking candles.

The good father, with much courtesy of manner and many inquiries about America, recognizes
the American minister as an " Excellency." He
invites us to see the holy spring.   It is in a deep
chamber amidst the rocks.   He gives us a drink
of its clear, cool water.   Then we follow him to
a sombre room still below.   This chamber has a
stony forbidding aspect.   It is almost on the
rugged edge of a precipitous rock.   It is, or was,
a retreat for the insane.   There is only one
patient now.   He is not there to receive us ; but
the iron rings, oxidized with time, are there, fixed
in the stone floor.   This humble ferruginous
memento of the days when the crazed were
treated worse than the criminal, excites much
interest.   In vain we question the father about it.
He only knows his prayers and his illuminated
missals.   Science, with its ameliorations, has not
to him any of the modern medicines for a mind
diseased.   However, we do glean with the aid of
my Dalmatian, Pedro, who talks modern Greek
with the orthodox father, some hints of this asylum.   From these hints we evolve this story of the
convent :

The legend goes, that many years ago, a shepherd tending his flock on the summit, where the monastery stands now, went to sleep one hot afternoon. In his sleep he has a dream. In the dream he is advised to dig in a certain spot close to where he is lying and "he would hear of something to his advantage." He digs and finds a horseman mounted on a beautiful white charger, with bells hung round the animal's neck. The horseman makes a behest to the sleeping shepherd.

He is enjoined to dig again, according to directions. He digs and finds an old picture. It represents exactly the horseman whom he had seen in his dream, even to the bells round the horse's neck.

A superstitious importance is attached to the discovery. This is strengthened by the fact that the shepherd,—who previously was quite an imbecile,—the moment he touches the picture becomes possessed of the most extraordinary knowledge in all matters. The picture is recognized. It represents St. George. From the fact of the bells round the horse's neck not being painted but real bells, the picture, when it was discovered by the shepherd, was and is still called "St. George of the Bells." In consequence of the sudden change which took place in the mental faculties of the shepherd when he touched the picture, a popular belief was engendered, and still prevails, that the picture possesses healing qualities in respect to persons diseased in mind. That persons slightly deranged, and more particularly hypochondriacs, derive much benefit from a sojourn in this monastery is a fact in support of which many examples are cited. Its splendid position, bracing air and regular diet, free from all excitement may have more to do with the cure than the healing qualities attributed to the picture. Where the picture was discovered this church and subsequently the monastery were built.

It is the view under the clear sky and tonical air rather than the picture that we have climbed the mountain to see. The distant view more than repays for the exertion. Beneath is "a sea of glass like unto crystal, which was before the throne." The near view is as wild a spot as the imagination could desire. Around and below are rocks piled on rocks, gray granite rocks, somewhat red with iron-rust, and amidst them various trees and shrubbery. At one *coup d'œil* we see the shores and isles. As we gaze, the full moon rises out of Asia on the south-east, and the full red and purple blaze of the sinking sun makes its long shadows and mystical lore in the west. Diana with her bow of silver, and Apollo with his arrows tipped with roseate light,—brother and sister,—unite to glorify the isles, out of whose myths in ancient days rose those Hellenic creations which the world has accepted as aptly interpretative of nature!

The good father bids us ascend to his reception-room in the second story. As we ascend we pass an open door and enter the ante-room. It looks like a little arsenal. With the aid of my Dalmatian interpreter, Pedro, I question the father, pointing to the three guns and a big cavalry sword hanging against the wall :

"So you, like my servant's apostolic namesake Peter, use carnal weapons upon these serene heights of devotion ? "

The good father's eyes sparkle and snap. He lifts off from the spike on the wall an American Martini rifle. He opens its breach tubes. He clicks it, with another snap of his Greek eye. Then he responds with a smile :

"Yes, Excellence. We must be ready ? We cannot tell in this lonely spot when we may be attacked."

" But the sword, good Father Arsenius, what of the sword ? Is it a relic of the ' Peloponnesiacum Bellum ;' or is it one of the evidences of your ancient Spartan spirit and valor ? Is it an Archaian souvenir, or an Arcadian cheese-knife ? Or is it an heirloom of your family out of the more recent Greco-Turkish revolution ? "

He catches the raillery of my ironic talk. He seizes the old sword. He handles it like an old soldier of Macedon. With Spartan brevity he rejoins :

" Excellence ! It is good for bad heads." Pointing to the Bithynian coast, he adds : " Brigands have been here from yonder shore ! "

It is indeed a lonely spot. The promontory, extending out to the sea, further east on the isle, was once a convenient resort for brigands from the main land. There now lives, alone on its extreme point, an old monk, who was formerly a prodigious brigand chief from the mountains of Asia.

In the monasteries of the Princes Islands the old monkish establishments are obsolete. I believe that they in some sort are under the control of the monks of Mount Athos. But from what I observed in the monasteries at the Princes Islands, the rigid rule against the admission of females is not applied. Most of these monastic communities debar all female creatures ; yet they have the poor taste to allow within their precincts huge tom-cats. These are procured from the outside, of course. The communities are kept up by the admission of members from without, and as some of the monks have entered the monastery in early life, the image of womankind has faded completely from their memory. In fact, the question is often asked outside as well as inside : " What sort of creatures are women, anyhow ? "

At Mount Athos not a female of any kind, not a cow, nor a she-cat, nor a mare, nor a ewe, is

allowed within the sacred precincts. No female
is allowed to exist upon their sacred ground ;—and
yet travellers have said and avouched that female
fleas live long enough here to breed, until the
nuisance becomes a positive martyrdom. These
pests are bred from the filth in the cells ; and the
dirty appearance of the monks indicates that they
assist this breeding. But nothing is so thoroughly sweet, elegant and clean as the monasteries
in and around Prinkipo, of which St. George of
the Bells is a chief ornament.

The good father invites us to his principal
chamber. It speaks of feminine neatness and perpetual purity ; quite unlike the exclusive masculine
style of Mount Athos. Its dress is of white lace
on sofa and chair and at the windows. He orders
his hand-maiden to bring us refreshments. Along
with fresh water from the well below, she tenders
us on a silver salver a dish of conserve of roses.
You take a spoonful of this dainty dish, and dis-
solve its honeyed atomies with toothsome delight ;
then a draught of the cold water, followed by the
inevitable mocha in a tiny cup set in a silvery
fingan of filigree. Thus refreshed you look
around. The white walls are not altogether bare.
Here are pictures of St. George and the Dragon,
King George of Greece and his queen, the patriarchs of the Orthodox Church and Abdul Mejid,
the liberal Sultan of twenty odd years ago. Here,

too, is Abdul Asiz, his son, on a gray charger, passing in front of his soldiers. He dresses in Turkish breeches of voluminous size now obsolete. The Czars of Russia also depend from the white-washed walls. Many cards of celebrities lie upon a dish on the table. The dish is two feet in diameter. It is decorated with a fine painting of the Saviour and his apostles, and a verse in English from Matthew xii., 1st verse. It is a gift from an English visitor. An ornate lantern of Turkish make,—the kind used by families on the dark streets of Stamboul before gas or American petroleum gave their light to the Orient,—is upon the table under the gay-colored chandelier. A beautiful and large Easter egg, with a resplendent picture of the Conception and Ascension on its shell, hangs by blue virginal ribbons to the wall. Is not blue the favorite color of the Immaculate Mary? This is a present from Russia. A gilt horseshoe hangs over a thermometer, and this completes the furniture of the reception room, where our reverend "papa" in his long black gown and rubicund visage, holds court.

We enjoyed many pleasant visits to the monastery of St. George of the Bells. In none of them, however, did we see the mounted horseman. He doubtless was an illusion of some insane devotee or inmate of St. George. That saint always appears as a cavalier. The bells are here, as they

BEATING THE "SIMANDRO"

are on the other monasteries of the isles. The
clangor which is beginning to arouse protestations
against the use of bells in cities, has no reason
when applied to such a locality as this isle. The
vibrations and music of the monastery bells touch
tender chords of memory, and seem appropriate
to those ceremonies which awaken the best emotions of our nature. While I was not impressed
with the magnitude of the arsenal of St. George, I
could not fail to moralize upon the incident in its
association with the bells. The *morale* took the
form of Longfellow's poem after looking at the
arsenal of Springfield. It was prompted by the
sound of the bell upon the distant monastery of
Christos, floating to us upon the still evening air
with solemn, sweet vibrations, which gave to the
poet's soul the voice of Him who was the Prince
of Peace.

When Mohammed II. captured Constantinople,
although he granted many privileges to the Greek
Church, he prohibited the use of bells. The bells
annoyed other populations ; but he allowed them
to be used in the churches and monasteries of the
Isles of the Princes. There they still remain.
These islands were then exclusively inhabited by
Greeks. No other people were disturbed by the
resonance of the bells.

There seems to have been much prejudice
among certain sects in the East against the use of

9

bells. I have seen in Jerusalem a heavy resounding oak board, which, being struck by a metallic
bar, calls the religionists to prayers. In the interior of the court of the old Greek monasteries,
there is often seen a monk who calls the congregation to prayer, not as the Moslem does, from
the minaret with his shrill appeal to Allah, nor by
the bells which were permitted to remain upon
this island, but by a bit of board called the Simandro, which is generally used instead of bells during
worship.

After a small contribution to the good father,
and many farewells, we mount our donkeys and
go home by the moonlight that now floods the
isle. It is too late to make a visit to the other
monastery. That is reserved for a promenade on
foot, as it is near our villa.

GREEK FATHER ARSENIUS AND HIS SABRE.

CHAPTER IX.

THE GREEK AND OTHER MONASTERIES OF THE ORIENT.

In a beautiful volume by Rose Elizabeth Cleveland, the sister of the President, there is a clever essay on the monastery. Aside from much transcendental remark upon the cloistered life, the essay has the merit of a succinct statement of the rise and object of monachism. Miss Cleveland makes a contrast between the chivalric and haughty soldier of the Middle Ages, and the humble monk in sombre cowl and scanty gown stiffened " by reason of his abstinence from the sinful luxury of ablution." She calls these men the aristocrats of society, the bulwark and ornament of the church. Royalty bowed to them.

Her estimate is evidently taken from Gibbon's chapters, and Gibbon's chapters have been toned by his study of the Greek convents which played so significant a part in the history of the " Decline and Fall." The rise of this body of self-sacrificing recluses—shadows of the living amidst other shadows — she traces back to Antony of Egypt. She fixes their *locus in quo* amidst the region of

tombs and stone-covered caves filled with the
bones and dust of human skeletons. Therein was
their place of penitence. In strange contrast with
this picture were the elastic monastics of later
times, such as Walter Scott describes and such as
these isles knew in the time of their prosperity.
They were men of scholarly worth, and yet they
appreciated physical comfort. The Benedictines in
the Latin Church are praised for their general bene-
faction. They were the agents for the spread
of Christianity, civilization and learning in the
West, while penitential cloisters gave refuge to
the inherent monastic spirit which Miss Cleveland
classes among the natural diseases of mankind,
when carried to excess. She regards the rise
of these soul-hospitals as the result of an indeter-
minate feeling among men, hovering between the
old world of Paganism and the new one which
ushered in dimly the Christian faith. This is the
life Jerome followed and Chrysostom eulogized:
"Afar from the shadow of roofs and the smoky
dungeons of cities, came the mystic light from the
unseen world."

Miss Cleveland closes her paper with the entrance of Charles V. into the monastery and with
the divine pillar of Simeon. She comprehends in
her sketch a truthful, though I think an exaggerated view of the strangest institution to which
man ever consecrated his religious energy. These

isles are full of the evidences of this cloistered energy. When we visit Halki, Antigone and Proti, we perceive better illustrations of it than the Turks allowed to remain in Prinkipo.

The temperament of the Oriental tends to religious emotion and elevation of soul. It leads to the different forms of mysticism which have prevailed in the monastic life. There are various names given to these monastic people. There is one especially translatable. It is that of Quietist. How far at the present time religious contemplation forms a part of the life of the monk, has not yet been revealed, and certainly not to the tourists who visit the celebrated monasteries in the East. Many enter the monastery because when they become old and after a life somewhat irregular, they desire to repent in solitude. Some have been engaged in trade and have had disappointments. A gentleman who visited Mount Athos made inquiry and found that the love of tranquillity, pure and simple, without any religious enthusiasm, had overcome a grocer from Corfu, a tailor from Byzantium, a merchant from Syria, a sailor from Cephalonia and a leech-gatherer from Larissa, in Thessaly! One would surmise that the last-named person would naturally feel disinclined to solitary contemplation ; for there could be nothing so haunting and horrible as the memory of blood-sucking !

The motive which impels so many to take the monastic vow, and which they keep with great fidelity in these Oriental monasteries, is the love of tranquillity. This grows upon the devotee, like any other habit. It is a great temptation for a class of men to forsake the world, and find their happiness in some hermitage, especially in a land where there is so much balm and beauty of scenery, and where the human kind brings so much care and trouble. This class become weary of a world where there is perpetual revolution in human thought, and restless progress in human endeavor. There is a great fascination for them to abide in such a "laboratory of all the virtues," as Mount Athos has been called.

There have been some, however, who have degenerated after selecting these monasteries for life. They return to the earth with its activities and pleasures. I have in my mind the experience of a German, who recanted before he entirely gave his mind and vow to the work; for, after reaching Salonica from Mount Athos, he made a candid confession. Although he had little care for the enjoyments of this world, he had not elevated himself in the scale of righteousness by his secluded life. When he returned to the flesh pots again, how he devoured the political newspapers, magazines and reviews! How hungrily he foraged in the libraries of his consul! Thus he demonstrated the emptiness of that life which was inside the cloister, and which shrank from the heat and dust of political and social activity.

It is nearly forty years ago since Curzon wrote his "Visits to the Monasteries of the Levant." It is a comprehensive book, and gives in detail all that is worth knowing as to the architecture of the monastic structures and the spirit of their recluses.

That which inspired his book was his collection of ancient manuscripts. These he had picked up in various out-of-the-way places in his travels. They were of white vellum leaves. While admiring the antiquity of one and the golden azure of another manuscript, there arose memories and reflections of the strange places from which they came and the strange people from whom he obtained them. He gives an account of the most curious of these manuscripts and the adventures connected with what he calls the pursuit of his venerable game. Most of the monasteries which I have visited in the Princes Isles have old manuscripts or antique Scriptures. These are the first thing the monk shows to the stranger. Besides the Holy Scriptures, there are many writings which have been composed within the precincts of the monastery. They have reference to the rules of Christian life. Some of them promulgate the doctrines of the heresiarchs, which in the early ages of the Church created so much confusion and rancor. The

author, Curzon, however, does not dwell so much
upon his trophied manuscripts. He grows eloquent by the contemplation of the picturesque and
superb natural situation of the monasteries.

He tells many curious stories about his mode
of procuring the rare manuscripts which he collected in the Orient, many of which have been
placed in the British Museum. He travelled
many miles at great risk to find them. On one
occasion he was after a Syrian manuscript of great
value. It was alleged to be in an old monastery
in Egypt, near the Natron lakes. He took good
care to carry along with him some persuasive elements not recognized generally among the literary
amenities, but he was so anxious for the manuscript and a Coptic dictionary of which he was in
pursuit, that he filled his carpet bag with some
bottles of *rosoglio.* This is a liqueur to which the
Orthodox Greek monks are partial. Many of the
monks even on Mount Sinai comfort themselves
with this spirit. It seemed to be potential,—
more so than a golden fee. Curson gathers the
monks around him. He fills their cups with the
sweet, pink *rosoglio,* and the monks with much talk
about good-will and humanity. Now Curzon
knows that there is a famous old crypt, in which
the manuscripts are kept. The monks have no
idea of the precious souvenirs below their cells;
but at last, by social persuasion, they discover a

FINDING RARE MANUSCRIPTS.

narrow, low door which enters a small closet. This is the crypt. It is filled with manuscripts to the depth of two feet. Lying there *perdu* are the loose leaves of the Syrian manuscripts, which now form one of the chief treasures of the British Museum.

"Ah! at last!" he exclaims, "here is the magic box! It is a heavy one."

The boozy monks shout out:

"A box! A box! Bring it out!"

"Heaven be praised!" they scream; "we have a treasure!"

They pull out the box, and thus is resurrected some most interesting manuscripts. They have been buried in this ignoble literary grave for cent- uries. Let the guild of letters drink bumpers to Curzon, the literary detective of the ages,—and drink deep in the pink *rosoglio!*

I have read a story of a famous monk,—I think he was of Alexandria. He belonged to the early day,—perhaps in the fourth century. He went through all the austerities of the desert, and wound up in one of the cells on the borders of the Matron lakes. He was followed by many of his faith. They lived separately, but they assembled together on Sunday and had a sort of prayer meet- ing. They were totally abstinent. A tourist gave the saint a bunch of grapes. He sent it to another brother; that other brother sent it to a third brother; at last the grapes passed through the hands of some hundreds, and came back to the saint. He was happy in the abstinence of his brethren, but he refused to eat himself. This was the same saint who killed a gnat which was biting him. It made him so unhappy that he retired to a marsh where the flies had immense power,— equal to a Jersey mosquito,—but he stood the insectivorous infliction like a high-toned, chivalric, middle-aged and manly monk. His body was so much disfigured when he went back to the monastery, that his brethren only knew him by his voice; and even his voice had a strange sound, like that of a buzz-saw in motion.

One of the romantic legends which haunts the neighborhood of the monastery on Mount Sinai is that connected with the disappearance of a convent. There is yet heard, between the Sinaite mountains and the Gulf of Suez, the music of its bells. It floats down on the breeze at the canonical hours. The Arabs declare that they have been within the convent, but that the moment they cross the threshold they lose sight of it. The Bedouins have similar legends about other convents. Some of these supposititious convents are buried beneath the sand. Others have a bodiless hand, ringing the vesper bell.

On the top of Mount Sinai, which is scarcely thirty paces in compass, there is not much room

for any structural or musical performance. The
dignity of that mountain comes from another
source !

Considering the beauty of this world, the loveliness of its Tempes, the splendor of its Olympian
prospects, is it not strange that so many of our
kind creep into caves in their monastic fanaticism?
The Orient especially has had whole flocks of
hermits roosting in pigeon holes upon the sides of
mountains. Some of these caves are so high and
some so far below the surface that we can only
liken the monks who live in one or the anchorites
who burrow in the other, to animals. In the time
of the Crusades, when the Saracen was roving
about the Eastern world, his favorite diversion
was hermit-hunting. In the early Greek frescoes
frightful representations of these chases are pictured. The Saracen on horseback with long spear
punctures the monk and hermit. There is something heroic in this monastic constancy to a faith,
that never seems to be outworn,—a constancy
which leaves home, riches, even thrones and all
mundane pleasures to seek for tribulation. These
men retire to the very dens of the earth, subject
themselves to cold and hunger and all the agonies,
trusting that their pain in this world may be their
felicity hereafter, and that those who bear the
cross to-day will wear the crown to-morrow.

CHAPTER X.

THE monasteries of our neighbors in Prinkipo have but few monks. These seem almost entirely engrossed with secular affairs. They look after the lands and the funds. They make grain and wine, and at the same time keep up their religious exercises on proper occasions. If you would have the monastic life of the East in all its fulness and variety you will have to go to Mount Athos. There you find about three thousand monks, not to speak of a population of seculars who reside in the vicinity and who may amount to three thousand more. There are many monasteries, the monks of which vary from twenty-five to three hundred. It is very difficult for a stranger to obtain accurate information as to these figures. The Greek is not a statistician. He answers no question with facility and satisfaction. If you ask him a question, as I have asked the monks on this island, his answer invariably is, "Nobody knows," or to put it in the Greek, Ποιος το εξεῦζε. The truth is, nobody here cares an *obolus* about the antiquities or history of the monasteries, or their imperial founders. The modern Greek priest cares as little for that of which we inquire as he does for Homer and his divinities. Let us, however, try the experiment of inquisition with our nearest neighboring monastery.

Within half a mile of our villa, up the mountain, is the monastery of Christos. It is being rebuilt. It is not so old as the others upon the isles, but the structure is more extensive and stately. It has a revenue as well from the Greek orthodox establishment as from its tillable land. There are a half dozen monks who attend to the gardens and raise the grapes and make the wine, which is the favorite *vin du pays* of the isles. They purchase grapes in large quantities from the Asian vineyards, which lie in a southerly and easterly exposure over the long range of land across the channel.

To this monastery is my morning walk. There is a half-way place under the broad sheltering arms of the pines, where a score or more of people can rest on a circle of stone seats. From here you can look down into the Alpine vale below, covered with vineyards, figs, olives and cypresses. To complete the sylvan scene the pine forests skirt this valley. On reaching its top, on the right and among the pines, are a dozen splendid tombs. They are walled up on the side of the hill near the monastic group of buildings. Here the rich and

the notable are buried.   The crown on their monuments indicates rank and station.   Here are the
tombs of the patriarchs of the church.

As I wend my way up to the monastery upon
this quiet Sabbath day, I find a freshly laid circlet
of rare flowers upon one of these monuments.   It
is a new monument, made since we have lived
here.   In the shadow of the trees fronting the
monastery are a dozen or more of elegant carriages
and dog-carts, with liveried drivers.   Something
unusual is going on.   I enter the alley that leads to
the church, pass between the line of beggars hold-
ing out their boxes for *piasters*.   There is a crowd
of peddlers selling bread, in rings a foot in
diameter.   This bread has the look of pretzels.
They are piled artistically, ring on ring, upon huge
platters carried upon the heads of the venders,
or are placed upon tripods.   The bread is called
simits.   The picture will show the vender.   I
enter the church.   It is commodious and full of
people of all classes.   Where could they come
from, and so early?   From the village a mile or
more below?   I suppose so.   There is a sweet
canticle being sung by trained boys.   Is there a
funeral?   I see no coffin and no corpse; for at
Greek funerals the body is exposed in the coffin.
Many large candles are aflame ; and many of the
people, especially those in elegant toilet, hold
smaller lighted tapers.   A bishop in full canonicals,

VENDER OF SIMITS.

crozier in hand, and a hat gorgeous with gold, and a stole of most beautiful satin with gold embroidery, enters the pulpit. Around him stand other priests, some in purple robes, some in their plain black dresses, all with the strange black hat whose crown is rimless, save at its top! The chant is taken up by the priests. The candles are decorated with white and black ribbons. Many of the visitors are in mourning. Some are weeping ; but it is not a funeral. It is the customary mass for the souls of the dead. It is usual, as I learn, forty days after death to have such ceremonies when the family can afford it. The chant ends. The flowers are carried out to the tomb, and with them three large mysterious baskets. These baskets are draped in crape, and ribboned with white and black. I follow the crowd of villagers and peasants who throng about the tomb. Here the baskets are emptied. Each person rushes pell-mell to obtain some of the contents of the baskets. These contain flour, boiled simply with water and salt. Some eat portions on the spot. The women fill their handkerchiefs with it and the boys their hats. All struggle and almost fight over the sacred emblem, which has been blessed. It is a curious ceremony. When done, the parties immediately interested re-enter their vehicles. The gentlemen light their cigarettes. Much bustle ensues. The soul of the departed is supposed to be quiescent and pacified! Not-withstanding the solemnity of the sweet music and that the candles are beautifully symbolic of the reillumination of the soul, and despite the old pictures of the Saviour, the Virgin and the saints with their golden aureoles and radiant glories, which make the scene impressive, yet the *finale* with the bread and the mob of folk who rush to eat and bear it off, is not consonant with the solemn beauty of the ceremony and scene.

The Greek congregation is not particularly reverent, although the rites are ceremonious. I cannot but feel that in their devotion they have not intensely the religious feeling or emotion. I have before me a statement which confirms my remark: A lady visits one of these churches with a friend who is a Greek devotee. The latter is a fashionable woman. She conducts her friend in a courtly way around the church during service, to look at the pictures of the portly and sad-eyed martyrs. She lights a dozen or more of tapers to show her pious zeal; and as she lights them, as the story is told, she hums in an undertone the *barcarolle* in Masaniello, muttering between the staves:

"The Virgin! I shall give her four candles. Is not my own name Mary? Look! What a pretty effect! Note her gold hand and her silver crown with the light flashing on them! Now comes St.

BEGGAR.

'George, — I like St. George. He shall have two candles. Who is this? Oh! St. Nicholas; I cannot bear St. Nicholas. I shall pass him by!"

Her companion ventures to intercede in favor of St. Nicholas.

"Very well, then! As you wish it! There is one candle for him! but he never was a favorite of mine! There are two saints in the calendar to whom I never burn a taper, St. Nicholas and St. Demetrius."

It is not to be ignored that in the church ceremonies there is need of some gentle warder. What with the bowing and the whispering and the laughing and the fidgeting of those who are gathered in a Greek church; what with the lattices of the gallery where even yet in some places the females are shut as it were in a prison, and the chanting of the priests in some sort of reckless music, there is not enough to attract the ear with sweetness and gentleness, or to impress the beholder with veneration. Ah! I forget the gorgeous stoles of the priests. The clergy seem to hold the Eastern Greek in thrall by their superb attire. So it is with the head-dress of the priests. The very hair upon the head of the Greek priest has a patriarchal air. It may, like a crucifix, or a torch, or a sacred candle, give an added solemnity to the scene. Perhaps it is known to the reader that the Greek priests are not permitted to use

either razor or scissors. They can only reduce
their beard by plucking it out. This is an old
Jewish law. They do this plucking with such skill
as to make their locks look elegant without being
too abundant. In part they resemble our American Indians, who pluck their beard from their
faces, though they never worship God by tearing
their hair. I have seen some of the Greek priests
who must have omitted this species of martyrdom,
as their back hair was done up in coifs after the
feminine fashion. The Greek priests have a
splendid physique, from which even their feminine
head attire does not detract.

A stranger in a strange land,—almost unnoticed
except by the beggar who asks alms of me,—I
pursue my way after the ceremonies of Christos
church, to the *Diaskalon*,—the Greek name for
the grand plateau and restaurant. The flags
of all the nations deck its central pavilion.
Scattered at various elevations are these same
funereal people at the tables and chairs under
the pines. They are inhaling the aromatic
pleasures which mingle with the fumes of the
coffee and tobacco ; and therewithal the recent
mourners of the church are solacing themselves.

From beneath the wooded coverts we catch
glimpses of the bluest of seas and the clearest of
skies, broken by the mountains on the mainland
and isles, whose grandeur never ceases to attract

the vision. Resting here, I reflect on the strangeness and remoteness of the scenes of the morning. They are a curious blending of classic Paganism with Christian rites. The very crosier of the Patriarch, with its eagle and serpent is copied from the *báton* of Jove, and a hundred incidents remind me rather of the Hellenic mythology than of the monastic and Christian life which is here professed.

The Greek church and ceremony which I had the pleasure to observe at Christos did not please me as much as the mosque and its ceremony. The mosque has a simplicity of beauty. The Greek church has its altar, which is separated from the church by a screen, but it has neither aisles nor side chapels. The screen is ornamented, as is the church, by pictures of saints. Shade of Raphael! What pictures! How hard, dry and horrible they look. The Greek Church will not have images, it is said. Surely these pictures are the likenesses of nothing in heaven, or on earth, or in the waters under the earth. No Catholic in Spain would have dreamed of decorating his favorite saint with such votive offerings. Besides, the decorations in gold and silver on hands, eyes, ears and nose give such a comical effect, that the beholder only enjoys it as the caricature of art, and not as an aid to religion.

Many of the pictures that I have seen in the

Greek and Coptic churches, and many of the manuscripts, are adorned with grim painted illuminations. They are from colors composed of various
ochres. The outlines are first drawn with a pen
or brush made by chewing the end of a reed
until it is reduced into filaments. This pen is
then nibbled into proper form, after the ancient
Egyptian method. With this reed, or pen, the devotee fills up the spaces between the etchings with
his colors. The Virgin is generally dressed in
blue; the other figures are of a brownish red, and
they all have a curious cast in the eye. The artistic work is hardly equal to that of the ancient
Greek or of the modern Italian, but yet many of
the oldest churches and some of the rarest books
of the Old and New Testaments, as well as the
manuscripts of many classic works have thus been
glorified by much rude art.

The ceremony of blessing the grapes, to which
I have referred, is another example of classic
reminiscence; nor is it confined to the Orthodox Greek church. There is a Catholic Armenian
church in the village of Prinkipo. Upon one
Sunday morning we were invited to be present
to witness the same ceremony in that beautiful
church. The church was arrayed with all the
flowers of the season. An immense basket of
grapes stood upon the gorgeous altar. The Patriarch, who is a brother of the Armenian banker,

Azarian, conducted the services. It was a touching and reverent recognition of the kindly gifts of God. But, after all, is it not taken from the similar ancient Greek ceremonies which were intended to honor Bacchus, who "first from out the purple grape crushed the sweet poison of wine"? The great world, as Tennyson has it, may spin forever down the ringing grooves of change, but how much of the changeless remains! The very images of Greek beauty in feature are here, worshipping the god of the vine, in the church of Jesus Christ.

> "Vulgar parents cannot stamp their race
> With signatures of such majestic grace."

The priest of Apollo stands confessed at the altars of Prinkipo!

The Greeks have a good deal to answer for. Their faults are numerous, but they are superficial. As in other nations, so among the Greeks, the scum rises and is prominent. The *timeo Danaos* and the wooden horse have demoralized them in history.

The Greek is not to be confounded with the Levantine. The latter is a mixed race, from Italy, Malta, France and other western lands. The Levantines are Franks and so called. They are born of the early adventurers from the time of the Crusades to that of the Crimean war.

There is much to be said about the religious
devotion of the Greeks in association with these
monastic isles and structures.   I know that they are
reproached for their weakness and their indiffer-
ence, when their empire was crumbling, before the
Latin conquest, led by the Fourth Crusade under
Dandolo and Baldwin.   It is said by Mr. Pears, in
his history, that while the Moslem was thundering
at the walls of Stamboul and when the city was
again about to succumb, that the Greeks of the
hierarchy were disputing about non-essential articles of their faith and doctrine.   The empire of
the Greek fell, but his faith lives.   It will not
be disputed but that he has an ineradicable love
of liberty worthy of his lineage.   Nor will he rest
until the Hellenic race is enfranchised.   But how
can we reconcile the condition of his church and the
Ottoman state in Turkey to-day?   The Greek
rayah, as yet, is a *serviteur* of the Sultan.   He
wears the red fez.   It is the badge of subjection.
He seems to wear it willingly.   He is ready to
take office whether as Vali of a province or Caï-
makam of a district, as minister of state or grand
vizier, and when his sons are dubbed as Beys and
Effendis they eagerly seek position and promotion
in the offices of the government.   His blue Fanar-
iote blood runs through a line of linguists, statesmen, diplomats and soldiers, celebrated as the
favorite servants of the Ottoman Sultans.

Nor is this more marvellous to those who read the stories of the Greek revolution than the orthodoxy of the Greek Church, which in Turkey is content to be the subordinate *imperium*, with its Patriarch, under the Imperial Majesty enthroned at Yildiz and supreme at the Sublime Porte!

Perhaps we do the race of Leonidas and Demosthenes injustice. But after observing recent events in Turkey, it may be said that if the Greek people of Turkey—five millions strong—are waiting for the palingenesis, or new birth, they did not show it when Bulgaria raised the sword to cut the Gordian knot of the Berlin treaty, in September, 1885. The Greek *rayah* was then a helpful subject of the Ottoman.

The distinguishing feature between the Latin and the Greek churches should be understood. The very word " orthodox " presumes on the part of the Greek a fundamental, dogmatical difference. That difference lies in the rejection by the Greek of what is known as the double procession of the Holy Ghost. The Greek, and following it the Russian Church, repudiates as an interpolation the word *filioque*, in the creed of the Council of Constantinople of A.D. 381. The Greek went further and charged five heresies against the Latin. They are enumerated in the sentence of excommunication pronounced by the Patriarch against Pope Nicholas I. These heresies include :

First. The doctrine that the Holy Ghost proceeds from the Son as well as from the Father.

Second. The practice of the Latin Church of fasting on the Sabbath.

Third. Its sanction of the use of milk and food prepared from milk in the first week of Lent.

Fourth. Its prohibition of priests from marrying.

Fifth. Its withholding from presbyters and bishops the right to baptize persons with the Holy Chrism.

Sixth. The use of unleavened bread in the Eucharist.

And as the sweeping conclusion, a repudiation of the papal claim of supremacy.

Another thing may be said for the Greek Church. It never claimed, like the Latin, any measure of temporal authority; only spiritual jurisdiction. But this was more in theory than practice.

If I were to seek for the glory of Greece, I would not go to the Acropolis; nor to Thermopylæ; nor to the art of Phidias and Appelles; nor to the ancient theatre or the modern chamber where Deleyani and Tricoupis debate; but to their heroic adherence to their orthodox faith. Whether that faith be pure or impure, whether its Protestantism is better than that of Wickliffe, Huss, Luther, or Calvin; whether it was wise or not in its times of trouble, when Polycarp died, or Byzantium fell—it has been consistent and heroic

ŒCUMENICAL PATRIARCH DIONYSIUS V.

even unto death, under tremendous stress of circumstances, and amidst the fiercest fires of persecution. Five hundred years before Wickliffe—
seven hundred before Luther—the Greeks maintained against all comers their orthodoxy and
primitive doctrines and early practices. The New
Testament came to all Christians in their opulent
tongue. The Nicene creed, that settled as early
as A.D. 325, the Arian controversy as to the Trinity
for all Christendom, came out of the first Œcumenical synod of over 300 Greek bishops under the
presidency of a Greek bishop of Spain. The
Greek Church "safe-guarded the Niceno-Constan-
tinopolitan, Ephesian-Chalcedonian symbol of the
Trinity" in the form left by the fourth Œcumenical
synod. What contests it has had in its own
bosom! what struggles with Caliph and Pope!
what persecutions from Saracen! what contempt
from Protestantism! But it has never yielded to
the edicts of power, the force of arms or the flames
of persecution. Enduring all the tribulations of
martyrdom and the contumely of arrogance, it is
still a living evidence of Christian faith; and
these isles have witnessed as they look out toward
Chalcedon and Nicæa, the scholarship and devotion of an intrepid race of ecclesiastical heroes.
If the orthodoxy of the Greek is a petrified religion, it is a petrifaction which is monumental.

CHAPTER XI.

ONE of the pleasures of our summer resort at Prinkipo, after donkey-riding, fishing, promenading and inhaling the health-giving air, is to make trips to the adjacent mainland and isles, even to the ecclesiastical vicinage of Nicæa, and the historic places of Nicomedia. These latter places are eastward, upon the two extreme points of the Sea of Marmora. They are only separated from each other by a mountainous tongue of land, a tongue which speaks eloquently of a mighty past! The voyage can be made in a sailing *caïque*, in a launch, or by the post boat. It can be made in a day. It is hardly fifty miles to Ismid, or Nicomedia. It is a longer trip to Nicæa, now known as Isnid, which can be better made *via* Broussa, when the brigands are asleep. Isnid is the famous locality where the Nicene creed and its controversies made war a chronic habit in the early days of Christianity. We are projecting several of these trips.

This morning is dedicated to Halki. It is the

154

Sabbath. No more beautiful day ever dawned in the East than that which ushers in this bright morning. The sea is of the deepest ultramarine blue with stretches of light in swaths that break its uniformity of color. A little breeze ruffles its surface. A few white-winged *caïques* move quietly, seeming to be more at rest than in motion. The clouds make shadows over the mountains. The slopes of Asia, east and south, are magical in beauty. The roseate aurora of which Homer sings, hardly fades from the lustrous glory of the sky before we are off to Halki, the isle of copper. It lies just west of us, only a mile distant. It is within our view from Prinkipo. It has two prominent main-tops of mountains, each crowned with large yellow buildings. One is a Greek commercial college, and the other a Greek theological seminary. Our launch, the "Sunset," is ready. The Maltese captain and his crew are unusually affable. They are cultivating their best graces ; for on coming up from Stamboul yesterday we had a breezy time around the Moda Point, and our new flag blew away, and they looked as if they were under the patriotic ban. Alas! that this, the only emblem of the great Western republic now on these waters, should have had such an inglorious burial in the Propontis. Who will find it? Who return it? Who will know it? The other day, while stand-

ing on the quay, as the " Kearsarge " first entered
Prinkipo harbor, I heard a talk among the fishermen about its "*drapeau*." They spoke in Greek ;
but Pedro, my Dalmatian servant, translates.
Said one :

" The Greeks have colored their blue stripes,
and changed them to red since their late fiasco
with Turkey. It is a Greek ship."

" Oh, no," said his companion ; "it is the tri-
color of the French—red, white and blue, modified with the stars."

" Nay, not so," said a third : "there is a new
nation in Africa and it is sending out vessels.
This is the flag of the Congo Confederation !"

No one dreams that a nation of sixty millions
swear by this starry ensign, and that the " Kearsarge " had vindicated it under the eye of antago-
nizing British and curious French people, off
Cherbourg.

This flag is beginning to be known here by its
" Sunset " coloring, which Drake sang so vividly
and which our launch illustrates *eo nomine.* So
that when we reach the *scala,* or landing, we
have a greeting from all the fishermen and other
scala-wags who adorn the quay. The steam is
already up ! Away we dash for the Copper Isle !

Our little launch is filled with pots of flowers,
and with our blue flag at the fore, signifying that
the ministerial " Admiral," is on board, our

LEGATION STEAM LAUNCH "SUNSET," OFF PRINKIPO.

old star-spangled banner at the stern, rather the worse for wear, and our gay scarlet cushions on deck, we make a sensation as we move over the sea not at all inglorious for our remote country.

This island of Halki derives its name from the copper mines which in ancient times existed in it—halkòs (χαλυὸς), in Greek meaning copper. The Turks call it *Heïbely*, that is, bag-like ; because of the resemblance of the two hills on either side of its principal plain to saddle-bags thrown across the back of a horse.

There is little to add to the description of the monasteries on this island given in " Iles des Princes," excepting one or two slight errors to correct. The author of that book speaks of the personage who restored in 1680 the monastery of the Virgin Mary as " Nicosios Panagiotaki." It makes him a native of Scio, old Homer's isle ; whereas his proper name is Panagiotaki of Nicosia, in Cyprus. The American reader will be happy to know that he was the great dragoman of the Sultan, when dragomans were more distinguished and less common than at present. They will also be pleased to know that he was not from Scio, but from Cyprus. In the library of this monastery are to be found some fifty or sixty old manuscripts, mostly relating to ecclesiastical matters, written on parchment and dating as far back as the sixth century.

In a remote part of Halki lived, up to four years ago, an old monk.   A certain mystery was attached to him.   He was formerly a wealthy merchant and a highly respected member of society. One day, about thirty years ago, he left his house in Pera, in the morning as usual, to go to his business.   He did not, however, make his appearance at his counting-house that day and did not return home in the evening, in fact, he did not return at all.   Inquiries were made.   About a month afterwards he was discovered in a retired spot of Halki. There he had built for himself with his own hands a wooden hut and was living in it, having assumed the garb of a monk. Neither the solicitations of his wife, children or friends could induce him to return to his home or explain his strange conduct. He sent them all away. He lived for nearly twenty-five years in that hut, subsisting on herbs and presents from charitable people. Money he would not accept, but bread and other perquisites he did not refuse.   He spent his time in study and prayer. Of late years he was held in great veneration by the inhabitants of the isle. When he retired to Halki, he left behind him an excellent business and a fortune of nearly $100,000.

Why anticipate these incidents? They make Halki interesting. My portfolio is crowded with memoranda of this historic and monastic isle. They concern its three monasteries, its commercial school, its natural position in the sea and its paradisiacal beauty and situation. What convents! what tombs! what buried patriarchs! What biographies associated with the Paleologii—John VIII. especially! What ravages by fire and war! What grandeur of Greek dragomans, like the famous Nicosias Panagiotaki! What funereal cortèges by sea! what Phanarotic ability! These added to the natural beauties of the isle, transmute the copper of Halki into the golden ingots of history and chivalry.

The time is propitious to search for the secrets of Halki. Every page of Gibbon calls aloud. The round tower of the Genoese beckons! A thousand years, eloquent of historic glory, almost forgotten by our new hemisphere—years in which eunuchs, emperors, empresses, patriarchs, clerical and domestic, local and foreign wars, come and go like rainbows. These all invite us to study Halki!

We had arranged to have with us Admiral Woods Pasha. He is an English gentleman, formerly of the English navy. For the past twenty years he has been in the Turkish naval service, and has reached, for a young man, quite an exalted place in the service. For several years he was a professor in the naval school at Halki. Since the Turks have been threatened recently with disintegration, he is expected there

again to lecture on explosives, torpedoes, and naval
warfare generally.   In these matters he is peer-
less as a student and accomplished as a practical
officer.   To him Halki is an open book.   For him
all its pretty bays, nooks, and paths, its monuments and monasteries, its social, historic and personal memories serve to illuminate the open volume.   His sister accompanies us.   She speaks
modern Greek, and interprets for us.   The Admiral Pasha speaks Turkish like a native.

We reach the isle.   We land on the *scala*, at
the door almost of the naval college.   The marines
perceive the Admiral, for he wears the undress
uniform of his rank.   They make salutation as
we enter the gateway of the huge building.   Like
most of the monster buildings in the East it is
painted yellow.   It was used once as a *cazerne* or
barracks.   As a consequence there is a mosque
near by.   This is signified by the white minaret.
It is vacation in the college now.   We find, as is
the case in all edifices—public and private, in this
country—that the inside of the college and grounds
is more inviting than the outside indicates.   We
find ourselves, under the convoy of a Turkish
naval officer, within grounds laid out with great
beauty, but in a neglected condition.   Flowers,
creepers, rare shrubbery, and trees, make a picture
none the less interesting, because *en déshabille.*
The Admiral Pasha relates many tales of these

VIEW OF HALKI FROM PRINKIPO.

grounds. These tales relate to the days of Mahmoud II., who massacred the Janissaries. That
Sultan used to come here from the capital to have
a revel, sending for the attractive beauties of the
isle and making merry like an old feudal lord of
the manor. His son, Abdul Mejid, was also accustomed to visit here for days together, but not in
such a hilarious fashion. Abdul Mejid's son, Abdul Hamid, the present Sultan, has never been here.

The grounds are in sad decay. The naval cus-
todian tells us that this year a sum is set apart for
the renovation of the grounds and buildings.

We enter the building. There is nothing to
note except large rooms with furniture once rich,
now faded, and chandeliers that would do honor
to Dolma Batché or Peterhoff.

"Here is the chamber," says the Admiral,
"where, on the visit of the allied fleets after the
Crimean war, we gave the allied officers a grand
fête and heavenly dance. Did you note these
rude pillars unpainted on the first floor? Well,
I had them put under the floor to support the
dancers. It was done in a few hours on a hasty
summons."

"By you?" I ask.

"By my orders! The timber was prepared in
Stamboul, brought down here in the afternoon, set
up in style before night, and we danced over it till
morning! How's that?"

11

" I did not think, Admiral, that the Turks were
so energetic."

"Oh ! they are great on spirts, when the ' occasion sudden ' demands exertion."

As it is vacation no students assemble to gratify
their curiosity at our unexpected advent. When
my Dalmatian, Pedro, signifies that he desires a
half-dozen donkeys to be ready on our return from
seeing the naval school, we are surrounded by a
bevy of young Greeklings,—Arabs I was about to
say,—of the town. They do not use suspenders ;
sometimes they have a sash or belt like their
elders. Their pantaloons may be said to be like a
doubtful bill after a field day in Congress,—full
of amendments—amendments in front and rear.
Some are so much covered with patches as to
be a "substitute," leaving only the title ! These
gamins are not badly behaved. I am yet to see
any bad boy among the Greeks. When Pedro
indicates a wish for donkeys, a race begins for the
remote donkey stand. It is Epaminondas against
Lycurgus—Eschines over again for the crown
against Demosthenes. Around the corner come
the gamins with four donkeys and a horse ! I
mount the horse. The steed is fiery. Our sailor
George and servant Pedro assist us to mount.
Away we go ! We had become used to gaping,
curious crowds while in Egypt ; so that when the

housewives of the town rush to their windows to gaze at our procession, we are not embarrassed.

"Which way shall we go?" I ask the Admiral. "Up the magnificent avenue of cypresses, which takes us to the oldest monastery?"

He responds:

"Let us reserve that to the last."

No carriages are allowed in Halki. The only locomotion is by foot or donkey. Some years ago the attempt was made to introduce carriages, as the roads are suitable for them; but the very donkeys, together with their drivers, raised a thundering note of rebellion. The harness of the new *régime* of drivers was cut, the vehicles disordered, and the scheme abandoned. In Prinkipo the same sort of revolution failed. The private carriages triumphed, and there was no power in the donkey battalions against the gold of the Hellenic bankers.

Halki plumes herself on her freedom from the aristocratic carriage. Her paths are paths of peace, and her ways are ways of pleasantness. In fact, there is a quietude and beauty about her solitary meandering walks that make her more attractive to the monastic or studious mind than her more fashionable sister isle.

We take up our line of march to the lofty top of the mountain, where the theological seminary with its piles of yellow-painted stone and beautiful,

ample grounds give the finest view of the islands
and the two continents.

I have said that it was difficult to find any literature concerning these isles outside of the modern
Greek. This I cannot read. But one capital
object is always apparent without seeking other
than tablets of stone set in mortar; and that is
the prevalence of religious enthusiasm as associated with these isles. The monastery is ever up-
permost. It was quite as convenient for the state,
as a prison and refuge, as for the church to per-
petuate Greek teaching and tenets. These tenets
are especially saturated with the reclusive life. No
place in the Eastern World, unless it be Mount
Athos, is so fitted for the solitary musings and reflections of the cenobite as these isles. There is no
place so fitted, I may add, for the anchorite also.
Both words are as Greek as the habits of the
Greek fathers of the Christian Church. The word
cenobite is from Κοινός, common; and βιος, life. It
signifies a community, in opposition to the anchorite, who was a solitary hermit, from ἀνά, back,
and to Χωσειν, retire.

This isle of Halki is the home of both of these
recluses. This the sequel will show. It is an illustration of the excesses of that pious zeal, which
led the early fathers to retire into caves and convents, as if in the very face of the teachings of

Him whom all confess, who sought to be affable and social in his intercourse with mortals.

The convent of St. Trinity, most conspicuous from land and sea, is the one within whose courts we now are. It used to graduate yearly two hundred students, for the Orthodox priesthood. The past year there were but sixty-seven graduates. Is this a sign of our utilitarian age, which is even invading this great theological centre of Oriental orthodoxy? In comparison with the number of students of the commercial school, 167, this showing is like Jean Paul Richter's father, poor but pious. It was not so formerly, in the days of Ottoman persecution, or before that, in the time of the Greek domination, with St. Sophia as the crowning edifice of the Christian world!

The convent we now visit is called in Greek *Hagia Triäs*, or *Triàda*. Its founder was one Photius. He is called illustrious; but whether he be so or not, depends upon those who are interested in the vicissitudes of the Eastern Church. He was one of the learned patriarchs, a leading mind and conspicuous figure in the ninth century.

The convent fell into ruins when the Turks took Constantinople. It was rebuilt in the sixteenth century by one Métrophanos. He, too, was a celebrity in Orthodox annals. He was the son of a tile-maker of a little town on the Bos-

phorus, Haskëui.   He became an archbishop of
Cappadocia, and afterwards patriarch of Constantinople.   He abdicated on a charge of simony
against him.   The story told of him is, that on
retiring from the patriarchate, he received the
two dioceses of Lamia and Chios.   He sold the
first and retired to the second!   He liked the
thirty pieces.   Still he was and is renowned and
revered by his fellow-churchmen and by scholars.
He was a crank on one subject.   He was wild in
his endeavors to recover the manuscripts which
had escaped the Turkish conquest of 1453.   He
recovered many of them.   A catalogue of his find-
ings was found in 1572.   After his death his collection was scattered.   It is recorded that a
learned diplomat, Ghislan de Busbecq, who first
brought the lilac into Europe and who lived three
months on Halki, in the sixteenth century, sent
a cargo of wonderful manuscripts into Europe.
I have been in the receipt of many letters from
American scholars, anxious to know about many
missing manuscripts.   They are supposed to be
yet concealed in the crypts of St. Sophia or in the
dusty mosque alcoves in and around Stamboul.
I have been besieged to bring them out of their
stony tombs and mummy cerements.   It may be
proper here to say that all such attempts are
vain.   The lost books of the Greek classics, frag-
ments of Livy or Pausanius may be exhumed ; but

my efforts, like those of my predecessor, the author of "Ben Hur," have been in vain. Only a few treasures remain in the library of the Holy Trinity of Halki. If the precious classics were ever there, the changes and chances of time, war and fire have left of the "fund of Mètrophanos," precious few of the relics which he gathered with so much scholastic zealotry.

The marks of fire are seen on the smirched foundation stones of the present edifice of Trinity. During the Greek revolution, in 1821, the convent was burned. It was again built by the patriarch Germain IV., in 1844; so that it is comparatively new. The old building of Phocius was then changed into a theological seminary; and so it remains.

To reach the spacious paved courts of this Trinity convent we pass around and up the mountain, through shady woods, whose grounds are not cumbered, like those of Prinkipo, with rocks. When you attain the summit you have the finest prospect of sea, sky, isle and continent I have ever witnessed. From the promontory you may not only gaze down into the Swiss vales of the isle, but off into the shores of Asia and Europe. The great city of Constantinople seems to be nearer and more resplendent in dome and minaret than from our villa at Prinkipo. From these terraces of Trinity the mountains of the horizon, seen under their hazy attire, are lit up at sunset with a glow of russet, pink, purple and gold which would be anything but conducive to the study of Greek or metaphysics. At Naples, when evening paints her colors upon the sea and the isles of the bay and in the very lustre of the air, one must close the shutters, in order to think, read and write. Is it not a marvel how the students of these isles can gaze into recondite lore when nature spreads for the eye such an illuminated volume of the good and beautiful?

After some inquiry we find a priest to show us the inside of Trinity. He appears. He is of bare head, of good face, but as dumb as an oyster. Even our fair dragoman, Admiral Wood's sister, could not coax much information from him. The fact is, that he did not know as much as we did about the convent and its history. However, as he was unlocking the church door, I observe over its portals the sign of the Trinity, three in one—a triangle, with an eye in the centre, symbolic of the eternal All-seeing One. At each angle is the initial of the Father, Son and Holy Ghost. Around this triangle is a radiant golden glory. Some Greek sentences below tell when the church was rebuilt and by whom. The words are of new Greek and unknown to us. On either side are other emblems. One is that of an open book or tablet of stone. It is the law. On the other

side is a golden cup with a cross above it. It is
the sacred chalice or sacrament. In the vestibule
of the church is a strange picture. It is as old as
these emblems. It is black with the smoke of a
million candles burned from the ninth century to
the time of the destruction of the church. It
represents three angels entertained at a feast. It
is the Annunciation, I suppose. Within the
church are the same pictures which are seen in all
Greek churches, and which I have seen so often in
Russia and in Constantinople. They consist of
biblical scenes, from old chaos and the creation
down to the birth of the Saviour. In these pictures you will see reproduced in horrid art the
Grecian features. The nose is prominent. In the
vestibule are the tombs of many patriarchs. We
are led to believe that one worn smooth by constant walking over it is that of Phocius. But in
the American mind it is of little moment who
is Phocius to it or it to Phocius. Only the
carved skeleton of old Phocius is seen. The
only living things about the convent are to be
found in the library. Here are books ; and John
Milton says that a book is a most reasonable
creature. " It is a life beyond life,—an immortality
rather than a life."

Let us to the library. There we are joined
by a director of the college. He is arrayed in a

priestly stole, and his head is clad with the cylindri-
cal hat, the rim at its crown. He has abjured
the pendant veil from the hat for this occasion.
But like the typical Greek priest, he has a black
beard. His hair, too, is long and curls. It is
parted in the middle, and neatly brushed behind
the ear. He is courteous, and is anxious to give
us all the satisfaction he can. He presents us to
the librarian. Ah! I must not forget him! His
name is Constantine. He has been here seventeen years. He is seventy years old, and gray
where he is not bald. He is not a ready, oral lin-
guist, but here our fair dragoman comes to the
front. We rejoice for an hour among these im-
mortals of the alcove. The librarian shows us
his catalogue. He shows us books in fourteen
languages. Many of them are quite old and Oriental. He displays many old manuscripts in
Greek. One Testament is 1200 years of age. It
is on illuminated parchment. It looks old and
tired. The library smacks a little of the French
Revolution, or of the encyclopedists of France.
It must have come out of freedom of the Greek
mind, aroused by the excitements at the end of
the last century. There is a goodly company of
mathematicians in one alcove ; but most of the
books are upon logic. Others pertain to "the
Fathers."

I asked Constantine : " Have you no novels

here? Do your students never read fiction?"

He colors a little as he replies:

"I read all the time,—mostly novels. It would be tiresome here else. One of the patriarchs died, and his niece brought us quite a lot of novels from his library. The students don't read them."

"How many students graduated this year?" I ask.

"Only eight, and only six of these are to be priests! It is not as it was." He sighs an orthodox sigh, and resumes.

"Ah! we have the same old banquet when the young men go out into the world. If any of them do not become clergymen, they have to pay £15 extra for each year that they have studied here."

Woods Pasha is rummaging among the old books. He finds a history of the Sultans in English. It is of the year 1610. It is full of rare wood-cut portraits. He calls me to him. He reads the first sentence.

"See! Excellence! what a race is here! What an author! He derives the Turkish race from the *Tenori* (Turkish) or Phœnicians—the ancestors of Carthage—the soldiers of Hamilcar, Hanno, Hannibal and Hasdrubal, and the merchant princes of Carthage! Is not such a derivation almost comical?"

I recognize the big volume. It is the counterpart of one presented me by Senator Wagstaff, of

New York, just before I left that city on my
mission. It came over with his family from England some 200 years ago !

I am all interested in the volume. The admiral resumes—

"This volume goes on to say that it is a marvel
that from so small a beginning such a power as
that of the Ottoman developed, at which the
world grows pallid--"

"Ah, my dear Admiral, that was written in
A.D. 1610."

But the admiral grows intensely interested.
He asks the librarian :

"If I should want to read or borrow this book,
can I have the privilege ?"

"Yes," said Constantine, "come at any time—
even at midnight, and you are welcome to all we
have !"

I said to the gentle bookworm :

"I wonder you Greek folk never care in your
grand ambition to rival the wandering Ulysses, and
in your persecutions and trials here seek an Odyssey from the Orient, to America !"

"Ah ! Excellence !" said he, "I should have
gone there fifty years ago. It is now too late. I
must lay my bones here."

Then I pondered on a glimpse I had caught of
a vagrant sentence in an open volume of the
library. It was from Dr. Arnold. He says, in his

comprehensive way, that on the destruction of the
Athenian fleet in the harbor of Syracuse, B.C. 413,
depended the fate of the world. But for the victory of Rome, the energies of Greece during the
next eventful century would have found their
field in the West no less than in the East; and
then Greece, and not Rome, might have conquered
Carthage. Greek, instead of Latin, might have
been at this day the principal element of the language of Spain, of France and of Italy; and the
laws of Athens rather than of Rome might be the
foundation of the law of the civilized world.
Syracuse was a breakwater which God's provi-
dence raised up to protect the yet immatured
strength of Rome! The learned teacher of
Rugby might have carried his supposition farther, and hung on his hypothesis the possible condition of the Christian religion with a patriarch
instead of a pope, giving the canons of faith to
the Latin races of the world! These early Greek
fathers of the church, who recognized the great
white Slavonic czar as the chief father of their
religion, might now be giving ecclesiastical and
civil law to the majority of civilized nations!

There is a fountain in the stony court under
the broad shade tree. The antique church, the
monks' apartments, and the patriarch's chamber,
the scene of many a wedding festival,—these
with a prospective marriage ceremony, are in

reserve for another visit, for we shall go again to
the theologic college to drink in at sunset its wonderful prospect toward the north where Stamboul
shines afar.

We now take a path to the south-western portion of the isle, where the commercial college sits
serene at the top of another mountain.   There
are no carriages on the isle, and yet the roads up
through the pine groves are as substantial, wide
and clean as if they were in the *Bois de Boulogne.*
Each of the pine trees is a picture, and the
ground beneath them, carpeted with the needles
and cones, makes the forests here much more eligible for picnics and invalids than the forests of
Prinkipo.   In fact, the lay of the land, the winding
roads and by-paths, the seats for the pedestrian
and lounger, and the general beauty, surpass our
more pretentious isle.

We arrive at the top of the mountain of the
commercial school.   Here are pretty gardens.
Here, too, is a tomb of much elegance.   It is a
tomb of a patriarch of the Orthodox Greek
Church.   There is a tomb of an English minister
of Queen Bess's time.   He fought for one of the
Sultans in the Danubian country.   The college
is semi-religious, although commercial.   Soon we
are joined by one of its directors, and by the jani-
tor and several of his servants.   It is vacation.
The students are absent.   We enter the court-

yard and dismount. A priest with a pleasant beaming smile—not the kind of beam referred to in the Scripture—brings out a big key, and the ancient church is opened. There is no troublesome unshoeing or slipping, as when we enter a mosque. It is a little church and quite young. It is only 800 years old. It is black with age and the soot of burning candles. All the available space in the two apartments and even in the little altar room is filled with images of saints. One saint twice produced, Saint Macarius, has a long white beard that touches his sandals. Like all images in the Greek churches, these pictures, hands and all, are covered with either gold or silver or some metallic imitation. The faces are not covered. They look out of the shiny aureoles. Some rare relics are here, and exceptionally old books, but the antique effect is tawdry. The church is as neat as it can be in its dress of lace and gold. There are carved seats, which look old in the dim religious colored light from windows of antique style. There is a vitriol lamp burning before the Virgin. Faded flowers, silver chains, crucifixes, volumes of the Scriptures, and chants, —these give a mysterious awe to this antique edifice hid away in the mountains, which once knew and felt the power of the great Greek hierarchy and empire of the East. Tapers by the score are piled up on a table. There is nothing, however, musty in the little pent-up edifice, for the smell of myrtle or pine gives a delicious sweetness.

As Pedro talks modern Greek like a native, being born on the borders of Epirus, we communicate easily with the priest. We find him not only a healthy and hirsute person, of fine physique and pleasant manners, but of unusual intelligence as to his own religion.

The director gallants us to the long *salle à manger* and dormitory. These accommodate 167 students, and are as neat as can be. We visit the library. It did not interest. It was made up of Greek and French books. The latter are of the age of the French Revolution or before. Rousseau lies quietly beside Buffon : the one a beast and the other a writer about beasts. Obsolete literature is plentiful. We glance at a globe which represents the world, including our United Colonies in the time of John Smith of Virginia. Then we enter a long corridor, decorated with sketches of ancient Greeks, Homeric heroes and fathers of the church. We seek the open air, feeling as if we had been buried.

Again we mount our donkeys. Sending off one of the gamins to order our launch, we go round the isle to the little bay in front of the college, down to the water side. There we find a restaurant and garden. The proprietor gives us lemonade and coffee, and a bouquet for " Madame."

We remount to take a path through the forests to a little old church under ground, cut in the rocks. It is the same kind of old church as the rest, only with a different name. This is called "The Holy Spirit." The Greeks always have a restaurant or tavern near their religious home, just as the Moslem has a mosque near his barracks, or a fountain near his mosque.

We do not find any person taking care of this "little church round the corner" of the white cliff, where we venture. We are free to go upon the premises. Here is a bed out in the air, and another in a little cave near the church. Fuel is gathered from the pine trees—we beg pardon, not "from," but "under" them ; for it is forbidden to take the cones from the trees, only those that fall are taken. Charcoal is already binned for the winter. Could a more secluded spot be found on this uninhabited part of the isle ? On the other side more than a thousand people live. There the streets are roomy and nice. The town reminds one of a town in Italy or Spain, except that the houses are better and more comfortable. They are of wood. Halki is a sort of rival of Prinkipo as a health and summer resort ; but the best class live in Prinkipo. The rich people and grand villas are in Prinkipo. I cannot help but conclude that Halki has more natural beauty of site, forest and shrubbery. Owing to the scholastic and other associations of Halki, there is more interest for the Greek on this isle. When one sees the remnant of this grand race, lifting up still, though under adverse institutions and circumstances, the banner of the cross, one cannot help pondering upon a history that began with the heroes of Troy, and even yet listens delightedly to the oratory of Delyani and Tricoupis under the shadow of the Acropolis.

Our next visit is to the church of St. George. It is reached through the cypress avenues, as the picture represents. St. George seems to be a favorite with the Greeks, especially in these isles. The king of Greece is popular, not only because he is an amiable and equitable ruler, but because his name is George. In a great many churches this saint, who is of Cappadocia and has a marvellous history, is always pictured as slaying the dragon. In the painting at St. George's monastery and church in Halki, he is painted as rescuing a damsel in distress from the fangs of the monster. The artist has discreetly and graphically made the dragon climb half way up the haunches of the saint's gray charger, and has so arranged the dragon that George runs his spear into his opened jaws and clear through the animal, making the weapon truly lethal. It is not the pictures of this church that allure the visitor, although there are in the new church dozens of pictures of saints of the best Russian art. They are presents from Russia.

But the situation is the attraction. The long double alley of cypresses, three deep, leads the pleased traveller up to the monastery. The main building is on a precipitous bluff of rocks. From its terraces and under its cypresses Prinkipo is in full and near view. It looks off to the east and south. St. George monastery, too, has a history, but there is not so much of antiquity or tradition about it to give smirch to its saints or a dim religious light to its richly dight windows. It is rich, however, in this world's goods. It is the proprietor of some twenty houses in a long row upon the terrace, above the cypresses. These it rents. In the Middle Ages it was connected with the church of Chalcedon. Now, where is, or was, Chalcedon? It is on the way to Constantinople, which we shall soon travel in another chapter. All these scenes make us moralize upon events which carry us back to the first centuries of the Christian religion.

CHAPTER XII.

ANTIGONE AND PROTI—HISTORIC AND OTHER INCIDENTS.

THERE is not much to be seen by the eye upon the island of Antigone. But its classic name gives it a flavor of the Greek, while its three monasteries have a rare, eventful history. The island was formerly called "Panormos," which means in Greek "a harbor safe on all sides." The Turks call it "Bourgas-Ada," the Island of the Fortress, owing to an ancient fortress which existed there, but of which there is no trace now.

The monastery of the Transfiguration is on the summit of the highest hill of this island. It was pulled down by order of the Sultan Murat IV. in 1720, in consequence of a procession with torches which, according to ancient custom, went round the monastery on the night of Good Friday in that year. The Turks, seeing the lights and the commotion from across at Kadikeui, became alarmed. They demanded and obtained an edict from the Sultan that the monastery should be razed to the ground. Contrary to what the author of "Iles des Princes" says, there are plenty of ruins and

monuments connected with the monastery remaining, and even tombs of exiled princes with the
bones carefully preserved.   The author of " Iles
des Princes " falls also into an unpardonable error
regarding the little island of Pita, which he places
between Halki and Prinkipo.   He cannot surely
have visited the islands at all or else he would
have known that Pita is just in front of Antigone.
It helps immensely to make the little harbor of
that island a safe retreat.   Pita is uninhabited and has no interest whatever attaching to
it, except an ancient cistern with a quaintly carved
pillar in the middle.   This shows that in former
times the isle was inhabited.

Antigone is a melancholy isle compared with
Halki and Prinkipo.   Is it because so lugubri-
ously named ?   Poor Antigone, the forerunner
of Juliet even as Haemon, her betrothed, was the
antitype of Romeo ; for did she not sacrifice herself when entombed alive, and her lover kill
himself by her corpse ?

Every isle of Greece thus perpetuates some in-
vention or myth in which the tragic element
plays its part.   The birds of Antigone circle all
about us, then fly off, organize into companies and
battalions and return to us with a wail which
Greek fancy might translate into some woful song.

Upon the sides of the mountains, beyond the
cliffs, are lanes through the shubbery—lanes for

the goat and sheep. As we pass beyond the point a wreck is seen with one mast standing. The proofs are written in the chaotic rocks of the shore, of how earthquake and tempest have wounded and shaken the isle. The colors of the rocks are various, some black as the porphyry of upper Egypt, some brownish-red as the iron can paint them, and some as white as snow.

As we regard it a duty to take possession, *pedis possessio*, of each one of these princely isles, we array our boat in greenery and flowers, and start upon this September morning for Antigone. The wind is fresh. The curl of the lilies upon the blue sea gives us warning; but as the wind, whose nautical moods I study, is not from the south, we venture over the two miles of azure. Before we turn the point of Halki, the ferry from the city steams around that rocky isle. A wave of a handkerchief from some one on board indicates that our *capoudji* (messenger) from the Legation is on board. As business is always before diversion, we whisk our launch around and pursue the steamer into the harbor of Halki. Our *Capitano* must have had something aboard besides his *esprit de corps*, for he jams our launch "Sunset" against the side of the big boat, until my better half begins to forget her duty as passenger and speaks words of command in several dialects at once; and my Dalma-

tian *serviteur*, Pedro, regains his profane tongue,
which is Italian. We soon capture our mail-
bag and messenger. We read our letters from
home, fresh out of the pouch, and then, ho! for
Antigone!

The weather is a little hazy, partaking something of the captain's condition. We cannot see
the distant mountains of Asia except in dim
outline, but the sun shines on the minaretted
and domed glories of Stamboul; and that is
enough. Antigone has quite a population. They
are nearly all, if not all, out on the pier to
greet our strange flag; but as they charge a
mejidie (or dollar) if we stop at the pier more than
five minutes, the Captain makes money by hailing
a *caïque* at half that sum. We land in that
little frail craft and in a tossing sea. The crowd
is attracted by our flag and the infrequency of
such a vessel at the port of Antigone. Once this
was quite a busy commercial place. The
heavy stone walls of the harbor, and the solid
walls of the villas, red and black with iron-rust, indicate that formerly here was a substantial people.
The drives are all for donkeys; no carriages are
allowed. But we dispense with donkeys, and are
content to saunter upon the terraces, where we
are observed by such members of the families of
the town as had not appeared on the quay to receive us. Many of the houses have elegant ter-

raced gardens. Some of the houses are as quaint as those of old Amsterdam, with points, angles, gables and balconies overhanging the street. After some observation of the town and a glance at the crowning monastery we re-embark, not without a transient souvenir of the isle. This consists of a huge watermelon, upon whose sides the Greek artistic vender has made two drawings by scraping the green rind. The first sketch is plain enough to decipher ; but can the reader guess what the other one is. It is a fire-engine, such as the *pompiers* of the towns and cities of the East regard as the refinement of inventive art. It is to be regretted that I cannot reproduce the picture here.

Fires are very frequent in Constantinople and its adjacent villages. The structures are wooden, dry and frail. The streets are narrow, and therefore the fires are very destructive. There is much smoking of tobacco by the Turk. There is such a general use of charcoal and braziers, such a general carelessness in using the cigarette and *chibouque*, together with the matted floors that fires are frequent. The last thing that I saw before I left Constantinople was the practice of the fire brigade under the tuition of their chief. He is a Hungarian nobleman. He is providing modern means to put out fires, especially in Pera. The little engines, a caricature of which suggests

these incidents and which the *pompiers* carry
along with such hideous cries, are not bigger than
the ordinary engines which we have to water our
garden at home. They have but a single chamber.
This is about eight inches long by three or four in
diameter. They seem rather to nourish a fire.
The firemen themselves are said to be selected for
personal strength and activity,—I should say for
lung force. On their heads they wear a broad
cap. They are naked to their waists.

Do you ask how is the alarm of fire given?

I answer: Upon the elevated Seraskierate
tower of the War Office in Stamboul there is a
guard who watches. When a fire occurs, he
beats a big drum, and shouts wildly, " *Wang gin
var,*" which, literally interpreted, means, "A fire
there is!" This assembles the firemen. It
alarms the people. The tower of Galata is also
used for the same purpose on the other side of
the Golden Horn. If it be in daylight flags are
flaunted from the tops of these towers, indicating
by their color and arrangement where the fire is,
and by night other signals are used for this purpose.

Before sailing homeward to Prinkipo we may at
least glance at, if not land upon, Proti. Proti is
the first, as the word signifies and as the map
shows, of the nine isles on the way from Constantinople. It is by no means the last of the nine

in historic and monastic interest. Its houses are few and scattered. But one tree decorates its summit. A few others surround a house. The sides of the isle looking toward the city are scarred by wave and storm. It is not so attractive nor so much frequented as the sister isles of Halki, Antigone and Prinkipo. Whether it be fire, or goats, or man, or tariffs, its forests are gone. Much of its beauty and all of its productiveness have departed. How often have we to remark this fact in the Orient! Dr. Stanley has said the same on the aspect of Palestine. He refutes the presumption of its limited resources in ancient days, by its present depressed and desolate state. But doubtless the aspect and advantages of the land have greatly changed. So it is with all these lands, including the Greek isles and the Asian mainland. Asia Minor and Syria could once have brought forth ten times their present product and have supported ten times as many as their present population. This sterility involves the question always asked in the Orient : " Can these calcined and stony places ever have been a land flowing with milk and honey ?"

Proti is associated with Halki in several pretty narratives. It once had another name. Greek and Turkish nomenclature for places always represent some sensible object. Some of the names are quite poetical, others quite commonplace. This isle of Proti appears to have been formerly styled also " Acconœ " or " Acconitis," from the quantity of whetstone which was once to be found on it, the Greek word *accona* (Aκόνη) meaning whetstone. By the Turks it is called " Khinali Ada," Reddish Island. Proti had formerly a fine harbor and populous village on its eastern side, but they have disappeared. Only a few remnants of ruins are left, among which are two large-sized cisterns of the Byzantine period. These indicate the spot where the old village was situated. The harbor has been washed away by the sea. The present village occupies quite a different site.

There were three monasteries on this island. The smallest of these monasteries was that built by the Anatolian, General Vardane. It was destroyed on the 20th of February, 1807, by the British fleet under Admiral Sir John Duckworth and Rear-Admiral Lewis. That fleet comprised ten men-of-war. Among them may be mentioned the two-decker, " Endymion," and the " Ajax " of 74 guns. The latter caught fire accidentally and was entirely destroyed. After forcing the Straits of the Dardenelles and destroying part of the Turkish fleet, which was lying at Gallipolis, this fleet came and anchored in the harbor of Proti. There it remained eleven days. The Turks, in order to prevent the English from getting water

and fuel from the island, sent a small detachment of sixty determined men from Kadikeui,
who, after some difficulty, succeeded in landing
and entrenching themselves in the monastery.
The English landed a party and attacked the
monastery to which they finally set fire. The
Turks, driven from their stronghold, offered a fierce
resistance. After killing a considerable number,
they at last drove the English out of the isle, and
before the latter could return in stronger force, the
Turkish detachment was saved from its perilous
situation by the inhabitants of Halki, who came in
their *caïques* at night and took off the Turks. In
recompense for this service and their bravery, the
Halkiotes were granted by the then Sultan, Selim,
exemption from taxes, a privilege which they continue to enjoy up to the present time.

CHAPTER XIII.

PLATI AND OXIA—SIR HENRY BULWER'S FATAL LIT-
TLE ISLE—HIS DIPLOMACY AND HIS ECCEN-
TRICITIES.

FROM any eminence in Constantinople, upon a clear day, two isolated rocks apparently leap out of the Sea of Marmora—the classic Propontis. But they are not merely rocks. Oxia, in Greek, means "late in the day," or "Sunset." It is thus named because the sun lingers last on its prominence. From one point it looks like the pyramid of Ghizi. We have not yet been upon it, but we have been around it. It is not inhabited except by snakes. Our visit is, therefore, reserved. But we have accomplished the other little isle, Plati. It is the Oriental custom to name localities from some concrete quality, association, or object. What Plati means in Greek I can easily surmise. Although it is some 300 feet above the sea level, still it is a plateau. It can be cultivated nearly over its whole area, which is at least 150 acres. The name is derived from the Greek word πλάτη, which means a flat or broad surface. It is the same root for our word plain, or plaza, or plat. Plati is due west from Prinkipo and due south from Constantinople. It is some fifteen miles from the city.

These twin warders of the archipelago—Oxia and Plati—are conspicuous figures in the sea. They have each an individuality, not merely physically, but strategetically. The power, whether Greek or Turkish, that held Constantinople, used them as sentinels to warn of the approach of the Genoese or knightly enemy. Their isolation made them capital prisons. Within their horrid caves, now used for cisterns, the convict was immured without hope. Sometimes the loose and abandoned visited them for the worst purposes of lust and escapades of deviltry. Pirates sometimes concealed themselves there. But during the Greek rule, the Greek Church erected monasteries upon them. The remains of these are still seen upon both islands. There was a church, or oratory, on Plati. Its *débris* is found near the castle by the sea. Several times, when the dogs of the big city became obstreperous, or the horses sick, the former were deported to the rocky and barren islet of Oxia, and the horses there found their paradise. In the place where the hermits were once established, civilization gave eternal rest to the animal creation. Sometimes these isles were used as a target for the practice of the Ottoman naval guns.

The *oubliettes*, or dungeons, were once the
scene of a singular freak of justice. Two eminent
patricians had a quarrel. One was a Greek, Basil
Bardas; the other a Roman, Scliros. They
fought the first duel recorded in the Greek annals.
The story runs that the Emperor Constantine VII.
exiled them—one to Oxia, and the other to Plati.
They were consoled, however; for, as by a cruel
irony, they were placed near each other, and one
suffered like the other! Constantine ordered that
their eyes should be put out. It was the pleasant
pastime of these Greek rulers to burn out the
eyes. But on this occasion the Plati prisoner escaped, and there was no adequate compensation.

These isles have associations more interesting
to Americans than those which are philologic, historic, geologic, or æsthetic. Plati is best known
as the isle of Sir Henry Lytton Bulwer. The distinguished diplomat came to Turkey after his service at Washington as English minister. He
followed here Sir Stratford Canning, the greatest
of the English ambassadors. How 'Sir Henry
obtained this isle and what he did with it, and what
associations cluster about it in connection with his
name, would furnish a strange, eventful history.
These concern the biography and eccentricities of
the man and the minister, as well as the qualities
and condition of the isle itself.

There are those in Washington who remember

Sir Henry. The Clayton-Bulwer treaty was a fact
of his accomplishment. Scarcely any public man,
from Judge Douglas's time to the present, but has
taken a hand in the discussion of this treaty and
its obnoxious clause so inimical to certain Isthmian interests and ambitions of the United States.
Among the rest, in an humble way, the writer
hereof made a report on April 16, 1880, in favor
of its abrogation. The report developed some
matters not generally known. It concerned the
Monroe doctrine and an interoceanic ship canal.
The President had urged in his message the policy
of the canal being under American control. He
urged the necessity of such control as a part of
the guardianship of our coast line. Although
New Granada in the railroad franchise of 1846,
and Nicaragua in the Hise treaty of 1849, recognized the American protectorate, the latter treaty
was not ratified because of Mr. Clayton's alarm
lest a collision with Great Britain would follow.
The Mosquito king played its little, buzzing,
stinging pårt. Mr. Clayton disavowed the Hise
treaty to the English minister, Crampton ; but
begged the English not to allow us to appear
cowardly by the abandonment of " great and splendid advantages." Mr. Clayton begged England
to give up her Mosquito protectorate and share
with us the authority over the transit. In this
awkward way the negotiations proceeded until

April 19, 1850, when the partnership with Great Britain was consummated. This was done under the adroit management of Sir Henry Bulwer. Both parties agreed never "to erect or maintain any fortifications commanding or in the vicinity of any ship canal, or to occupy, or fortify, or assume or exercise any dominion over Nicaragua, Costa Rica, the Mosquito coast, or any part of Central America."

England often violated this treaty. But why particularize? It is a long story, in which such statesmen as Cass and Buchanan, Clarendon and Napier, Ousley and Dallas, Clayton and Bulwer, and recently Clarendon, Blaine, and Frelinghuysen have figured, and always with an inconsequential result for us. The subtle crystallization which Sir Henry Bulwer produced remains like a wall of adamant across the line of our policy and the Isthmus. Our puny statesmen have tilted in vain against this wall with their javelins of straw.

The English employ such trained diplomatists as Bulwer the world around. But his chicanery and selfishness overtook him at last. His Nemesis was the genius of Plati. The rock upon which his career foundered was this islet to which the prow of our little launch is turned.

Sir Henry has left various impressions here upon those who knew him. I was not in Congress when the treaty was made. I do not remember

ever to have seen him at Washington. He is
described as a most engaging and charming gentleman. In social etiquette and style he had no
peer. He was tall and thin in person. His nose
was hooked and peaked ; his face was long and
grave ; his eye was like a flash of lightning ; his
upper teeth protruded, and his mouth was set a
little awry. Despite these *gaucheries* he was not
unhandsome. I fancy that he was not unlike his
elder brother, the great novelist. In conversation
he was unrivalled. He was a capital *raconteur.*
He liked to emit startling paradoxes. He was an
admirable speaker. Whether he was sincere or
not, he made all seek his society and like him.
His voice was measured, low, musical, and persuasive. He was most at home in intrigue. In
this he displayed the *timbre* of his character. He
went into a diplomatic contest *con amore*, vizor up
and lance pointed. He generally pierced the
armor of his antagonist. He usually won, for he
did not disdain to use all the arts known to the
old style diplomacy, which he held was fast fading
away. Altogether he is described to me by the
physician who attended him and by the captain of
his yacht as a most extraordinary and fascinating
man, but replete with whims, of which the owner-
ship of this isle is by some accounted one of the
most peculiar.

He was ambassador in the time of Abdul Mejid,

whom I remember seeing on my trip here in 1851. No more worthy Sultan, unless I except his son, the present Sultan, Abdul Hamid II., ever did more for the reform of his Government or made more sacrifices for the advancement of civilization. He is known in the East as the Haroun al Raschid of modern times. Sir Henry Bulwer had, therefore, many opportunities of aiding effectually in the regeneration of the East.

Sir Henry conquered the good-will of this Sultan of happy memory, by some special efforts about the succession in Egypt. As a consequence, or reward, the Khedive of Egypt made him a gift of this isle. He began its improvement. He erected the two castles—one on the shore and the other on the summit. It is said that they were intended as miniatures of his own ancestral home at Knebsworth, England. He had another whim. He thought to raise cattle on the island. In fact, he stocked it with some cattle of the rarest breed. A storm of a fortnight, before the days of steam ferries here, prevented adequate provender from reaching the isle. The cattle perished and so did the enterprise. He seldom lived on the island. His wife visited it frequently, but only to remain a short time. Sometimes with friends he stayed over night and had a good time, but his health was infirm. He could not follow very far a certain jocund disposition without hurt to his physical system. He was odd about his health. His doctor tells me that he saw him every day for four years, and that he used to take a different pill at the end of each dish at his meals. It was one of his caprices to have frequent imaginary ills and pills. It was the remark of Guizot about him, that "if Bulwer were ill, look out! Mischief was sure to follow his pills." Guizot had reference to Bulwer's tact at Madrid in the matter of the Spanish marriage of the Duke de Montpensier, son of Louis Philippe. Sir Henry must have had a bad spell about the time he inveigled Mr. Clayton to sign away an American protectorate over the Isthmian ways.

How he used to chuckle over his diplomatic triumphs! Some of them were won in Roumania along with Halil Pacha, a festive companion and a good fellow, a colleague of Bulwer in Roumania. How he used to laugh over his circumvention of Mr. Clayton! These are a part of the traditions and gossip yet at Pera, which is called the ant-hill of politics.

He had curious characteristics. Sometimes it was thought that he was mean in money matters; but the owner of our launch, Mr. Jones, who brought out a steam yacht for him from England, and used to ship him about these isles and the Bosphorus, tells me that at times he was extravagantly and unexpectedly generous. He was often timorous of society. He would hide from his embassy and friends for weeks at a time. It was his whim or his respite. His doctor says that once, while attending him at Cairo, he insisted on spending three weeks with an old English farmer out of that city, where, amid the chickens, donkeys, dogs, and hogs, he was content to live on the homely fare and under the simple cottage thatch of the peasant, whom he never afterward failed substantially to remember.

It is a part of the reminiscences about Sir Henry, that while he was resplendent in social life and exquisite in personal taste, he was not to be relied upon. His word was not absolute verity. It was not exactly unveracity. It was imagination, all compact. It was a desire to please. He was princely in his entertainments. After he was no longer ambassador here, he returned on some speculative mission. He held the same old high carnival daily and nightly with his epicurean friends. What he did to embarrass the American missionaries here I do not exactly know. It had some reference to the American (Robert) College. Its then President, Dr. Hamlin, in his book, handles him without gloves. He held him to be as destitute of public probity as he was of private morality.

As Dr. Hamlin was outspoken as to this personage, I may quote what he says, in his published volume :—

"The case of the college was at length laid before Sir Henry Bulwer. He was a man, of no principle ; but he knew that to carry the measure would get him credit in England. He took hold of it with the intention of carrying it through. After a long time, and wearisome delays, he wrote me a note, saying that the question was decided, and that, within three days, I should have leave to go on.

"I next received a note from him, telling me that I had made an unwise and inconsiderate bargain, in purchasing that place, and the consequences should justly fall on my own head. He saw no reason why the English Embassy should have any further trouble with regard to it !

"It was a treachery so base that I made no reply to it, and had nothing more to do with Sir Henry Bulwer. I felt curious, however, to know the reason for such a sudden facing about. Nor was it at all difficult to find.

"He had received a magnificent 'gift' from the Pasha of Egypt, with a request that he would arrange some important and pressing affairs with the Porte.

"Another was sent to the Countess G——, one of Sir Henry's mistresses, and, of course, he undertook the Pasha's business. Among the conditions made by A'ali Pasha, in return, was, that he should throw that college question overboard which he accordingly did, as not worth a moment's consideration. It is a good specimen of Sir Henry's character. In similar circumstances he would have thrown overboard any English interest with equal coolness."

As an illustration of the *morale* of the diplomacy of Sir Henry Bulwer, let me record a fact. In May, 1860, Prince Gortschakoff addressed a circular to the great powers of Europe as to the condition of the Christians in the Balkan peninsula. It suggested inquiry to verify the facts, so as to bring about some amelioration. Sir Henry drew up a list of the questions which he sent to the British consuls throughout the Empire. He accompanies it with a circular of his own. In this he intimates the way in which he expects the consuls to answer. As a sample of his shrewdness, not to say old-time diplomacy, in his circular of the 8th of August, 1860, the following passage occurs :

"Your conduct in this crisis will be duly watched by me, and my opinion whether favorable or the reverse, communicated to Her Majesty's government."

This threat had its commentary in the action of one unfortunate consul. He failed to receive the circular, and wrote too plain spoken a report. He afterwards apologized for it when he saw the circular, and wrote a second destroying the effect of the first.

This lack of private morality is not treasured against him so much as the lack of public honor. Of his acquisition and disposition of this rocky islet there is much said. After the isle was given him, Sir Henry, in 1854, spent $75,000 in its so-called improvement. He did not keep it long, but somehow, in some peculiar circuitous way, he resold it for a round sum to the then Khedive of Egypt, Ismael Pasha, who yet lives as the best or worst type of a millionaire who has wrought a great fortune out of the misfortunes of his country.

One of the stories which remains as to this isle is, that when Lord Lyons was appointed in Sir Henry's stead as ambassador here, he called on Lord Palmerston at the Foreign Office in London to receive his instructions. After they were given, Lord Lyons took his leave, saying:

"My lord, is there anything else you can say as to Turkish affairs and my duties?"

Lord Palmerston replied "No."

Lord Lyons said "Good-by."

As he reached the door and was about to make his exit, Lord Palmerston called out:

"My lord! Yes! One thing I forgot. Never own an island!"

It was this island of Plati to which Palmerston referred. It lost Bulwer his place, for he sold it for a large sum to a party interested in his service. He lost his office by the indelicacy of the transaction.

Now that we know the later history of the isle, let the launch steam up. Ho! for Plati! Let us see what are the graces of the isle which attracted and outwitted the clever diplomatist.

Before we dash away from the *scala* let us take an observation or two. With a good glass the two castles upon this rocky islet are visible from Prinkipo. We make preparations to launch out for it and lunch on it. Our Dalmatian *serviteur*, Pedro Skoppeglia, prepares the latter, while our Maltese *Capitano* Vincenzo takes the rudder in hand and gives his order.

The launch is newly upholstered. It looks as gay as a jaybird. The cushions have been newly covered, and the flag looks its prettiest. The sea is quiet. No white horses are capering over its smooth azure surface. A few fishermen are dropping their nets. They look picturesque in their red sashes, baggy breeches and fez caps. They are half Greek, half Ottoman. A few ships lie at anchor in the harbor. The Asian coast, with its mountain curves on the north and east, is faintly lined against a sky which has but a few fleeces of clouds in the east, hiding the snowy tops of the Mysean Olympus. The sea is intense in its azure, except where there are rich bands of green, and the gulls sit like white flowers on its bosom.

The water is as clear as a fountain in July when one "sees each grain of gravel." Lake Tahoe, in Nevada, is not more lucent than this water of the Propontis. A gentle breeze ripples it with sunshine, and makes a myriad of glittering diamond points which decorate its blue robe. A few *caïques* and *feluccas* with white wings are in the distance, whose horizon is stained here and there with the Cardiff coal smoke emitted from the steamers bound from Constantinople to the Dardanelles.

What a picture is that to the northward! Stamboul, like an *odalisque* in her *yashmak* of finest tulle, seems to emerge from the blue deep. Like a picture of Turner, a semi-ideal glimpse of Venice or some weird mirage of Orientalism, it seems a fairy city of the sea. It is set on seven hills, and, although a dozen and more miles off, it looks as unreal as if woven by unseen fingers in aerial looms—an unsubstantial dream of a country that never was on sea or land, which "great-browed Homer ruled as his demesne."

My wife suggests a possibility of fishing at Plati, or on the way. At once we are environed by a picturesque group. We choose a four-oared *caïque* with a canopy, and two sturdy Greeks. The *caïque* itself is a picture. On its inside is a clean floor covered with Turkish rugs of rich colors. The wood-work is stained with golden hues.

The outside is of green, red and white, daintily dashed or strewn with flowers not inartistically painted. You cannot tell stern from bow, so airily tip-tilted are the graceful ends of the boat. Our lines and bait are ready. We take a turn in the harbor with the launch, which was named by its owner, Mr. Jones, from whom it was leased, in honor of a pet name I have heard frequently: "Sunset." Then we take the *caïque* in tow and leave the quay with much *éclat*.

Before we leave, let us take a glance at the old town, with its bath-houses and stone quays. What is that moving object far off to the Asian shore? Is it a duck or a seamew? The glass reveals it! It is an amateur in a flatboat, with paddles, which the man deftly plies. Our little screw gives a few saucy, splashy turns, for the admiration of the fishermen and Greek gamins of the quay, and we are off for the west, —America-ward! Halki is neared. Her big yellow barracks by the shore, with the Turkish naval school, her Greek theological college on the northern summit, and her wooded and lovely curved mountains, resembling a Mexican saddle or an inverted *caïque* —these detain the eye, but not the launch.

A breeze springs up as we pass the hotels Calypso and Giacomo on the craggy shore of Prinkipo. The superb villas which crown the bluffs are on our left. The breeze starts the pris-

matic windmills in motion. The flag over the
Azarian water tower is our own star-spangled
banner. It kisses the breeze, and we salute the
starry emblem. Boys are swimming in the bay.
The mountains, nearly to the top, seem to sway
in the wind with their pines. The pretty nooks
and twisted rocks of the shore, the gardens pro-
fuse in scent, flower and rare trees pass by as if
we are indeed in dream-land, with pleasure domes
magically evoked out of sleep. Soon we pass on
the south side of Halki. Its rocks are broken,
cavernous, and precipitous, as if lashed by a thousand storms. Along this south side of Halki is
a beautiful harbor. We pass round point after
point of Halki, until between Halki and Antigone there opens a vista scarcely credible for
its loveliness. Chatak-Dagh, the highest mountain of the mainland of Asia, is in our rear, 1500
feet high. It fills the gap which we look through.
The shore line and mountains make a landscape
over which and through which there hangs an
interpenetrating lustre and distant unveiling which
would make Bierstadt wild with artistic enthusiasm. These isles take on a different dress when
observed from the sea.

We forget to look at yonder avenue of cypresses
on Halki. They lead up to another famous monastery, where many a Greek exile has been housed
and many a marriage ceremony has been per-

formed. The rocky ledges of Antigone, near which we now sail, are rugged and lofty. They are not devoid of trees, which give garniture to their sides and ledges. Here sea birds live in great numbers. As we turn to look back again the dark coves of Western Prinkipo are revealed, and beyond the southern end of Prinkipo, little Niandro lies, almost in ambush, at the feet of St. George's mountain, which looms up as if it would rival Olympus, whose head is shrouded in the white clouds anchored over the Mysean mountains.

Now, if we could keep right on, on, on, where would we land? Get the map and see. It strikes me that we would strike Lemnos isle, to which the Empress Irene was banished when it pleased her lord-treasurer to show his harsh authority over the murderous mother whose bones lie somewhere on the Isle of Prinkipo. Or if we missed Lemnos, going due west, we would come up against the coast of Thessaly, and almost under the shadow of that other and more classic Olympus as to which there is much to be said when the roll of Homer's heroes is called.

Our boat turns now to the isle of Bulwer—Plati. It looks near, say five miles. I strive to sketch its outlines, for its exterior seems as yet only a blank rock. Its castles are dimly lined and nebulously white. We look back. Great shadows

from white fleeces of clouds are moving over the
Asian shore, and old Olympus has not yet come
out of his tabernacle. The wavering line of the
Asian shore to the south is pencilled on the edge
of the horizon. It soon vanishes around Modena's gulf and is lost in the sea.

Passing the checkered and streaked cliffs of
Halki and Antigone, noting the walls here and
there to prevent land slides and excavations from
which iron and copper have been taken, observing
the clean-tilled brown and red earth which the
olive and cypress ornament, smelling the scented
shrub or machie which gives its fragrance to the
air, we turn again to look back; and lo! St.
George's monastery, on southern Prinkipo, is a
white dot on the green eminence. We pass the
southern shore of Antigone and note upon the
narrow shingly beach the men who hunt birds,
steal their eggs, and gather oysters or some other
crustacæ, which abound on these shores. They
have boats. We run close to the beetled crags,
colored and speckled like the increase of Jacob's
flocks, while here and there are big boulders held
aloft in the arms of stout rocks which frost and
earthquake have tumbled from the scarred mountain sides. Antigone rises sheer 500 feet. Her
side is full of caves. What are those white flowery
specks mingled with the rock and greenery? We
soon ascertain, for have we not discovered and

aroused the gulls and cormorants that here nestle?
They come out of their nooks by 'the thousand,
and keep up such a clamor that it seems like the
angry protest of a bird mob against the invasion
of their haunts by our launch.

These are the birds which make Marmora and
the Bosphorus so full of life, even when the hot
air silences all other noise and motion. They are
never disturbed or killed by the inhabitants.
They have a monopoly of the isle. They are
gentle, as all inhabitants of the isle,—which is
named after the heroine of Sophocles,—should be.

This tameness of the birds is not limited to the
Island of Prinkipo. All through the mosques and
groves and walls and gardens of the old city of
Stamboul you hear a universal twitter and the
fluttering of wings which indicate the life of the
birds. The sparrows fly in and out of the houses.
The swallows, which seemed partial to my presence,
fix their nests in every convenient arch in and out
of the bazaars. The pigeons are maintained by
many, and have a mosque of their own named
after them. The gulls rival in number the turtle-
doves, the one having dominion of the air and
the other of the woods and cemeteries. The
halcyons fly in long ranks up and down the Bosphorus, as if restlessly intent on some very
earnest business; while the grave and dignified
stork sits upon the towers of Anatolia and Rou-

melia, and upon the cupolas of the grand mauso-
leums. The Turk never harms these birds.
Every bird has a little office of trust which it exe-
cutes for this wild, reckless and sanguinary Turk.

Now we steer direct for Plati. Its profile is a
semicircle. It has dark gaps in its sides. There is
a white building on its shore and another on its summit. A few more whirls of the "Sunset's" screw
and there is revealed the two Anglo-Saxon castles.
No houses yet appear. The smaller sister, Oxia,
is more like a pyramid. In fact, it is about twenty
times as large as the pyramid of Ghiza, but not so
symmetrical. As we draw near it takes on a rough
aspect. These twin isolated rocks, as we approach,
become quite tall and roomy. I should say that
Plati—Bulwer's Isle—is at least a mile in circuit.
Looking to the north-west there appears in dim
outline the European coast. The white specks
are the houses of San Stefano. There the famous
Turco-Russian treaty was made, and there the
Russian army lay in wait ready for a spring at, and
into, Constantinople.

As we approach the little isle the haze lifts.
The desert of blue water is oased by a splendid ship in full sail, bearing the Greek ensign.
It moves like a vision of beauty and leaves
no cloud upon the sky. It hides between the
isles we have passed, then reappears. It is moving toward Modena, which is the port of the

‧ancient capital of the Ottoman at the foot of Olympus.

Now we are within a hundred yards of Plati, but as we cannot land in the launch, we embark on the *caïque* with the fishermen, and are rowed into a little cave, where we are saluted by the seneschal of the castle. He is an old man, an Armenian, George by name. His last name is the last thing we inquire for. Every one here goes by the Christian name, even the Turks ! The castle is then, indeed, inhabited. Its towers and walls have a relict radiance of past glory. As we enter the chief room an enormous chandelier attracts attention. Then the fresco of the walls, the mosaic of the floors, and the tessellated pavements of the courts all speak of occupation and sudden decay. Everything is quiet. No birds sing : not even a cicada chirps. Not a ship or boat is in view. The sea is still. It seems like that primeval time before the winds were loosed from their caves. The water glistens and glows under the July sun. The haze clears away almost entirely. The city of Stamboul rises out of the blue elements. The minarets and cupolas of the mosque of Suliemanyeh—the best specimen of the ‘Osmanli structural genius—and the minarets and dome of stately Sofia, seem to gesture upward and swell with new grandeur. Turning to the east, every one of the nine isles are marked in clear outline, except little

14

Pita, which plays hide and seek behind Antigone,·
and Andirovitha, which lies prone like the dragon
under the shadow of St. George of Prinkipo. The
clouds still enshroud Olympus on the south, but
the outline of the Asiatic coast is becoming more
definite.

The lower castle is much the larger. It has
many chambers—reception rooms with fireplaces,
as if it might have been comfortable in winter.
One of the rooms is a large frescoed hall. It has
various bookcases, but no books, only painted titles.
They give added mockery to this shell of a
castle. Here is "The History of Mehemet Ali ;"
there the "Histoire des Arabes ;" yonder, Rob-
inson's "Palestine," and again here D'Ohsson's
"Tableau d'Empire Ottoman." Over a Turkish inscription I find one most characteristic volume,
contents omitted—"Notes of Machiavelli and
Montesquieu."

After looking about the castle on the shore, we
mount the hill by a path. We are conducted by
the Armenian. He tells us that he farms the
property and that that is his consideration for
being its *châtelain.* I ask : "Do you make anything out of it ?"

"Some years a little. Not much this year."

"How many hands do you employ ?"

"We have," he replies, "eight persons on the
island, including my boy here, Antoine, and my

wife, who keeps house in the upper castle. The other men are flailing the oats now and caring for the six cows and one bull."

The path to the upper castle had once been laid out with skill and fringed with flowers. The *fleur-de-lis* has left its remnants here on the borders. We pass old fig-trees that never fail to live where there is a mouthful of dust, a few olive, ash, and locust trees, remains of old buildings, oratories, convents, and *kiosks*, and pedestals of carved marble and broken heads of columns, doubtless ravished from old temples and never worked into the projected architecture. Then we stand in front of the main castle. It is surrounded by foliage. It has even in its ruin a fairylike look. "Perhaps in this neglected spot" Sir Henry hatched many a diplomatic egg, or revelled in many a bout with his *attachés* and friends.

There is a little touch of the Arabic in the Gothic of the building which destroys its unity. Large rocks and boulders lie about its esplanade. Sheafs of grain are stacked, and some maize and melon patches are on the terraces.

The building above is not so stately as the castle by the sea, but it is in better preservation and is prettier. The rocks are clad in a red lichen ; and vines in good condition are in eligible places. Here and there are garden spots, in which are gourds, pistachio nuts, melons, artichokes, and

tomatoes in good growth.   But the business looks
as if it had gone to seed ; so do the peasants, in
their Turkish fez, red Greek sash, and baggy
breeches.   The only healthy and handsome gentleman on the isle is the bull.   We come upon him
unexpectedly.   He makes a quiet remark in his
own tongue, upon which I retreat suddenly.   I
am happy to see that he is tethered to a stake, which
he could not pull up, by a chain he cannot break.
His five cows serenely chew their cuds, and give
no sign of surprise at our presence near the harem.

We stand in front of the castle.   The *chât-
elaine* appears.   She is not romantic nor pretty,
but polite.   The two men stop their flail and
come down the circular steps that lead to the por-
tal above.   On this circled terrace are trees of
luxuriant growth and tangled vines in flower.
The front of the palace has its windows and doors
arched with brown and white stone from Chios.
The floors within the rooms are of marble mosaic,
and are not yet disarranged by neglect.   The ceil-
ings of most of the rooms are low, and where the
rain has not entered, are as clean as when just
frescoed.   There are mirrors all about, in the dining, library, and other rooms.   The colored glass
gives a dim religious light to the chambers.   But
the feature of these apartments is the imitation
book-cases.   These are cupboards, but their doors
are neatly painted with the binding and titles of

works of all kinds. This seems to have been the
ruling passion of Bulwer—this outside display of
literature. I ask George to open one of the
book-cases. Ostensibly it was a library of volumes on the English, French, German, and Turkish *cuisine*. He opens it, and a lot of bottles
filled with the *vin du pays* appear. This evokes
a smile all round; but George does not tender us
a perusal of the contents of these brittle books.
Here are books entitled "Wine Drinkers,"
"Geography," and "Metaphysics." Over one
door of this library is written in French: "*Il
faut vivre avec ses amis.*" Over another is the
same motto in Turkish. It seems strange that
Bulwer should seek such a secluded spot, where
friends could rarely come, and where, if the traditions are correct, he was rather limited in his selection by number and sex. What a commentary
these chambers furnish of the elegant man of the
world—this type of the accomplished strategist
in the wiles of diplomatic war!

Upon these marble floors lie piles of oats
and broken straw for the kine, while the sound of
the flail keeps time where the golden bowl used
to flow and the viands of the epicure were wont
to steam. Now the common vegetable used for
the peasant's soup—called *sobitha*—a kind of seed
or nut, is spread in one room, while in another the
worm-eaten wooden floor has lost its power even

of storage.   Upon these desolations the soft hues
of the stained archways give a melancholy lustre,
which the mirrors yet unbroken on ceiling and on
wall reflect in multiform shapes.   Some pictures
are in the *salle à manger*, but they are not as fresh
as those I saw on the tombs of Egypt, four thousand years old.

We pass up a stairway of white marble,
which is perfect, and the only perfect piece of
work remaining.   Streaks of white light here shoot
through the round windows.   Here, too, is another
illusory library.   One cupboard has a lot of supposititious volumes entitled, " Is Wine Beneficial ? "
another in German—" Drunken."   Secret recesses
repeat these illusions.   Here, over the bedstead,
in an alcove, is a case of " *Rêves* "—Dreams !
The bedstead is elegant, but the family of the
Armenian peasant sleep upon the coarse quilt
which covers its gilding.   Over the fireplaces are
volumes of " Day Dreams," another of " Visions."
The outlook over the castellated terrace up-stairs
shows the superb sea in its ultramarine robe, and
Stamboul the Beauteous !   The upper rooms
are hot and close.   Some of the doors are screens
of flowers in *appliqué*, upon cloth, picturing vine,
leaf, and grape upon both sides.

These rooms are painful to behold, like the
wreck of a proud man in the glory of his youth.
Upon the floor below, in one of the rooms,

there lie the *disjecta membra* of an alabaster vase of proportionate elegance, and chased with the vine, leaf and fruit. I asked George if he thought the ex-Khedive's agent in Constantinople would sell this.

"Yes, he would. In fact, it had been once sold to an American, but he had never taken it nor paid for it. Ali Effendi, at Kioskontak, on the Bosphorus, is the agent. See him!"

We passed out into the court. It is not large, say 100 feet square. It has a fountain, but no water. It has flowering shrubs, but their scent is wild, as if the tangle of time had deprived them of sweetness. Weeds, weeds, weeds—all, an epitome of the life of their former owner. Some of the walls are tumbling down, and have props, but the arches spring perennially beautiful in their various stones from the island home of Homer. The general color of the building is white, so that the stains of time and weather are plainly apparent. Still the towers remain, and the castellation is clean cut against the sky.

The best-preserved portions of the castle are the stables. They are quite roomy. What did Sir Henry want of horses on so small an isle? I stumbled over an old grist stone made to grind the grain—as old as that which Mungo Park's negresses used when he was investigating Africa—the counterpart of that which is seen in Egypt to-

day. I can understand its utility here in this
lonely place. There are fishers' nets lying about
in which my feet are entrapped. Their *raison
d'être* is also apparent, for Marmora is the sea for
fish *par excellence.* I can appreciate the pleasure
terrace beyond the palace, looking west, for here
the sentimental diplomat of the Bulwer type could
profitably muse as he looks off toward sunset
and Washington, where his Clayton-Bulwer treaty
is still discussed. I can appreciate also the garden
of figs and melons between this terrace and the
western end of the isle—a wild, incongruous romance on durable rock ; for have we not regaled
ourselves upon the fresh fig and the delicious melons ? I can imagine a utility in the little lizard
which flashes into the sunlight out of the rocks, to
give my wife an ejaculatory surprise. Even the
snails which cling to the shrubbery have their use, if
only as a bait for fish. I can well imagine why the
kitchen, with its ovens and wood-house, is separated
from the castle, and which still has its use as a
chicken-house. The old petroleum cans that lie
around have their use as buckets. I can understand the compensation which a place of this isolated kind,—so full of remoteness from the "cries
of the people who do come and go, "—furnishes to
the jaded intellect and the palled taste of the hot
and stifling city. I need not read Ruskin to give
emphasis to the utility of beauty, such as this pano-

rama establishes, with breezy fretwork upon the blue sea, and its inspiration drawn so closely from the fountains of nature. But I cannot fancy what on earth Sir Henry could want, on such an isle, of such stable room for a great stud of horses, who could not caper very nimbly here without falling off into the Marmora sea.

Perhaps the solution is found in the Quixotic spirit which erected these castles in such an out-of-the-way spot, or perhaps in the spirit of some of the mock volumes whose titles I read in the lower castle halls, as, "Themes on the Impossible," or "L'Advantages de la Lune et du Soleil Comparés," or "Charmes du Mariage par un Garçon de 80 ans;" for in their different-colored bindings, blue, red, and green, these odd and *outré* titles to textless books render them pretty toilets to the eye which thirsts for the realities which are not within.

I said nearly every object here indicates decay. There is an exception in front of the castle. It is a good *bas relief* of St. George and the Dragon and an elegant monogram of "H. L. B." This cipher is all that remains to attest the personality of the accomplished diplomatist, who, in making these structures, built more than a Spanish castle. The figments of his brother, Sir Edward Lytton-Bulwer, and the poetry of the son ("Owen Meredith"), who glorified Florence Nightingale by a song as sweet as that melodious bird itself can sing, have left their permanent impressions upon our time. But these ruins of mortar and stone, glass and wood, have no meaning except to mark the swift decadence of the statesman who erected them, and of the fall from power of the ex-Khedive, Ismail Pasha, who owns them.

Thus moralizing, we take our way, after making remuneration to the Armenian keeper for his politeness in showing us the realities of these castles, which seem from the Bosphorus and from the other isles like unreal *chateaux en Espagne*, or castles in the air. We find at the landing the good launch "Sunset" sitting like a bird upon the sea, impatient to show off her brand new flag to these warders of this once strange diplomatic *chateau*. Our ambitions take a more apostolic turn, and, forgetting diplomacy and its eccentricities, we steam over the clear blue water to Antigone with our fishing *caïque* in the wake. There we enter the *caïque*, and fish for *grand poissons*, while the launch darts around the isle for the sustenance of our bodies, *i.e.*, lunch. What we caught is nothing to nobody. But we brought home a splendid many-hued string of memories with all the flavor and zest of castle building, without the glamour of antiquity.

CHAPTER XIV.

PRINKIPO AS A HERMITAGE—CLOISTERED AMENITIES
—A RICH LIBRARY.

"THERE is the making of a monk in every man,"
says Miss Cleveland, in her essay on monasticism.
As its complement, it might be said that there is
the making of a nun in every woman. Man is
more than half a recluse. More than half the
time he prefers to be cloistered. Certainly, if he
have studious or contemplative tendencies, and
had the opportunities and books, he would not
mind much isolation from his fellows. John Bun-
yan and Cervantes could fill up their time delight-
fully, even in jail. Men in these Eastern climes
have sought and yet seek the cave and the monastery. When the world palls, or ambition is slaked,
or the passions are paralyzed, men, and women
too, seek diversion in the hermitage. This occurred to me when I first looked at my Prinkipo
"Castle of Indolence," and isolation. I was ready
to say, as I looked at the enchantment of shore,
sea and sky: "Here is Nature's grace! Here are
the open windows of heaven! Here dawn and
eve color the vault and deck the blue waves.

Here are cosy nooks and seats of vantage, far from
public work and resort.   Here

> "Let health my nerves and finer fibres brace,
>   And their toys to the great children leave;
>   Of fancy, reason, virtue, nought can me bereave."

After a visit to the hermit of Halki, I was more
than ever disposed to bless my stars that, for a
time at least, I had the privilege of a home remote
from all worldly associations, and even from the
usual noises and excitements of the isle.   After a
little, however, my sociality began to assert itself.
The little children, the very dogs, chickens and
donkeys evoked it.   Within our villa and garden
there were few or no intrusions.   I was content to
dream and read, to read and write, until ordered
up the mountain for a sanitary stroll.

When I came to this villa my first adventure
was to the library.   The son of the proprietress
had been crowned at Cambridge, England, as first
in classics.   His library, though not large, was
pleasing and select.   I remembered what Caliban
had said of Prospero in the Isle of "The Tempest:"

> "Remember to possess his books!"

I had practised on this Shakesperian edict.   One
of my victims was our city landlord.   I levied on
him before I began to prey on the villa library.

That is why and how I had become master of a library of my own.

The hotel most famous in Constantinople is the Hotel d'Angleterre. It used to be kept by Missirie. The soldiers in the Crimean war called his hotel " Misery." My experience in 1881 was that, since it has been kept by the Greek. Logothetti,— " word-bearer,"—it was well kept. I had then the best room. overlooking the Bosphorus and the Sea of Marmora. and I ought to have been content. It was not misery. I was content

In rummaging around in the old and odd places of the hotel I found that travellers to the East for fifty years had left books and what not. and that they were gathered in the dusty holes and recondite shelves of the hotel. I used to spoil my clean linen by exploiting these places for literary spoil. One book which I found was the volume of an Austrian secretary at Moscow. quite confidentially giving a narrative of naked facts about Peter the Great and his diabolism. Only one other copy of the work was ever found. That one was discovered by Eugene Schuyler at Naples. The rest. in the interest and honor of the Czars and their *régime*. had been destroyed.

On my return to Constantinople. in 1885. I went rummaging again. I found that volume gone. Making a bargain with M. Logothetti. I " launched " off to Prinkipo quite a lot of these waifs. They are before me. Here is one! It has on its fly-leaf the name of Lady Mary Wortley Montagu. But can it be her signature? If it were, it would be doubly enhanced. It is only a Gazetteer of the "known world" in 1815, with "improvements" by Dr. Brookes, of London. It is printed for J. Bumpus. It opens with a map of the world of 1815, from the "best authorities." The imaginary and abstract lines—like the poles and circles—are in the map, in geometric symmetry; but between Capricorn and Cancer—the goat and the crab—in Africa, is "Negro-land,"—a vast space. There is hardly a name between that of "Hottentot" and "Barbary." What a filling of space, since by the De Brazzas and the Stanleys, by the Spekes, Livingstones, and Bakers!

Among the definitions of this Gazetteer is this: "That a hill is a small kind of mountain!" This remarkable book begins with four "Aa's." They are rivers in Samogitia, Picardy, etc. It ends with Zytomicrz—a town in Poland,—but pasted at the end of the zeds, is a poem whose last verse is:

> "And woman—woman ever bright!
> I loved thee most, when least sincere."

The Gazetteer spells Michigan, *Michagan;* Chicago as a river or village is not even named. Turning mechanically to the word "Limburg," the Gazetteer says: "It is the place for excellent

cheese." "Limestone, or Maysville, Ky.," is in
the catalogue. Pennsylvania is celebrated for
neither coal, iron, nor oil ; but for potash, furs,
skins, and wax. Philadelphia—the Turks call it
Allahhijah—had then only two thousand Christians. I beg pardon ; that is the old Philadelphia
near Smyrna, where there was one of the seven
churches. The capital of Penn's State is said by
Mr. J. Bumpus, to have grown so fast that in the
lifetime of the first person born in it, it contained
forty thousand people. As my mother was born
there, it was not exactly a city of brotherly, but of
motherly love ; and I am proud to have it said in
the Gazetteer that it is near New York and has a
magnificent State-house and a Philosophical hall.
Illinois is set down as a river in Indiana. New
Haven is celebrated for its card-teeth, college, and
buttons. Ohio is a State with five districts, of
which New Connecticut is one. There are "no
slaves" there. Marietta is its largest town ; but
Chillicothe is the capital. Massachusetts is well
watered and produces plenty of maize, hemp, and
copper ! It has a machine for cutting nails,—in-
vented by Jacob Perkins,—which makes 200,000
nails a day ! That State makes 1,900,000 gallons
of distilled spirits a year ! New York State has
wheat for its staple and abounds in fine lakes.
The city of New York is fifteen miles in length,
but hardly one in breadth. It has "no basin or

bay for the reception of ships, but the road where
they lie in East river is defended from the terrific
violence of the sea by some islands, which inter-
lock each other!" What a commentary on Long,
Staten, and other islets, and Hell-gate and its
dynamitic thunders and forces! Is New York
equipped for education and goodness? Yes. It
has "a noble seminary called Columbia College
and a magnificent edifice called Federal Hall,
where the illustrious Washington took the oath!
It has a botanical garden. In time of peace it has
commerce! In time of war it is insecure. It has
no marine force.

Philippi is recorded in the Gazetteer only as a
town in Macedonia. It is not said that Cassius
and Brutus met there at a cross-roads grocery to
drink the health of Augustus and Antony, before
Christ some forty-two years. Of China it is said
that it excels in kitchen-gardens and cultivates the
bottom of its rivers. It has trees on which is
raised tallow! The Chinese complexion is a sort
of tawny; and those who are thought to be most
handsome are the most bulky. The Chinamen
affect pomposity, but their houses are low. The
empire existed before Noah's flood. They drink
a liquor called "rack." It is not added what kind
of a *racket* it makes when exported into such
unknown realms as Wyoming and California!
Is California gazetteered? Yes. It is put down

as a peninsula. It is separated from the coast by the Vermilion sea. Of this my friend the publisher and learned author, Bancroft, of San Francisco, will take heed. Galvez found a pearl fishery in its gulf — I reckon — of Colorado. He found mines of gold of a very promising appearance. Most Californians use a girdle and a piece of linen for clothing; but further north the Californians use shells for ornament and live in caves. Its chief town is St. Juan, which makes a wine like Madeira.

Saratoga is a town and a fort. It is on the *east* side of the Hudson. Not to be prolix, the United States itself is summed up in this Gazetteer—as seventeen States. They are well supplied with rivers, great and small, springs, and lakes. In the large towns the houses are of brick; in the others and their environs, of planks; but eighty miles from the sea, in the Central and Southern States, seven-tenths of the inhabitants live in log houses. These houses are made of the trunks of trees. They are from twenty to thirty feet long and four or five inches in diameter. They are laid upon one another and support their ends into each other. The spaces between the trunks are filled with clay. They have two doors, which are hung with wooden hinges. These doors frequently supply the place of windows. Neither nails nor iron of any sort are used.

15

All this was long before the rivalry between Chicago, Cincinnati, and St. Louis.

To one interested in our census since 1810 this Gazetteer makes a picture of contrasts interesting and economic.

"'The chinkin' and daubin'" of even the log cabins of the 1840 campaign seem, to one who has passed through our civil war, as quite a rearward object of domestic architecture.

Comparing this description with that of Constantinople in the Gazetteer, how great the changes! These changes indicate civilizing energies even in the capital of Turkey. The description of Constantinople almost suits its present condition ; but not quite. Its towers and walls—its castles and multitudinous houses—are the same! St. Sophia, with its room for 100,000 worshippers, remains. The seraglio burned down some twenty years ago. A railroad now runs around those old walls, out of which the *odalisques* of Abdul Mejid peeped thirty years ago, when I first saw it. The bazaars are the same. The Jewish and Armenian traders are the same ; but the "great number of girls from Hungary, Greece, Circassia, and Georgia, for the service of the Turks," have greatly diminished. The ambassadors, now as then, live on the Pera side of the Golden Horn ; but the fifty thousand graceful *caïques* no longer ply upon the Bosphorus for general transportation. The Shirket company runs steam ferries up and down the straits, and the azure sky is stained with their coal soot and smoke. A car, run by an endless chain and by the vapor of water, lifts the passenger from the shore at Galata to the top of Pera heights. A street railway plies its work and sounds its horn not only upon the newly-widened streets of Pera, but even in the narrow streets of Stamboul, upon whose travel or travail there look out of the jalousies of the Moslem the beauties of the haremlik!

Outside of the great city are the same treeless hills and furrowed vales. Here and there they are green and laughing with cultivation, and not unspeckled with the splendid black and white sheep and goats of the suburbs. As far as the eye can see, the glorious panorama of mountain and water, with the grand prospect of domes, minarets, palaces, armories, arsenals, and barracks, is spread out for the wondering and admiring gaze. The old commanding situation for commerce and empire remains, and will ever remain.

The same Eastern imbroglio continues, from the same old motives, from the same great and greedy powers. Gradually the European elements are encroaching upon Asiatic features and policy. It may be that, before the new century dawns, the dreams of Peter the Great will be realized; or else that the Greek—under some noble impulse,

and from consenting and non-conflicting elements,
—may resume his worship in St. Sophia and his
control from the palace of Blachernae. It may
be that the capital of old Byzantium will become a
free port. All this is problematical, for the Turk
may remain under better conditions. Eastward
the star of empire may take its way, even though
it glimmer within the horns of the crescent.

But I was rummaging in my villa library among
the lost tribe of books of the old Missirie hostelry.
It is the same as ever—as in all libraries; for all
libraries when analyzed have their chance companions. Here is a learned treatise by Lord Lindsay
on "Christian Art," with its symbolism and
mythology, written originally for "Sir Coutts Lindsay, Baronet." It is said to have wings for the
artist to the gate of heaven! Its uncut volumes
are as clean as the subject; never having been
other than idealized by the sacred quality of the
author's mind. Next to these volumes is Eugene
Sue's "Martin the Foundling." It has his portrait in the French toilet of 1847. The book is
illustrated by Shepherd. It shows the prevalent
taste in unchristian art and literature four decades
ago. Hallam next kisses George Eliot's "Gipsy."
Plans of fortifications for Crimean struggles lie
dormant, next to books on the peace of Christ—
which passeth all understanding—of their proximity. Hepworth Dixon bounds into the arena,

along with a dozen books of highly-colored lithographs showing the "Dawnings of Light in the East!" A score of volumes descriptive of all the lands and peoples from Bagdad to Carthage, with here and there love-tokens sent as bookmarks, and flowers from Bethlehem, whose faint odors are all too emblematic! Mitford's full volumes on Greece sit down with "Gentle Elia," Bulwer's "Rienzi," Tom Moore's "Lalla Rookh," Cicero, and "Eöthen." But who spreads the feast for these anachronistic people? Who? Why, the very prince of the *cuisine* himself. Soyer makes a "culinary campaign," which he calls historical reminiscences of the late war (Crimean), with the plain art of cookery!

This culinary champion was a confederate of Florence Nightingale in the campaign which she made against the evils of war, in the hospitals of Scutari. In this volume he dishes up many historical delicacies. He makes up in succulence of detail what he lacks in literary proficiency! Perhaps no one in that singular war achieved more reputation than this great chief of the kitchen. He was a practical man. When not organizing his *suite* in the hospital kitchen for the disabled and wounded soldier, he was purveying in a kindlier office. That his life was not entirely fruitless of good, his volume fully demonstrates; for after his laborious campaign, in bidding adieu to his readers, he says:

"I do not intend to remain Soyer *Tranquille*, but I hope to be the means of causing a lasting amelioration in the cooking for all public institutions. Such a result of my labors, after my long culinary experience, ought to make an author happy indeed, and I hope for the future to be found as traced below." Here follows, as the curious *finale* of a useful and benevolent life, his own picture, as he sits felicitously over a glass of Chateau Yquem, in some celestial *cuisine* above the stars!

All through this odd volume of Alexis Soyer Miss Nightingale sings her quiet music of humanity—so sweet amid the sensual palate pleasures, that "we know not we are listening to it."

From all the ends of the earth and from all the æons of time come forth from Missirie's dusty volumes these controversial, didactic, military, theologic, descriptive, cuisinistic and classic folk—dressed in garbs as various as those which make the Stamboul bridge a perpetual kaleidoscope! Here, in Misery's hotel—as some one has sung, but whose music I cannot recall in verse—here the rage of controversy ends; zealots become friends, Socinians abide with Calvinists, and those other Calvinists or Kismetians of Mohammed meet Catholic and Quaker and

"Bellemarine has rest at Luther's feet."

I am forbidden by my wife and other powers to write for publication on political and social themes pertinent to this capital of diplomacy. Having, however, the cacoethes equal to any Scotchman, I must be writing something at odd moments. If I cannot make literature of a higher grade, may I not take glances at those who have been creators of that order of work?

It is difficult to find any "Orient pearls" not already discovered and strung. And yet these wonderful seas and waters ought to be gemmed at bottom: but where one would find pearls he only gets—sponges! It takes away my breath when I think of trying to write of some new thing here. Or, to keep to the metaphor, as in the pearl fisheries of the Red Sea, I am not unlike the diver who does not often obtain the pearls, but, reckless of sharks and death otherwise, he is content with filling his lungs for three minutes and loading his feet with a stone, and, dropping his ballast, to arise with one oyster, whose pearl is not always equal to the effort and occasion.

Yet what a sea for pearls of thought—pearls of great price—is this Mediterranean, which through divers ways leads up to this capital of capitals! The Mediterranean is called by the Turks the White Sea. It is blue, but cheerful as the white light of unclouded day. It is tideless, but what tides has it not witnessed in the affairs of men

—taken at the flood by some and at the ebb by others? It is the sea of historic movements as well as of musical cadences. Troy, Carthage, Byzantium, Athens, Rome, Alexandria — ever romantic and commercial, classic and barbaric! Over its waters Crusaders came; amid its isles Venetian and Genoese sailed. Now upon its bosom steamers of Russia, Austria, France and England ply with ceaseless interchange. But an American vessel with the star-spangled banner— never.

"SOYER TRÈS HEUREUX!"

CHAPTER XV.

Again the precept of Shakespeare is heard :

" Remember to possess his books."

Without them, Prospero had not one spirit to command! When I made the lease of this villa there came into our possession all the lore of the Cambridge scholar, much of which was all Greek to me, especially the modern Greek. It was my custom in the morning, when the air was cool and fresh, to promenade, book in hand, up to the half way seat on the mountain side. Here I could read undisturbed. Here, I re-read Homer, not merely in English, but in the original, with much marking and remarking between the lids of my scholarly landlord's copy.

The confessions of Jean Jacques Rousseau were found in this library, lying close to some religious Armenian literature. I perused them for the first time under these skies,—where Rousseau's father used to live and work too, as watchmaker to His Majesty, the Sultan! How strangely this senti-

233

mental yet gross Franco-Swiss philosopher, with his love of nature and nastiness,—his amours and his amiableness—impresses one! His style is so lucent and his artlessness so absolute, that one need not wonder that his social theories, arrayed in alluring garb, caught the fancy and enthralled the emotions of his time.

By adding some of my own favorite volumes to these bookish anchorites of our villa, I have reading enough. I can accomplish more than Horne Tooke did when he was in prison; for not only have I the "Diversions of Purley" in studying radically many tongues, but I can delve literally into the old earth herself, with Rousseau, in search of medicinal roots, to gratify my botanic fancies.

Besides having the launch and the free sea, the flag and "interterritoriality," I am as un-hampered as the botanizing bee or butterfly in our garden, that flies from flower to flower at its own sweet will. But this freedom of motion is not the idea of a hermitage.

One of the precious little diamonds in literature, which was presented to me by a D.D.,—whom we call the "Dreadful Dragoman," is that of P. Gyllii, on the "Topographia of Constantinople." Its frontispiece has the *imprimatur* and flavor of Munich. It was printed in 1632. It is two hundred and fifty years old. Two angels in the frontispiece draw up two curtains between classic columns, in order to display the old city with its mosques and khans. Beneath is a picture of the Seraglio Point. The houses were far apart then, and the foliage abundant. The same kind of boats float on the current as those of the present day. It is a picture of the city under the Sultans in its primal splendor.

I must not omit a glance into an unpretending volume by Edward Bulwer-Lytton, which illustrates the institutions of ancient Athens. If it be not accurately historic, it is provocative of the study of Mitford, whose nine volumes have each a significant picture, a rich text and learned notes. Bulwer not only illustrates the matchless genius and glory of Greece, but the interesting struggles which her states carried on in these colonial waters, upon whose bosom to-day ride steamers which the classic Greek with all his fleet Mercuries and potential Neptunes never imagined. Some of his chapters and scenes take me to the very boundaries of Bulgaria, where a Battenberg prince now keeps the Balkans in perpetual turmoil. I confess to a prejudice against Hessians, which these summer studies from this library have strengthened: but I must not confound Prince Alexander of Hesse Darmstadt with that venal scoundrel of Hesse Cassel, who sold his subjects to King George III. of England, to destroy the colonies of America.

From the perusal of these histories of human degeneracy, how happy to find the works of the "Gentle Elia." They bring back the remembrances of summer days, like those we pass here; and of delightful years, before diplomacy required reserve. His words "Spoken at the Mermaid!" and his sonnets of sweetness and quaint conceits give a vivacity which no carking care about Harpoot schools or Bulgarian atrocities can ever dispel from our diplomatic mind.

Here, too, is found hidden between Greek and Armenian tomes, Longworth's "Year Among the Circassians." It was published in 1840. It has some old lithographs of the interiors of Circassian homes. These are rude huts. Few articles of necessity and none of luxury are shown in the picture. Here is a man with a turban. He wears a black beard and a blouse. On his breast are a score of cartridges arrayed tastefully. He sports light stockings and the usual pointed shoes. A saddle and gun, a curved sword and a blanket, with an ottoman sofa or so, for reclining at meals, or for rest, make up the furniture. A fire of faggots is at one end of the hut. There a tea kettle is boiling. A graceful girl, in a pretty bodice of dark material, a skirt of light color, and a tasteful unique head-dress is the central female figure. A sheep at the door, and a brace of dogs near by, are the accompaniments.

INTERIOR OF CIRCASSIAN HOME.

The household is serving a Persian, Turkish or Jewish visitor with meats and cups of refreshment. The hospitality is unbounded. This is the scene, nearly a half century ago, before Schamyl was conquered and the Russian had triumphed over native valor and mountain fastness.

But the Turk had long before then conquered, by his gold and other agents, the beauties of these mountain homes, for his harems. Buying and selling slaves for wives was then a legal matter. The mountain beauties liked to be sold out of their rude modes of living into the luxurious ease of the grand capital. Any stranger who interfered with the affair of the *hadji,* or merchant, was left to the cold sympathies of those most nearly interested. The father, or husband, not only often acquiesced in the transaction, but it was not considered disreputable for an *oùzden,* or a freeman in good circumstances, to sell his own children. The advantages of a settlement in a good harem in Turkey, was the *animus* of this business which has given most of the women and mothers to the Turkish harems. Besides, these females received a pretty good education in Turkey, including religious teaching. Their condition was bettered. Marriage in Turkey, as I show in another chapter, is comparative freedom. It was not freedom they wanted, but ease and slippered luxury. Fancy gilded their future. They used to bring a higher price if they were something beyond a tobacco-smoking *hanoum.* Housewifery enhanced their price. Sometimes the best and prettiest were placed in establishments, where, under matronly care, they learned to read and write, acquired some Arabic and Persian literature, and were taught how to deport themselves gracefully and graciously. It mattered not if they were property, when, after they could display their graces of mind and body, they could rise to independence. They could be thus weaned from the dependence which made them submissive to the haughtier sex even in their own Circassian household. When ushered into a more entrancing sphere, let us not be surprised at seeing in these women of the Circassian mountains those gentle qualities, controlling the hardier sex, which form the most attractive features of the Turkish woman, with her languishing eye and splendid figure. The very Spartan vigor and fierceness of the Circassian man, which forbade him to see his wife except stealthily, while it destroyed much of his affectionate nature, gave to the female under such discipline and reserve a constrained and modest demeanor, which is a most seductive part of her loveliness. After many generations, and with the delights and comforts of her new home and the bath, she obtains a complete mastery over herself, and her Turkish husband and lord. That mastery extends to her children. This makes her a provoking conundrum to the Frank, and a fascinating dream to all who behold her.

The Georgian has a beauty quite different from that of the Circassian. The Circassian is dazzling, queenlike and stately. She has a fair skin. She is elegant in form. She is kindly and gentle in voice, but lazy in movement and without *esprit*. One of her own sex has said: "there is no soul in a Circassian beauty; and as she pillows her pure, pale cheek upon her small dimpled hand, you feel no inclination to arouse her into exertion; you are contented to look upon her and to contemplate her loveliness." The Georgian is a creature with eyes like meteors, and teeth almost as dazzling as her eyes. Her mouth does not wear the sweet and unceasing smile of her less vivacious rival; but the proud expression that sits upon her finely arched lips accords so well with her stately form and lofty brow that you do not seek to change its character.

I have an impression that the Georgian is quite a dominant element in Turkey through the mother. We lose sight of this in our confused estimates of the Orient and its domestic influences.

Ever since the 18th of September, 1885, the "ant-hill" of Pera, where the diplomatic people winter, and the palaces of Bayukdere and Therapia, where they summer, have been in incessant moil and toil over the perpetual question of the East. Many of the books which I found at Misserie's old Hotel d'Angleterre, and which I was allowed to import to Prinkipo, were on this subject. They were not diverting; and yet they were full of eventualities which never happened, and of prophesies of new phases in which fresh delimitations of frontier and changes of dynasties came and went in mosaic confusion. They show the futility of *à priori* reasoning. They were big with the fate of empires and of men, but otherwise little. One prospect appears all through this class of literature. It is a "Dawning in the East" which has never yet dawned. And yet where else should there be dawn? I open a volume with this phrase as a title. It was written at Bagdad in 1853. Was that locality too far East to enjoy a dawn? This writer indulged in roseate hopes for the Jews in Persia, Kurdistan and Chaldea; but the past thirty years have not verified his optimistic predictions, either as to Jew or Gentile. The Euphrates still runs down, the tents of the Bedouin are still on its banks and the projected railroad of the valley is still a dream of the engineer.

But the missionaries continue their work; and, although surrounded by Bedouins, we have the same good report every day of advancement in teaching the native as to his life and letters, and the prevalence of brigandage by Circassian villains.

My view of Turkey is more hopeful. From the Robert College, if permitted to continue its work, may come the redemption of the time and of Asia Minor, Syria and the Balkans. Princes may come and princes may go into these struggling lands, but at last the potent secret will be revealed, and the light of America will illume the forlorn peasant homes of these historic and much-vexed lands.

What next ? A weather-stained volume called "Turkey and its Resources," by Urquhart, published in 1853. The author is more economic than prophetic. He had inklings that the adhesion of the various parts of Turkey were soon to be a thing of the past ; and yet he was surprised that Turkey still was languishing and lingering. He finds the secret of this cohesion of empire in municipal organization. This was not an accident, in his opinion, but an organic principle of Arabic legislation. The free states of Greece were the models, in fact the origin, of this Home Rule, which binds the tribes of the East in some sort of unity. One of the strange things which this author discerned and which the Turks could not understand was : How can a free land tax commerce and survive. This problem is commended to my own countrymen for solution.

16

One volume, in gilt attire like a pasha at Bairam, fairly leaps out of its shelf to greet my eye with its large and elegant typography and its interesting contents. It is the fifteenth edition of Sir Edward Creasy's " Fifteen Decisive Battles of the World, from Marathon to Waterloo." Upon the fly-leaf I find the name of my landlord, with the script : " First in classics, Xmas '66. L. F. B." and on the cover, in grand style, two phœnixes, not one only as it is fabled, and over them " RUGBY SCHOOL." If the date were only contemporaneous with " Tom Brown," or Dr. Arnold, there would be added another employment for analogy.

On the occasion of urging upon Congress the erection of the Saratoga monument, I had said that Saratoga was one of the pivotal battles of the world. I find Saratoga in this volume. It is headed by Bishop Berkeley's poetic " Star of Empire," and Lord Mahon's pregnant words : " that the surrender of the thirty-five hundred fighting men at Saratoga, had been so fruitful of results, that it not only changed the relations of mankind and the feelings of England toward the American colonies, but it modified for all time to come the connection between every colony and every parent state." Mentally, I made the comment which the recent excitement about Ireland suggested. What eventful connections have since grown out of the insurgence of the thirteen colonies toward the vast colonial dependency of Great Britain!

Hanging on the wall in this suggestive library is a chart of the power of Great Britain. Every continent is represented. Her immense dominion is typified by various races pictured on the chart. Along with it, as the commentary, come to my mind the stirring words of Gladstone, as I heard them uttered at the Robert American College commencement in July, by a Celtic boy with a Bulgarian brogue, who recited the conclusion of the great oration on behalf of a statutory Parliament and Home Rule for Ireland! A pardonable patriotic pride in the college, and in the doctrine and in the contest at Saratoga, and even in the testy Englishman, General Gates,—whom I never could admire,—begat much toleration even toward the traitor, Benedict Arnold. For had he not, in disregard of orders, given his splendid personal courage to that pivotal battle, whose results the reluctant step-parent was all too slow to recognize, but which the world has not failed to honor?

It is one of the "Pleasures of Prinkipo" that in this library, and from Lord Byron's poetry and Michel de Montaigne's essays, I have taken fresh quaffs of nectared delight. Byron's fine appreciation of the East and Montaigne's scholarship, frankness and genius have filled up many golden hours and sped them with flying feet.

Byron, more than any other poet, not excepting
Lamartine, has disentangled the sensuous pleasure and historic appreciation of the Orient, and
woven the many-tinted threads into robes of im-
purpled texture.   If his " Bride of Abydos " is
silly, as a tale, its scenes of domestic seclusion,
and its gorgeous pictures of water, sky and earth,
diamonds, stars and flowers, never fail to be
quoted by the young who repair hither to fill their
golden urns of imagery, and by the old, who
renew here their early dreams of luxuriant life.

As a foil and contrast to this literature of the
Orient, I happen upon a half-covered volume of
Frankenstein.   It was penned fifty years and more
ago, when this sombre literature enthralled the
literary world.   But where now is the weird monster of Mary Shelley's prolific imagination ?   And
yet, in this day of marvels in physical science, the
creation of a human frame by human skill, and
endowing it with the principle of life, may not
seem as bold as it did in 1831.   But as a figment
of the brain, it is, as the author urges, of the same
type as the " Iliad," the " Tempest," and " Paradise
Lost."   Its first scene is laid in the region of the
frozen North ; but its bewildering magic emanates
from the Orient.   What Paracelsus and Albertus
Magnus taught, are they not prefigured in the
monstrous beings of the " Thousand and One
Nights ? "   The idea of constructing a being of gi-

gantic mould and infusing into it the vital spark,
together with the terrible Nemesis of the story, is
of the Orient, all complete. Beside, is not the
Orient the home of the Magi? Have not the
fire worshippers made its sacred fires perennial
and poetical? Even at this day, the naphtha of
Baku has its religious associations, to which the
muse of Moore gave melody. How small the
world of fact and fancy is! How near akin are
the delusions of the past to the science of the
present! Aye, even in these library shelves of
Prinkipo, I gaze with awe, not unmixed with
wonder, upon two books bound in bloody red,
which connect my daily diplomatic duty with the
poetry of the past and the rites of the Parsee.
The next chapter will elucidate the relation.

It would fill a volume were I to recount
the rich variety of the thesaurus of the library
which came to us with our villa. Here on one
shelf is Sir John Lubbock's "Origin of Civilization" and "Primeval Man." In strange juxtapo-
sition I find the complete works of Molière. On
opening the latter I find this commendation by his
editor: "*Deux siècles sont passés, dit avec raison
M. Bagou, et nous attendons encore.*" Molière's
genius of comedy has had more than his
two centuries, but wherever the keen French
wit predominates, as it does in the Orient, his
works are perused with much *riant* enthusiasm.

Alongside of Herschel's "Physical Geography," with its revelations of our earth and seas, lands and minerals, snows and rain falls, caloric and magnetism, I find a strange volume whose title is "Inquire Within Upon Everything." On inquiring, I find an interesting discussion which vindicates the letter H in the English vocabulary, or rather its omission, as being a correct mode of speech. In fact, this book answers all queries—from the killing of vermin to the style of a frock; from the selection of a dining-table to the carving of a turkey or the decoration of a room.

Here in one corner of the library I find, "Boner Hunting Chamois in the Alps;" in another place, "A Golden Treasury of Lyrics." "Zadkiel's Astrology" astonishes, by its proximity to "The Chemistry of Common Life." Macaulay and the "Waverley Novels" are snugly hid along with Thucydides and Plutarch. Paley shakes hands with our own Maury, and "Henry Esmond" with Homer, Æschines and the whole cohort of Greeks. Here is Carey's Gradus! It takes us up the heights of Olympus. But is there anything in the library pertinent to my own life in the East? Yes: "Chesterfield's Letters to his Son." I open it at page 301. It gives me advice for a most pressing emergency at the Porte. "Why is it," it asks, "that negotiators have always been the politest and best bred men in the

world in company?" Ahem! Then he proceeds
to say:

" For God's sake, never lose view of these two,
your capital objects: bend everything to them, try
everything by their rules, and calculate everything
for their purposes. What is peculiar to these two
objects is, that they require nothing but what
one's own vanity, interest and pleasure would
make one do independently of them. If a man
were never to be in business, and always to lead a
private life, would he not desire to please and to
persuade? So that in your two destinations your
fortune and figure luckily conspire with your vanity and your pleasures. Nay more; a foreign
minister, I will maintain it, can never be a good
man of business if he is not an agreeable man of
pleasure too. Half his business is done by the
help of his pleasures; his views are carried on,
and perhaps best, and most unsuspectedly, at
balls, suppers, assemblies, and parties of pleasure;
by intrigues with women, and connections insensi-
bly formed with men, at those unguarded hours of
amusement.

" These objects now draw very near you, and you
have no time to lose in preparing yourself to meet
them. You will be in Parliament almost as soon
as your age will allow, and I believe you will have
a foreign department still sooner, and that will be
earlier than ever anybody had one."

With one or two exceptions, which I will not
notice, I have endeavored to practice, and not
without some success, these Chesterfieldian pre-
cepts.   In fact, it was in pursuance of their suggestions that I was enabled to accomplish what
the President was pleased to commend in his last
Message, in behalf of American interests at the
Porte.   It was because of this accomplishment—
thanks to Lord Chesterfield—that I concluded to
return home, after diplomacy did not, and as my
new service does not, require so many and such
peculiar sacrifices to the graces.

CHAPTER XVI.

INFERNAL FIRE AND LALLA ROOKH—DIPLOMACY— THE ROMANCE AND POETRY OF PETROLEUM.

I CAME to take an interest in the matters indicated by the head of this chapter because my official duty required me to examine into certain petroleum frauds on our trade in the classic isle of Mitylene. This interest was spurred by some happy coincidences, partly literary and partly social. Thus it happened to "concatenate accordingly."

Twenty-six years ago I wandered into a store near my law office in Cincinnati, Ohio. It was kept by the Messrs. James. I opened an exquisite edition of Thomas Moore's "Lalla Rookh." That book, the dandyism of all literary Orientalism, was *en toilette* in gold and ruby—ruby predominant. I read the dedication to Samuel Rogers. When I opened the same volume, the other day, in my library in Prinkipo, the "Pleasures of Memory" returned. I recalled, by a system of mnemonics, my Cincinnati experience as a young lawyer—or, rather, as an inchoate lawyer, then studying how Law limped after Justice in vain;

for I am not aware that in the three decades
or more since, Law has overtaken her healthier
sister. Many a time since I have seen Law stum-
ble, just as she was about to join hands with Justice and assist the latter to bear the scales aloft.

Eheu! Posthume! How the years have glided
away since that morning of my life, when "Lalla
Rookh" was one of the sources of my inspiration,
and before petroleum had lighted my student's
lamp in this Eastern capital.

During one of the damp, foggy, gloomy days of
the past winter, a stranger from New York was
announced. I hastened to the reception room,
and while awaiting him I picked up, by way of
passing the time, that very volume of "Lalla
Rookh." It has followed the author around this
planet and gives much comfort by its sensuous
imagery and impearled ideas. But on this occasion this beauteous work was all aglow with its
ruby and gold. It lay next to a terrific volume
called the "Region of Eternal Fire," dressed like
Mephisto himself, and sporting gold-leaf all over
its diabolic cover. It was Marvin's account of a
journey to the petroleum regions of the Caspian
in 1883. The book, its cover, and contents de-
served the sinister title.

But what has the Nourmahal to do with these
subterranean deviltries? This much: That the
place in "Lalla Rookh" upon which I happened

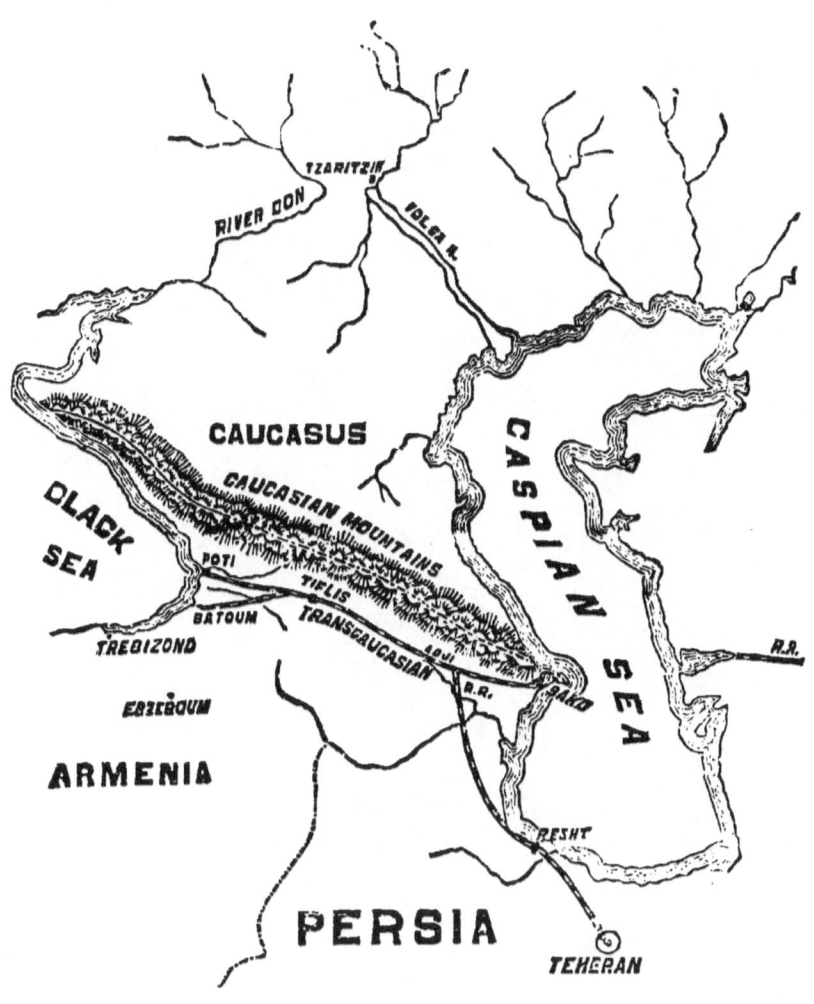

THE REGION OF FIRE AND PETROLEUM.

in my momentary vagary gives a description of Ivan's outlawed men—the worshippers of fire! It locates them near Yezd's eternal mansion of caloric—

> "Where aged saints in dreams of heaven expire;
> From Baku, and those fountains of blue flame
> That burn into the Caspian."

To this verse there is an annotation which indicates the historic facts to which Marvin alludes in his practical observations—viz., that about Baku, from early times, the sun and fire worshippers abided and that they kept illuminated the fires with vestal vigilance for 3000 years on a sacred mountain near Yezd, called Ater Quedah. He was reckoned unfortunate who died away from that mountain. Another note to Moore's verse says: "When the weather is hazy on the Caspian shore the springs of naphtha on an island near Baku boil up higher, and the naphtha often takes fire on the surface of the earth and runs in a flame into the sea, to a distance almost incredible."

This edition of "Lalla Rookh" was of 1849, and the notes were by the author as early as 1817; so that Baku, now so famous, and to Americans so troublesome and interesting as a competitor, is not a new place as a fiery resort or as a theme for literary exercise.

The odd coincidence of the proximity of these volumes on my table, and the other fact that I opened the poetic volume by chance upon the verse and notes quoted, gave rise to a new marvel. It was this : My visitor was an agent of the American Standard Oil Company ! He was *en route* to Baku ! He was about to sound the depths, volume, and values of these remarkable wells ! This visitor was the shrewdest man I met in the East. He was looking after his business and the new light of Asia with a watchful eye on Baku. He intended to go there. He did go. He returned and reported. He did not say much. He was writing it all up for his employers. I propose to do a little of this for my readers, since it combines the utilities of light and life with the elegance of poetry.

To do this I must draw upon Marvin's " Eternal Fire." Marvin is not a slow, infrequent, or unknown writer. He is voluminous. He was the correspondent of the London *Morning Post* on many a well fought journalistic field. He it was who wrote the " Russians at Merv and Herat," " The Russian Advance Toward India," " Merv, the Queen of the World," " Reconnoitring Central Asia," etc. He captured the Caspian, if ever man did, by way of penetrating its physical and political secrets.

Mr. Marvin's new Inferno is the result of

much research, for he has exhausted the literature
of petroleum as well as its physical phenomena.
That literature is by no means limited to " Lalla
Rookh." Names that give one the lockjaw to
pronounce, such as Gulishambamp, Markooriskopf,
Ogloblin, Mendeleiff, Gospodin, Polelika, and
others have given to the petroleum industry of
Baku and of Russia much chronicle and many
statistics. Yet Mr. Marvin's book seems to have
rather a tendency toward a high appraisement of
the Messrs. Nobel and their great genius for engineering, and properties in oil. I could not rise
from its perusal without that impression.

The engravings in the book of the Nobel works
are interesting, but I should say that Nobel *drew*
something in favor of Marvin for them. But are
not these enterprising Swedish men worthy of all
that is said and pictured? The brothers Nobel
have dabbled in dynamite and triumphed in torpedoes ; but their enterprise at Baku in laying
down the first pipe-line and by replacing barrels
with cistern steamers—in fact, by organizing an
oil fleet and making communication over the shal-
lows of the Volga by tank-cars, with depots over
Russia, and soon to be extended elsewhere—is a
romance worthy of celebration by pen and pencil,
a romance greater than that of which Tom Moore
sings. How the Nobel business is carried on, all
for cash,—how the brothers have passed crises in

the financial world,—how they have harnessed the Russian government to their petroleum-car,—how their business has become nearly a monopoly by reason of their peculiar mechanical skill and appliances,—is it not written by Marvin in a most fascinating manner? Whether you consider the material wonder described by Major-General Goldsword in 1870, when he saw natural petroleum gas fires which had been flaring more than 2500 years; or whether igniting in the furnaces of a hundred steamers on the Caspian and Volga; or the enormous subterranean reservoirs which science here locates; or the great ridge beneath the Caspian, from shore to shore and beneath the Caucasus, from sea to sea; whether this useful element be found beneath the barren steppes or under the mountain chains, or whether it rises in columns like the geysers of Iceland or the Yellowstone; whether, as at Findlay, Ohio, or at Allegheny City, Pennsylvania, it is made to move machinery and illuminate great workshops; whether its streams come forth in iridescent beauty—the iris out of whose black unfragrance comes the pigments for the painting of my lady's robe or her maid's frock; whether it exudes from the sodden soil or is used for watering the dusty streets of Baku; or whether it weaves by locomotion and the swift-flying shuttle of interchange a new civilization,—it is at once a theme for the muse of

Moore and the speculations of the bourse. If it be true, as is alleged, that a single man pricked the earth near Baku and wasted 50,000,000 or 100,000,000 gallons of good oil—enough to supply and light London for years—then poetry has lost its license, and should turn over its office to a tenth muse, which I christen the "Muse of Mechanism," to sing in oily numbers these natural glories and humanities of the earth.

Outside of the mercenary view of this burning question, it may be stated that the Parsee still lives; but fuel to feed his sacred fire is now an expensive item. Yet it must be supplied whenever a new temple is dedicated. Sixteen different kinds of wood, in one thousand and one pieces of fuel, are required to obtain the sacred flame. This is afterwards fed with sandal-wood, and the cost of the process averages $7500. There are still three large and thirty-three small fire-temples at Bombay! They are by no means inexpensive.

The fire worshipper is no longer paramount in Persia. Zoroaster no longer teaches his peculiar doctrine. Nine-tenths of the Persians are Mahometans. There has been a perpetual persecution of those who remain faithful to the fiery tenets of their forefathers. For twelve hundred and fifty years the Guebres (the name from which the Gaiour, or infidel, is taken) have survived. They pay their devotion to the life-giving

principle of the sun.   They do not worship the sun.
They worship God, its creator; the Being who
is supreme over fire and light.   The Guebres are
an honest race.   They are of the pure Persian
stock, when Persia was of some account in the
conduct and history of the world.   Most of the
Parsees reside in India.   Their homes are in
Bombay and in Calcutta.   Out of the hundred
thousand who survive, only about seven thousand
are left in Persia.   Their worship is singularly
beautiful, symbolical, and not at all unworthy of
the great demonstration which nature makes in
and around Baku.   It is by no means unworthy
of the auroral splendors of the dawn when its most
prominent observances hail the coming day!
That people which does not enjoy light and fails
to illumine, wherever and whenever nature makes
provision, are the laggards in the human race.
The fire worshippers love the light and their ways
are not evil !

Sometimes these fountains of naphtha create a
volcano whose sudden outbursts quite swamp the
little buildings around.   It is not a volcano of fire
so much as of hot mud.   Some time ago there
was an explosion about ten miles from Baku, and
a column of fire shot up three hundred and fifty
feet high.   The country was illuminated.   The heat
was perceptible miles away.   Little damage was
done, for there was no wind.   The volume of

muddy liquid thrown up was estimated in Russian, which I cannot interpret, except by the vague data that it spread itself over more than a square mile, and to a depth of from seven to fourteen feet !

David A. Wells, in his new book called " A Study of Mexico," regards the kerosene lamp as one of the motors of civilization in Mexico, only next after the railroad. In urging the reciprocity treaty with America he indicates how a bright, new, little kerosene lamp became to him the most remarkable and interesting object of importation from the United States to that country. It was to him " remarkable and interesting, because neither the man nor his father, possibly since the world to them began, had ever before known anything better than a blazing brand as a method for illumination at night, and had never had either the knowledge, the desire, or the means of obtaining anything superior. But at last," says Mr. Wells, "through contact with and employment on the American railroad, the desire, the opportunity, the means to purchase, and the knowledge of the simple mechanism of the lamp, had come to this humble, isolated Mexican peasant; and out of the germ of progress thus spontaneously, as it were, developed by the wayside, may come influences more potent for civilization and the elevation of humanity in Mexico than all that

17

church and state have been able to effect within
the last three centuries."

The same may be said, with even more emphasis, about our petroleum interests in Turkey. The
petroleum can and lamp play a double purpose ;
the one as a tin bucket and the other as a vessel
for the fluid which gives so much comfort to
the dark places of the East. It supplies, in fact,
the lamp of Aladdin, from whose friction sprang
rare and wonderful opulence.

It is generally supposed that Job was a rich
man. Perhaps many of his boils and broils came
out of the fact that he was an opulent liver. Considering the land of Uz as we now find it, one
would suppose there was very little wealth in it.
We have not a very clear idea of it. Job must
have worked several gangs of slaves on fruitful
ground in the desert. He had some connection
with the petroleum industry of the Euphrates,
although it has never been thoroughly acknowl-
edged. Job acquired his large fortune from the
uncertain element of the petroleum wells. Sometimes they gave him abundance ; at other times,
like the wells around Pittsburgh, they gave him
nothing. There can be little doubt that when his
wells caught fire, it spread fire on the prairie, and
not only destroyed houses, and flocks, and children,
but reduced Job to a considerable amount of profanity and scalding sores. Whatever may be said,

however, about this remarkable man, it is very certain that before his time—many years before his time—the Dead Sea, the *Asphaltum Mare*, was the result of a vast eruption of which oil was the principal ingredient. Its surface is below other sea levels. The earth's crust must have been rather thin there, so easily was it ruptured. Otherwise the five cities of the plain might to-day be rivals of Chicago or Birmingham. The Dead Sea is very salty. In boring for petroleum saline springs are often tapped. But for the tap in the crust, when Lot fled from Sodom, Jordan might not have been deflected from its course, and Canaan might still have been a land for the sacred lyric muse beyond all the music of the Methodist or the rhapsody of the Russian devotee.

There is no doubt that petroleum bubbles up to the surface of the Dead Sea and that the sun's rays solidify it. This is asphaltum—the purest bitumen. It is known in Egypt as the element by which the mummies were made up for immortalization. Herodotus (I seldom quote him without thinking of his title as "the father of liars") has made several remarks about petroleum. I will not quote, for fear I may be challenged to the proof. I turn to Plutarch, who had a sense of veracity. He confirms Herodotus and we will take Herodotus into our confidence for this occasion only. Plutarch describes certain remarkable phenomena in which fire is an element. In fact, the oil to which he calls attention was burned in the ancient lamp. It was known to the Romans as Sicilian oil. From Persia to Italy, from Hafis to Horace, the lamp which gave its sweetness to love and its glory to the Augustine age was fed from the burning spring of the Orient—the same wonderful phenomena of which Zoroaster was the prophet, and the Parsees the devotees.

It is not my purpose to make a disquisition upon petroleum. The genius of man is penetrating the crust of the earth in its every part; and from the shores of the Caspian to China and Japan, from Formosa to the Punjab, aye even out of the lost Atlantis, in the Bermudas, the Canadas and Pennsylvania, this element of fire leaps to the surface at the touch of the diviner's wand.

It is, however, to the United States that this industry owes its highest refinement and perfection of distribution. The carrying of oil from the springs to the refineries in pipes, over thousands of miles and from hundreds of reservoirs; the genius by which through chemistry this oil is purified; the immense Standard Oil Company, with its capital of twenty odd millions; our exports, which from New York alone are over forty millons of barrels, nearly all refined,—call up an image of prosperity in an olden trade.

One drawback to the use of petroleum has been recently developed. It is very doubtful, judging by the terrible explosion recently on the "Petriana," one of the tank steamers, whether or not it is possible to work the petroleum vessel. The crew having taken naked lights into a tank-room which had been somewhat strained in a gale, the gas was fired. Great loss of life ensued, and the inference is that if petroleum is ever used for fuel in locomotives and ships, there will be plenty of accidents after this pattern. This trouble is likely to be obviated.

Whether you consider this petroleum development in the nebulous glimmer of ancient and religious history, or in the blaze of modern science applied to labor-saving machinery, is it not marvellous? Whether it make out of the Caspian a grand commerce and revolutionize and perhaps rescue people who have, like the Armenians, lost their nationality and home, this marvel may again be, as it was to ancient Greek and Roman navigators, a Pharos arresting attention and giving safety to the almost despairing barks of human hope and happiness. Is it therefore wonderful that the ancient world, seeking a religion with mysterious rites, should find in this awful and unknown element of eternal fire its sacred symbol and worship? The Greek had his Vulcan, or Hephæstus ; but the Persian, with like

aspiration, made fire not merely the emblem
of the divine intelligence, but of God himself !
The Jews connected fire with Jehovah. The
burning bush revealed their God. A sacred flame
burned unceasingly in the temple. When, therefore, from the soil or from the fissures of the limestone of Baku the gas issued, it became a light
through the labyrinths of devotion into the unseen world.

When Moses was a child, a thousand years before Christ, the disciples of Zoroaster made pil-
grimages to Baku. Its sacred soil was known to
the Saracens as early as A.D. 600. The Parsees
here worshipped until the conquering iconoclastic
Moslem, with his one ineffable, invisible Allah,
destroyed the temples of fire and the illusions of
the Magi. As late as the twelfth century pilgrim-
ages of the fire worshippers were permitted under
Persian conduct. Since that time we have accounts of this strange fire, and its utilities in giving light, in slacking lime and in cooking victuals.

Petroleum is the " Seneca oil" of our own Indians. They used it for medical purposes. " The
Russians drink it," says a writer, "as a cordial !"
What will not a Russian drink, regardless of odor
or vigor? It was good for "sore heads ;" for
scorbutic pains, gout, and cramps. It was early
an article of commerce. It had its factories. But
never until lately, except perhaps in some of the

lost arts, has it been used as a motor of machinery and a factor of progress. While it has flamed about Baku, empires have risen, ripened, and rotted.

CHAPTER XVII.

THERE is one portion of the Bosphorus on the Asiatic side, known as Kandilli. The whole harbor of Constantinople is in full view from this point. From time immemorial it has been called the place "gifted with lanterns." Just below it, is the modern Turkish village of Beylerbey. From one village of Turkey and its quiet life you may learn of all. Here are the houses and cottages, the little mosque, the bay - trees, and the cemetery. Yonder is the good Imaum, the Hanoum to be respected, and the Pasha in all his dignity. There is the country bumpkin at his marriage, too bashful to venture through the midst of the young girls of the village to fetch away his bride according to the usual custom. Sometimes, but rarely, you see a sottish son or wild daughter who furnishes the topic of multitudinous gossip for the many mothers-in-law. That street Arab is eating *simits* — the ring-shaped bread with sesame seed upon its shining surface.

Here, in short, are all the ups and downs of humble fortune ; but among them all is preserved the beautiful Oriental custom of taking home to the family the evening presents.

I have a special memory of Beylerbey, not so much, indeed, of its charming environments, as of a brief interview I once had there with a royal personage. He was the last of an ancient line—a prisoner of state ; alas ! confined by the decree of the Sultan within the appanage of the palace demesne. What his offence or treason was I never sought to know. It makes me sad to think of him. It is not safe to become too familiar with such victims of Oriental despotism. I saw him but a few brief moments. I looked upon him ;— and for this indiscreet curiosity alone I—yes I, the Envoy Extraordinary and Minister Plenipotentiary of the United States of America, came near forfeiting my existence. I had to run for my life —to fly to my little launch, which was the only vessel in the harbor bearing our ensign—at that time. Surely this ought to be a lesson to Congress, in respect of our decrepit navy ! Diplomacy compelled me to pocket the indignity I suffered. Disagreeable as this incident was, it had its ludicrous aspect as the reader will see further on.

Beylerbey was not always a place of confinement for prisoners of state. In ancient days it

was a favorite pleasure retreat of the Byzantine
emperors. It had then its famous Greek church,
Chrysoxeramos—of the golden tiles. When the
Turks came they gave the place the name of
"Joy Unceasing." It long remained the chosen
residence of the Sultans, who preferred the Asiatic to the other side of the Bosphorus for the summer season. It still retains much of its imperial
enchantments—and entanglements, as I found out
on my first visit, but not with " unceasing joy."

Among the several palaces on the eastern side
of the Bosphorus are the palaces of Istavros,
Chengel, Keui, Kouleh, and Kandilli, but the palace of Beylerbey is the most beautiful and renowned of them all. It was built by Mahmoud
II. for a summer residence. It rose like an ex-
halation to sweetest music. It was planned in a
dream, beneath the shadow of an Oriental mountain, in an hour of golden luxuriousness and indolence, and carried into execution during a fit
of elegant caprice.

When the beautiful Empress Eugénie visited
the Orient at the opening of the Suez canal, the
reigning Sultan, Abdul Aziz, went to many excesses of magnificent courtesy, including the dedication to her use of the Beylerbey palace. It was
then completely refurnished. The upholstery was
of velvet and satin. The decorations of the chamber of the Empress were copied from those in the

Tuilleries. A magnificent *caïque*, marvellous beyond the dreams of Cleopatra, was built expressly for Her Majesty. It had all the Oriental appointments and rich carvings in gold, while everything was ready to be served in European or Asiatic fashion to gratify her womanly and regal caprices. There were also special services, thoroughly Turkish, with all their environments. Upon the princely dining table there were rare silver services, Broussa silk napkins, embroidered with gold and silver, and golden dishes studded with turquoises, and everything to give Oriental taste and tone to the repast. The Sultanas actually drank champagne to the Empress' health. For the first time, these Mussulman ladies sipped the liquor forbidden by Mahomet. It made the young hilarious and the old happy. Singers and dancers gave variety to the regal welcome. The Empress learned to smoke cigarettes, perfumed with Orient odors. She had near her two charming young women of the East, as interpreters and companions. One of them was Nazli Hanoum, a princess of Egypt, and grand-daughter of Mehemet Ali. Her life since these joyous scenes has had its mournful experiences. One of these is associated with the writer. It came innocently enough from our courtesy to this fair Mahometan Albanian at Prinkipo, which led to certain illegal proceedings recorded in this volume.

There is a kiosk, almost wholly of glass, at each end of the sea-wall, which protects the palace grounds of Beylerbey. The interior of each is furnished with a broad divan in blue and straw-colored satin. Behind the wall there are terraced gardens rising in tiers, one above another, where flowers and fountains abound. Upon the highest point of the grounds are the ostrich gardens; and formerly there was a rare menagerie there. All the animals are gone except the ostriches and a lone tiger. I emphasize the tiger. Hereby hangs my tale.

The palace is upon the lower terrace of the garden, not far from the Bosphorus. It is a building of three stories. It is of pure white marble. It is ornate in style. It is not palatial in extent, but it is a gem of Oriental architecture. The broad vestibule leads into a grand central chamber which is lighted from the roof. Here is a staircase of unequalled beauty and superb decoration. Marble columns support the galleries of the floors above. Walls, floor and ceiling are of marble. It the centre of the main hall is a grand fountain, with innumerable jets shooting their sheafs of silver with a murmurous music into the quiet air.

From this central hall various rooms open. Here the Grand Duke Nicholas, after the treaty of San Stefano had relieved the city from Russian

occupation, held high court and carnival, following
the example of the Empress Eugénie. Here rat-
tled and clanked over the marble pavements the
spurs and sabres of the Russian officers. Here the
then young Sultan, Abdul Hamid, came to make his
courtesies to the Czar's representative.

But of more vital interest to me than all these
scenes of departed pomp and pageantry was the
last remaining animal of the Sultan Abdul Aziz's
menagerie. He was a royal Bengal tiger. I made
my homage to his royalty as he couched and pant-
ed in his confinement. "He was the sole relic of
old Priam's pride!"

It is not unusual in the palaces around Constantinople to illustrate the parks and gardens
with some very vivid pictures of natural history.
The Sultan has within his grounds at Yildiz
several aviaries of rare birds. He has a remarkable collection of pigeons, and, along with a small,
but very select, menagerie, some 200 fine horses.
These horses are exercised in a riding school where
the Circassian guards sometimes exhibit their feats.
His Majesty is accustomed to shoot wild fowl,
which are decoyed to his little lakes within the
palace enclosure. And, like other and more ultra-
Oriental princes and emperors of the Tartar race,
he occasionally summons for his recreation a
sweet singer, or a conjuror, or a dwarf, or all of
these together; but in their midst a young tiger,

whose antics are more terrifying than harmful, is
not unfrequently introduced for the gratification of
the company, or the delight of the harem.

In an excursion to the Bosphorus from our Isle
of Prinkipo I had the honor of gallanting, under
a special firman from the Sultan, a company of
some twenty-five ladies and gentlemen. They
were mostly of American nationality. After
observing the wonderful riches of the treasury at
Seraglio Point, with all its crowns, bâtons, arms,
scimitars, robes of state and royal jewellery, and
the usual touristic visit to Dolma Batché, the most
beautiful palace in the world, our launch bore us
across the Bosphorus to the palace of Beylerbey.
Sauntering through its sylvan shades we come to
the ostrich farm upon the lofty heights. They
may be tame birds, but they show considerable
fierceness when we observe them. No one ventures in their midst. But what most attracts our
attention here is a cage, some forty by thirty feet,
in which is confined the royal tiger. He is the
prisoner to whom I have referred so touchingly.
No doubt he has many strange graces and accomplishments and, doubtless, some crimes to atone,
but I am not sufficiently "close to His Highness"
to note his graces or vices. I keep a respectful
distance, for his cage looks old and shaky. Its
iron bars are suggestively slim. The tiger lies
in a crouching attitude with eyes ablaze, as if

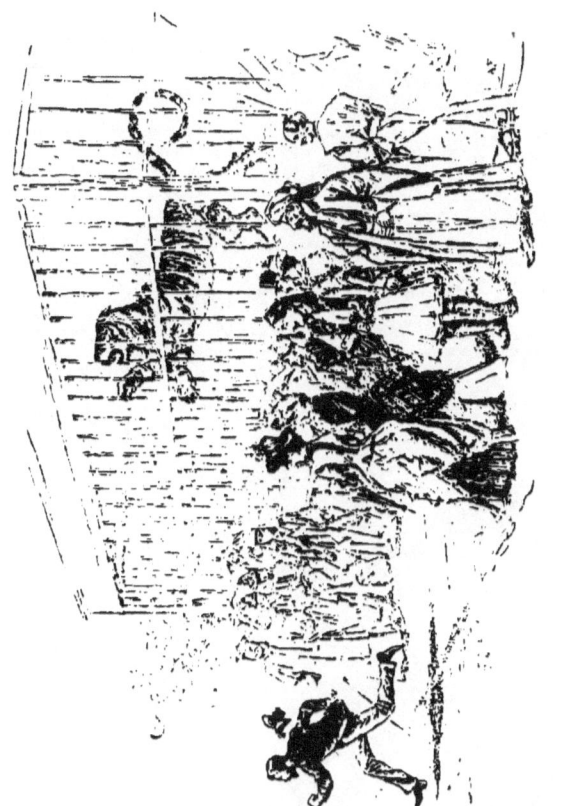

TIGER-HUNT FOR THE MINISTER.

intent on gratifying some carnivorous propensity. Some of the company playfully pitch pebbles at him to arouse him. I do not. I stand in the middle of the road.

He does not notice the rest of the company. Evidently he desires to receive no one of less rank than a Plenipotentiary. *Horresco referens!* In the twinkling of an eye, he springs, not at any of the company, but at the Envoy! In fact, this Oriental monarch would have the American Minister one with himself. No doubt he intended to do me a special honor, to take me into his embraces—to fall upon my neck and hug me. But what would my democratic constituents think of such a submission to an autocrat? This selfish thought comes on me like a flash of light—an inspiration. I turn my back hurriedly on royalty. I throw diplomacy to the winds. I flee "the presence" with a celerity and certainty that were never surpassed on the swiftest "star route" of the plains. When the company assembles at the palace below, to re-embark on the launch, I am told, amidst much hilarious chaffing, that I had outstripped the swiftest flight of Mercury. But I maintain that in spite of the succulent two hundred and fifty pounds of our cavass, and other weighty persons present, including some unctuous females, the tiger showed a royal discrimination in picking out a Minister Plenipotentiary for his prey.

"Afraid?" What! an American afraid of a royal
personage? Never! Besides I had no time for
fear. "Undignified retreat?" Let me amend.
It was not a "retreat." It was more like one of
General Joe Lane's field evolutions, of Kansas
fame. It was a swift countermarch in the face of
the enemy, executed in the most dashing style to
the rear!

I once came upon two grizzlies in California;
they were in a — cage. I never loved a ferocious animal outside of a cage or menagerie. I
have never seen any such in a state of nature,
except a supposititious hyena in upper Egypt
among the tombs, and a jackal between Jaffa
and Jerusalem. I met the latter by moonlight
alone, but I loved him not. It is not necessary
to see the tiger in his lair to appreciate his
moral qualities. I have talked with wild Kabyles
in Algiers, and with officers of the British
army from South Africa, and have heard them
detail their lion-hunting adventures.

One of the officers of the British Indian
army told me a story worth repeating. It was
about the famous Jäagt in the Island of Singapore. He was a man-eater; I mean the Jäagt. I
will let this son of Mars—the officer—relate his
adventure in his own grandiose style, and with all
its Brobdignagian proportions. He describes the

tiger as running through the jungle—away from
him.

"As soon as I saw" said the British officer,
"his eyes burning like coals of fire, I knew he
was the famous man-eater. He had a little child
in his fangs, and, upon my honor, was about to
leap over one of the pits, which are sometimes
dug in the jungles, and bear it off to his fastness
among the rocks of the hills! My first impulse
was to open fire on the brute with my sixteen-shot
revolving breech-loader rifle, but when I saw the
child, I hesitated."

Here I raise my hands in holy horror, and my
eyes express the utmost concern as the officer
resumes :—

"I hesitate," said he, "but a short time. I
pick out a spot where the intermaxillary joins
the temporal bone. I fire. The child drops un-
harmed from the tiger's broken jaws! It is one
of the best shots of my life!

"This shot brings the ferocious animal to bay.
I see the great gouts of blood, dropping from
his jaws as he lashes his sides furiously with
his royal tail! He crouches for a spring. Is he
not a royal specimen? His side shines in the
sun like satin striped with burnished gold. I am
almost dazzled with its brilliancy. I do not want
to spoil such a trophy. I aim for his eye. I send
a bullet into his brain, just as he makes his spring.

18

He falls stone dead at my feet! I restore the child, a beautiful boy, to its distracted mother who lives in a bungalow, near by. Upon my honor, the sight of the lady's joy and gratitude over her rescued child almost unmans me. She is the wife of a huzzar officer. I order one of my retinue to remove the hide from the slain animal. I present it to her a few days afterwards for a rug. I would not have taken a thousand pounds for it."

But this was not the end of the gallant officer's tiger story. After a moment of suspicious silence on our part, he said:

"Do you know, gentlemen, I have sometimes been slightly embarrassed at the suspicion with which those unfamiliar with life in the jungle receive our accounts of its adventures? Now, mark the sequel. Twenty years after this incident, I was in the smoking saloon of one of the Peninsula and Oriental steamers, with a lot of officers and civilians on their way out to India. We were whiling away the evening, comparing our hunting reminiscences. Among other exploits, I recounted this adventure in Singapore. Just as I finished it, a little ensign whom I had noticed listening to the story with strange excitement of manner, springs from his seat with uncontrollable emotion. He runs to me. He throws himself into my arms. He exclaims:

"'General! general! I am that rescued child,

and the lady is my mother! She cherishes that tiger robe as the chief of her choicest treasures! Oh! my brave, brave, preserver! Have I found you at last?' If you can credit it, there was not a dry eye in the party."

I relate the brave officer's story, not alone for its own interest, but in order that its moral shall maintain the veracity of my own tiger tale. It is with great reluctance that I tell it. I would not be discredited. Still I have a suspicion that that officer is a lineal descendant of Ananias and Sapphira; and that the young ensign displayed fine histrionic talent.

Nearly every one in his callow youth has a partiality for an animal. Some take to a horse, some to a squirrel, some to a dog, some to a parrot and some to a canary. My partiality was always for a cat. There is something in the affectionate nature of the cat, whose purring leads one unconsciously and gradually on toward a tender regard for its congener—the tiger! In visiting the menagerie, I always look first for the tiger's cage. Look into any book upon vertebrated animals at the figure of the tiger! You will see it pictured as a model of strength and grandeur. The ancients said that the peacock was the most beautiful among birds and the tiger among animals. Where is the animal of its size that can leap so easily as the tiger, four times its own length? It is said while its

physiognomy is far from fierce and, unlike the
lion, is of a placid and pleasing air,—that no correction can terrify, and no indulgence tame it.
But it is erroneous to suppose that the tiger is un-
tamable.   Why should not any feline be tamable?
The cat is the most domestic of animals.   Shakespeare calls it the "harmless necessary cat."
Augustus, the Roman emperor, kept a tame tiger,
and Claudius had four of them at a time, as a
royal pleasure.   This fact is verified by a beautiful mosaic, discovered near the arch of Gallicius
in Rome.   Kean, the tragedian, possessed a puma.
It is a fierce feline.   It followed him about as
docile as a dog.   Sarah Bernhardt has a young
cougar as her playmate!   I should prefer them
when quite young.

It was the custom of the early emperors in
Byzantium to have a tame tiger near them.   The
fakirs of Hindostan have the secret of making
tigers as tractable as kittens.   But after such kittens come to the age of discretion, I would not
play with them, if I were a fakir.   As a general
rule, I would not advise either emperor or fakir
to be too familiar with the tiger.   Like other
specimens of royalty, its favor is fickle.   It has
the trick of its ancestry.   Through caressing, it
may be tamed for a time, but very few people
either in or outside of India would go its security
to keep the peace.

In Asia the type of royalty is the tiger. In ancient Rome, the symbol of empire was the eagle. In France, it is a rooster. Is it not Emerson who says that these symbols of strength are selected from the predatory kingdom? It may not be generally known, but it is true, that the beaver was proposed in America as the emblem of our hardworking, industrious and sagacious people; but the beaver was laughed out of our national crest. In its place was substituted a bald-headed robber.

Not being able to account for the tigerish propensity exhibited toward me at Beylerbey by anything that I had ever done to the animal, for I always defer to him, even in a menagerie, by taking off my hat before his cage, at a respectful distance, it at last occurred to me that I had never sufficiently atoned for a bit of school-boy composition. Its theme was "The Tiger." I cannot fully recall its tenor, but it did not do justice to the magnificent savagery and superlative strength of his nature. I simply said that it was an animal three feet high and eight feet long. This was unjust. Had not Buffon seen one in the East Indies, fifteen feet long? This, however, included the tail. "Allowing" says the naturalist, "four feet for that, it must have been eleven feet from the tip of the nose to the insertion of the tail." Goldsmith saw one in the

Tower nine feet long. I am now satisfied, from a hasty glance in the cage at Beylerbey, that the tiger is at least twenty-five feet long and seventeen feet high! It is announced in books, that he has a yellow hide, and an average of some twenty-five very black stripes. I am now satisfied that the hide is of a sanguinary red and that its ebony stripes may be counted by the hundred. In my composition I related how it was the object of sportive expeditions in Bengal; that the hunters go forth, armed with rifles, in a *houdah*, on the backs of trained elephants to kill the tiger; and I have never since disassociated the elephant from a tiger. The general opinion is, that the tiger springs upon the elephant to reach the hunter. I did not question its correctness in my speedy movement down the hill of Beylerbey. My tiger seemed to have elephantine proportions. As the Irishman said of the elephant—it had a tail at both ends of the animal. My movement at that particular juncture outdid any latter-day toboggan slide. It gave rise to an excess of specific levity, from my companions; but I gave to the retreat all my specific gravity. It was accelerated by a wild scream from the animal, more horrid than the roar of the lion: *tigrides indomitæ, rugiuntque leones.* I had yielded to the indomitable. Is it Byron, or some one else, who says : "There is a pleasure in the pathless woods." I never enjoyed myself in palatial grounds so much as I did on my retreat from the caged animal at Beylerbey; for I went down through the terraced groves regardless of paths. I did not retreat before an ordinary, unrenowned beast. No! I learn that this is the identical tiger referred to in a volume by Lieutenant Greene of the United States Army. He saw it in 1878, after the Russian war. He speaks of it as "a far-famed tiger of great beauty and wonderful size." So that this hero of the jungle is not unknown to literature. How often has he avoided the poise of the spear in his native home! How often has he leaped upon the Jumbos of the jungle! Of this there is no record. It is said that death and the gods are shod so softly that their tread is silent. The paw of the tiger has death beneath its velvet. But when I fled from his paw I took courage from this comforting verse about the Pale Horse and his rider:

> " ———poisoned with a kitten's claw,
> The man escaped the tiger's jaw!"

Tiger-hunting was always a favorite diversion with me—in books. I have read Captain Shakespear's "Wild Sports of India." I had followed him upon the elephant. I became as brave as a Shikarree up a tree, with a bullock below for a bait, and a "man-eater" crouching in the thicket

—but this was in a book! I have swallowed many of the swelling tales of the Nimrods of the British Indian army; and have blessed the intelligent lungoor-baboon, which warns other animals of the feline approach, by swinging with prehensile grasp from tree to tree, uttering much Simian profanity.

The roar of the tiger and the trumpeting of the elephant give a resounding glory to the hunt of the tiger. The more distant these notes of battle to my ear, the better! I was told in Northern Africa, by a Gascon resident, that the lion killers run little risk, as they take care to gorge the animal with a calf or so before attacking him. In reading up the literature of the tiger, I am inclined, from my experience at Beylerbey, to make a series of rules, *nunc pro tunc*, for the governance of the tiger hunt, *seriatim* thus:

Rule I. If the tiger be interrupted by the approach of any other animal, do not try to shoot at the other beasts. How any hunter can coolly look at a tiger, selecting the best place in his body for the bullet, is to me marvellous; yet I have read of hunters scanning his withers and girth, locating his lung, liver and vertebræ, with as much *sang froid* as if the burning of his optic coals were not vital with savagery.

Rule II. Scan, with heed, the anatomy of the head, before going for the brain.

R<small>ULE</small> III. In the selection of a spot to which to tie a heifer as bait, find a place near a lofty and easily climbed tree.

R<small>ULE</small> IV. Do not forget to grease the trunk of the tree behind you as you climb up.

R<small>ULE</small> V. Approach the tiger, if at all, when it is sleeping.

R<small>ULE</small> VI. If this be not profitable, carry a vial of chloroform. This conquers the nervousness of the animal, but it requires more nerve for its application than some Nimrods possess.

R<small>ULE</small> VII. If your elephant meet a tiger and, being frightened, runs into a tree and upsets the *houdah*, do not stop to rearrange the elephant. Leave yourself for the nearest tree. Such a tiger is not worth a scent. Let him go !

R<small>ULE</small> VIII. When you see a tiger in the gloaming sharpening his claws against a forest tree, see that your native aids go ahead to absorb his undivided attention. They are not expensive.

R<small>ULE</small> IX. If you perceive the tiger to be dead, do not be in a hurry about skinning him. He has been known to punish, after death. I have read well authenticated cases of tigers whose aorta or cerebrum have been fatally shot; but the tiger easily overcomes the *vis inertiæ*.

R<small>ULE</small> X. When you desire to sit on a damp mound in an Indian jungle, to watch for tigers, arm yourself with quinine balls.

RULE XI. When the tiger charges, as mine did at Beylerbey, with his ears back and his body almost even with the ground, do not try to subdue him with a piercing glance of your own masterful eye.

RULE XII. If it be a tigress that charges, do not rely too much on the gentleness of her sex. She is not a cold blooded animal like the bear and she warms to her bloody work.

RULE XIII. When you are advised by your Shikarree that the tiger is lying in a wide open space, where the grass is higher than your head, do not go into the high grass. There is peril in handling the gun under the circumstances.

RULE XIV. If your gun is a repeater, be sure to carry more than one charge; otherwise you cannot be safely regarded as having a battery with you for the assault which is necessary.

RULE XV. Be sure that your gun has proper penetrating power; for the tiger is a mass of sinew, muscle and bone.

RULE XVI. Do not negotiate the tiger's skin prematurely; for you may discover before you commence skinning that you have only tickled his hide with a non-lethal weapon.

RULE XVII. In removing the tiger's skin, under the belief that he is dead, better commence at the tail, as many tigers have been known to revive at the other end, under the operation.

RULE XVIII. Do not attack the tiger without a breech-loader ; for if you should in your nervousness pour the powder in on top of the wad, you might obscure your vision of the tiger, and he would likely have an advantage, owing to his peculiar eyesight, enhanced after the manner of burglars, by prowling at night. In case of such obscuration, wait until a wind arises to blow off the smoke before renewing the attack.

RULE XIX. Do not cultivate a mercenary spirit as the inspiration of a tiger-hunt. Although the Indian Government may offer a large reward for the skull of this ferocious beast, it is well to cultivate a disinterested spirit. Give all your mind to the sportive exhilaration.

RULE XX. It is well to have at least twenty elephants in line before you charge on the jungle ; otherwise, the contest may be unequal.

RULE XXI. When the tiger screams, it is well to consider it as an intimation that he has prepared his dinner and wishes to dine alone.

RULE XXII. If you are surrounded by a tiger and a tigress and several cubs, and escape through what the East Indians call the "swearing" of a common monkey, remember to treat the monkey thereafter with respect. Do not, in addressing him, use the word "monkey." When you speak of or to him, call him the *Semnopithecus Entellus.*

RULE XXIII. Inasmuch as the peacock is in-

digenous to the forests of India where tigers most
do congregate, and is a rival of the tiger for beauty
of form and color, and besides is an ally of the
monkey in warning other animals, including man,
of the dangerous proximity of the enemy, speak
of the peacock with respect.   Praise its melodious
voice and dilate on its tail.   Its vociferous
" hauk !" " hauk !" should not be repeated in vain.
It deserves recognition.   These birds of Vanity
and Juno are friends of mankind.   They deserve
recognition in a tiger country.

RULE XXIV. If a superannuated jackal, who
has been expelled from his pack, makes its familiar yell, look out for the tiger!   It is his lackey.
It feeds upon his leavings.

RULE XXV. When chasing the tiger, and finding him in full retreat, if he stops, as he sometimes will, to tear up the tufts of grass hilariously
to clean his nails, raise the banner of non-interven-
tion as an American gentleman, and quote Horace
ad unguem.

RULE XXVI. If you have enough elephants in
your retinue to carry some coal-oil tar, it would be
a matter of safety to agglutinate the tiger's eyes
and ears, for that operation has the same effect on
a tiger as tarring and feathering on an unhappy
human wretch, where Judge Lynch holds court.

RULE XXVII. If your company is noisy
enough with their cries, drums, cymbals and

other clangorous music, retire from the hunt. You may thereby soften, if not frighten, the ferocity out of the tiger.

As a final suggestion. After you have him thoroughly dead, singe his whiskers! Otherwise he will haunt you. I need not say that my experience at Beylerbey was of similar import. I was, and am still, haunted by this animal. In my dreams I picture him in every attitude—crouching, standing, and fighting with fang and claw, as a royal animal whose only type in the human family is found in such scourges as Genghis Khan, or Timour, the Lame Tartar.

I return to Prinkipo after this jaunt more or less timid about animals, especially the "felinæ." This timidity is increased by an adventure with a watch-dog in our villa. He has returned and finds us as new occupants. As a good dog he resents our tenancy. He bites the tenant.

Our front gate is not latched. It is pushed gently open and a dog bounds in. I am in the arbor with my wife. The gardener rushes in to catch the dog. But the dog has only come to his old home. He is likely cross by reason of his exile. We had stipulated that he should be taken away from the villa. The cook and the maid said he would not bite. They gave him something to eat, while we collected around him. The cook said:

"Why don't you caress him, and he will soon know you."

I venture to do so. In a moment he snaps savagely, but happily the stiff shirt wristbands and doubled up sleeve of my woollen undershirt take the grip of the teeth. Only a slight scratch appears on the wrist, without breaking the skin. The indentation of the teeth is exquisitely shown on the stiff wristband. He is no apprentice in the art of printing—this dog.

I resort to the library for consolation. I peruse Buffon, Jardine and Goldsmith. At last I find consolation in Aristophanes who, in speaking of another wild beast, advises in his comic vein to have nothing to do with such creatures; and especially, to "let the tigress suckle her own whelps."

As a sportsman, in the literature of tiger-hunting, I close this chapter with a regrettable announcement. The famous Parsee tiger slayer, Hormusjee Eduljee Kotewal, has just died in a Bombay hospital from the effects of "a mauling by a cheetah." Ah! had he been a good Parsee; had he carried with him a bottle of naphtha from Baku, or a jug of coal tar from Oil City, how easily he could have subdued the cheetah! The Bhandsa State would not now be in tears over the death of its brave forest inspector. He died game. His record is high. He shot, during life, a hundred tigers. Peace to all their ashes!

CHAPTER XVIII.

Sometimes I add a volume to my repertory, fresh from the mint of London or Paris, which is perused under conditions of indolence and seclusion. One of these volumes, which held me by its fascination and glitter of style, its wealth of research and strangeness of learning was Flaubert's "Salambo." It opens the mystic chambers of Phœnician life. It gives new glimpses of the Commercial Republic in her pristine days. It presents the strange religious rites of Asia and Africa in their wildest orgies. It displays Carthage when she was the rival of Rome, in an aspect to make others weep with Marius over her ruins. The volume is very realistic, especially when read in sight of those Bithynian shores where the merchant princes of Carthage once traded, and where their conquering triremes often swept through the waters of the Propontis.

"Salambo" is the bewitched and beauteous daughter of the great Hamilcar. Her counterpart one may see at the Greek church or at the *scala*

287

every day here at Prinkipo. I confess to a dis-
appointment in the volume, however, for the hero
of my youthful enthusiasm, Hannibal, the famous
son of Hamilcar Barca, is barely mentioned.
True, he was but a youth when the stirring scenes
of the war with the mercenaries, of which the
book treats, was in progress. Still the intrepid
boy is sufficiently outlined for the reader to see
him as " father to the man."

Hamilcar was often put to straits to save Hannibal from the demands of the priests of Moloch.
They sought their human victims among the sons
of the eminent. The learned novelist makes the
teacher and guardian of the boy come from that
mysterious shore which is peopled with turtles,
which sleep under the palms on the dunes. The
faithful Iddibal enters the presence of the anxious
father to render an account of his stewardship over
the boy. " No one yet suspects ? " The old guardian swears that the mystery has been kept. " I
teach him to hurl the javelin and to drive a team."
" He is strong—is he not ? " asks the proud and
anxious father. "Yes, Master, and intrepid as
well ! He has no fear of serpents, thunder or
phantoms. He runs bare-footed like a herdsman
along the brink of lofty precipices. He invents
snares for wild beasts. In the last moon he surprised an eagle. The animal, in its fury, en-
wrapped him in the beating of its wings ; he

strained it against his breast; and as it died, his laughter increased."

Hamilcar bent his head, well pleased at these presages of his son's greatness! "But" resumed the teacher, "the boy has been for some time restless and disturbed. He gazes at the sails passing far out at sea. He is often melancholy. He rejects food. He inquires too much about the gods; and he wishes to become acquainted with Carthage. How is he to be restrained? I have to make him promises. I now come to Carthage to buy him a dagger with a silver handle set in pearls."

This is one glimpse at the boyhood of the Carthaginian hero, who made "Rome howl" in the might of his glorious manhood. What a career was his! And how tragic in its ending,—like that of all the great conquerors—Alexander, Cæsar, Napoleon! He became a prisoner on yonder shore of Bithynia. It is just across the channel of Prinkipo. There, it is said, in the so-called castle of Hannibal, he took poison and died.

There is a romance about Hannibal which had strange attraction for me when I was a child. I felt a pity for the little boy when his father, just before journeying with him to Spain and when he was only nine years of age, dedicated him at the altar to an eternal Nemesis against Rome! I attached myself to his fortunes and gloried in his tri-

19

umphs.   How he subdued the Spanish princes;
how he aroused the Roman senators by his successes; how, after protecting Africa and Spain, he
moved on to Italy; how he crossed the Pyrenees
with half a hundred thousand footmen and 11,000
horses; how he deceived Scipio, and how he crossed
the Alps into the valley of the Dora Balteau,—
each incident is a romantic chapter with a lofty
climax, which must always allure the fancy of the
young and amaze the mind of the old.   At Cannæ
he played havoc by destroying 70,000 men.   Italy,
almost Rome herself, succumbed to him.

The immense sacrifices and movements of these
ancient rivals so disturb the even flow of history,
that we almost forget Philip of Macedon and his son.
The brother of Hannibal joined him in Italy, on the
banks of the Metaurus, where his army was worsted
and the brother was killed.   Then Hannibal was
on the defensive.   Never in the annals of mankind
was there such a long campaign as he made in a
hostile country, without assistance from home.
When Hannibal withdrew from Italy he was met
and beaten by Scipio, and thus ended the second
Punic war.   Then Scipio began those services by
which he attained the civic crown.   These events
happened more than 200 years before Christ.   It
is 2069 years since that tomb across the Prinkipo
channel received the remains of this wonderful
soldier.   Rome had demanded the punishment of

Hannibal as a disturber of the public peace. He set sail for the land of his Phœnician ancestors. He landed at Tyre. After some adventures at or near Ephesus, he sought these shores, made memorable by the siege of Troy, and since the scene of many contests of priest and king, caliph and emperor. He was received at the court of the king of Bithynia, whose realm extended from the Euxine and Propontis, on the north and west, eastward, and including those places now famous for their ecclesiastical history—Nicomedia and Nicæa. Its people were Greek colonists. Their descendants to-day are Greeks. The inland, as we see it from Prinkipo, is mountainous. It was then, and is yet, wooded. Near the sea there are fertile plains, which 2000 years ago were in a high state of cultivation, with villages sprinkled over its plains and slopes. Along its shore, toward Ismid, there is a railroad whose rumble invades the ear as I write. It is an unaccustomed sound in the Orient. It is tempered by the moaning of the wind through the pine trees of Prinkipo.

It was in this land of Bithynia that Hannibal at last found asylum. A Roman embassy went to the king and demanded him. For fear of falling into the hands of his enemy, to whose destruction he had been dedicated fifty-six years before, he destroys himself. This event happens at Nico-media, then the capital of Bithynia, and now known as Ismid. It is at the eastern end of the gulf of that name, to which, every day, I see the Turkish postal steamer voyaging, with its solitary white plume of vapor floating over the sea between the snowy range of Olympus and the wooded heights of our enchanted isle.

This son of Hamilcar Barca, the Thunderbolt, almost fulfilled his destiny. He only failed to make Carthage—the mistress of the world—*vice* Rome conquered. He reduced Rome to a dire emergency. Hasdrubal, his brother, rolled down the Alps with an army that gathered like an avalanche as he moved into Lombardy. What with his elephants and troops, with which he had left Gaul, he drew tribe after tribe of the cis-Alpine Celts to his standards. But the Roman senate had not then degenerated. Rome had a consul, Nero. He was the man for the crisis. He was associated with old Livius,—as tough and obstinate an old Roman as ever led on a legion or rode in a triumphal chariot. Of stores, money and men Rome had been drained. Cannæ was still remembered. But a senate which had voted a triumph to its defeated soldiers, and never despaired of the republic, was not to be disturbed by panic. Although Hannibal was in the south and his brother in the north, or, in the language of that time, although two Hannibals were in the field and striving by all the arts and devices of skill and strategy to draw toward each other, and thus to destroy Rome and carry out with strenuous ferocity the vow made by their father, still Rome did not despair. After much pressing the Roman consuls outwitted the "sons of Thunder." It was the consuls who united. It was the double Hannibal who was separated.

What an assemblage was that army of Hasdrubal! The known world had been ransacked for its hordes. Here were Iberian Celts in white *bournous;* their brother Gauls, half naked, rank with savage Ligurians; mountaineers of the maritime Alps from Genoa and its vicinity; Nasamones from the region of Morocco; spearmen from the Nile—and Lotophagi, who lived upon a fruit that cured home-sickness. These flank the Carthaginians "in cubic phalanx firm advancing" in the centre. Numidian horsemen from the tribes of the desert swarm on the wings, upon unsaddled steeds. The van of the army is made up of Balearic slingers from Minorca and Majorca, whose art I have noticed among the Kabyles of Algiers. The artillery is in the line of colossal elephants, guided by Ethiopians. It makes a living pachydermatous wall of defence. With javelin, sword and spear, the soldiers march; with mallet and spike the elephant-drivers ride, ready to kill the beast when it becomes unmanageable!

For the Roman array read Gibbon's first chapter.

In divisions of 1200, with breast-plated and helmeted ranks they meet the enemy. Their red crests shine like fire in the light of battle. Their javelins are light and are easily borne, with the short-sword for thrusting and cutting. In quiescent order the stern legions form. Every soldier is a single combatant. Each horseman is a skirmisher. Nero commands the right wing, Livius the left, and Porcius, the prætor, the centre.

History records this great test of Roman valor by recounting the defeat and death of Hasdrubal. The head of the defeated general is carried as a trophy upon the hurried march of the Roman army. It is thrown into the camp of Hannibal, who then looks upon his brother's face for the first time in eleven years. Horace pictures the scene in his verse, and Livy tells of the delirium of Rome over the result. The senate is in perpetual session. The temples are filled with worshippers. Thanksgiving is proclaimed. Pleasure and business revive. Hannibal remains in the land, but his power is broken. The battle gives Rome two centuries of triumphs. Hannibal still holds Southern Italy, but Rome has conquered. *Carthago delenda est.* Still it is this Hannibal—our neighbor of Bithynia—who was the first in a period of 619 years, according to Gibbon, who had violated the seat of Roman empire by his presence as a foreign enemy.

I have mentioned, in the preceding chapter, a
volume by Sir Edward Creasy. It is entitled the
" Fifteen Decisive Battles of the World—from Marathon to Waterloo." He makes the battle of
Metaurus one of these pivotal battles, because
upon it hinged the supreme power, either of
Rome or Carthage. The historian likens the
issue to that of Waterloo. Napoleon was only a
later Hannibal. One fought seventeen years
against Rome, the other sixteen against England.
The historian carries the parallel even to Scipio
and Wellington. When Hasdrubal fell at the
Metaurus the fate of the world and that of Hannibal also was sealed. It was not a struggle
between two cities or empires, but between the
commercial spirit of Africa and the civilizing laws
of Rome. It was a contest between the Indo-
Germanic and the Semitic family of nations ; between art and culture on one hand, and industry and adventure on the other. Everywhere on
the historic sea which surrounds us the struggle
was witnessed. Here the Phœnician contended
with the Greek two thousand years ago. To-day
the congener of the Phœnician, the Arab, contests
with the West. Rome annihilated Carthage;
will the Turk remain when pressed by the same
potential West ?

What remains of Carthage ? The periplus of
Hanno, from which Flaubert constructs his won-

derful novel ; a few coins ; some verses in Plautus ;
some remnants in the Franco-Phœnician peninsula,
and the fourth ode of Horace !

" Quid debeas Roma, Neronibus
   Testis Metaurum flumen et Hasdrubal
   Devictus. "

So apocryphal is its history that Byron was
compelled to rescue from the oblivious pen of the
" Blind Muse " the name of that consul, Nero,
who made the unequalled march which deceived
Hannibal and defeated Hasdrubal. To this victory of Nero it might be owing that his imperial
namesake reigned at all. But the infamy of the
one has eclipsed the glory of the other. " When
the name of Nero is heard, who thinks of the consul ? "

So I may say, looking across the Prinkipo channel, within a few miles of the rolling plains of
Bithynia :—

Who, in looking into the eternal Oriental
imbroglio, would dream that 2000 years ago at
Metaurus, or perhaps at Zama, the conflict was
begun, and temporarily ended, between the Indo-
Arabic-Asiatic-Oriental races and that other ele-
mental force which we now call "the West" ; and
that the dust of the Carthaginian hero who once
held Rome in awe reposes in yonder little dead
kingdom ? Arnold says, " The victory over Han-

nibal at Zama made it possible for the isolated city of Carthage, thirty years later, to receive and to consolidate the civilization of Greece, or by its laws and institutions to bind together barbarians of every race and language into an organized empire, and prepare them for becoming, when that empire was dissolved, the free members of the commonwealth of Christian Europe."

Who now dreams that the leader of that Punic host was the precursor in time—and counting the æons, how brief the time—of that adventure which, without the mariners' compass or steam, followed the African coast far beyond Sierra Leone, " doubled the Cape," and explored the coast of Norway and the islands of Albioni and Hiberni! Phœnician navigators anticipated the Congo and other enterprizes into Central Africa. Their fleets made a great trade with the tribes of the *terra incognita*. Carthage, when beaten by Greece in commerce upon these shores —the Ægean, the Pontus, Hellespont and Propontis—made her commercial career on the Western Mediterranean. She had great men like Hamilcar and his great sons ; but her fall was signal. and calamitous. She was too much commercial and not so warlike as she seemed. Her factions ravaged her before she was ruined by Rome. She depended too much on hirelings. The rich merchant—the " ancients," as Flaubert describes them

—fought by a substitute from Minorca, Greece, Gaul or Numidia. There was a tariff on life. Her mercenaries, like the Hessians hired by George III. to fight against America in 1776–7–8—were brave enough, but they did not fight like the sons of the soil, contending for national life or personal ambition. Zama was the end of Carthage. There she yielded her sceptre.

The story of Hannibal after he was beaten at Zama by the Romans loses none of its romance by the lapse of two thousand years. He first sought refuge at the court of King Antiochus, in Syria. Afterwards he went to the court of King Perseus, of Bithynia. Here he was betrayed by one of the legates whom Perseus had sent to Rome. Then he was tracked to the house which Perseus had given him. There he had lived a lonely life, with only one servant. When the servant informed the old soldier that all chance of retreat was blocked by more than the usual number of soldiers around his house, he gave up all hope of escape, took the poison which he carried with him, and at the age of seventy, in the year 183 B.C., this, the most remarkable man of antiquity, next to Alexander and Cæsar, died.

When I learned that the grave of Hannibal was very near our vicinity, I happened to mention it in a letter to America. Thereupon the independent and not too reverent press of my country

made every sort of picture of the great Carthaginian. Some delineated him as the great elephant
of that name in Barnum's show. One pen-artist
went so far as to picture him as the same elephant,
pushing his way over the Alps, with trunk, trappings and all the impediments attached! Such
mistakes are liable to occur in the hurry of the
American press. It was a natural mistake. It
gave me some sadness. From the numerous
wood-cuts which illustrated the newspaper accounts of Hannibal's Bithynian grave, I am tempted to reproduce an etching as a good specimen
of American art in its compact imagination as
evolved for that occasion. As the reader will see,
the artist—lest his exaggeration should seem to
be conceived in too humble a way to suit an Oriental theme—gives his pen boldly to the portrait-
ure, so as to carry conviction of the truth of his
story. He circumstantially depicts the American
minister as a visitor at the grave of this departed
hero! Doubtless his inspiration is drawn from
Mark Twain's inconsolable sympathy at the grave
of Adam in Jerusalem.

Not the least of my enjoyments—*sub silentio*—
at Prinkipo is the perusal of letters from old constituents. Some have taken me for a minister of
the gospel, commended me for my change of life,
and given me sedate advice. Some have asked
impossible things that I should request of the

government of Turkey.   I wrote to a friend about
my location of the grave of Hannibal.   I
thought it would interest him as he had once been
consul to Tunis, which included old Carthage in
its jurisdiction.   I received a most sympathetic
reply.   He greatly appreciated my kindness.   He
asked me to drop a tear for him over the grave of
the Carthaginian hero ; to invoke his *manes*, and
whisper gently at his tomb that he, the late consul—not of Rome but America—had lived long on
the soil of Carthage, and, like Marius at Utica, had
sat down upon the ruins of Bursa to contemplate
the scene of Carthaginian greatness.   He concluded by hoping that I would make a libation on
the grave to the repose of the ghost of Hannibal.

But the most jocose account of my discovery
was written by a valued friend, a Chicago editor.
He of course heard that I had discovered the
grave of his favorite hero.   He determined
not to be out-done in describing the scene.
Concluding a long account, he pictures the
minister standing over the grave of the hero,
his lachrymal duct dripping with sympathetic
tears, which plash on a marble tombstone in-
scribed : "HANNIBAL, B.C. *Anno* 186. *Requiescat
in pace !*"   Among many touching episodes he im-
provises the following : "The minister's wife was
not so much overcome by emotion as he was.
'Why,' said she, 'dost thou weep for Hannibal?

Pray—dam—oh! dam thy tears! Has he not been dead two thousand years? After such a long absence will you not soon meet him in a brighter and a better world?'" The minister, let it be here recorded, was in no hurry to meet his departed friend in the brighter and better world. The editor's account of the scene is so realistic and pathetic that it almost makes me weep—for the credulity of human nature.

HANNIBAL'S GRAVE.

CHAPTER XIX.

ASIAN SHORES—NICÆA AND NICOMEDIA.

THE country along the Asian shore is not less
celebrated for its fertility than for the comfort it
gave to the early Greeks. It was from the remot-
est times thickly studded with cities and towns,
with their teeming multitude of people. It is
still populous and prosperous. What land can
vie with it in interest? Its mountain peaks
were once the abodes of the gods. Its ranges
still form the natural boundaries of grand provinces, and shelter fruitful Piedmontese valleys
in their warm embrace. To the classic fancy they
are crowned with rich foliage above terraced
slopes like Judea of old and blooming under rare
cultivation. The terraces remain; but the bare
peaks point forestless to the passing clouds in silent
protest against the waste of past generations and
the indolence of the present. What land has
scenes of more romance, or names more familiar to
the reader of biblical and secular history! Its
nomenclature, even after thousands of years, woos
the archæologist and artist to their work, and

revives in the mind of the tourist lofty themes of the ancient days when the hosts of Troy and Greece were embattled on these plains.

It is a pleasant jaunt in the launch across the channel to Kartal, where there is an old abandoned silk factory, owned by one of our neighbors on the island, who is a Swiss. The large hall with its clean, white, stone flooring is there. Fifty silk-stands are there, but they are silent. They speak the sad tale of an elegant industry abandoned. The water gave out, and therefore the industry failed. Around the establishment the fig-trees are hardy, for they care little for water. But the earth is parched, and the fruit thereof is pinched and poor. It is not of present enterprises I would speak now and here. The past dominates.

This part of Asia Minor, into which I am accustomed to look almost every morning from the Isle of Prinkipo, is known as Anatolia. It is a peninsula,—a vast plateau, falling by stages down to the three seas. It is a spur of the great plateau of Central Asia. Its climate is balmy and tropical. It was the seat of empire. Its very position is so admirable that it influenced immensely the early civilizations which here contended.

The great cities are gone. There are few monuments of former grandeur, and scarcely any roads leading into the mainland. Of commerce

there is almost none left. Industry and patience
still bring something out of its soil ; enough for
its inhabitants, but dissolution seems to mark
large portions for its own. In the western portion and in the vicinity of the seas the land is
arable and populous. The eastern portion is a
pasture ground for the Turkomans. It has a
splendid history in connection with the Christian
and other faiths. Its population, once twenty-five
millions, now hardly exceeds seven millions, of
which two millions only are Christian.

There are two classes of Moslems here : those
who wander about, and those who are settled.
The settled tribes are descendants of the conquerors, the Seljukian Turks. The Seljukian
is always spoken of with respect, for he has preserved his ancestral virtues, — dignity, courage,
loyalty and religious fervor. The Moslem in
Asia Minor looks upon Turkey in Europe only
as an encampment. At Broussa, Koniah and
other celebrated places in Asia Minor, is to
be found the true centre of the Mahometan empire. Whatever may be thought of its political
or economical situation, the travellers whom I am
accustomed to meet, and who return from their
excursions into this wonderful land, bring back
stories overrunning with enthusiasm. They praise
the beauty of its scenery, the grandeur of its
mountains, the richness of its lands, the magni-

tude of its forests, its rain-falls so copious, and its rivers so large ; and above all its ancient monuments and its strange village life heightened by the unstinted hospitality of its people. Here in this region is found the Valonia oak, one of the principal trees in Asia Minor. It not only produces an acorn whose husk is used in tanning and which is exported in considerable quantities, and produces quite a revenue, but it gives to the landscape many graces and beauties, of which the tourist is not unobservant.

The Turks had accumulated enormous wealth at their old capital of Broussa, in Asia Minor, before Constantinople fell beneath the prowess of their scimitar. When Tamerlane, the Tartar, struck the Turkish power on the plains of Angora and made the great Sultan, Bajazet, his prisoner, he found such a quantity of treasure that the coins and precious stones were weighed by the *oka*, which, as stated in a former chapter, is a Turkish measure of nearly three pounds. We must remember, however, that this is merely tradition, and that everything told of this extraordinary Tartar must be received with some grains of allowance. Doubtless he shed more blood and made more trouble upon the face of the earth during his thirty-six years of reign than any other personage of history. The Alexanders, Hannibals, Cæsars, Attillas, Charlemagnes and Napoleons, were harm-

20

less as babes compared with this stalwart conqueror and sanguinary scourge of the human
family.

How much of interest there is associated with
the history of Asia Minor! It might be called the
cradle and the grave of our race. Its very form
makes it a theatre of contention. Here are two
continents near to each other. Asia defiantly
thrusts her foot between two seas, and Asia
Minor becomes a battle ground where the tribes,
even of far-off plateaus of the continent, march
and countermarch to the conquest of the West.
Across these now placid waters Assyria and Persia empty their hordes. Here Darius leads, over
his bridge of boats across the Bosphorus, seven
hundred thousand soldiers into Europe. His son
moves out of Persia into Cappadocia, which is at
the eastern end of Asia Minor, with an army in
which forty-six nations are represented! Behold
them as they cross the Hellespont! They are a
million of men. They march for the conquest of
Greece, but at set of sun "where are they?"
Alexander, too, marches over and encamps on
these historic shores. He resumes the march and
never stops in his conquering career until he
crosses the passes of the Himalayas. There he
moves down upon the rich lands of India, subdues
its princes and weeps for more worlds to conquer.
The Roman legions grew luxurious on the plains

of Asia Minor after they made the East the prey of
their eagles. Never was there such a theatre of
war, conquest, spoil and splendor as Asia Minor!
The Balkan peninsula, between the Black Sea and
the Ægean, bids fair to be a repetition of its history. What is Asia Minor now? In almost every
issue of the newspapers of Constantinople we read
of the Greek, Kurdish, Circassian and Turkish out-
laws. Brigandage makes it almost impossible to
travel over these historic and sacred regions without a strong escort. Much depends upon the
governor of the province, as to whether the
tourist has safe conduct, or the missionary protection.

Asia Minor is not only celebrated for its ancient
wars and modern troubles, but its every province
is rich with the memories of St. Paul and his companions. From Tarsus, where he was born, in
Cilicia; from Aleppo to Antioch, across the Bay
of Scanderoon to Pamphylia, Lycia, Caria, Lydia,
Mysia, and the other mystical and musical names
of which the New Testament is so full, and where
Christian churches were early established,—there
is everywhere some memory of the great apostle
of the Gentiles, and some sign of the sufferings
and victories which finally made Asia Minor
the most profitable and prosperous part of the
Christian vineyard and the Byzantine empire. The
seven candlesticks of Asia shed from hence their

refulgence into Macedonia and beyond into Europe. At Ephesus is still shown for Christian
veneration the cave of the "Seven Sleepers,"
and the holy dog which guarded them in their
more than Rip Van Winklian nap of two hundred
years.

It is a matter of regret that, owing to an unfortunate illness, I was unable to make a contemplated trip to Nicæa, Nicomedia and other places
of ecclesiastical celebrity along the shores of the
Gulf of Ismid. At one of the villages where we
were expected to land the people of all nationalities had made great preparations to receive the
American Minister. The Moslem governor called
on our missionary, the Rev. Mr. Pierce, and asked
permission to ride with him to the landing to meet
and greet us. Mr. Pierce begged him not to make
any demonstration, as the visit was to be merely a quiet tour. But the village authorities insisted that they would be guilty of inhospitable conduct if they did not show the respect which they
felt. As there was no telegraph to countermand
the news of our visit, the Governor, with all the
village magnates, and the Armenian clergy, went
with the Rev. Mr. Pierce to the landing. There
was a large cavalcade to escort us to their village.
Some five hundred, as I was informed, were on the
road at the entrance of the village to do us honor.
Moreover, the village streets were cleaned for the

occasion, an event which the Rev. Dr. Dwight informed me was unparalleled in the history of that country.

The guide-books tell us very little about the most interesting environment of Constantinople. The most suggestive of its historic pleasure resorts, next to the Hippodrome, with its serpentine column—which often gave Delphic responses when it stood on the Greek island in its pagan days,— are the precincts of Chalcedon and the shore which runs eastward along the Propontis and from there to Nicæa and Nicomedia. This shore is in sight from the heights of Prinkipo. Along it runs the railroad to Ismid. One of the most interesting short tours, especially if you take a sailboat or a steam-launch, is along this shore. It is not only celebrated for the ecclesiastical councils, out of which our Christian creed came with emphasis and durability, but it is no less famous for its early classic associations. Chalcedon lies in a vast plain. That plain was once the rendezvous of the troops which were wont to depart from Constantinople on their Asiatic campaigns. It is indented with beautiful bays. Near one of these bays is the garden of Haider Pasha. It has a shady fountain and a plantain grove. The fountain bears a Greek name—Hermageros. Nothing can exceed the beauty of this spot. I do not see that its charm has been lost by having

Kadikeüi near by. This village literally means " the place of the judge." It stands on the site of the ancient Chalcedon, whose ruins are the remains of structures in which were once heard the Grecian oracles and Christian councils. One of the legends of this place is that it was first settled by the Greeks before even ancient Byzantium. At that time some colonists came out from Greece to found a new state. They consulted the oracle at Delphos to know at what point they should settle. The oracle said, " Opposite to the blind." This was interpreted to mean, on the peninsula opposite Chalcedon. Chalcedon is opposite Stamboul. For, as it was argued, the founders must have been blind to prefer Chalcedon and neglect such unparalleled advantages as the waters of the Golden Horn and the Bosphorus, which glorify the present harbor of Constantinople.

There are many warlike stories about the taking of Chalcedon by the Persians. It was besieged and mined by them. It has often been taken since and devastated, alike by Greek, Byzantine, Goth, Arabian, Persian and Turk. Belisarius figures much in Greek history. Gibbon has given him an immortality. Here is the spot where his palace was erected at the end of his service. Out of the remains of his palace has arisen the finest structure in Stamboul,—the mosque of Suleimanyie. Even the transient traveller cannot

be at a loss to fix this point, for there is a tower
and lighthouse near by, whose lights, at the season of Bairam, form a double crescent which is
reflected in the water. The promontories along
the shores were decorated in ancient times with
temples. In fact the whole littoral sweep from
the lighthouse to Pendik, from which the pilgrim
caravans still start for Mecca, is full of historic
interest.

The fourth Œcumenical council is known as
the Council of Chalcedon. This is therefore a
spot of ecclesiastical renown. It is now, however,
merely a railroad station. Here was once a
famous church. It was built by Constantine on
the site of the Temple of Apollo and demolished
after the fall of Constantinople. Its materials
served to finish one of the grand mosques of
the city. Now on this not neglected spot there is
heard the shriek of the locomotive as it moves
eastward on its way to Nicæa and Nicomedia, heralding a new gospel for the worshipper of mam-
mon ! It is not altogether modern and prosaic, for
doth not its path lead both to the glory and the
grave of Hannibal ! Not far from its track Belisarius once cultivated his vineyards. I doubt if any-
one but myself has ever found the grave of Hannibal. I saw it in a vision—not of Patmos but of
Prinkipo ! He died in the neighborhood of what
is now the railroad station of Guebsehe ! No one

in the neighborhood knows anything about the
tomb, or the Carthaginian. You will inquire in
vain for it. It is always a little further off; in
fact it is an unattainable object,—a will-o-the-
wisp. There is an old ruined castle in the neighborhood. This is often visited. It is Hannibal's
castle. It is not apocryphal! It is not apoca-
lyptical. Its architecture belongs to the Middle
Ages, and it is not very worthy of that. Its name
makes it a standing anachronism. Its ruins are
near some thermal waters, which the emperors
of Byzantium were accustomed to visit with their
families. We can lave in these waters, but Hannibal,
alas! although he perished at the ancient Lybissa,
and although the spot is certainly located at the
famous camel-stables of the caravan times, before
the railroad came, Hannibal and his tomb, I fear,
are forever lost to local habitation.

There are evidences at that place of many
tombs. Near by is a splendid mosque which reminds the traveller of a mosque of Broussa. Here
not unfrequently some traveller of wild archæological genius rushes with frantic delight to a large
tomb with a domed roof, hoping that he has discovered the long-lost grave of Hannibal; but it
only turns out to be the burial place of a Hanoum—a woman of the good old time, who was the
mother of forty daughters! The daughters are
buried on either side of her; twenty in each grave.

Must this search for Hannibal and his tomb go on forever?

Nicæa, the once proud capital of Bithynia, is a more interesting than healthy spot. It was founded not by Alexander, but by another son of Philip of Macedon. It was on a lovely plain. It is described by an ancient historian from the standpoint of a stone placed in the gymnasium whence its four gates could be seen. In vain do the English and other tourists, who go there to shoot birds, seek this central stone. Antiquarian travellers have visited it, not so much for its classical associations, as for the religious struggles of the early church which occurred here. The city was beautified upon a Grecian model, and the Romans gave it some utilitarian improvements, as was their wont. It was the capital of a proud nation; but like other Eastern capitals, it had its distresses by earthquake, and its sieges by soldiers. For some time it stood a barrier against the progress of Mahometan invaders, and many a Saracen and Turk fell weltering in their blood before its Christian defenders. It was not until the latter part of the eleventh century that the Turks obtained possession of it. Soon after a crusade changed its condition; for within ten years it fell before the Grecian host, which invested it by water and land. Gibbon tells the story that numbers of boats were transported

from the Sea of Marmora to the lake Ascanius.
These were filled with soldiers, but before the
attack the banner of the Greek emperor floated
above the towers. It then became the Greco-
Roman capital of Western Asia. But when the
Seljukian Orchan—the ancestor of the present
Sultan—arose, the city and the rich treasures col-
lected within its walls fell a prey to the Turk.
Thereafter Nicæa became known by the less ven-
erable and less impressive name of Iznik.

There is but one Christian church remaining to
recall the ancient creed and glory of Nicæa. But
as long as the Nicene Creed—which was here first
promulgated—is repeated by the faithful it will be
a bond between all Christians and the Eastern
Church. That Nicene Creed is recited in its original tongue by the peasants of Greece. In Russia
the great bell of the Kremlin tower sounds during
the time its words are being chanted. This creed
is repeated aloud in the presence of the assembled
people by the Czars at their coronation. It was
at the first council of Nicæa that the fathers—who
are so often quoted—met to form this summary of
Christian faith against Arianism, and to discuss
the supremacy of the Bible, the power of the
Pope and the Church, the Sacraments, Original
Sin, Predestination, Justification, and above all the
question upon which they differed most, the doctrine of the Incarnation. This latter question was

set at rest by the Nicene Creed. The council met in the month of June, A.D. 325. Its creed was signed by three hundred and eighteen bishops. It is substantially the same creed which Christianity has accepted at 'its various councils and conventions held during the progress of time, and which it declares to-day. It was confirmed, slightly changed, by the council of Constantinople, A.D. 381. It is said to be worked in brilliants on the robes of the highest church dignitaries of Moscow. Notwithstanding all the efforts for harmony which this creed inspired, the unity of the Church of Rome with that of Greece, or rather with that of Russia now, or with that of the Church of England, or with either of them, though often attempted, has never been consummated. The creed remains ; but the exact place or building in which the famous council assembled has not yet been ascertained. Whether it was in the church, which gave a foundation to the ruined mosque of Orchan, or in the Christian temple, of which there are some remains, no one can tell.

This country of Asia Minor speaks in every broken pillar and every fragment of stone, not only of the sojournings and teachings of the great apostle of the Gentiles, but it recalls those early days of fiery zeal when the fathers of the Church met to crush out error, and to perfect a creed which survives through the lapse of centuries.

The creed remains, vital and mystic, but the
swamps and thickets and lakes around the ancient city of Nicæa mark a place of desolation—
fit haunt at the advent of the hunting season
for—what? For the hunters of Constantinople,
in search of duck and woodcock, and sometimes of
the wild boar.

Nicomedia, another city of Asia Minor, was
built in 264 B.C. by Nicomedas, king of Bithynia.
He called on the Gauls to help him in some of his
wars. There are some sweet Gallic accents yet
observable in the dialects spoken along the shore
of Marmora. Nicomedia was not only great as a
city, but greater as a Roman capital. Its greatness has been handed down to us by Roman his-
torians. Here Pliny was pro-consul. Here he
resided and wrote letters to the Emperor Trajan,
describing the monuments, advantages and importance of the city and its surroundings. It is
thought that Pliny first started the idea of con-
necting the waters of the lake of Sabandja with
the Gulf of Nicomedia by means of a canal, and
thus cause the waters of this lake to join those of
the river Sakaria, which empty into the Black Sea.
Herodotus—or his annotator—discusses this pro-
ject, and I received many letters from American
students propounding many difficult engineering
problems about this important matter.

Dioclesian embellished Nicomedia with a taste

and expense that were unparalleled. It became only inferior to Rome, Alexandria and Antioch in extent and population in classic days. It is celebrated for one of the first general edicts of that emperor commanding the persecution of the Christians. This was in the fourth century. Gibbon relates many interesting details of the martyrdoms of that early day, and especially one holocaust at the end of the fourth century, when a Christian emperor, who was an Arian, caused a ship containing eighty bishops, who belonged to the orthodox faith, to be set on fire in the harbor of Nicomedia. They perished for their creed. Here was the home of Constantine. Along with its rival Nicæa it underwent many sieges, but it is principally renowned, along with Nicæa, for being the seat of early Christian councils. Now like Nicæa, it is principally attractive to the hunters, who go out with shot-guns from Constantinople to kill snipe and other game in and around its swamps. The flamingo and the stork are common upon its ways and house-tops, but all the interest left in this capital seems to surround the great soldier of Carthage—Hannibal, whose stern parent was very far from being one of the Christian fathers.

CHAPTER XX.

BROUSSA is a city of Asia Minor. It stands in superb contrast with the relict cities of ecclesiastical glory. It is a thriving business city, with a history worthy of the founders of the Ottoman Empire, who are here buried. I have been at Broussa, but I never surmounted the top of Mount Olympus. It is becoming quite a summer pastime, which our American friends of Robert College— including those of the gentler sex—enjoy. They camp out upon the heights and enjoy the prospect, and inhale health. Mrs. Washburne, the wife of the president of Robert College, gives us a description of her experience the past summer in tent life upon Mount Olympus.

If from the heights of Prinkipo so much can be seen, how much more from the top of Olympus, which is seventy-five hundred feet high? From its lofty dome can be viewed the Sea of Marmora, with its islands, gulfs and promontories, on one side, and the Dardanelles and the countries around it, on the other.

The eye takes in the lakes on the east, where were situated Nicomedia and Nicæa, and the mountains of Bosachan to the west. Such a wide expanse of water; such magnificent ranges of mountains, and such a lofty standpoint give a ground of vantage that elevates the observer far above the turmoils of our little world. And what a land! What seas are overlooked from this more than Alpine height! Here one stands wrapped in thought, not alone because the scenes below have been illustrated in crimson letters by Persian, Greek, Roman and Turkish armies; not merely that Broussa—the most interesting Moslem city next to Constantinople—which lies at the foot of the mountain, was the capital of the first Turkish empire, and still retains the bodies of its early heroes and Sultans, but also that from this elevated point can be seen what is now the ignoble point of Ismid, where was once the proud capital of Bithynia, the famed city of Nicomedia. It was once the residence of emperors; but now it is only a memory! We have not to ascend Olympus to see it. It is almost within the range of our vision from the hills of Prinkipo.

It would be a pleasant thing to compare our Mysean Olympus with the Olympus which Homer has peopled and glorified with the divinities. Both mountains are within the jurisdiction of our legation. The Olympus which the won-

drous mythology of Greece gave to the world
is just over the boundary of Greece. But it is
also within the precincts of Macedonia, which is
in Turkey. My servitor, Pierre, has been on the
heights of the Grecian Olympus with a company of
engineers. He was their purveyor. He knows
all about the monastery of Saint Dionysius, before
which and its ministers the light of Apollo has
shone and the eagle of Jove has flown. He is
acquainted with the guides, who are known as
" clefts," called so, perhaps, because they are familiar with the rocks. Having ascended the classic
mountain, he gives me an account of its holy oaks,
catalpas, arbutuses, pines and firs, and the glory of
the adjacent mountains. From its summit one can
overlook the sea, as to which Pierre becomes eloquent in his description. He forgets his French
and other alien tongues in telling the glory of the

> " Long line of foam, the jewelled chain,
>   The largesse of the ever-giving main."

He relapses into his own language of Croatia,
with whose coast he is as familiar as I am now
with the inlets and seas about Prinkipo. Within
view of Olympus are the shoreless cliffs of
Ossa.

How glorious and great is the peak of the classic Olympus ! To the north is the level plain
diversified with woodlands. On the opposite side

of the water are the promontories, one after another—Athos, Tomina—and beyond these some
of the islands of the Ægean lift themselves
out of the blue waves into the beautiful blue
sky.

This wonderful home of the gods, this Grecian
Olympus, which fills such a grand page in our mythology and rhetoric, is now undignified by many
saw-mills turned by its obedient streams. Thus
are the naiads enslaved and the dryads dishev-
elled of their leafy glories, while the waters plash
and the wheel turns, and the saws eat their eager
way into the timber that is sent thence to Smyrna,
to Constantinople and even to Egypt. *Non
constat* but I am now sitting in a chair whose
ligneous fibre grew under the very shadow of the
throne of Zeus. I revert to my callow college
days. I ask: Where are Venus and Mars?
Where the glories of that wonderful company of
gods, with Jove above them all by his great
looks and power imperial? Gone into the
dim yet deathless traditions of the past, which
made this mountain so weird in its witchery
and sacred in its power over the poetic Greek
imagination. What poet of the future will sing
" Olympus Lost" ?

The classic Olympus has now come down to this :
that the most conspicuous tradition of our Homeric mount connects itself with a bear. The

21

legend is told by the monks of St. Dionysius. When that saintly father was ploughing on the mountain side, he was forced to leave his ox with the plough in the furrow. While away, a bear came along and ate up his ox. The saint on his return discovered what had happened. He— No, he did not curse and swear, but he was very mad with the bear, and he determined to punish bruin in a way not to his taste. With a power that belonged almost to the supreme Zeus himself, he seized and harnessed the larcenous ox-lifting bruin. Forever after that bear had to drag that plough. He became quite tame and grizzly in the honorable service of Ceres. When the family of bears found what his saintship had done with their fellow, they incontinently turned tail and fled the Mount Olympus, just as the snakes scurried from Ireland when they heard that St. Patrick had landed.

While the Macedonian Olympus soars high in the clouds of classic lore, it cannot compare, except in the number of its peaks, with our own Mysean Olympus. The classic Olympus has a triple crown. Olympus of Asia Minor has but two summits. Although the classic Olympus has a name which signifies the "Shining One," and is called the white, the dazzling, and gleaming mount by the Greek poets, it may as well be stated in prose that no part of this Homeric

Olympus is within the limit of perpetual snow; while our Asian Olympus never fails to shine with its white perennial crown ! No one can gainsay that the surroundings of the classic Olympus are something magnificent. Its effect is grand. Here is Ossa. It too has magnificent views. It commands a wide expanse of sea beneath its aspect. Olympus is nine thousand feet high; but its weak point is that the country on one side is almost wholly excluded from view. This is owing to a double line of summits. Scholars who have ascended its classic eminence find it no unworthy position for the gods It has a serener ether than belongs to our lower nature, and there is an odor of sanctity around its monastery. The early Greek believed that its atmosphere was never disturbed by wind, storm, snow or clouds. It was always divine. The clouds below its tranquil summit were the beautiful gates of heaven to the sensitive Greek. When Jove rolled them back, Apollo gave them hue and beauty. What a palace was that of Jupiter ! What a council-chamber that of the other gods ! What a course for their chariots and races on the summit of the mountain !

But to enter these mystic scenes and precincts is to go beyond the limits prescribed for this volume. Lest I awake the ire of Homer or his students, I will not further make comparison between the two Olympian heights. The best I can do is to come down from these heights and flights and describe things as they are to-day in this ancient wonderland. If we were to describe the various peaks upon the classic Olympus and the legends connected with them, the classic mountain might be reduced to a lower plane than that of the Olympus which the learned regard with so much pedantic devotion.

Shakespeare has made the scenes about our classic Olympus interesting. His genius seized Pelion and piled it on Ossa in a wild way. Ossa is a smaller rock than Olympus; but what huge rocks they are! When the vale of Tempe opens to the sea between them, it is a picture of Claude, representing beauty at the feet of strength!

Along the coast of the Ægean, Pelion lies near Ossa, and along with Mount Olympus they look across the sea to the scene of the great Trojan epic.

It is a custom, even to the present day, among the Grecian Christian women when they are *enceinte*, to slide down one of the smooth places on the side of the classic mountain. It is a sign of a happy deliverance. And as they slide, they sing a peculiar song in Greek. It has reference to their future destiny, or that of the expected child.

There is still another eminence nearer our home,

THE ARABY-TURKISH CARRIAGE.

though less classic and historic than either of the Olympii. It is a Turkish *Dagh*.

One of the best points of observation for a view of the landscape in and around Constantinople is the Mount Bougourlow. It rises only a few miles behind Scutari on the Asiatic side. When you climb to its summit the panorama of the Bosphorus and the Sea of Marmora is spread beneath you. This mountain is not only frequented by strangers who desire to survey the prospect, but by the Mahometan women, who go there in good weather to pass the day under its pleasant trees. They go in little companies. Sometimes the harem goes. The women watch their children at play; they chat; they listen to itinerant music; and they have their picnic of grapes, bread and sherbet, topped off with a smoke of the fragrant weed.

The ascent to this mountain is by no means easy. The roads are hardly passable. The principal vehicle is the arabi — a lumbering carriage drawn by oxen. But it makes up in gaudy finery what it lacks in speed. There are many little plateaus to break the ascent of the mountain. Here you can rest. On each plateau are seen families of both Armenians and Turks—resting on their lazy route upward. The situation is so high, the sea breeze so grateful, the temperature so refreshing, and the dealers in coffee, water, sherbet, pastry and confectionery are so numerous that the spectacle upon the top of the mountain is as festive as the wide-spread panorama below is sublime. The women sit upon the grass under their sun-shades. They are clad in their varicolored and shining silk dresses. Some recline beneath the shade of the sycamores and plane-trees. The gayety and novelty are enhanced by a bevy of Greek girls. You easily recognize them. They are known by their diadems of braided hair. They amuse themselves with the dance in movements which require little exertion, but which are full of the poetry of motion. These performances you may see repeated at the " Sweet Waters."

This scene is seductive with attractions, but your ascent to the mountain is for another purpose. Here the eye roams over the prospect of the great city, with its domes and minarets upon the west. On the east is a vast plateau or prairie. Over it runs the old road of the caravans. It leads out of Scutari into the very heart of Asia. On the north is the Black Sea and old Cimmeria, — the land of blackness and blockheads! On the south is our own island home of Prinkipo flanked by Bothnia and Troy. Turn where you will every prospect pleases. Not the least of the delights is the circle immediately around you. Here are the Zigani playing upon the fiddle. They chant ballads in their strange gypsy dialect. Here pleasure, innocence and gayety abound. The groups are as joyous as one could wish to see. One feels tempted to remain here long As the company descend the mountain shouts of wild laughter from the arabis answer to each new plunge of the awkward vehicles. Horsemen dash down as recklessly as if they were on a level. Everything bespeaks a scene entirely Asiatic and far removed from the Europe which is in view from the summit. In such glimpses we catch rare views of the harmonious blendings of Greek and Turkish life, suggestive of the blendings of the two races which gave so much force and romance to the Mahometan empire in Europe.

The founder of the Ottoman dynasty, Othman, was an extraordinary person. He left not only a great name, but a sovereignty over the greater part of little Asia. Starting with an army of only 416 horsemen, he increased it to 6000. When he died he left neither gold nor silver behind, only a spoon and a salt-cellar, an embroidered *caftan*, a new turban, some flags in red muslin, a stable full of horses, some yokes of oxen for the laborers of the farm, and a choice flock of sheep. These sheep were the ancestors to the imperial flocks which were fed at the foot of Mount Olympus, and this man was the ancestor of the imperial rulers of the great Ottoman empire.

Orkhan was his second son and his successor.

He had great skill in ornamentation and evidently was romantically inclined, for the buildings which he caused to be erected are covered with poetical inscriptions. Whenever he founded a college he also established a soup kitchen. The villages which are called after his name are numerous. His reign was unsullied either by barbarity or violence. He is known as the Numa of the Ottomans. What I wish to remark in relation to this family is this : Their tombs at Broussa are noted in history. The munificence of these princes toward Broussa has its monuments in the charitable institutions which they erected. Niloufer Khatoun was the first wife of the Sultan Orkhan. She founded one hundred and eleven charitable institutions. Some of them are in Nicæa. She passed the end of her life at that place in quiet retirement, and was always regarded as a most excellent and pious princess.

It may be thought that the Sultans are not permitted to marry outside of their own religion. They are not so restricted in choice. It is a fact that the strength and glory of the Ottoman dynasty has been sustained by the marriage of its Sultans with Christian women. The virtuous princess Niloufer, whose body lies near the walls of Broussa, was a Christian, and she is in such contrast with Roxolana, another Christian wife of a subsequent emperor, that it is well to regard the one and discard the other.

CHAPTER XXI.

EUROPEAN SHORE—SAN STEFANO AND THE TREATY.

SAN STEFANO is always in sight on a clear day from the Princes Islands. It leaves one indelible historic impression. It is connected with the war which began in the autumn of 1877 between Russia and Turkey. Of that war and its various fortunes I shall speak in a more elaborate volume than this—"The Diversions of a Diplomat"—which I contemplate publishing. The diplomacy in which Lord Salisbury—who was the agent of Lord Beaconsfield—took so conspicuous a part at that time, is associated with the very room where I now pen this chapter. Here, no doubt, Salisbury dreamt dreams and saw visions. The device of Midhad Pacha—then grand vizier—to disarm the hostility of the European congress or concert by proclaiming a liberal constitution ; the adhesion of England to Turkey ; the isolation of the Czar ; the crossing of the Danube, upon which the Great White Father of all the Russians invoked the blessing of God as he gave the order to advance ; the move on the Balkans ; the cries against the infidels ; the sacred hymns of the old Greek Church

329

heralding the Slavonic army—all these are a part
of that conflict which had its consummation and
mise en scène at San Stefano.   In that movement
the Russians had two hundred and twenty thousand men, and the Turks about the same number.
In soldierly bearing and qualities these armies
were nearly equal.   They were equally enthusiastic
and brave.   In arms the Turks were, perhaps,
better off than the Russians.   Three hundred
thousand American rifles, the Peabody-Martini
gun which is still to be seen in the hands of the
Turkish soldier, had been stacked for the emergency in the barracks of Constantinople.   Iron-
clads filled the Golden Horn.   Germany supplied
the Turk with cannon which were as much superior to the old bronze guns, as the Martini rifle was
in advance of the old Revolutionary musket of our
fathers.   The Russians were, perhaps, superior in
cavalry.   The Cossack was then thought to have
no equal.   This was before the day when the
Arab of the desert with spear and horse broke the
squares of the flower of Albion's infantry in the
Soudan.   But the fighting was not to be done on
horse-back.   The Turks were in their own country.   They had the mountain range of the Balkans, so celebrated in military history from the
time when Darius crossed the Bosphorus to fight
the Scythians.   Bulgaria then, as now, was the
objective point.   Generals Gourko and Skoboleff

led the Russian armies. As the people of many of the towns through which the Russians passed were adherents of the Greek Church, they welcomed the Russians as deliverers. Priests, monks and girls met the Slav soldiers with flowers and benedictions.

The Turks were aroused. Their armies were concentrated upon the Balkans. All Europe beheld their magnificent fighting at the Shipka Pass. Plevna became almost another Thermopylæ in the way of the advancing Slav. The Czar himself soon found his presence necessary to inspire the stolid Russian soldier.

The advance was easy, until all at once the Shipka Pass was found to be defended by the Turks, and Plevna made its heroic resistance! In spite of the gallant fighting on the part of the Turks, the Russians found themselves south of the Balkans. Was there a panic in Constantinople? Was there terror at the Porte and dismay in Dolma-Batché and the palaces? Was there a packing up of archives? Was there to be another hegira of the Mohammedan and another exodus of the Jews? All this has been said.

The intensity of religious emotion was invoked in the rank and file of the Russian army. The splendid ritual of the Greek Church was called in to take the place of the drum and fife. With

uncovered head, the sad chants peculiar to the
Greek Church gave solemnity to the scene. It
was no summer holiday,—that fight in the Balkans. At length Osman Pacha, who so long
withstood the skill of Todleben, surrenders with
his army. Plevna falls. It is the turning-point of
the war. The Russians push down toward Constantinople. With an audacity unequalled they
press on towards the Bulgarian capital, Sofia,
where for the first time since A.D. 1434, a Christian army is seen.

"On to Philippopolis!"—"On to Adrianople!"
The victorious Russians press on, until on the
last day of January, 1878, the minarets of Constantinople appear.

The passage of the Balkans was a wonderful
achievement. It was a terrible struggle amidst
the storms of the winter season. Even as I now
write, in this balmy clime, and so near the Balkan
range, the snow is blocking its passes.

How far did that war limit the power of Turkey? By what miracle did the Caliph of all
Mahometanism survive the conflict of race and
religion? This is not the place to seek the *casus
belli*, or to criticise the strategy by which the Russian army reached the plains of San Stefano. On
the memorable third of March, A.D. 1878, the little
village, whose white houses now appear upon my
vision, was the scene, after a month of negotia-

tion, of the celebration of the peace by what is known as the " Treaty of San Stefano."

This village is not without some American associations. It is the place where Commodore Porter, of " Essex " fame, first fixed the American Legation. It is situated on the Sea of Marmora, and within six miles of the Golden Gate, from whose towers I have gazed upon the grand campaign, where the vast Russian army was encamped.

But it is most distinguished as the place where the treaty between Russia and Turkey was made. That treaty was made by General Ignatieff. It was set aside afterwards by the treaty of Berlin, owing to the energetic protest of the Powers. The protest was backed by the British Navy, which was anchored between the islands of Halki and Prinkipo, in the same blue waters through which I am accustomed to glide in our American navy of the Orient, the steam-launch " Sunset."

It was thought when the Russian army came in sight of the minarets of Stamboul that the rule of the Turk in Europe was forever ended,—that his encampment was broken up and that he would retreat into Asia. Judging from the enormous number of refugees who fled before the advancing Russian army, this was then a reasonable expectation.

There were other Powers, however, to be dealt with before Russia could be permitted to fly her flag from the dome of St. Sophia. The English fleet passed up the Dardanelles. There, on the plains of San Stefano, were rolled back the waves of Russian invasion which almost swept over the walls of Constantinople !

The war, not to speak of the treaty, which was more or less abrogated afterwards at Berlin, had the effect of greatly circumscribing Turkish dominion in Europe. It severed Bosnia, Servia, Herzegovina, Montenegro, Roumania and Bulgaria, and portions of Thessaly from the empire. But the Moslem domination over a large portion of Turkey in Europe still remains. Judging by recent events, the power of the Turk is stronger to-day than it was ten years ago.

Although the village of San Stefano has a place in diplomatic history, it consists of only about twenty or thirty houses. These houses are large. They are owned by wealthy Greek merchants who inhabit them during the summer. When the Russians were preparing to move on Constantinople, these houses were occupied by the Grand Duke Nicholas and his staff. There is a quay upon the Sea of Marmora upon which the village fronts. During the winter and spring of 1878 there could be heard at these Princes Islands, floating across the waters, the music of the Russian bands. It is not unlikely that this alien music was heard by the young Sultan, who had only a year or two before that time come into power.

The Russians remained at San Stefano during the armistice. The officers, and after a while some of the men, were allowed to visit Constantinople. It is said that they behaved themselves in a most exemplary manner. Certainly they pleased the merchants of the bazaars. It is reckoned that six millions of rubles in gold, a sum equivalent to $4,600,000, were then paid into the shops by the Russians. During this time although there was a mercantile *entente cordiale*, the treaty hung fire. The Russians became impatient at the dilatoriness of the Turks in signing the treaty. The 3rd of March rolled around ; it was the anniversary of the Czar's accession ; and the negotiations were abruptly ended. At one o'clock in the afternoon the troops were drawn up as for parade. The horses of the Grand Duke and his staff were saddled. Still the Turks delayed to sign the treaty. Couriers dashed fleetly between the house of the Grand Duke and that in which were the negotiators—Ignatieff and Savfet Pasha. At last the Russian menace was heeded. The intended attack upon the city was turned into a " Review," and the army was informed that the war had ended.

It has lately transpired that, when the Russian army was near Constantinople, Count Schouvaloff telegraphed to the Czar that England would not interfere with the occupation of the city by the Russians, provided no attempts were made by the Russians to seize Gallipoli and blockade the iron-clads within the Golden Horn. The Czar trusted to Schouvaloff. He was the ambassador at London. He believed that the city would be occupied without British intervention. It is alleged that on the receipt of this dispatch the Czar telegraphed to General Gourko at San Stefano commanding the troops to march into and occupy the city. Of course, the dispatch was in cipher; but it could not reach San Stefano without passing through Turkish hands. It is said that the Turks so transposed the ciphers that when the telegram was received by Gourko it was utterly unintelligible. The general had all the shrewdness of his army at work upon the dispatch,—but in vain. Thus, two most momentous days passed by; and the British cabinet meanwhile were advised by the Turkish minister at London of the peril. The British cabinet immediately directed the minister at St. Petersburg to state to the Czar that the occupation of the city would be regarded as a *casus belli.* The result of the curt dispatch was the treaty and not the occupation.

This remarkable statement is vouched for by Dr. Blowitz, the Paris correspondent of the London *Times.* "Upon what a slender thread hang everlasting things!" How it ended, we know. The

Grand Duke telegraphed to the Czar the same night that the great and holy mission which he had assumed, of liberating the Christians from the Mussulman yoke, had been accomplished. Thereupon preparations were made to re-establish the old diplomatic relations at the Muscovite and Ottoman capitals. Thereupon the Grand Duke and his suite danced the *Cracovienne* on the marble pavements of Beylerbey ; not as a conqueror, but as a guest of the Sultan !

CHAPTER XXII.

IN a former chapter I have stated that Murray's guide-book gives it out that the women of Prinkipo are the most beautiful in the world. I am ready to believe that Murray, on this topic, is nearly, if not absolutely, veracious. I will not say that every one is a Miranda or a Una, or even a Helen; for there are many females on this island who are neither youthful nor attractive. But, according to the best standards of taste, there are more beautiful women here than I have ever seen among the same number in any other part of the world. Perhaps it is because they are modelled upon the eclectic principle of the ancient Greek artist who, to make one perfect form, selected from many beauties the conspicuous loveliness of each. The Greek blood upon this island is of a purer strain than can be found upon the mainland of Greece. This is also the case in the Cyclades and other Grecian islands nearer the ancient capital of art and genius. The classic costumes are not quite the mode of Prinkipo, but they still remain the fashion in the inland of the Greek pen-

338

GREEK WOMAN FROM THE INTERIOR.

insula and many of the islands of the Ægean.
Now and then, here in Prinkipo, you may see young
Greek girls dressed in European style, but seldom
without retaining the jacket of embroidered silk
and the coiffure, which remind you of the ancient costume. The chiselled features of these
young graces show the classic model. Greece is
now best represented in her old colonial depend-
encies. In the islands the living models of Phidias, Praxiteles and Lysippus are by no means rare.
Whatever changes the latest fashions of Paris
may make, they do not affect the graceful classic
dressing of the hair. It is still parted in waves,
just as we see it in the antiques with which every
archæologist is familiar. These waving bands
flow over the temple on each side and are encir-
cled by a large braid forming a sort of crown. I
am not prepared to say that these braids are always genuine. Their different shades of color
suggest a suspicion of the ancient as well as modern art. Nor am I prepared to discriminate very
greatly between womankind, in grace of form and
movement. Still one would have to be blind not
to see in the evening balcony-groups of Prinkipo
many a beauty whose very pose suggests the classic type. Even the touch of the finger to the
forehead in repose—" like one who with a pleased
look leans upon a closed book "—gives a serenity,

proportionateness and beauty altogether unique and Hellenic, and rarely seen elsewhere.

Visitors who write about Turkey more frequently go into raptures over the Turkish woman than over her Greek sister. Is it because the beauty of Turkish women is only partly revealed? The best writer upon the Orient whom I have read, "Eöthen," is an exception to this rule. He seems to have been more enamored of the beautiful descendants of the old Ionian race, whom he found along the shores of Asia Minor and in its splendid cities of Beyrout and Smyrna. But his picture of the Smyrniote lady is somewhat dim, as if he were under a spell. He sees Greek beauties everywhere in these cities, even in the humblest mud cottages. They are all attired with magnificence—"their classic heads are crowned with scarlet, and loaded with jewels, or coins of gold—the whole wealth of the wearers." Thus far he writes with considerable fidelity, for the Greek woman wears her dowry or fortune upon her person. It is an investment made for safety, as well as adornment. It has its convenience also, for the suitor, instead of going to a public office to ascertain, from the will of her father or the record of public taxes, the value of her estate, can, while he admires the contour of his mistress's head, reckon it therefrom. When "Eöthen" gazes long and longingly at the features of the Greek he finds some artificiality.

" Their features," he says, "are touched with a
savage pencil, which hardens the outline of eyes
and eyebrows, and lends an unnatural fire to the
stern, grave looks with which they pierce your
brain." Evidently he is becoming more or less
inflamed, for he says further on : " Endure their
fiery eyes as best you may and ride on slowly and
reverently, for facing you from the side of the
transom that looks longwise through the street,
you see the one glorious shape transcendent in its
beauty ; you see the massive braid of hair as it
catches a touch of light on its jetty surface—and
the broad, calm, angry brow—the large black eyes,
deep-set, and self-relying like the eyes of a conqueror, with their rich shadows of thought lying
darkly around them,—you see the thin fiery nostril, and the bold line of the chin and throat, dis-
closing all the fierceness and all the pride, passion and power that can live along with the rare
womanly beauty of those sweetly turned lips."

This rhapsody comes from a man whose travels
through the Orient were of a most sedate and
philosophic quality, and who is quoted after fifty
years as no other writer upon these lands has
been quoted. Evidently this gifted writer went
clean daft upon his inspiring theme. What a
climax he makes in his description of the Greek
beauties ! He falls into an ecstasy when he says :
" But then there is a terrible stillness in this breath-

ing image ; it seems like the stillness of a savage
that sits intent, and brooding day by day, upon
some one fearful scheme of vengeance, but yet
more like, it seems, to the stillness of an immortal,
whose will must be known, and obeyed without
sign or speech. Bow down! Bow down, and
adore the young Persephone, transcendent Queen
of Shades!"   .

What should " Eöthen" have said when he en-
countered, as he often did, the genuine girl of the
desert ; not in the palace or harem, but in the tent,
surrounded by the associations which gave to the
East its sweetest lyrics. Sometimes such an Arab
girl is known to sing her songs from native inspiration. One of these songs echoes in my memory as it is sighed rather than sung beside the fountains of Damascus. It is a melancholy strain, but it
has the essence of contrast and patriotism, which is
the spirit of poetry. She praises her russet suit of
camel's-hair as dearer to her than the trappings of
a queen ; the humble tent as better than the towers and halls of the splendor around ; the frolicsome
colt as more beauteous than the gorgeous mule
of the pasha ; the barking of the watch-dog as a
sweeter sound than the melody of the lute ; and,
as a climax, the rustic youth, unspoiled by art,
poor but free, with whom she will roam the desert,
though all the pampered sons of wealth should
seek to woo her from his love.

Closely assimilated with the Grecian woman in beauty, and having each her own peculiar loveliness, is the Armenian, Persian, Hebraic and Ottoman woman. All are, in one word, of Oriental type. Artists have portrayed the large black eye, its languid lustre and liquid splendor; the heavenly arch of the brow, and the delicate softness and smoothness of the skin which tell of the bath and its constant use. But no one can picture the beauties of these Oriental women. The rose, the pearl, the alabaster, are but feeble symbols of their loveliness. Their courtly ease, low sweet voice, innocent jocund laugh, and the honeyed talk, make a poem of enchantment surpassing the sensuous imagination of Keats. It may be that the Armenian women are of the earth and earthy; but their graces betoken the nearness of their country to the Garden of Eden, and the absence of the aftermath which sin brought from thence into the world. The Turkish woman does not dress as gaudily as the Persian, nor does she bloom so much in the fictitious glories of painted womanhood. She has her own mode of pencilling the eyebrow and arranging the veil which defies competition. But when called for an out-door promenade in a long and graceless *feridjie* she does not show that elegance which one might possibly see if he were allowed within the harem. The contrast between the indoor dress, both in Persia and here farther

west, and the walking attire, must strike every
traveller who has had the privilege to draw it
from life.

The more characteristic charms of the Circassian, while she may be passing fair, consist of a
tall and well formed figure, dark eye-lashes and
bright chestnut hair ; but sometimes that element
of the old Tartaric strain—a high cheek bone or
wide mouth, is too prominent a feature. Her
charms are more or less concealed by the veil.
Diamonds and other jewellery illumine her hair.
Her dress is brightened and colored to attract the
eye and rivet the gaze.

The Lady of Lima is one of the beautiful flowers of the great Spanish plant on our own hemisphere. She is said to be all eyes. The way she
wears her *saya y manto* gives her such a coquettish
and bewitching air, that, if all her other features
were ugly, she would be rescued by the glory of
her eye and garment. The Lady of Lima has
been known unconsciously to entrance her own
husband in passing along the street ! Although
only one eye is visible at such times, the orb of
the Spanish ladies is of such a large, deep, liquid
black, that her glance through her *crêpe* mantle
from China becomes auxiliary to many a heart-
breaking infelicity. The Peruvian and Andalu-
sian beauty is but another type of the Oriental

woman under American and European acclimatization.

It would seem that the blonde is just now most affected by the Turkish women. Fair hair, and blue eyes or gray, are not, however, admired by their Persian sisters, although in Persia a fair skin and florid complexion are much sought after. But, strange to say, that even though nature may have been unstinted in her gifts to these Eastern women, art is not seldom called in with her rouge and powder. I am told that the beauties of the harem, in Persia at least, are like full blown peonies. I have seldom seen a Turkish woman who rouged her face. She may paint her eyebrows and powder her neck, but rouge does not seem to be one of her adornments. The Persian generally gives her suffrage to the jet black, almost blue-black, long hair. After the Egyptian and Oriental method, still seen upon temple and tomb, it is worn plaited into a number of tiny braids whose ends peep forth coquettishly from beneath the veil. But neither in Persia nor in Egypt, nor in Turkey, is the contour of the ankle revealed by the walking attire. For four thousand years the women of the East have been under formal and constant restraint before their lords and masters. They will not uncover their face before any man except their father or husband. Therefore they put on an outward dress that makes them all look alike. This costume was borne from the East to Andalusia and thence to Spanish America. The veil of the East is, therefore, not only an Asiatic but an American institution.

In Turkey, thirty odd years ago, when I first visited it, the trousers, that are yet common in Persia, were the rage. Then much female paraphernalia were crowded into these voluminous trousers—which were gathered at the ankle—when a Turkish lady desired to make a promenade abroad. I have noticed that during the intervening time the Turkish women have learned to correct the ungainly gait which came from wearing slippers at the extremity of their stockingless legs—a custom which even Byron remarked was "one of the disenchantments of their beauty."

I have tried to describe the women of the East; but how can my pen, with its sameness and tameness of words, picture the rare form and alluring graces of these maids of the Isle of Prinkipo? If they are not good,—as Miranda remarked of her lover in another enchanted isle,—then good spirits will try to dwell in such forms of loveliness. As some one sings : "Nature herself disjoins the beauteous and profane ; and beauty is virtue made visible in outward grace." Ah! if one could always incarnate within these outward forms the Florence Nightingales of our earth, where could be found more exquisite caskets of the soul with-

in ! A friend who saw this rare woman here during the Crimean war tells me that she was held in
the greatest honor among both men and women.

" How," I asked, " did she look ? how was she
dressed ?"

The answer was :

" Her short brown hair was combed over her
forehead, while her childlike and wasted figure
seemed to give more grace to her goodness.
When I saw her in her black dress—which was
held by a large enamelled brooch, surrounded
by a wreath of laurel (an offering of the soldiers), and her little white cap with a white crape
handkerchief thrown over it, leaving but a border
of lace to be seen, she was the picture of a nun,
"breathless with adoration !"

This was the woman of heaven's own type of
beauty, the angel of the hospitals, the pearl of
the camp. I asked for more particulars as to her
personality. My friend responded :

" She had a Roman nose, small dark eyes, keen
yet kind. She was orderly and ladylike in manner."

All of this is in sharp contrast with the luxurious gifts and physical graces of these women of
this isle of princes and princesses.

But because Florence Nightingale was too good
to be less than an angel, we must not forget that
there may be still some Circes, Calypsos, Helens,
Sapphos and Aspasias. But happily they are rare

among the Christian women whose devotion is the soul of the Orthodox Church. Such women are the rule. If there be others they are the exception.

Would you have me be more particular as to these island goddesses? I meet them in the promenade, dressed as queens and as gracious to all as Minerva was toward Ulysses. I see them moving amidst the pine forests, their little high-heeled white shoes hardly deigning to touch the ground, the realization of Burke's picture of Queen Antoinette; for never lit upon this star more resplendent visions of immortal beauty!

It is impossible to particularize, although I have one in my mind's eye, as I write. Is she Helen of Troy, or Venus reincarnated? When likening these beauties of the isle to Homer's heroines, I do not refer to other than their bodily graces. Venus is a goddess. She can take care of herself. Helen is not an odious person. With all her faults I love her still. She was not hateful even to old Homer. As I recall her she is frail but not abandoned. She struggles with virtues on one side, and a softness which overcomes them on the other. Sometimes she is repentant, but always fair. Fate seems to rescue her fame; and fate is never wanting when the "machina" is necessary for the whirl of the Greek epic. There are places in Homer where, as in his speaking horses and his blood-distilling myrtles, even Pope confesses that the machine would have been better than the monstrosity. But Helen is sufficiently natural for our daily contemplation, and far more alluring than many of those who have passed as fashionable beauties.

If not Helen, then her typical sister is here upon these isles of Greece.

I see her apparelled in pink satin, moving in stateliness through the sylvan dells. Sometimes she can be seen under a yellow or scarlet umbrella, —"serious as those intent on love,"—with her gay cavalier, whose summer hat is adorned with a variegated ribbon of a broad swath! The scene is Greek. Grecian graces pervade the isle despite the *mode.* They fill the air with visual enchantment and honeyed sounds. True, these graces and Helens are dressed *à la Parisienne* or, recently, on Viennese patterns, and even in Pera fashion. But no toilet can conceal and no dress enhance the glory of their beauty.

In several passages of the Iliad we have descriptions of the Grecian ideal of the beautiful woman. Powers, when he makes his Greek slave, and Canova, his Venus, copy the statues of Phidias or the effigy of that Helen who was *teterrima causa* between Greek and Trojan.

In Book xiv. of the Iliad we have a poetic picture of the dress of the Grecian woman 2500

years ago.   It was very simple.   After the inevitable bath and the fragrant unguents—Oriental customs—she ties up the radiant tresses and casts a
white veil over her hair—the original *yashmak*.
Then she has a mantle for her whole body—
the *feridjie*. Then she hangs her pendants
and puts on her sandals. This was the dress
which the magic girdle of Venus enclosed when
Juno borrowed it to please the god of Olympus,
and in which many a Circassian beauty is arrayed
to please her pasha. It was the dress of goddess,
princess and lady, until its simplicity was corrupt-
ed by the later Asiatic fashions, which Isaiah describes in his third chapter.

But it is Helen's beauty that I take to be the
best standard of ancient Greece. Homer gives us
her portrait. He pictures her at the loom. All
his heroines are industrious and work golden webs.
But he does not give as full a catalogue of her
special beauties as we would like. Her mien is
majestic ; her graces are winning; she moves—a
goddess ; she looks—a queen ! She has the celestial descent. Her charms make men fight nine
years on her account. But what is the color of
her eyes and hair; how tall is she ? These questions
remain unanswered. Although the Greeks preferred the goddess of love to be golden-haired, and
worshipped Juno as blue-eyed, yet in general,
among the Greek females of our isle the blondes

are exceptional. There are some among the Turkish women whose mothers are doubtless Circassian blondes; but then, their eyes are dark as night, and wonderful as meteors. Our Prinkipo Helen is pure Greek. She affords opportunity for the display of her charms and her wavy, graceful figure. She does not conceal her form under the ungainly *feridjie*, although sometimes, like our Greek lady from Bourdour, in the picture, she dresses elaborately. Besides, she is devout and that helps her, as it does the Turkess. There is no doubt of the fact, that the many kinds of prayers and their frequency in the Greek and Moslem ceremonies tend to make the person willowy in grace and facile in movement. These prayers are to be executed with minute and easy exactness of limb and motion. The Turks pray at least five times a day. The Greeks make genuflections whenever they pass a church or the image of a saint. I cannot reckon from theological data how much movement there is required in the Greek ceremony, but the Moslem demands twenty-six postures for each prayer. The very devout use many courses of eight postures each. Nine times eight is an excellent number,—which, with the concluding postures, make seventy-four. Then there are special prayers at certain seasons, which my informant enumerates as follows: "for Ramazan, for the seven holy nights; for drought, famine, pestilence; the funeral

26

prayer, the battle prayer, the marriage prayer, and many others, each of which must be executed in its own way with the utmost particularity. The slightest deviation or mistake destroys the merit of the whole, and the performer—I mean devotee—must begin anew." This constant genuflection from early childhood makes the form lithe and the vertebræ curve in lines of loveliness. No one ever tires of meeting such courtesy as both Turkish and Grecian people of both sexes bestow. Piety and Beauty meet each other ; Goodness and Grace kiss each other !

I would not depreciate the women of other climes, nor extol personal charms above mental culture and virtuous merit. The Greek woman may have at her tongue's end a dozen languages. Her time at school has been so absorbed by them that she has, perhaps, neglected to acquire other information and discipline. She, however, becomes a wonder for sweetness of voice. Her articulation runs the gamut as her ancestress touched the lute. Much less would I make undue encomium upon the Turkish women, who are greatly secluded from the world of letters, learning and social intercourse. Still it is true that for physical grace the Greek beauty has no parallel but her own. The blondes of Boston, with glasses before their acute orbs; the brunettes of Baltimore, with their easy flow of talk; the girls

of Norseland, with their golden tresses and ceru-
lean eyes ; the senoritas of Seville whose beauty
made Byron beatific,—all pale before the maidens
of Prinkipo, who as much excel his Maid of
Athens as she excelled the dowdy and gaudy
girls who figure in the novels of " Ouida."

CHAPTER XXIII.

THE TURKISH WOMEN—A PRINCESS OF EGYPT INDEED — AN ESCAPADE.

BUT are there no Turkish ladies on your isle? Yes, my fair or stern reader, there have been about fifty here this summer. Six reside immediately in the rear of our villa. Their house has the sign of Turkish seclusion at its windows—the *croisée*. They walk out over the hills with the children; no man accompanies them. It is their custom never to promenade with their husbands or their male relatives. Their children are as pretty as pictures. The women are *yashmaked* in white tulle over head and face, and this group has white *feridjies*. They look like a bevy of Dante's ghosts, moving in the gloaming of the evening, or sitting upon the hillside, as quiet and mysterious as the dumb folk of Rip Van Winkle's vision. This group is not so attractive; but there is another group who live by themselves near the Calypso hotel. They are the wife, daughter, and sister of a Bey, with their female companions. They are veiled, but not much. Sometimes I meet them unaccompanied by their

TURKISH WOMAN.

Nubian eunuch, and when the veils are coquettishly *en abandon.* They take donkey rides
around the isle, morning and evening. They
sit upon the animal with all the grace consistent with their clumsy outer garment, the *feridjie.* Their head-dresses shame the new-born
snow. Their *feridjies* are of all colors : one is
of golden yellow, one of royal purple, one of
white silk, and one is as blue as the Bosphorus.
The eldest has black silk. They wear the neatest
of French boots.

The other evening these ladies were mounted
and in a blithesome mood. The donkey-driver is a
Greek ; he, too, was frolicsome ; in fact, the keen
air of the isle gives to all jocund spirits. The
ladies were arbitrary ; and on their request the
driver pushed the animals up hill and down dale,
while the riders screamed and laughed like children just out of school. One of the fair company
rode an obstinate donkey. She was left behind.
My Dalmatian *serviteur,* Pedro Skoppeglia, and
myself were on a rush behind them upon our donkeys. May I not mention, *sub rosa,* that my wife
was not with us on this occasion? The lady who
drops to the rear calls to the driver in vain. He is
occupied with the other three ladies. But we do the
work of punching up her donkey, and away she flies
like John Gilpin. We gallantly drop to the rear as
we approach the village. They draw rein until we

turn down a street, when the belated one drops
her veil to bid me "*Bon-soir.*" I, too, must drop
the veil. I said that my wife was not there.
Do you ask me, "Was she beautiful?" She was of
Circassian mould and passing fair. She was the sister of the Bey. "Were the others beautiful?" Yes,
of various types. The lady of the *bon-soir* was golden-haired. She had dark melting eyes, eyebrows
of faultless arch—and arch ways corresponding.
Her color was that of a sunset rose, creamy, tinged
with pink. The old song I heard in Damascus
came back to me with its refrain : "Beautiful was
the pomegranate; but the wild bird sang to the
rose." She needed no such toilet as the Oriental
women of Isaiah's description. She sat upon her
animal like Helen—if Helen may be supposed to
have ever sat upon a donkey, except metaphori-
cally. One must have recourse to Oriental metaphor and exaggeration to color her photograph.
Her shape, was it not as graceful as that of the
cypress? The shafts of her eyes beneath her
lashes were unsparing. Thus the poet of Persia
would sing of her :

"Oh! Queen Rose, thy slave is beggared; his
whole heart is only one wound. Smile but once
again and his head will touch the stars!"

I believe I mentioned that my wife was not
there. Besides, there is a certain reserve which
one in my relation to the American ensign had

TURKISH WOMEN ON A DONKEY RIDE.

to sustain upon the island. The best I could do was to request my wife to make advances to the fair Turquoises! This she did through a mutual friend, a Swiss lady of their acquaintance. Then followed an invitation to a sail in the launch around the isles, and a picnic *al fresco* in the beautiful bay of Halki. Surely no Congressman who voted for that launch and reads this chapter, will regret such tender advances in the direction of the *haremlik* by a prudent minister and discreet husband. Yet—yet, the wild bird will sing to the rose.

Seriously, while these ladies understand French, as do their relatives, the question arises :

What else do they know ? They do not attend to the cooking in their homes. That is all done for them, and generally out of their households. Their slaves do all their home work, except embroidery, which Helen and Penelope and the rest of the Homeric heroines performed as a ladylike employment. There arises a new Eastern question,—and after all it is a question much mooted among medical men,—whether our fair sisters should enter largely upon and join in the mental toil and tournament of active life. Exceptional culture on this isle has not, as has been contended, removed the " fittest " women,—those physically perfect and most likely to add to the production of generations of high-class brain-power,—

from out of the ranks of motherhood. The sweet girl-graduates of Greek descent here — whether of raven or golden hair — are in no danger of losing their vital forces as women by excessive study of something beyond the languages and graces ; for languages and graces seem to be drunk in with their mothers ' milk. The Oriental woman, says Flaubert, is hard to understand, as we are not permitted to know her. But this is not the case with the Greek, who never could assimilate with the ultra-Oriental customs. After all, from my observation here, I accept as true to life the description of a happy home life and wife as well depicted by an Oriental king, Solomon. He says :

" Who can find a virtuous woman ?—for her price is far above rubies. The heart of her husband doth safely trust in her ; she will do him good and not evil all the days of her life. She riseth also while it is yet night, and giveth meat to her household, and a portion to her maidens. She girdeth her loins with strength and strengtheneth her arms. She perceiveth that her merchandise is good ; her candle goeth not out by night. She layeth her hands to the spindle, and her hands hold the distaff. She stretcheth forth her hands to the poor ; yea, she reacheth forth her hands to the needy. Her husband is known in the gates, when he sitteth among the elders of the land. Strength and honor are her clothing; and she shall rejoice in time to come. She openeth her mouth with wisdom; and in her tongue is the law of kindness. She looketh well to the ways of her household, and eateth not the bread of idleness. Her children arise up and call her blessed; her husband also, and he praiseth her. Favor is deceitful, and beauty is vain; but a woman that feareth the Lord, she shall be praised."

Has the curriculum in our female colleges been productive of such ornaments of home as the Wise King describes?—is the question yet to be decided.

The British Medical Association, through its spokesman, Dr. Moore, epitomized one side of the question, when it said: "This higher education will hinder those who would have been the best mothers from being mothers at all; or, if it does not hinder them, more or less, it will spoil them, and no training will enable themselves to do what their sons might have done. Bacon's mother, intellectual as she was, could not have produced the 'Novum Organum;' but she, perhaps she alone, could and did produce Bacon."

The other side of the question might well be illustrated here, for in language dissenting *pro hâc* from the Association, it may be truly urged that where there is naturally good intellect and a good physique, and where these are sustained and improved by judicious feeding, exer-

cise, and employment, we should have no fear
of subjecting girls to any strain which the ordinary forms of so-called higher education would in-
volve.   We do not believe that either they or their
offspring would be in any respect the worse for it.
The question is a personal one ; and it is only on
personal qualities that it can be rightly decided.

It cannot be rightly decided by flippant flings
at the Ottoman women, nor at the time-honored
custom of "shamefacedness" in women which Paul
commended.   The Greeks to whom the Gentile
apostle addressed his admonitions were not then,
and certainly were not in the time of the empire,
so pure that they could throw stones at their later
Turkish competitors for empire.   "The Greek
emperor," said Gibbon, "demoralized, with his
uncurtained harem, the very Turk."

It is very seldom that a stranger, even if he
knows the Turkish language, and presumes to in-
terrogate, ever has occasion to receive a response
from a Turkish woman.   I have read of one or
two instances, but perhaps these are travellers'
stories.   In a volume written some forty years
ago, its author, the ubiquitous Mr. Smith, says,
that while he was in some distant province, making a sketch of a Saracenic mosque, he was kindly
invited within by the Ulema.   While engaged in
his sketching, several Turkish ladies passed by.
Curiosity getting the better of them, they turned

their wonderful eyes, first on the artist, and then on his artistic performance, and inquired with almost American power of question, but with Oriental poetical expression :

" Whence come you, O my soul ? Whither are you going to travel ? Oh, Allah ! who taught you to place upon paper what you see before you ? "

Was it possible that Turkish ladies should have so transformed themselves in a moment by the sight of an ensanguined Englishman as to have rivalled our Yankee power of interrogation ? I cannot believe it, nor that " the approach of some great white turbans cut short the conversation, and compelled the damsels to beat a retreat."

It is a frequent question, What have the Turkish women to do when they meet ? As far as I could judge, in passing a group of them at the Sweet Waters, I never saw them lacking in the quality of loquacity. They have great powers of conversation. " *Loquunter Maria, Sibilla, et ab hoc, et ab hac, et ab illa.*" Instead of " Maria " insert Zeuleika ; instead of " Sibilla " read Fatima ; and then let the *hoc, hac, et ab illa* run at their pleasure.

It is always a source of astonishment to the stranger in the streets of Constantinople or Pera that so many ladies of the harem are seen driving around in their broughams, and shopping without any attendant, not even the Nubian. Their *yashmaks* have become so thin that the police have had their attention called to them, yet without making much reform in that particular. In private life a wonderful change has been made in the costumes of the Turkish women. My wife has a couple of dolls which illustrate the latest phase of Turkish progress in this respect. The Turkish dress of thirty years ago is almost obsolete. The Turkish ladies like, where they have an opportunity, to talk of the innovations that have been made in their costumes and customs.

It cannot be true now, as it was four decades ago, that the women of the harem, after the first little offices of the Koran, pass the remainder of the day in *ennui*. Some of their time must be spent in dressing and changing their ornamentations. The bath is always handy, and in winter season they no doubt nestle much under the covering of the *tandour*. But not now, in summer, do they bury themselves among their cushions, and thus in perpetual *kef* pass their time away in the land of sleep and dreams. Habits of industry have invaded the harem. Thus utter idleness has ceased to be an attribute of the Turkish female.

The sentiment which fills the Frankish beholder when he views the Oriental female is a perpetual theme of laudation, as well in prose as in poetry. The swan-like woman, " rubbed with lucid oils," or the Asiatic eye, like the first rise of moonlight, — "large, dark and swimming in a stream which seems to melt in its own beam,"— these and other fervid pictures show how poetic sensibility has endeavored to wreak its observation and feelings upon expression !

When Theodore Gautier visited Constantinople he did what many tourists undertake : he described some of the unveiled beauties of the harem, and made some delineation and coloring of its inmates. After some conscientious misgivings, he indites this paragraph :

" 'But how do you know this?' the reader is about to say, no doubt, scenting some gallant adventure that I have failed to recount. But my knowledge," said he, " has been attained in a manner the least Don Juanish in the world. In wandering in the cemeteries, it has frequently happened to me to surprise involuntarily, some lady adjusting her *yashmak*, or having left it open on account of the heat, trusting for security to the solitude of the place. That is the whole story."

Such an experience is not unusual to those who sojourn in the East. It has often been my fortune, or misfortune, to come unexpectedly upon some of these beauties of the harem when aloof from their eunuch or other guardian. Those on our isles are fond of labyrinthine rock rambles. I often came upon them in covies of a half-dozen in the sweet nooks and shades of the woods. It always struck me as strange that they should have so much care for their faces when they did not seem to be otherwise fastidious.

My experience, however, in the harem has been limited. The adventure which I will now narrate is a little beyond the limitation. When visiting Constantinople some six years ago, and while stopping with our consul at Therapia, certain Turkish ladies made a call at the consulate. One of them was an Egyptian princess. She was a cousin of the Khedive, and a grand-daughter of Mehemet Ali, the great Albanian soldier of Egypt. I happened to take a cup of tea with her, and this, to be mutual, required that she should drop her veil just a little. She was widowed, and lived at that time with her mother in one of the palaces on the Bosphorus. I need not say that she was beautiful and accomplished—Ayesha, the favored wife of the prophet was not more so. "Her eyes were brilliant, and yet human, like the reflection of stars in a well."

When we were visiting Egypt, in February, 1886, I received a note from the princess to call at her palace. She desired to prefer a request of the Sultan, whom she knew to be my friend. The request had reference to some diamonds. They had been mortgaged by her husband, and she desired to recover them. This request had a touch of romance about it. I ventured, in company with the vice-consul, to make the call. Her palace is quite after the manner of the *haremlik*, which I had frequently seen when the birds were flown. When I enter it I find the inevitable colored eunuch. He dismisses the consul and solemnly directs my steps up the winding staircase, at the same time using the most singular sound, —not pronounceable, or translatable into type,— by which to warn all the females of the household of the approach of a man and a Giaour. I surmount the stairs with much timidity. The number of heads which pop out of the doors of the various landings, and which are withdrawn with sudden surprise, astonishes me. At last I reach the apartment of the princess. There I find her seated upon an ottoman. After making the salutations and many inquiries, and a statement of the business, we smoke our cigarettes together, and drink our tea. We talk of palms and palmistry, of Egypt and England, of Arnold's "Light of Asia," and American petroleum, of the beauties of the Bosphorus and the navigation of the Nile. After this interview I am escorted by the same colored gentleman, amid the same indescribable noises, down the winding stairway to the door. On the way down, one of his sable highness's ejaculations scares one of the resident young ladies. Not being aware of my proximity, she is ascending the stairs.

At the terrible sound she rushes for the banisters. She attempts a speedy covering of her head. She is embarrassed. So am I. I, too, rush for the banisters,—for support,—and thus we meet. There is no screen, and no scene; but there is a hasty parting, all too hasty; while the eunuch gives out another tremendous sound, as if all the Indians of the "Wild West" were incarnate and vociferous in his person. I reach the sweet and balmy atmosphere of Cairo, with considerable perspiration. This is my wildest adventure in a harem.

It so happened, during the past summer, that this fair princess desired to pay some Moslem rites upon the grave of her mother, who died the summer before upon the Bosphorus. She came to Constantinople. Her physicians ordered her to Prinkipo. There she took a house near ours. As in duty bound, I make my devoirs. My wife invites her to ride, in our launch, amid the isles of our beautiful little archipelago. Without much reflection, I procure a carriage, drive to the villa of the princess, and tap the knocker. Her man-servant comes to the door, and soon she appears, radiant in all the beauty of her white tulle *yashmak*, and as stately as became one of the line of Mehemet Ali. I assist her into the carriage. She sits by the side of my wife and they make the vivacious French incandescent with their talk. We drive to the *scala*, where the flag and the launch await us. Unfortunately, at this time, one of the ferries from Constantinople comes in and lands about a thousand passengers. They see the Giaour, with a stove-pipe hat. He is gallanting a Mahometan lady. The rumor reaches the Kaïmakam, or governor of the island. We return to the *scala* after our sail among the islands. We drive her to her home in the carriage which is waiting. What is the result? Before I take the boat that day for Constantinople, my driver, horses and carriage are arrested by order of the Kaïmakam!

This is, indeed, an adventure not provided for by any instructions from the State Department. At once I send a remonstrance to the Kaïmakam, against the arrest of one in the employ of the American minister. It is couched in unabridged terms, such as are embraced in the word inter-territoriality.

It is needless to say that this proceeding reached the prefect in the city,—and I fear the Sultan and the palace also. There had been an apparent infraction of the Turkish law which forbids a Mahometan woman, unless of princely rank, to be seen upon the street with any man, and more especially a Christian. The plug-hat made a *prima facie* case. However, the matter was decorously settled, as it should have been; for the Kaïmakam had exceeded his authority. It was a matter outside of his jurisdiction. His conduct was arbitrary. He had no warrant or process for the seizure of the horses, the driver, or carriage. If there had not been an Oriental princess in the case,—who exhibited some sensibility in relation to her royal independency, which perhaps she had overstepped,—the matter might have figured in our diplomatic correspondence. As it was, the affair was properly settled without a pursuit of the governor. My impression is that he did not know the quality of the lady, nor the capacity of the minister. I had occasion to remedy at the palace any seeming mischief which might have been done. The princess left us the next day, which was the beginning of Bairam, in order to sacrifice a sheep upon the grave of her mother. She was a devout Moslem, as well as a most charming and intelligent woman.

I am sorry to undignify the Kaïmakam of the Princes Islands, who produced so much trouble in this romance of the princess. Since I left the island he has become an ex-Kaïmakam. This means an unknown quantity not only in algebra, but in politics. He was removed from office. He had been unmindful of the relation of *meum et tuum.* He overdrew his salary, by more than a thousand dollars, an act without legality on his part, or satisfaction on the other part.

CHAPTER XXIV.

FAREWELL TO PRINKIPO AND ITS PLEASURES.

EARLY in the fall (1886), we commence preparations to leave our home at Prinkipo. These preparations look beyond Constantinople. Before they began the President had kindly extended his permission that I should return to America. In fact, I had intimated to him that it would be agreeable to me to resign my office, as nearly everything possible to be done to place it in running order had been accomplished. Through the favor of the Sultan, and the partiality of Säid Pasha, his accomplished minister of foreign affairs, and with the intelligent assistance and counsel of Mr. Garguilo, the dragoman of the legation, I had so far pursued my instructions from the Department of State as to complete two treaties which had been suspended during nearly a dozen years. The first involved extradition, and the next the question of expatriation and naturalization.

The American reader will be pleased to know that the business of the legation at Constantinople by no means gives the leisurely and slippered ease which might be inferred from a perusal of these pages. There is no time in which something may not be done to forward the interests of the American people, and especially of the teachers, preachers and printers who are, through American benevolence and means, permeating and smoothing down the ancient ways of the Orient. But, whether encouraging this work, or keeping up with the current events of American newspapers, or watching the operation of the Turkish life-saving service; or whether riding around the suburbs of Constantinople and trying experiments in ploughing, as an amateur farmer, whereby I have sometimes relieved the tedium of absence; or whether making an excursion to Egypt, and its temples, tombs and other historic lineaments; or whether upon the Acropolis observing the new developments of archaic statuary as photographed by the modern artist; or whether bounding by day and night upon the Ægean, under the terrific impulses of an equinoctial tempest, —I have found enough leisure in my active life in the Orient for some of that sedate and quiet repose which so many believe is the only occupation of an American minister at the Sublime Porte.

Having thus successfully accomplished my mission here, all this delightful wintering and summering amid these resorts of historic grandeur, and at this theatre of diplomatic contention, are easily relinquished for the gratification of home tastes and predilections. After much consideration, and many lingering farewells in my heart before they were spoken in the word, my mind is made up. It is now the *animo revertendi.* Not the least difficult to sever among the attachments which I have formed in the Orient is that for this paradise of Prinkipo. But the soughing of the wind presages the autumn ; and the dropping of the leaf upon the mosaic pavement of our garden, and the brown tinge of the foliage, make our withdrawal from the pleasures and precincts of this Eden of the East less regretful than it would be in the vernal season.

Not unfrequently there were some lively breezes upon the Marmora. The south wind always brought its waves, and though the little launch was capable of mastering them, it was not so comfortable, especially for the ladies, to be on board during these emergencies. More than once, when we started from the bridge in Constantinople, the seeming calm of the sea was disturbed and the waves dashed over the sides of the vessel. On such occasions, we had to run behind the island of Halki for shelter. As the launch was often decorated with flowers, and especially the hydrangea, it presented quite a gay appearance with the red cushions for the seats and the rugs for the floor. But when the waves were rough, these flowers looked as if they had been on a spree, and returned to the garden considerably demoralized.

We selected a calm time and a good photographer for our farewell view of the scenery of the islands. Nature never gave to mortal man a more beautiful day, a more serene sea, a more azure sky, or more balmy air for a last visit to loved and familiar scenes and associations. As I look about me, preparatory to this journey on the launch, I feel that nature gives to the weary eye under such a sky and amidst such scenes, a balm that does not come even from sleep in a less favored climate. Here is the very home of the *Kef*,—of dreamful repose in a sunny sheen bathed with the mildest airs. The landscape changes its mood with every vista of observation. The sea copies the land in its coquettish phases. Soft are the midday sighings amidst the *bosquet* of the pines. On the placid shores the waves forget even to make their drowsy melody. No fountains play on the terraces ; no purling streams gurgle on their way to the sea ; no torrents bound from the mountain steeps ; no sound is heard except the faint chants in the churches and the monasteries, as they float by in waves of softest melody. Here is blissful rest ! Looking through the avenues of the trees, down upon the waters of the Propontis, I see the distant sails becalmed, with here and there streaks of smoke from the funnels of the great steamers bound for the Dardanelles, or the little boats, looking ever so small, carrying the mail to Modena or Ismid. Is there any motion on the surface of the sea? No. Look again! Is it the shimmer of the sun on the blue surface? No! it is a breeze so mild that the nautilus of the Southern seas might safely spread its tiny sail.

Fanned by this gentle breeze, we begin our farewell photographic trip. Our first course is to the front of the town of Prinkipo, with its craggy heights and superb buildings and its inlets and shadows. These our photograph speedily captures. Then turning around a rocky point, upon which sits as a miracle of beauty a little domestic temple, we anchor our vessel and bid "all hail!" to the fishermen hauling in their nets from the rickety platform. They are acquiescent and submissive, these fisherman, and give themselves to the lens of the photographer without effort to escape. After a feeble attempt to take them all, while they are manning the ropes and bringing their burden of fish to the pebbly shore, a wild, strange being presents himself upon the long platform of the pier! His advent is greeted with a roar of laughter from the fishermen. He is saluted by his name, which is none other than Demetrius. He is not of the ecclesiastical kind. But he is of the orthodox race, and thoroughly Grecian. He carries a basket in which he has been gathering some provender among the islanders. He has a rough cap upon his shaggy, curly black hair; and a coat and pair of shoes which no beggar on the bridge at Stamboul would envy. Pedro, our Dalmatian servant, and George, the sailor of the launch, surround him. They press him along to the conspicuous front of the picture. He is taken, in much better company than he is accustomed to. As soon as his picture is finished and his recompense paid, some of the villagers who have gathered upon the shore pick him up bodily and pitch him into the sea.

Of course this was a very rude proceeding. On my remonstrance, the villagers expressed regret. They said that they had often done the same thing to him before; that he could swim like a duck, and that, like a cork, he was light in the head and therefore not properly the subject of homicide by drowning. He does not drown. He soon swims out and clambers up the pier. He makes no protest. He likes his ducking; for does it not bring him reward? I am free to say that never have I seen in the Orient a man who, before his involuntary douche, needed washing more than did Demetrius.

The English engineer who leased our launch to the government for the use of our legation, lives on the western shore of Prinkipo, upon a perpendicular cliff overlooking a deep and delightful shady cove. Upon the rocks which form the cove a summer house is placed with exquisite grace. It is the house of my friend Jones, the lessor of the launch. He is not at home to give us our farewell, but his family come upon the cliff, and along with the villagers they look wonderingly at our photographic operations. It is a pretty point of observation for a picture. The dim islands of Oxia and Plati are in the hazy distance. Halki, with her red rocks, is but a mile away. Above its minarets and Turkish naval school and its long yellow buildings we discern with a glass the lazy inhabitants curiously observing our performance, while a winged *caïque*, and three Greek priests in a boat, pass by. They shake their heads solemnly at the damp, unpleasant body of Demetrius, who stands a most pitiable and limp object upon the pier. Along the road upon the shore we perceive carriages and donkey parties. They seem to be floating along in a mirage of sunlight. We hear the tinkle of the bells on the water donkeys.

We do not linger long at this our favorite spot. We put off from the shore. We stop the launch in the open sea near Prinkipo so as to make its picture and that of the island of Halki whither we soon shall sail. We are intent on seeing once more the beautiful bay upon the eastern side of Halki.

The landlord of the restaurant, or *Diaskalon*, sends his boat to us as soon as we anchor in the bay. He greets us upon his shore, loads my wife fairly down with flowers from his abundant garden; and after many compliments to America, and a bottle of wine, a cup of coffee and a smoke, we are about to return when the insatiable photographer assails the landlord and his company. He takes the whole group, amidst surrounding foliage, in which every prospect pleases, and the very sun, as well as our host, seems to smile.

Our intention had been once more to visit Oxia and Plati, so as to take a view of the palaces of Bulwer and some of the beautiful scenes upon those rocky islets. But by this time the breeze freshens and we are content to fire at long range at these singularly romantic spots. On returning to our home we stop before the monastery and church of St. George upon the rocky promontory of Halki. The long avenues of cypresses which lead up to it are reduced pictorially in a twinkling, by the refinement of art. The prettiest part of this church is on the outside; although it has recently been renovated and glorified by new pictures and adornments from Russian co-religionists. Most of these churches, for reasons already hinted, are not attractive. These old and stained churches within the Turkish dominion, which are so rigidly orthodox, are in great contrast with the temples and basilicas of which Moscow and St. Petersburg furnish the best examples. The new Temple of the Saviour at the former, and St. Isaac's at the latter place, have no equal for the splendor of their pictured adornments, the gracefulness of their architecture, their innumerable lighted tapers, their gorgeous vestments, their rare and original music, and for that wonderful mystery of the gilded iconostos, or altar screens, heavy with masses of metal and jewels and the pictures of saints. The choirs in the cathedrals of Russia are conducted with extraordinary precision and harmony. In this harmony there is no organ or other instrumental music.

We return to Prinkipo. In the afternoon we make a detour of the island. This is done with the purpose of photographing one souvenir from the spot where the Imperial palace of the Empress Irene once glorified the earth. It is now only a hole in the mountain. But we fill it with solid objects of historic interest. What the sunless treasures of this Imperial palace were will never be known, especially as the treasurer had not been heard to audit the catalogues. But we find memories outside of this vacancy. They are Homeric and Hellenic. Stretched on the shelly shore are some idlers, while others "whirl the disk," if they do not dart the javelin. We meet our Albanian guide and his dogs. He is embroidered as if for a gala time. Indeed I notice that carriages are on the road to a grove near St. Michael's church, where there is a table spread. It is covered with dainties, fruits, wines and meats for a hundred people. The place is very select for such an entertainment. It is a church *fête*. The breakers on the east shore of the isle begin, with the creamy, dry Sillery of their crests, to anticipate the feast; and on the west side there is what Byron called the "Sunset glow of Burgundy." Children play about in the fragrant bushes. But not a word awakes those historic people who once revelled here and whose dust is not even folded in tombs.

On our return to our villa in the evening, we find "Far-Away Moses." He is purchasing much bric-a-brac and material for us to export to our home. Mark Twain has made him immortal, in his "Innocents Abroad." But our photograph gives to this remarkable Israelite a pictorial costume which is a sample of the best appearance which a Hebrew may make in Turkey!

This almost closes our album. Last, though not least, come our own household. They are all present for the picture which we desire, including even our old "Amty," the cook. Pedro stands prominently upon a pedestal like the

"FAR AWAY MOSES."

Dalmatian hero of many an incident of the classic Olympus or of his Croatian home. Our gardener is not on hand, except by deputy. Xenophon on this occasion is represented by Epaminondas. My wife's little Armenian maid stands upon the steps beneath " old Amty," who has the emblem of her vocation, a ladle, in her left hand. But a better picture is taken of the family group outside the grilled gate of the villa. Pedro is there mounted upon a horse, as if he were the Don Quixote of our expedition, while the minister, like Sancho Panza, upon a donkey, modestly turns his back to the instrument. An English helmet temporarily destroys something of the nationality of the minister. But our photographic mania does not end until our two female servants of the household are caught as it were in masquerade ; the maid Marie being dressed as a Turkish lady, and Theano in the present Greek costume of her class in the island.—Here " night's descending shadow" hides the view, and we close the camera.

A few weeks more and the summer will be ended. Its luxury of flowers and leaves and the bright blue of the skies and the brighter blue of the seas around our islands will have passed away. The green of the woods will soon turn to russet and gold, at the touch of the frosty autumn. All the endearments of this wonderful and beauteous land will soon pass into the realm of memory. Even the freshness of the "Sweet Waters" will pass away; the dark green cemeteries, the monuments and columns, the hippodrome, the mosques and minarets, the fountains, and the chosen haunts with which we are familiar,—these will pass away with their enchantments, associations and attachments, but never shall the blissful days of these isles of "eternal summer" pass from our fond recollection. They will remain among the bright oases of our life.

A few more days we linger at our lovely home. We make our adieux to neighbors and friends upon the island and do the necessary packing for our long journey. Better to leave it now in the cool beauty of its refreshing haunts, than later, when November brings its mist and chill, to make the solitude, which is so pleasing, lonesome to a sense of pain.

What will the groves be, when winter rules and makes this clime less clement? We do not desire the solitude of dearth or death; but rather that of the hill and valley, where "the harvest of a quiet eye" may brood and sleep in our own heart. We do not desire to see the mansions here,—so lately filled with music and jocund with domestic joys, and the gardens so full of pleasance and fragrance,— deserted of both flowers and houris. We do not wish to wait until the clouds,—which are now white as wool and rolling in light masses, over the hills of Asia,—become black with storm and thunder.

The ways here are sufficiently untrodden now, but what will they be when even the donkey-boys cease to accelerate the tourist, and the peddlers have gone South with the birds, to the isles of the Grecian archipelago? The privacy of the pine forests, the brown of the vineyards, the silence of the warblers, and, above all, the cessation of the crowds of people who come here for recreation, will make Prinkipo and "the Princes," enchanting though they are, too secluded for a diplomat or a tourist.

The story of our summer is told. The wreaths begin to wither on the tomb. A thousand thoughts and studies hang over them. But these are not dead garlands. The Angels of Memory will resume their places at the gate of this paradise. The flaming sword drives us into the old and busy world, under the glaring sun and the uncloistered heat and dust of our earnest and active American life; but amidst all the turmoil and worry of that life, we shall turn to the " Pleasures of Prinkipo ";—

"In the shadow of thy pines, by the shores of thy sea,
On the hills of thy beauty, our heart is with thee."

www.ingramcontent.com/pod-product-compliance
Lightning Source LLC
Chambersburg PA
CBHW030948110726
47900CB00004B/1180